WE ARE NOT THE SAME

S.J. Cunningham

WE ARE NOT THE SAME
by S. J. Cunningham

ISBN 978-1-964369-01-3
Paperback Edition

This is a work of fiction. All the characters in this book are fictitious, and any resemblance to actual persons, living or dead, is purely coincidental. The names, incidents, dialogue, and opinions expressed are products of the author's imagination and are not to be construed as real.

This edition published by S.J. Cunningham:
www.sjcunningham.net

PROLOGUE

The gathering is a swell—a buzzing cacophony, brash and discordant. Megan can't make out individual words amidst the noise and laughter. People bump into her without recognizing her—without even *seeing* her.

She is invisible.

Music plays from a hidden speaker. The deep bass pulses and thumps. Bodies move together, coupling and uncoupling, in time with the beat.

She takes another long swallow of beer from the cup in her hand. She barely tastes it.

The damp from an earlier rain chills the air, but now, the night sky is clear and bright.

On the patio outside, the flames of a fire tentatively reach upward out of damp wood, struggling to burst free. Someone throws a log into their waning depths, and sparks erupt. The wood lets loose a high-pitched squeal. It is a living, breathing thing, burning alive and aware of its fate.

She sees *him* through the flames. Joe Wright. That easy smile, those dark, almond-shaped eyes. He is smiling at *her*, the girl who is not Megan. The girl who, until yesterday, had been Megan's best friend. Megan can barely stand the thought of the girl's name slithering through her mind— Sutton Schultz. The name hisses like a snake, sly and silent.

Megan had thought that Joe might look at *her* that way, with that wide bright smile and laughter in his eyes. But tonight, he doesn't see Megan at all.

Instead, Sutton is perched on Joe's lap, close to the fire, laughing. Her face is close to his. She knows that Megan is watching them, and she's enjoying it.

Megan wants to look away. She doesn't want to care. But she stares anyway. She can't stop herself.

The music has slowed its tempo, and the notes suddenly coalesce and make sense. The words become clear. *You still have all of me.*

An unknown partygoer thrusts another red solo cup into Megan's other hand. She glances around, but the person has disappeared into the crowd. She swallows down the second draught of pale amber liquid. It is semi-flat, yeasty, and makes her stomach feel full and uncomfortable.

Her attention returns to the couple behind the fire. The flames flicker, and the heat blurs the objects of her focus, causing the bodies to waver and tremble. Like a dream. Joe bares his teeth and catches the lobe of Sutton's ear between his white incisors. Sutton squeals, her head thrown back, throat white, lips very red, eyes rimmed with black. Her blond hair falls over his shoulder, and he catches a lock of it between his fingers. Tugs hard.

Megan takes a step back, sways. She's about to fall. She can already hear them laughing at her as her footing falters.

Suddenly, an arm wraps around her waist. It remains there until she is steady. She looks up into another face, harder and more mature than Joe's boyish features. Megan knows this other boy who is looking into her eyes—Dan Armstrong.

She has never said anything more than hello to Dan. She doesn't think she's ever really even thought about him. Embarrassed, she tries to right herself, but her movements feel fuzzy and soft. She wants to laugh, but she can't tell if her lips are cooperating.

He smiles. Is he laughing at her? She isn't sure.

He says something to her, but it's hard to hear him over the voices, the music, and the buzzing in her head.

He steadies her and leads her away from the fire and through the sliding glass doors into the house.

She wants to stay and watch *them*, but Dan's pull is insistent.

They are not supposed to be in the house, she protests, but she follows him anyway. She looks back over her shoulder—one last glimpse of *them*. They don't look back.

She and Dan emerge into the kitchen, which is now littered with red cups, pizza boxes, and nearly empty bags of potato chips and snack mix. It's quieter here. Soft music is playing from another room.

A giggling, pink-faced girl that she knows from her English class is standing against a counter with a boy Megan has known since kindergarten. The girl's name is Chloe. Chloe Nicholson. Chloe raises a hand and says something, and the other boy makes a face at Megan. She's supposed to laugh, but she doesn't. She frowns instead. Their voices are far away, like they're underwater.

Chloe asks Megan if she wants another drink. But Dan, still by her side, shakes his head and waves it away, answering for her.

He leads her through a doorway and into a living room, where he guides her to a sofa. She sits, and he disappears.

A couple is locked in an embrace on an armchair beside her. She averts her gaze and is about to leave when Dan returns with another red solo cup. She holds up a hand, but he pushes it toward her. *Water*, he says. She sips it at first, then suddenly, very thirsty, gulps it down.

It doesn't take long before her stomach gurgles, and she feels queasy. She places a hand on her midsection before standing and quickly shuffling down the hallway to find a bathroom. Thankfully, someone comes out, and she hurries in.

She shuts the door and manages to make it to the open toilet. She throws up all of the liquid, then stares into the bowl. Dried flecks from the contents of someone else's stomach stare back at her, mingled with her own sick. She wretches again and again until nothing is left.

When she finally stands, her head hurts. She splashes water on her face. In the mirror, her eyes are puffy and red, and her skin is blotchy. She looks grotesque.

She wants to cry.

I have to get home, she thinks. But she has no idea where her friend Holly, who has driven her to this party, has gone.

So, she walks back down the long hallway toward the room with the sofa.

In her pocket, Megan runs her fingers over the solid form of her Razr phone. She could call her mom for a ride. But the phone is for emergencies. Her mom has made that clear. And this is a tragedy, a humiliation, and a drama. But only to Megan. Her mother would resent the inconvenience and then be furious to find out that Megan, her perfect child who never does anything wrong, has been drinking.

When she returns to the living room, Dan is talking to a beautiful girl who Megan has seen before. Crystal Karlik graduated two years earlier. Megan wonders what Crystal is doing here with these kids. Kids like her. Crystal is standing very close to Dan, gesturing with her hands as she speaks. Her fingernails are long and purple-pink, the color of the summertime flowers on the rhododendron bush in front of Megan's farmhouse.

They see her standing in the doorway, and Dan walks away from Crystal. He doesn't turn around when Crystal calls his name. Instead, he looks very closely at Megan's face, and the attention makes Megan look down at the floor.

He is asking her questions, but she can't answer. Her mouth feels sour and her head hurts.

He takes her hand, and they walk out of the room, back through the kitchen and outside into the cool night air. The chill makes Megan feel slightly better. She can breathe. They continue to the front of the house where cars are parked haphazardly in the driveway.

Crystal follows them. She yells words Megan can't understand. Others join her, and when Megan turns around, she sees *them*. Sutton and Joe.

Sutton runs up to Megan and puts her hand on Megan's arm, pulling her back. Dan is tugging her in the opposite direction, and Megan is temporarily caught between two worlds.

She pulls free of *her*. They are not friends. Not anymore. She might have said that aloud, but she's not sure.

Dan leads her toward a car. It's cherry-red and low to the ground. When she climbs into the seat, her jeans slide on the shiny leather.

Crystal is beside Dan again, her rhododendron nails bright against his black t-shirt as he climbs into the driver's seat. Is Crystal his girlfriend? If Megan is taking him away from her, then she's no better than Sutton. But Megan doesn't think that's right. This girl is bossy and demanding. She seems more like a sister than a girlfriend.

Dan pulls away from Crystal, and he offers Megan a half smile as he twists the key in the ignition. It's now just the two of them, and even though her head is pounding and her throat hurts, she feels safe here. And happy to be insulated from the faces of the people she's grown up with.

The car roars to life with a low rumble. The exhaust is acrid in her nose. Dan powers down the windows. Then he maneuvers in reverse through the line of cars and backs out onto the road.

It isn't yet midnight, but theirs is the only car on this rural street. Dim lights from nearby homes blink as they travel past.

He accelerates along a stretch of roadway, and she feels like they are flying. She laughs—a real laugh—and the wind blows her hair away from her face. She leans out the open window. Her hair streams behind her, an auburn curtain. She closes her eyes as the wind washes over her.

Dan takes a bend fast, and the tires squeal as the back end of the car shudders on the wet roadway.

She laughs again. The buzzing in her head has subsided and her mind feels as clear as the stars above them. The half-moon is bright when it peeks out from behind the clouds.

He downshifts as they come to a series of bends in the road, but they are moving faster than they should. They slide, and the car's engine rumbles. Megan doesn't know if he's taking her home, and she doesn't care.

When they stop at an intersection, he doesn't move right away. She looks over at him. He leans forward and kisses her. She is surprised and slightly hesitant. She must taste terrible, but he doesn't seem to care. His tongue finds its way into her mouth. It is unexpected, and nice.

She knows that she'll probably feel differently in the morning, but right now, this is where she's supposed to be.

It may have been seconds or minutes before the high beams of a pickup truck blind them through the back window. The truck's horn blares and its engine growls.

Dan swears and gestures aggressively in the rearview mirror, shifts into gear and plows forward. They accelerate. The truck follows too close behind.

Megan blinks and squints in the glare. The wet asphalt of the road in front of them shines in the headlights.

Dan shifts, and they shoot forward. She hears the truck's

engine accelerate behind them, but it can't keep up with the little red car. She laughs again, and he looks over at her and smiles. He touches her knee.

A hard thud and a lurch on her side of the car knocks her teeth together. Dan jerks the wheel. They are careening sideways across the road.

They spin like a top—like a carnival ride—out of control. Bright lights flash. Megan is disoriented.

Tires screech, and the engine sputters. Another thud—harder, jolting. Her body is flung forward and held in place by the seatbelt tight against her chest. Her head lashes back against the headrest then sideways. She has no control. They are tumbling, turning, flying, soaring. She looks over, and Dan is floating in space, frozen in time. His eyes are wide, and they lock with hers. She laughs. Or maybe it's just a smile.

She turns her head. Something dark and solid comes toward her. They are moving in slow motion, but she doesn't have time to think.

And then…

A thousand stars burst from her head, out of her eyes, nose, mouth.

The stars become sparks of fire and light. Brilliant. They shoot from her hands and feet. From her chest.

She is the maker of the sparks. Her body *becomes* the sparks, the light. Countless glowing embers breaking open, breaking apart. It is terrifying, fascinating, unbearable.

Just as she thinks that her body doesn't exist anymore—that it has dissolved into the ether—the disparate parts of the universe start to come together, rushing toward her—*as* her. She is hypersonic, condensing at a velocity beyond words. The essence of her contracts at the speed of light until there is a final, dazzling implosion. She is everything and everything is her—inside out, upside down, and all around. She holds the universe, and it holds her. Her breath is the wind, her tears the ocean, her laughter the fire. She pulses and everything comes alive. She swells, bloated with herself. Her final scream is primal.

And then silence. Peace. The faraway sound of a horn. She sleeps.

CHAPTER 1

SUTTON-NOW

S utton Schultz's phone buzzes, and she stares at the name that lights the screen.

Mom.

Sutton steels herself to answer. If she doesn't pick up, the woman will just keep calling. Or worse. Sutton does not want a repeat of the situation a year earlier when she hadn't answered the incessant buzzing of her mother's phone calls. The woman had called the police, and two uniformed officers came sniffing around the mobile home to perform a welfare check. It had taken weeks to convince both Tommy and Andre that she wasn't a snitch. It had taken months for their neighbors in the trailer park to acknowledge them. And it had taken even longer to recover from Tommy's rage at the entire situation.

Sutton is aware that she is rubbing her jaw where it had once been broken.

She presses accept. "Yeah, Mom?" she asks quietly. She tries to make her voice sound rested and upbeat. She's not sure she knows what that sounds like anymore.

"Hi, honey." Her mother's voice is thick and bright and too sweet. They are both pretending. "Just calling to check in. Everything okay?"

From the tiny kitchen, Tommy walks into the room and scowls at her. Then he scowls at the squalor around her—

clothes, empty food wrappers, other paraphernalia. "Can you clean this place the fuck up?" he says from the doorway.

Most of the mess is his, but Sutton knows that she needs to do a better job of tidying up. She needs to be a better housekeeper.

Sheepishly, Sutton rises from the stained polyester couch and walks past Tommy. She tries to hide the fact that she is on the phone.

His bulky frame moves in close so that she has to angle her body in the narrow hallway. She eyes the fist-sized crater in the faux-wood paneling next to her and makes herself small.

He grins in a mean way, pleased that he has made her flinch, and she enters the bedroom she shares with him and closes the door.

He follows and pushes it open, staring at her.

The phone is against her ear. "I'm fine, Mom," she says, emphasizing the word so that Tommy knows she isn't talking to a guy. He gives her another scowl, but he walks away. She knows he's out there, listening. The walls in the trailer are barely thicker than cardboard.

She sits down on the edge of the unmade bed.

"I haven't heard from you in a few days," her mom says.

"I've been busy."

"Doing?"

"Working," Sutton says and shuts her eyes. She doesn't want to lie to her mother, but she has no choice. Not that it's any of her mother's business anyway. She's a grown-ass woman. She can do what she wants. But she lets the falsehood lie between them.

"Oh, that's wonderful," Angela Schultz says. Her words have changed from honey-sweet to a waterfall—flowing and gushing through the line. Sutton can hear the force of the hope in the older woman's voice.

Sutton runs a hand through her unwashed hair, then picks at a scab on her arm.

There is a pause.

"And what are you doing at your new job?"

A moment of panic grips her. She hadn't thought that far ahead. "Doctor's office," she says. "Pediatrics." She shuts her eyes again. It's a stupid lie. Her mother is a nurse, which is no doubt why the lie had come so easily. But Angela Schultz will see through this in an instant.

There is another pause. Longer.

"Pediatrics," her mother says slowly.

Sutton doesn't answer.

"For what doctor?"

"Uh—" She hesitates, then says, "Dr. Richards." *Stupid*, she thinks again, using that name of all names.

"Richards," her mother repeats.

Sutton waits. It's not out of the question that there might be a pediatrician called Dr. Richards in Beesonstown.

"And what are you doing for this…Dr. Richards?" Angela's voice is slow and thin. Gone is the honey and the waterfall.

"You know, whatever they need. Answering phones, patient preparation." That sounds right to Sutton. *Patient preparation.* She remembers the last stint she had in that terrible low-income residential rehab program. There were definitely women there—aides or assistants—doing the messy, lowly work that the actual nurses didn't want to do. In Sutton's make-believe job, that's what she does too.

Sutton hears a noise in the other room through the wall. A sharp tapping, then a long snorting inhale. Her heartbeat quickens, and she forgets for a minute about her pretend job and her mother's questions.

Very soon, Tommy will become rageful. Maybe if she just stays here, silent, he might leave her alone.

Her mother's voice breaks back into her thoughts, and Sutton startles.

"Sutton, your dad and I—we're here for you. We want you to know that. Whatever you need. If you need a break for a few days, you always have a place to stay with us. Your room is waiting for you."

Sutton remembers her childhood bedroom. The white wicker furniture—twin bed, dresser, and matching desk set—bought from some local retailer when she'd been twelve years old. The bed is probably still made up in the white bedspread with the tiny pink rosebuds. Her sheets would be white, crisp, clean. A pang of nostalgia hits her so violently that she nearly doubles over. She attempts a shallow breath, and a whimper escapes.

"Are you there? Are you all right?" her mother asks.

"Mm-hmm," she manages. Her lips are pressed together.

"Is it the date?"

For a second, Sutton doesn't know what her mother is talking about. And then she remembers.

In less than two weeks, May 28 will dawn. It comes quicker every year, and now it feels like every waking moment is just one step away from the date. She wonders if time passes at all or if every second is just empty space around which that day orbits.

She breathes in and out, craving the darkness and the sweetness of oblivion.

Twenty years. This year marks twenty years since her best friend was killed.

Megan had been beautiful, kind, smart, and giving with a presence that radiated warmth and love. If she had graduated just two weeks later—if she'd never gone to that party—Megan would have studied veterinary science, specializing in feline care. She remembers her friend's fervent love for the cats.

On the Richards' farm, the family had treated cats as just a step above rodents. And Megan had tried to save them all—the abandoned strays, the barn cats, and their constant litters. In high school, she'd made it her mission to adopt out as many kittens as possible, but nearly as many had come back as were given away. Every cat that had been returned, fallen ill, or died had broken Megan's heart just a little bit more.

She had been so damn *good*. And Sutton hadn't been able to stand it.

"Sutton?"

"I'm here."

"You know," her mom says softly, "that accident killed more than just Megan that night. That boy destroyed more than one life."

"I don't want to talk about this."

"Maybe if you address it, though, Sutton. Maybe if you're able to let it out and process those emotions—"

"Stop," Sutton interrupts. It's not the first time they've had this conversation.

"I can give you some names—"

"I said stop," she says, louder this time. Then softer, "I've gotta go, Mom."

"Would you shut the hell up?" Tommy screams through the wall.

"What was that?" her mother asks.

Sutton swallows, takes two deep breaths. "It's okay." Her voice is barely a whisper. She says it as much to herself as she does to her mom.

"Is that *him*?" Angela hisses. "Did you let him come back? How could you let him come back after everything he's done to you?"

Her mother doesn't understand, and Sutton can't explain it.

"We bought that place for *you*, not for him. You need to tell him to leave."

Tommy has left in the past, but he always comes back around, and Sutton always lets him in. Despite his temper, despite the outbursts, despite all of his habits, he is her constant. He is always there. And this is what she deserves.

"Did you hear me?" Angela raises her voice. "I want him gone."

"I can't—He has no place to go."

"I don't care about him, Sutton. I care about *you*." Her mother's voice is a desperate, plaintive cry. "He's not *good* for you, honey."

"I said, *shut...up*." The voice is deep, slow, menacing as it comes closer. His heavy footsteps cause the trailer to bounce on its steel beam foundation.

Sutton hangs up on her mother and quickly tucks the phone under the mattress before the door swings open and slams against the drywall.

Tommy's beefy body fills the doorframe, and though she quakes inside, she has learned not to cower. She stands and moves toward him. It's risky, but if she acts weak, he'll treat her as weak, usually with a hard backhand to her face.

"Aww, baby, I'm sorry," she purrs, running a hand down his bicep. It's thick and solid, mostly muscle. "It was my mother. I got rid of her."

She feels his anger slow from a boil to a simmer. The soft touch works with him sometimes when she remembers.

"What did she want?"

"Nothing. The usual." Sutton isn't sure what this means, but Tommy seems to understand. She's never met Tommy's parents, and he's rarely mentioned them. At various points in their relationship, he's told her that he had grown up in

Ohio, Michigan, *and* Indiana. It's possible that all of this is true. It's equally possible that none of it is true. She knows that he moved to Pennsylvania when he was in his mid-twenties, ostensibly for a construction job, and made this place his home.

Now he's twitchy like he always gets after he does a line, but at least he hasn't done a speedball—a combination of coke and heroin—which makes his behavior completely unpredictable. Still, after an eightball, she's never sure how paranoid and violent he might become.

"Fucking bitch," he mumbles, and Sutton stiffens. She's not sure if he's talking about her or her mother. Either way, she doesn't like it.

Tommy sniffs hard and swallows down the phlegm in the back of his throat. He has a stale smell about him. It's not quite the ripe smell of body odor, but a subtler unwashed, unclean smell. He reaches out and paws at her, rough when he grabs her right breast. He squeezes hard.

Sutton can't help it. She flinches and moves ever so slightly away.

Time stutters. Tommy's hand is suspended in the air between them. He looks at her from beneath his heavy brow, and then his brief moment of surprise becomes fury.

His hand finds her throat. His fingers close around her neck and squeeze.

She is barely able to suck in a thin stream of air, and she claws at his wrist. When her fingers curl around his, trying to free herself, he squeezes harder. She makes a rasping noise as her airflow is nearly blocked. His hand is a vice, and he lifts her from the floor. The blood collects in her head. Darkness encroaches from the sides of her eyes. Pinpricks of light and color appear, and her feet dangle. The black rushes in and her fingers go limp.

"Who was on the phone?" she hears him demand. She

tries to answer, to tell him what he wants to hear, but she has no voice. No air. *This is it. This is finally it.* A sense of relief floods her.

And then, cruelly, the light rushes back toward her, breath filling her lungs painfully with a great whoosh.

Her body is flying through the air, and she bounces back on the mattress. Her arm smacks the frame of the bed with a loud crack, and her eyes start to water.

Tommy sees her damp eyes and laughs. "You're such a baby."

She is holding her arm and gasping, gulping air. It hurts when she swallows.

"You know what? Go ahead and cheat on me." He walks toward the bed, and his hulking form looms over her. He may be about to rape her, and she won't fight it. But he doesn't. He just leans in close. "You want to sleep with some other guy? Be my guest." She can smell his breath, both metallic and rotten. "I'll offer him my sympathy right before I kill you." His voice is barely more than a whisper, and Sutton stares at the ceiling, at the brown-yellow blob that looks like the shape of an angel with outstretched wings.

Go ahead, she thinks. *I deserve it.*

Then he hits her in the face with a closed fist, and her world goes black.

CHAPTER 2

JOE-NOW

The photographer yells, "Mr. Wright, just step slightly to your left and look over at me with that big smile. Jenk, you keep your left hand on the wheel and give me a salute with your right hand."

In the background, Ed, the contact from the ad agency, is playing the Wright Automotive Group jingle on his laptop, though it is completely immaterial to the photo shoot itself.

When the road's been rough and the drive is a fright,
You can't afford to be wrong, it's gotta be Wright.
Wright Automotive!

Joe Wright always feels stupid doing these photo shoots even though he knows it's necessary for business development, customer relations, and name recognition. Keith "Jenk" Jenkins, the burly tight end who is posed in the cab of the brand-new black pickup truck next to Joe, has recently finished a record-breaking year. There's Superbowl chatter for the upcoming season, if the team can keep their defense intact. In addition to that, Jenk has been dating a popular actress, which has elevated his celebrity status and with it, the status of both the team and Joe's car dealerships.

The Wright Automotive Group has the official vehicle

contract with the team, which means that many of the coaches and players drive vehicles from Wright in exchange for advertising, charity events, and promos.

Joe knows he shouldn't complain. Today, when word had leaked that Jenk would be onsite filming at the dealership, a group of fans had to be held at bay by the team's security personnel. And Joe's salespeople had managed to sell thirty cars over projection. The day wasn't over yet.

"Mr. Wright," the photographer calls. "Keep that smile bright for me! Jenk, you're perfect."

Joe smiles harder, and his cheeks hurt. He catches sight of Vivian out of the corner of his eye, and his wife is smiling hard right along with him, even though she's not a part of this particular shoot.

For this promo, they're giving away two trucks and two sedans in correlation with the team's training camp at the end of the summer. It's only May now, so leading up to training camp, the team and dealership will embark on a complete marketing campaign—social media, television commercials, billboards, advertorials, podcasts, newscasts, print and radio advertising. The works.

One campaign will feature Joe, who has hit the genetic lottery. He knows this, and he hates it. He's been told that he could have easily been cast in the latest round of Superman movies—black hair, piercing blue eyes, bright white teeth, chiseled jaw, slightly suggestive smile. This, too, he knows is true. At thirty-eight, he's still in his prime, and because of the campaigns over the past eight years, he's become nearly as famous in the city as the players he features in his ads. Though he's not quite as popular as Jenk.

The other campaign will feature his wife, Vivian Wright, the former Miss Pennsylvania. Vivian has long siren-red hair, ocean-green eyes, and the highest cheekbones Joe has ever seen. On top of it all, she's brilliant. Before Vivian came along, the dealership catered to one rural neighboring county. Joe's father, who started the business over thirty-five years ago, had done well, and Joe may have run the company in much the same way.

But once he'd met and married Vivian, the size of the business had quadrupled. They moved their headquarters from their tiny home in the country to right outside the city. They bought up failing dealerships and rebranded. They hired the best mechanics, the best salespeople, the best customer service representatives.

And they have the best commercials.

With a happy marriage, two beautiful young daughters, a chain of successful dealerships, and more money than he knows what to do with, Joe should be over the moon with happiness. Most of the time, he is.

Vivian floats over to the photographer, murmurs a suggestion. "Great idea," the photographer says. "Joe, can you stand on the running board next to Jenk and wave?"

Joe grits his teeth but smiles anyway. The goal is to get views and clicks, and sometimes you have to look ridiculous in order to do that. He suppresses a sigh.

Jenk, he notices, is watching Vivian, too.

Fat chance. Even if the actress were a nonfactor in Jenk's life, Vivian would have zero interest in the pomp and flash of a football star. Vivian is a creator and a business-woman—strategic, steady, methodical. She would have absolutely no interest in standing along the sidelines cheering on a sports personality.

No, Joe thinks with a healthy amount of pride and con-fidence. Vivian stands beside Joe or she stands alone.

"All right," the photographer finally calls. "Got it."

Ed appears from the sidelines. He rubs his hands to-gether. "Okay, everyone, fantastic job," he says over the still-looping jingle from his laptop speakers. He approaches Jenk as the hulking man climbs from the cab, and Joe approaches Vivian. "That was okay?" he asks.

She shrugs and gives him a small smile. "It was fine, I think. You looked a little tense. We can see how it turns out."

She pats his arm. He tries not to take it personally.

Ed has said his goodbyes to Jenk, who is trying to catch Vivian's attention. Joe rolls his eyes slightly and raises a hand before he turns his back on his famous co-star. Vivian ignores Jenk altogether. The man's security team quickly approaches to accompany him to the large black luxury SUV that is waiting, concealed, inside a bay of the repair shop on the other side of the lot.

Ed comes up to them. "Great job," he says. "Remember, we'll be shooting at the stadium tomorrow morning for the commercial, and we've got studio time reserved on Sunday."

"Are we doing Viv's spots, too?" Joe asks.

Ed nods. "We'll knock them all out."

A loudspeaker crackles from high on a nearby pole, and then the voice of his receptionist Nora announces, "Mr. Wright, please report to the front desk. Mr. Wright to the front desk."

A shadow of annoyance passes over Vivian's face. They rarely use the loudspeaker system, which has become nearly obsolete. Vivian has lobbied for the removal of the system and the speakers for years, but the cost to remove them is outlandish. Joe had argued that they weren't hurting anyone right where they were.

Vivian continues talking with Ed while Joe heads inside. He walks past the crowd of Jenk's fans, still waiting for the tight end to reappear. Even though they must know his actress girlfriend is on location somewhere in Canada shooting a new movie, they yell for her too. Amazingly, a few of them also yell for Joe, as if his star has been brightened by the proximity to city sports royalty.

As he passes the rows of shiny new vehicles in all makes, models and colors, he pulls out his phone and sees three missed calls from his mother. He frowns. Sandra Wright had worked at the original dealership for years and supported his dad for the length of his career. She wouldn't dare call Joe's cell phone in the middle of the day if it wasn't an emergency.

There are no text messages from her. Just missed calls.

"Hello, Mr. Wright," Eric, one of his top salespeople at this location, calls out. He stands with a couple who gawk at him before bending their heads together and whispering to each other. The woman flushes and gives him a small wave of her hand.

"Hello, there," he calls back. Addressing the couple, he asks, "Finding anything that suits you today?"

"Oh, yes," the man returns. "We'll definitely be going home in something new."

Joe winks and points a finger. "Now that's what I like to hear." He flashes the woman a brilliant smile, and she beams.

He's still smiling as he pulls open the main double doors. Nora is sitting at the large round kiosk-type desk in the middle of the showroom floor. His smile fades.

"I'm so sorry, Mr. Wright." Her voice quavers just a bit. Joe is not a strict boss. At least, he wouldn't describe himself as such. But he does expect that his employees follow protocol. Using the loudspeaker to call him in from a marketing campaign is definitely not protocol. He is about to tell Nora as much when she says, "Your mom has called here twice. She said she couldn't reach you on your cell, and I thought it would be more efficient to just use the loudspeaker. I know it's not standard practice."

Joe glances down at the phone still in his hand and feels a flicker of apprehension. He gives Nora a tight smile. "Thanks."

Before he can reach his office door, his phone buzzes and he sees his sister's name. He presses accept and holds the phone up to his ear. "Paige?" He shuts the door behind him. Through the glass walls of his office, he notices that Nora is looking at him. When they lock eyes, she looks away quickly. He wishes he'd put some blinds on these windows. Vivian had said that blinds would make him seem unapproachable. There are times when he would rather not be approached.

"What the hell, Joseph?" Paige stage-whispers into the phone. "Where have you been?"

"I've been here. Working." He's not going to get into it with his sister. The woman is four years younger than he is and has never seriously worked a day in her life. She's gone from living off their parents to living off the alimony payments of first one, then another, then a third ex-husband, all of whom have been nearly twenty years her senior. "What's wrong?" he demands.

"Mom has been trying to get in touch with you."

"I *know*, Paige. I was just getting ready to call her back."

"Well, you can't right now. She's in with Dad."

"In where?"

"In the emergency room."

"Dad's in the emergency room? Why?"

He can hear Paige inhale, taking a long drag on the clove cigarettes she smokes. She thinks that they make her look sophisticated. Joe thinks they make her look desperate. "Look, I'm not sure how much they've told you, and God forbid anyone in this family be honest with each other."

Paige is right about that. The unspoken motto of the Wrights seems to be, *If we don't talk about it, it didn't happen.* They are experts at very quietly, very discreetly, sliding some money under the table and making their problems disappear without a word. This is another thing that Joe has no intention of discussing with Paige.

"You should probably just come here," Paige finishes.

"Come where?" he asks. "To the hospital? Which one? Is he in the city? Is he *okay*?"

"He's—yes, he's…okay." He catches the hesitation. "And no, he's not in the city. He's in Beesonstown."

"Oh, Jesus," he says. The hospital in Beesonstown is only suitable if you have absolutely no other options in the world. Even then, Joe just might choose to take his chances without any medical attention at all. "Can we get him transferred?"

"Yeah…I don't think so, Joe. I don't actually think he's going to be in here long. You should just come home."

Joe sinks down in his chair and leans back. It's not that he lives that far away from his parents' house in Conway. It's not much more than an hour and a half drive. It's just that he tries to avoid going home at all if he can help it.

After college, when he started taking on more responsibility for the dealership, he had planned elaborate trips with his friends over the holiday season to avoid going home. Then when he and Vivian had married, he'd insisted that it was easier for them to host holiday dinners, first as a couple and then as a family with their children. That way, he'd argued, Vivian's family could attend, and the family wasn't making two trips in one day. Paige hadn't seemed to care. She was either off enjoying a new relationship or skulking quietly into the home of whoever was hosting. And if his parents minded, they'd never said a word.

He tries to think of the last time he had even stepped foot in his parents' house—the big four-bedroom brick home on the hill overlooking the Mitsin River where all of his high school friends had gathered for bonfires, cookouts, and parties, once upon a time. Until they didn't anymore. Until that last time.

His office door opens and Vivian walks in, her pretty face questioning. He mouths "Paige" to her, and she nods, taking a seat in one of the chairs across from him.

Paige had said their dad was going to be okay. He latches onto that. "I just don't know if it's going to be possible for me to come home right now, Paige. We've got some marketing work happening over the weekend."

Paige makes a noise through the phone. A combination of an exhale of scented smoke and a scoff. "You know what, Joe? Do whatever you want to do. You always do anyway."

"What's that supposed to mean?"

There is a pause. In that pause, Joe anticipates all of the unspoken words and accusations that his sister clearly wants to lob at him. But she doesn't. She just says, "Nothing."

He locks eyes with Vivian who is still staring at him questioningly. To Paige, he says, "I'm going to need to talk to Viv."

"You do that, Joe." Paige's voice is overly animated and filled with sarcasm. "You talk to Viv. I'll take care of Mom and Dad."

"I'll call you back."

"Whatever. I need to go back in."

He ends the call and presses his lips together while he puffs out his cheeks.

"What's going on?" Vivian asks.

"I'm not sure, other than Dad is in the hospital, Mom is with him, and Paige thinks I should come home."

"Then you should go."

"I can't go, Vivian. There's so much happening here. And there's you and the kids."

Vivian looks like she's about to say something then

reconsiders. "Paige wouldn't tell you to come unless it was serious. She didn't give you any indication of the problem?"

"No. She just said something about our lack of communication skills—which she certainly demonstrated—and repeated her request for my presence. She *did* say that she didn't think Dad would be in the hospital for long, which makes me think it's not overly serious."

Vivian gives a little shake of her head. Her red hair bounces against her slim shoulders. "He's in the hospital right now?"

"Yeah, in Beesonstown of all places."

Vivian doesn't react. She was born and raised on the other side of the state and doesn't understand the nuances of the area in which he grew up. She doesn't know that Beesonstown has become a haven for low-level criminals and drug users, or that when travelling back to Conway, it's as if you've essentially gone back in time to an area and an era that hasn't seen either progress or decline. It's just...status quo. Same families, same schools, same businesses passed down from generation to generation. Joe is amazed by its ability to self-sustain the way that it has.

Vivian says, "Then you will go now to the hospital and find out what's going on. I'll join you later, either at the hospital or your parents' house once I've made all of the necessary arrangements here and at home with Bonnie."

Bonnie, their live-in nanny, is always at the house, so Joe is slightly more concerned about the business than the children. That should disconcert him more than it does.

But it's more than only concern for the business; he doesn't want his wife at his parents' house. She's never spent any real time in Conway, and she doesn't understand. While his upbringing was affluent, comparatively speaking, hers had taken place in an upper-class area where she'd been surrounded by people just like her.

Joe hasn't shared much with Vivian about Conway and about his old friends—the kids who'd grown up in houses that hadn't been updated for generations, who'd worn hand-me-down clothes, who'd floated down the Mitsin River in tubes trailing coolers for fun in the summertime, who'd chugged cheap, warm beer in fields and listened to country music. She wouldn't understand any of it, and he doesn't want to relive it.

"I'll go," he says. "You stay here and hold down the fort."

She shakes her head. "I'm coming."

He looks at his wife, whom he loves, admires, and respects. But in that moment, something red and hot bubbles up from a primal place in his body.

Before his temper gets the better of him, he stands and moves toward the windows that overlook the front of the car lot where all of the newest and most expensive models are kept. The dealership is situated off a major highway, with a stop light directly in front of the business so that it's easy and convenient for customers to pull in and out of the parking lot.

As he gazes out, a passing vehicle revs its engine and soars through a red light. Another driver blasts a horn.

There is another reason he doesn't want to go home. One he can barely admit to himself, let alone to Vivian. In two weeks, it'll be twenty years since the accident that changed everything, just as much as it had changed nothing, of how his life has progressed. Joe had faced no consequences for his role in the events of that evening. He had simply walked away, washed his hands of all blame, all fault, all reproach.

He squeezes his eyes shut.

Vivian has come to stand beside him. She places her hand on his shoulder.

He flinches without meaning to.

She notices, and removes her touch quickly.

He has hurt her feelings.

"I'm coming with you," she says again.

He clenches his jaw. He doesn't say anything else even though he wants to warn her that if she comes home with him, she'll likely end up hating him as much as he hates himself.

CHAPTER 3

CHLOE-NOW

"Mom, Tori asked if I could spend the night."

Chloe Nicholson is sitting at her desk in front of the soft glow of her laptop. Instead of working, she's scrolling on her phone, looking through the latest photos of a beautiful family's social media feed. Twelve-year-old Emma is standing in the doorway of Chloe's home office waiting for a response to her demand with a derisive look on her face. This expression, now a permanent fixture on her daughter's face, has appeared gradually over the past few months. Since she's been hanging out with Tori, Chloe thinks wryly.

It's Friday afternoon. Emma is done with her schoolwork for the day, and her chores have been completed. It's one of those rare free nights with no scheduled activities that makes Chloe twitchy.

"Not tonight," she says to her daughter, offering no further explanation aloud.

Tori is a tennis friend, handpicked to some extent by Chloe. The girl's family looks good on paper. The father is an orthopedist, and the mother is a corporate attorney for some Fortune 500 company in the city. But Tori and her family make Chloe uncomfortable. The parents seem far too lenient, often indulging the whims of their three children. Their oldest daughter, for example, has just decided to take a gap year from college after already completing freshman year. Though Chloe wonders if the girl actually *completed* anything. And the mother seemed pleased with this development. As if a gap year was something to be celebrated instead of cause for concern.

Tori, the youngest of the family's three children, never meets Chloe's eye when she speaks. Chloe at first attributed the behavior to her quiet personality—a quality that Chloe had initially deemed desirable. But it's been nearly half a year since Emma and Tori became friends. And in that time, Tori matured rapidly, her thirteen-year-old body unusually developed for her age. The child is evasive, and that's not the kind of healthy influence that Emma needs at this formative age.

"But why?" Emma's voice is plaintive. A whine. "You never let me do anything."

"That's not true. You do plenty of things." She gets ready to tick off all of Emma's activities, but before she can speak, Emma responds, "Yeah, with *you*." It sounds like an accusation, and though Chloe winces, she doesn't let on how much her daughter's words sting.

Emma had been such a sweet-natured child, always smiling and giggling. She'd been a delight. And for a time, her daughter's gentle temperament had even brought Chloe and Jason closer together. That hadn't lasted, of course. Her ex-husband had been far too unconcerned about life in general. The man had absolutely no plan or ambition. No drive or vision. He has always seemed content to simply exist.

When Chloe had been in college, still reeling from the aftereffects of the events of her life, Jason Lawrence's laidback nature had attracted her to him. Two years younger than her and from her hometown of Conway, he'd been easy and uncomplicated, yet understanding, when the rest of her life had fallen apart. And that had been enough for a time, until Chloe realized that there was more to life, and she had something to prove.

Even years later, after their marriage had slowly deteriorated, their divorce had lacked any kind of drama, complication, or emotion. Chloe had filed and Jason had simply signed the papers and moved out, taking nothing but his clothes. It had been easy, and Chloe had trouble understanding those other mothers who'd gone through complicated and messy splits that had ripped each other to shreds.

Life could be easy if you simply decided on a plan and followed through.

Which is why Emma's sudden change in temperament frustrates Chloe. There is no rhyme or reason for it. Since she'd turned twelve, Emma's moods have vacillated from indifference to near rage, and she goes out of her way to make Chloe feel like the bad guy.

Elaine, Chloe's therapist, assures Chloe each week that this is normal behavior, but it doesn't feel normal to her. Chloe had certainly never acted this way as a child, even when she'd had more than enough reason to do so.

Chloe just wants to protect Emma, who has no idea what's out there waiting for her during the upcoming, unpredictable teenage years. If that means Emma hates her for a little while, Chloe is just going to have to accept that.

Someday Emma will understand.

"Can Tori come over here then?" Emma tries.

Chloe sighs. "How about you and I make some popcorn and watch a movie? We can even pick something that's PG-13. How does that sound?" She smiles brightly at her daughter.

Emma rolls her eyes. "That's not even a thing anymore," she mutters.

She's not about to argue with a child over movie ratings. "Better yet, it's so nice outside. Why don't we go to the park and take a walk before dinner." She says it as if it's a brilliant idea and hopes Emma doesn't catch on to the fact that Chloe is attempting to encourage her to exercise more.

Her eyes just barely shift down to Emma's pink shirt stretched over her belly and the still developing buds of her breasts. Tennis and golf haven't quite been doing the trick. Chloe remembers what it was like as an overweight, unpopular teenager. Her parents had been absolutely no help with their baked goods and carb-laden dinners, and while she and her brother Matt had eaten well, the plentiful food had done them no favors.

Chloe's mind starts to veer into dangerous territory—remembering some of the things that she'd done to make people notice her. Make people like her.

She doesn't want Emma to have to go through the things that she went through.

She blinks, forcing her mind back to the present.

Emma is still young for twelve, most likely because she's enrolled in Chloe's charter school curriculum. She hasn't had the same access to social experiences as other children her age. The friends that she does have, she's met through extracurricular activities chosen by Chloe after plenty of research. Tennis, golf, horseback riding, piano lessons. Activities that will make Emma a well-rounded, well-adjusted person before she goes off to college.

"I don't want to go for a walk with you."

Again, the word *you* is an accusation.

Chloe raises her chin a notch. "Okay, then. You can catch up on your reading. Have you finished *The Book Thief*?"

She taps her cheek with the tip of her finger. She will schedule an extra tennis lesson with Emma's coach for next week. They aren't at a point yet where a personal trainer is necessary, but it won't be long.

Emma stomps away angrily, up the stairs, without answering. The bedroom door on the second floor shuts more forcefully than necessary.

Emma doesn't yet have a cell phone. This is one issue that infuriates the normally milquetoast Jason. But, as Chloe had argued countless times, their daughter doesn't need a phone. There are more than enough ways for her to stay in touch with her friends. In fact, she's probably flopped on her bed right now, messaging Tori through a chat app downloaded to her laptop. Chloe has full access to the contents of the application and will check that later, as she does each evening.

What bothers Jason is that Emma doesn't have immediate access to *him*. But whose fault is that? If Jason were a more committed father, he would volunteer to take his daughter to some of her activities. Then he could actually see Emma in person. It certainly isn't Chloe's fault that Jason had decided to return to that backwoods town of Conway, with its lack of progress, resources, and culture. And it's not Emma's fault either.

There is a part of Chloe that's glad her ex-husband has moved away. It's difficult as a single mother, but it's even more difficult parenting a precocious girl like Emma with a clueless man like Jason always questioning her methods. He has no idea what it takes to raise a well-rounded child.

Luckily, she doesn't need to worry about that. Jason remarried Becky five years ago, not even a year after he and Chloe had divorced. Since then, he's been much too busy with his new family—his young wife, three-year-old daughter, and one-year-old twin sons—to pay much attention to Emma. That suits Chloe just fine.

There had been no need for a formal, court-ordered

custody agreement. With Emma's schoolwork and activity schedule, it had just made more sense for Emma to stay with Chloe full-time.

Jason can have his rural life in Conway and Chloe and Emma will keep theirs, an hour away, in upscale North Fairhaven, far away from the bad things that had happened in the past.

Chloe's email notification chimes, and she looks back at her laptop screen, at the message that's just come through. She skims it first, her mind shifting gears from parenting to work. Then she squints and reads the message more carefully.

Coincidentally, it's a request for her to meet in a few weeks with the superintendent of a school district not far from Conway. Chloe's company, the Academic Achievement Academy, has been implemented as a supplementary curriculum program for a handful of high-performing school districts across the state, and this is just the latest in the long line of requests to come in. Her combination of strict psychological monitoring with a creative and rigorous supplemental curriculum has seen unprecedented success in the students who have gone through the program. It's been called "groundbreaking," but Chloe hasn't created anything new. It's just that the way she's combined the monitoring and learning program seems to be working. Over the past year, the size of her company has doubled, and with it the money has flowed in.

This particular school district is interesting because it's not nearly as high-performing as the other districts that she's worked with. In fact, this area is fairly socio-economically depressed. If the Academy can achieve results there, Chloe may be able to pursue the federal funding necessary to expand the program throughout the state and the country.

She gets that tingly feeling in her fingers that happens

when an opportunity presents itself.

She starts to type a response and then notices the date for the meeting request. Tuesday, May 28.

She hesitates.

Of course, she had known that the date was coming up. She is always acutely aware of that day. She'd just been thinking of it, in fact, before Emma had interrupted. Chloe just hadn't planned for it to be thrust in her face. It isn't lost on her that this is the twenty-year anniversary of…all of it. How has that possibly happened? How have the years passed as if they were nothing at all? As if it was all just empty space.

She stares at the blinking cursor on her screen, tempted to request a different date. Any other date.

She thinks about Elaine and glances over at her cell phone. Maybe she should call her therapist and talk this through before she responds.

But she knows what Elaine will say. *Chloe, you need to face your shadows head-on. If not, they will always have power over you.*

An image of the handsome man and his beautiful wife—the family she'd just been stalking on social media—appears in her mind. She scowls and casts them away.

No one has power over Chloe Nicholson except for Chloe Nicholson. Not anymore. But the image of the man's perfectly coiffed dark hair and bright white smile stays on her mind—front and center, actually.

"No," she says out loud and takes three deep breaths, imagining the man's face disappearing from existence.

He has no power over her.

When she feels grounded again, she turns back to the laptop. Fingers flying over the keyboard, she confirms the meeting date and presses *send*, unconsciously humming a little jingle as she does so.

CHAPTER 4

DAN-NOW

Dan Armstrong attempts to loosen the bolts holding the motor to the transmission and mounts of the Mustang parked in his small, cramped garage. There is very little clearance on top of the bell cover, and even though he's already disconnected the gears and wiring and drained the fluid from the transmission lines, the task will not be easy without a hoist.

He scrapes his raw knuckles against the engine and swears.

It's cool in the dim, musty garage, but he's sweating with the effort and the frustration. He wishes he owned a better space for this type of work. He supposed he could trailer the car and haul it to his father's garage ten miles away in the mountains above Conway. But that would mean interacting with the old man, which he tries to avoid if he can help it.

Dan straightens and rubs his knuckles. Then he reaches behind him and takes a long pull from the bottle that has been sitting on the workbench. The beer is warm, but the malty taste calms him.

After he finishes the last swallow, he wipes his mouth with the back of his hand and places the empty bottle back down on the cluttered surface.

He catches sight of Amber watching him from just

outside the garage, eight-month-old Mason perched on her hip. The baby is red-faced and damp, as if he'd just finished crying. It only now occurs to Dan that he'd failed to enter the house after returning from work.

"Hey." He doesn't look at her directly, instead moving back toward the car.

"You weren't going to tell me you were home?" Her tone is immediately aggressive, which sets him back on his heels. It's just after four o'clock. Most people weren't even home from work yet, and he couldn't even get a few minutes to himself after a shift that started at six that morning.

"I just got here ten minutes ago."

Her gaze shifts to the small refrigerator he keeps stocked in the garage. "And yet you've already had a beer."

He sighs. "Did you want something other than to give me a hard time?"

She shifts Mason from one hip to the other. Her brownish-blond hair is long, wavy, and unkempt. Mason reaches up and takes a fistful of her hair in his chubby wet fist and places it in his mouth. Amber doesn't seem to notice. "The boys are doing their homework," she says.

Dan nods, not sure what response he's supposed to provide. It's what Henry, Luke, and Sam should be doing.

Amber walks into the garage, and Dan tenses. This is his space. The only space he has left.

"How's it going?" she asks, eyeing the Mustang. Mason hits her shoulder, vocalizing *dadadadadada*. Dan is under no impression that the baby is referring to him, and his chest is tight as Amber moves to peer under the hood, careful to keep Mason out of reach of the dusty shelves with their dirty old cans of paint and sharp tools hanging from rusty hooks on the walls.

"I need to pull the engine," Dan says in answer to her question.

Amber nods. She understands more about cars than most women he knows. Her dad and grandfather had both been car guys and engineers, and she picked up on the basics when she'd been a tomboy.

"Did you tell Teddy?" she asks. Teddy is her brother, the owner of the Mustang. A salesman of commercial office equipment in a neighboring town, he doesn't understand cars nearly as well as his sister, though he likes to pretend he does. He paid too much for the car, and when he realized he was in over his head, he'd asked Dan to fix it.

"Not yet."

"Don't you think you should tell him before you get too far into this project? He might not have the money to pay you."

Dan isn't doing the work for the money, so he doesn't respond.

There is a long silence—one that has grown familiar between them, but not comfortable. In that silence, so many words float around them, words that are never captured or released.

"How was your day?" Amber finally asks. She doesn't mean it. She doesn't care.

Dan shrugs. What was there to say? He was a diesel mechanic for the railway company in town. He worked on the huge engines and then he came home and worked on whatever car was waiting for him. His day was his day. Same day, every day.

She lets out a breath, nearly inaudible. "We're having spaghetti for dinner."

It is the third time for spaghetti that week. He knows he should be grateful that there's dinner at all. Pasta is easy, and it's cheap. Still, it would be nice to have a bit of variety.

He moves to the small refrigerator and pulls out another beer, silently daring her to say something. She doesn't.

Mason starts to blow spit bubbles and make louder noises. *Bub-bub-bub-bub-bub.* He pats his mother's shoulder with his fingers. The baby doesn't look in Dan's direction.

Dan uses a rusty bottle opener on the side of the workbench to remove the bottlecap. He takes another long drink. The liquid is fizzy and cold, and he has to stop himself from chugging the entire bottle. He isn't sure why he's even trying to hold back.

There had been a time, a long time ago, when he'd refrained from any kind of alcohol. It was a sort of punishment. But then he realized that drinking was what everyone expected him to do. It was who they thought he was. So, he did it more and more, proving the world right. And in the process, he proved himself right. He fully embodied what he was supposed to be. A loser.

He'd have been better off never having been born at all.

With some effort, he takes the bottle from his lips, lets it dangle from between his fingers, and stares at Amber.

She stares back, opens her mouth as if she's going to speak. There is a pause. "Dinner in twenty minutes," she says instead of whatever she'd been about to say. Her voice is tight, clipped.

She turns her back and walks across the yard toward their small Cape Cod–style house. He waits a minute then walks out of the garage in time to see the front door closing behind her. Even though she's had four children, she is still a good-looking woman. Shapely in all the right places, with a bright, easy smile and a quick laugh when there's something to smile or laugh about.

There had been a time when he'd thought she was his savior. What had happened to that girl? What had happened to them?

Dan had met Amber at church, of all places, during that

fateful period between the time that he'd been charged with vehicular homicide and the trial and sentencing. He'd been lost. His aunt Brenda had been the one to suggest that he attend services at the small Presbyterian chapel. Dan, who had been on the brink of complete collapse, would have agreed to just about anything to make the pain go away.

It had helped for a time. While the congregation hadn't been exactly welcoming, neither had they turned him away. Eventually, some of them even embraced him for his commitment and determination to try to make things right.

As if you could make things right after something like that.

The best part of the experience, by far, had been meeting Amber. Five years younger than Dan, she'd been a young teenager when he'd first seen her; tall, thin, coltish. Her teeth had been too big for her mouth back then.

She'd also been determined.

They hadn't dated, at least not then. But they'd developed a casual friendship, and she had been a support to him through all of the hearings, the trials, the mistakes made by his lawyers, and eventually when the sentencing had taken place, and he was sent to the county jail for two years.

They'd communicated by writing old-fashioned letters. He still has those letters somewhere. And it was through those letters that they'd fallen in love. When he'd finally been released, Amber was eighteen, and she was right there waiting for him.

While her parents had been less than thrilled with the relationship, they also had not forbade the two from seeing each other. Amber found herself pregnant with Henry almost immediately. Dan went to a trade school, became a diesel mechanic, joined the union, and started working for the railroad in short order. A year later, they'd welcomed Luke, followed quickly by Sam. Then ten years later, Mason made his appearance. Somewhere between life, work, and kids, they'd had a very modest family-only wedding in the backyard of her parents' house just outside of town. He never remembered the date.

Looking back, Dan isn't sure how any of it had even happened. It is as though life is a river, and he is just being swept along like a small twig or flotsam.

He stands in front of the open garage and downs the rest of his beer before heading into the house, which they've outgrown. Mason sleeps in the master bedroom with Dan and Amber, while Luke and Sam share a room. Henry, the oldest at fifteen, is the only one lucky enough to have any privacy. But once Mason is out of his crib, the toddler will need to move in with Sam, and Luke will have to share a room with Henry. Dan is already dreading the battles that will ensue with that development.

He inhales and exhales deeply before he pulls open the front door. When he walks inside, he's hit with a blast of noise and commotion. Ten-year-old Sam is bellowing what seem to be nonsensical words, Mason is crying. Luke is yelling at them both to shut up, and he presumes it's Henry who has just slammed a door from somewhere on the second floor.

Despite the cool temperature outside, the house is humid and smells of garlic and an underlying sourness, like stale cabbage and onions.

He can still feel the effects of the two beers, but the sound of turmoil makes him want another.

He walks down the short hallway toward the kitchen, the nucleus of the chaos. Mason is strapped into a highchair, his fists pumping as fat tears roll down round, red cheeks. Sam places his hands over his ears and is leaning very close to Mason's face, yelling the nonsense words, presumably to try to distract his brother. It doesn't seem to be helping.

Thirteen-year-old Luke is sitting at the scuffed and scratched oak table, scowling at his brothers.

Through all of this noise, Amber is standing over the stove, calmly stirring a pot of sauce with a wooden spoon.

"Jesus, Amber." Dan raises his voice so that he can be heard. "The neighbors down on Oak Street can probably hear the racket coming from this goddamned house."

She doesn't answer. None of the boys acknowledge his presence.

He opens the refrigerator to grab another beer, and as he does, he catches sight of the calendar held with two soccer magnets to the freezer door.

The date—May 28—is marked with an unassuming black pen in Amber's swooping handwriting. Luke has a soccer game that evening.

Dan feels an unexpected bubble of rage. *She knows.* She knows that date, and yet she writes something as inane as a reminder of a soccer game in the empty space. He nearly punches a fist right into the calendar.

The baby wails louder. Sam pulls his mouth apart with his fingers and sticks out his tongue, making a babbling sound. Luke yells, "Oh. My. God!"

"Amber, what the hell is this?" Dan demands above the noise.

Without responding to him, Amber twists the knob of the gas stove and lifts the large silver pot filled with boiling pasta. The pot is overly full and heavy. Some of the water splashes out as she moves toward the colander positioned in the sink on the perpendicular wall.

Dan knows he should take the pot from her and drain it. He should tell Luke to stop yelling at his brothers and set the table. He should pick up the baby and soothe him until he stops crying. He should help his wife.

Instead, he says, "Amber, I asked you a goddamned

question."

The hot pasta water spills into the colander, and a thick curtain of steam rises up, fogging the window above the basin.

She wipes her hands on the front of her jeans then starts to slide the pasta right into the pot of tomato sauce. The oven timer begins beeping, joining the rest of the noise in the room.

Dan takes two strides toward her, places his hand on her shoulder so that she'll turn around and look at him. When he touches her, she flinches and the lip of the colander catches on the edge of the bubbling sauce. The pot flips toward her, splashing boiling liquid down the front of her shirt and over her forearms and wrists. She screams and jumps back, tripping over the leg of Mason's highchair and coming down hard on her hip against the floor.

All this shocks the boys—even the baby—into silence so that the only sound is the beeping of the timer for the oven in which the garlic bread has begun to burn.

Amber's head is down, and her shoulders begin to shake. At first Dan thinks she might be laughing, but as quickly as he reaches to help her up, he stops. When she looks up at him, he can see that her green eyes are red and filled with tears.

Henry appears in the doorway, and Mason starts to cry again.

Amber pushes her hair back with her hands, transferring tomato sauce through the brown-blond streaks.

Henry pushes past Dan and reaches down. "Mom, are you all right?"

She lets her oldest son help her up, and then she goes to the sink and rinses off her arms, which are pink from the hot liquid. Her shirt is still covered with the steaming sauce.

Dan stands still, impotent, while Henry picks up Mason,

and Sam and Luke skulk off somewhere, anywhere but that room.

Finally, Amber turns to Dan. In an exhausted voice, she says, "I want a divorce."

CHAPTER 5

CRYSTAL-NOW

Crystal Neumann pinches out the last few greasy crumbs of potato chips from the bottom of the bag she'd picked up on her extended lunch hour from Munson, Munson, and Temple, Attorneys at Law. The small reception area where she works is brightly lit and pristine, and she scrolls through her social media feed on her phone in the quiet of the round cubicle.

Anita Hanson has posted her daughter Elyse's graduation photos, and Crystal studies the posed and filtered pictures of the beautiful young girl. Jessica graduated with Crystal. The fact that not only Anita but quite a few others her age have children graduating from high school is still unthinkable to her, even though she's noticed these photos of her classmates with their children for the past few years.

It was just yesterday that *she* was making that walk on the stage to take her diploma from the school superintendent.

She'd blinked and somehow finds herself sitting in this empty, nondescript, pink brick office building, not two miles from where she'd grown up. How has that happened?

Crystal, despite adoring children herself, has also managed to have no children of her own. Her husband Frank's two grown daughters from a previous marriage are close to her age, so of course she doesn't consider his daughters as *her* children, even though they all get along just fine. She also doesn't consider their raucous little boys and girls—five in total—her grandchildren. She is still young enough for those little ones to be her own.

Crystal wipes her greasy fingers on a tissue and throws it into the trash. She pulls her attention away from her phone and looks at the clock, which is slowly tick-tick-ticking on the wall above her. It's nearly time to leave. She will stop at the Save-A-Lot on her way home and pick up some ground meat to make hamburgers. Maybe she'll also get one of those pre-made cheesecakes that Frank likes for dessert. She won't eat much. Maybe just a small sliver of cake, since she's eaten more than she should today.

Lunch had been the highlight of the day, in fact. She'd grabbed two slices of cheese pizza at the New York–style pizza parlor a few miles from the office. Vince, the owner, had winked at her and called her "miss," making her blush. Feeling good, she'd taken a few extra minutes to return a dress, the size of which ran insultingly small, to the Chestnut Hills mall, a sad and rundown collection of empty storefronts and echoing hallways that still has one function-ing and semi-decent department store left in it.

The workday itself had been calm. Boring, even. After two months at this job, she is learning that Fridays at Munson, Munson, and Temple often tend to be quiet. And on this particular Friday, only Temple is in. Temple is a thin and irritable middle-aged man who combs his thinning brown hair in a swoop across his shiny scalp. Munson and Munson, a husband-and-wife team, are at a conference in Las Vegas, which seems mighty convenient and a little hoity-toity to Crystal, not that anyone asked her opinion.

Her stomach gurgles after eating the chips and she places a hand on the ever-expanding girth that she finds there. Monday, she will start her diet. Maybe she'll even bring some extra clothes and sneak in a quick walk on the Great Allegheny Passage, the rehabilitated railway trail that parallels the Mitsin River through the city. If the late spring weather cooperates, that is.

Temple is scheduled to be in court on Monday afternoon, and with the Munsons gone until next Friday, the whole week is promising to be extra slow.

The phone rings its muted trill on the desk in front of her, and Crystal checks the time again. She does not answer calls that come in on the general number after 4:30. It is 4:45, and she lets the call ring through to voicemail. It makes her uneasy to sit there while someone is so clearly trying to reach a human, so she stands and heads to the kitchen to make a cup of coffee in the common area. She pops one of the breakfast blend coffee pods into the machine. She shouldn't be drinking coffee this late in the day, but she knows it doesn't matter. She won't get much sleep anyway with Frank's CPAP machine inhaling and exhaling beside her.

She glances down the hall at Temple's open door, then walks toward it and taps gently. A light tinkling of classical music reaches her ears from somewhere within.

"Yes?" he mumbles, just loud enough for her to hear.

"Sorry to interrupt, Mr. Temple. Can I get you some coffee?"

He doesn't look up from the file he's studying. "No." Then he belatedly adds, "Thank you, Doris."

She hesitates. *Doris?*

Crystal has worked for Munson, Munson, and Temple for just a short time, but shouldn't he know her name by now? Just today, she interacted with him several times, and all the while he had no idea of her name. She's partly amused but also offended.

How has it come to this, that the nature of her entire

existence is so temporary and meaningless? She is so temporary and meaningless that people don't even bother to learn her name anymore.

She steps away from his doorway without correcting him and backtracks to the kitchen to finish preparing her coffee.

When she returns to her desk, a red light on the phone pulses steadily, indicating a message, and Crystal takes a few tentative sips of her beverage before she listens to it. This law firm is one of the few in town, and despite specializing in mainly property and estate matters, each of the attorneys tended to take cases outside of real estate law in their own areas of interest and expertise. Crystal doesn't know if this is a good thing or not, but it is the one thing that keeps this job interesting. She periodically finds herself with juicy gossip that she is forbidden from sharing.

She picks up a pad and pen, dials into the voicemail system, and then presses the number one to listen to the message. A tentative clearing of the throat precedes the words.

"Uh, hi. My name is Amber Armstrong. I'm looking for someone—a lawyer. I need, uh..." The words trail off. *"I want to get a divorce, and I guess I need a lawyer to do that."*

Crystal's hand hovers above the notepad. She knows this name, knows this voice. She knows it well, in fact.

The breathy voice continues quietly, as if the woman is trying to whisper but also trying to be heard. Crystal imagines that Amber Armstrong is at home with her house full of children.

"I would like to meet with someone as soon as possible. I'm not, like, afraid or anything. You know. For my...safety. But...well. I'd just like this to be over and done with."

Crystal visualizes Amber—a sturdy, curvy girl with

dishwater-blond hair, no makeup, and a baby permanently attached to her body. The last time she'd seen the woman had been a few months earlier at the Save-A-Lot. Crystal had planned to say hello and maybe invite the family for a weekend dinner, but Amber had walked past with a faraway look on her face. She'd had a baby strapped to her front in one of those pouches and another little boy walked next to her chattering away. Amber hadn't seemed to notice or recognize Crystal. That had hurt Crystal's feelings greatly.

The voice on the phone continues. *"I have four children. I'm not sure about…custody. But, you know, that'll have to be decided, too. Or visitation for…him. I'm not sure how any of that works."* A long exhale follows. *"Okay, please call me back."* She rattles off a phone number, which Crystal jots down on the notepad.

Crystal replaces the receiver and then sits back. *Well, hell.* She may not know Amber well, but she sure knows Amber's husband. Dan has been through so much already in his life. She wonders if he has any idea that a divorce is about to hit him, too.

It's hard not to think about Dan without remembering what happened all those years ago. In fact, Crystal realizes, the twentieth anniversary is coming up in just over a week.

The Munson, Munson, and Temple office is just down the hill from the site of the accident, and if Crystal were to look out the west window, she'd be able to make out the large tree under which a perpetual altar of stuffed animals, balloons, and other memorial items is placed.

The girl hadn't deserved to die. Megan. Megan Richards. Crystal says her name out loud in an attempt to keep the memory alive.

She had tried to prevent Dan from driving that night, but he hadn't listened to her.

For the life of her, she can't think why she'd even been there that night at a party with a bunch of seniors about to graduate. Not that it matters now.

She also can't figure out why Dan has never left Conway. She wonders if it's some sort of self-flagellation. She wishes he'd reach out to her like he had when he'd been a boy. When he'd been dealing with all of the stuff with his mother and his horrific, abusive, alcoholic father.

She wishes he'd need her again. No one needs Crystal these days. Except Frank.

Crystal sits there for a long while staring at the note she'd made on the pad in front of her. She contemplates crumpling it up and throwing it in the trash with her grease-stained tissue.

In the end, she pushes herself up and walks to Temple's office, the notes of a piano spilling out from his speaker. He is still studying the papers on his desk, but now he's making notes on a large yellow legal pad to his right.

Crystal knocks, and when he doesn't acknowledge her, she knocks again.

She catches the flash of annoyance on his face as he looks up. "What is it now?" His voice is curt.

"A call came in on the general line. Someone looking for a divorce lawyer."

"I don't take divorce cases."

Crystal pauses, waiting for further instruction. When he looks back down, she says, "Should I...call her back? Refer her to someone else?"

Temple sighs. "Sometimes Marie will take divorce and family court cases," he responds, referring to the female Munson. "I don't know what her client load is right now. Any details?"

Crystal glances at the notes she's jotted down, even though she doesn't need them. "Amber Armstrong. Needs someone to help her with both divorce and custody. Says she's not in any danger but wants to move quickly."

"Armstrong," Temple says slowly. His chin snaps up. "Armstrong," he repeats. "Dan Armstrong?"

Crystal shrugs though she knows very well the answer to his question.

Temple makes a crooking motion with his finger, signaling for Crystal's notes. She hands him the piece of paper, and he looks at it. "Amber," he says under his breath. "I think this may be related to someone I prosecuted as one of my first cases," he mumbles mostly to himself, staring at the note. When he looks back up again, he seems surprised to find her still standing there. "I'll give her a call. Thank you, Doris."

"It's Crystal."

He looks up. "Sorry?"

"Crystal. My name is Crystal."

He blinks. "Ah." Then he looks back down at the paper and picks up the phone on his desk. When she doesn't move, he flashes her a glance. "That'll be all."

Dismissed.

Crystal slumps slightly as she walks away. She organizes her desk, washes out her used coffee mug, and neatens the kitchen. From the common area, she can hear Temple talking to someone, and she assumes that it must be Amber.

At exactly five o'clock, she gathers her handbag and walks out the front door, locking it behind her. She doesn't bother saying goodbye.

She climbs into her used compact sedan, which is a few years old but still runs well enough. She waits a moment for the Bluetooth to connect. The speaker blasts a My Chemical Romance song, and Crystal quickly turns down the volume then presses a button on her phone. It takes another few seconds for the phone to connect, but when it does, she's surprised to hear the male voice on the other end. She thought it might go to voicemail.

"Dan," she says. "It's Crystal. I know it's been a while, but do you want to meet for a beer later?"

There is a long pause then a slow exhale. "Why not." It's more resignation than a question.

"Great. How about eight o'clock at Bud's?" Bud's is the most well-known and crowded of the many bars in Conway. It's also the cleanest and most reliable.

Dan agrees and Crystal disconnects the call. From the speakers, "I'm Not Okay" resumes its chorus.

She isn't sure what she's going to say to Dan, but she's not going to let him go through this alone. Not this time. Not again.

CHAPTER 6

CHLOE-THEN

It is May 27. Chloe can barely believe it. Just two short weeks before high-school graduation. Two short weeks before the rest of her life will begin.

She has relentlessly toiled over the past year, determined to mold herself into a new version of the girl she had once been. And while she no longer resembles the pudgy freshman with frizzy hair and pervasive acne who timidly entered the high school nearly four years ago, deep down she still feels like that same insecure girl. Despite her physical transformation, her inner demons continue to whisper, *You are not the same as them. You are a fraud.*

Through the tight peach-colored crop top that she's wearing, she can feel the prickles of sweat blossoming in her armpits. She holds her arms out as inconspicuously as possible, desperately trying to air out her underarms before the perspiration causes visible dark patches. She is disgusting.

She has, incredibly, found herself in the middle of an unsupervised end-of-year conversation between some of the most popular kids in her senior class. Joe Wright is holding court, his black hair shining almost blue in the sunlight filtering in through the window. There are others around him—Ryan Tolbert, Nate Kasinski, Sutton Schultz, Jeff Snyder, Megan Richards. But as always, Joe is the dark and handsome star of the show.

Mr. McPoyle isn't in the room yet, even though English class should have started five minutes ago. But it doesn't matter. They all have their post-graduation plans secured— college, military, trade school. Now, they're only showing up to school to socialize.

A year ago, Chloe would have never been a part of this group. She barely is now. But she'd gone to the gym nearly every day, counted every calorie, tracked every step she'd taken. And it had paid off. Even though she's not slinky and cool like Sutton or gorgeous and popular like Megan, they have allowed her presence. And she knows her place.

Ryan says, "Let's make this party completely off the chain, you know? Let's go out with a bang." He's referring to the gathering that Joe has announced at his house on Mitsin Ridge tomorrow evening.

"As long as it doesn't get out of hand," Joe says. He looks as though he might be regretting the decision to host the party. "And someone else is going to have to bring the alcohol. I have to have some plausible deniability in case my parents find out."

They look at Nate, who has two older brothers, both of whom are over twenty-one and home from college. Nate says, "Nah, sorry, man. I'm leaving for the Army in less than a month. I'm not going to get kicked out before I even start."

"I'm sure I can find someone to get it for us." Sutton winks at Joe, even though Chloe is fairly sure that Joe is dating Megan. Chloe had seen them together a few times in the hallway, and it had sure looked like there was something going on between them. Chloe hadn't been jealous or anything like that. Joe is way too good-looking for her to even consider a crush. But Megan is beautiful, popular, and kind. A rare combination. Chloe hopes that the two of them will get married and live happily ever after.

But Chloe notes the look that passes between Sutton and Joe. Megan is laughing at something that Jeff has just said and doesn't see what's going on between her best friend and her boyfriend. Chloe doesn't know Megan well, but she's always been nice to Chloe, even before Chloe was thin. She feels a wave of protectiveness over Megan.

Chloe isn't sure if it's this rush of emotion that causes her to say suddenly, almost unbidden, "I can get it."

The entire group stops talking and stares at her as if they've just realized she's there.

Ryan is the first one to speak. "Doughy Chloe's stepping it up." He reaches forward to give her a high five.

Chloe is offended by the use of her old nickname, but she accepts the friendly gesture. She hopes her hand isn't too sweaty and watches to see if Ryan wipes his palm after the contact. She doesn't think he does.

"How?" Joe narrows his eyes as he looks at her.

"My—my brother is twenty-four," Chloe stammers. She has no idea if she can convince Matt to do this favor for her.

Megan looks over and touches Chloe's arm. "You don't have to. Someone else can get it."

"No, it's fine. I can do it." She shrugs. *No big deal.* The prickling under her arms has increased in intensity, and she keeps her arms glued to her sides, hoping that the wet spots aren't too visible.

Sutton says brightly, "Great, it's settled. Doughy Chloe will bring the booze. Do you know what to get?"

Chloe stares at her. She opens her mouth and shuts it, and Sutton rolls her eyes. "I'll write you, like, an inventory list." She reaches over and rips a piece of paper out of the notebook on Megan's desk, then begins writing with a purple pen in swooping handwriting.

Chloe doesn't like Sutton, whose eyes are rimmed too

black and whose lips are colored too red. She is popular, but there are a lot of rumors about how many boys she's slept with. Even the unpopular kids in Chloe's friend group have heard the rumors about Sutton's abortion during sophomore year. Chloe has no idea if that rumor is true, but she usually gives Sutton a wide berth, just in case it is. As if her behavior might be contagious. She doesn't understand why Megan is friends with her.

Mr. McPoyle enters the room then, and everyone lazily scatters to their assigned seats. Since final exams are completed, he announces that they'll be watching a film adaptation of *Lord of the Flies*, which they have already read. There are collective shouts of approval from the members of the class.

Chloe watches Sutton out of the corner of her eye. She has not once looked up from her purple inventory, and the list keeps growing longer and longer.

How on earth is she going to convince Matt to get all of this stuff for her? She has some money saved up from babysitting; she'll have to use that, she supposes.

Chloe finds it impossible to pay attention to the movie. As the bell rings, she knows that the sweat has soaked completely through her shirt, and she keeps her arms rigidly at her sides. When they emerge into the hallway, Sutton thrusts the paper into Chloe's chest. "You sure you can handle this?"

Chloe glances at Joe, who is watching this interaction. She nods.

"Good," Sutton responds. She leans closer. "Try not to mess it up."

Megan joins them and gives Chloe an understanding smile, and then they walk away from her, leaving her there to study the piece of paper with a panicked, deflated feeling.

"Everything okay, Chloe?" Mr. McPoyle has appeared

from behind her, and she crumples the paper before he can read the writing.

She swallows and tries to smile. "Yeah. All good."

He glances down at the torn notebook page, and Chloe prays that he doesn't ask to see it. She shifts slightly so that the paper is hidden behind her thigh.

He furrows his brow but only says, "Just watch out for yourself, okay?"

She's not sure what that means, so she just gives an awkward shrug and nods in response. Then she hurries away from the classroom and disappears into the stream of bodies.

Two more classes to figure out what she's going to say to Matt.

Chloe's parents are not home when she gets off the bus that afternoon in front of the small house on Jefferson Avenue. Even though she has her driver's license, there is no available car for her to use. At least, not since Matt came home from college and just never left.

When she walks into the house, she can hear the plinking of his acoustic guitar from his bedroom at the back of the house. His door is shut, and she stands outside for a minute before she works up the courage to knock. The plinking stops, and then silence. She waits for a minute before rapping softly again. "Matt?" she says against the door.

She hears the creak of his bedsprings as he rises, and when the door opens, she detects a pungent skunky odor along with the milder scent of a burning candle.

Matt is overweight, and his face is oily and peppered

with acne, even though Chloe's quite sure he should have grown out of that phase by now. Something has dried a whitish color on the front of his black t-shirt, and his gray sweatpants have a filmy look to them. "Yeah?" He doesn't move from the door so she can't see around his girth.

She's not sure how to start, so she just says, "Hi."

He stares at her.

"What were you playing?"

He narrows his eyes suspiciously. "'Dazed and Confused.' Why?"

She shrugs. "It sounded good."

That makes him hesitate. But he just says, "Mom and Dad aren't home yet," and tries to shut the door on her.

Chloe blocks it with her foot. "I know." Their mother is a bank teller at a local branch and their father is a supervisor at the quarry just over the top of the mountain beyond the small city of Conway. Their parents had been old, relatively speaking, when their mother had given birth to Matt and older still when Chloe came along six years later. They are both thrilled that Matt is back home and living in his childhood bedroom, and neither of them seem bothered by the fact that Matt doesn't have a job and spends most of his time holed up in the house.

Chloe thinks it's weird.

"What do you want?" he asks.

She takes a breath. "I need to ask you for a favor."

He doesn't answer, but he also doesn't slam the door shut, so she takes that as a good sign.

"There's a party tomorrow night at a house of a kid in my class. Joe Wright."

"The one who plays football?" Matt asks, and Chloe raises her eyebrows. Joe plays every sport, or used to. "Yes," she confirms. "His dad is the one that owns the car dealership heading toward Beesonstown."

"There's no way you were invited to his party." Matt barks out a laugh, and Chloe can tell he hasn't brushed his teeth in a while. She wonders what has happened to her brother and feels sad for him and indignant about his dismissive comment at the same time.

"I *am* invited." It's like no one can even see how much weight she's lost over the past year. How much better she looks now. To the whole world, she's still just Doughy Chloe.

Matt says, "Okay, whatever. What does that have to do with me?"

"They've asked me to get the beer and stuff."

"You're not twenty-one."

She blinks at him for a second, but he doesn't make the connection. So she says, "I'm not. But *you* are."

"You want me to buy you beer?"

"And some other stuff."

"Stuff?"

"Like other alcohol." She reaches into the backpack still slung on her shoulder and pulls out the crumpled notebook paper with the swooping purple writing.

He takes the list and studies it. "This is going to cost a lot of money."

"Like, how much?"

"For all of this stuff?" His lips move slightly as he adds it all up. "A few hundred, at least."

Chloe's heart sinks. That will put a huge dent in her babysitting money. She wishes she would have thought of asking if she could take up a collection or something at the party. "Well," she says slowly. "I can cover it, I guess. Are you saying you'll do it?"

Matt looks from the paper to Chloe. He doesn't answer her question, but instead says, "You sure you want to get involved in this, Glow Worm?" He uses the childhood nickname that she loves, and for a second, she longs to fold herself against him like she used to do when she was a little girl and he was her big brother.

She considers his question. "I've known most of these kids for nearly thirteen years, Matt. And today was the first day that I felt like they even saw me."

"I get it. Believe me, I do. But did it ever occur to you that they don't see you because you're just too good for them?"

She doesn't answer.

"Here's what I think. You're going to go off to college, and you're going to kick ass. You're going to find your group, and you're going to have as many friends as you want, but only ones who matter. You're going to forget all about these losers."

She doesn't believe that for a second, and she slumps against his doorframe. She tries to think of something to say that will make him see just how much she needs this.

Before she conjures the words, Matt looks back at the notebook paper. "I'll make a deal with you. I'll do this for you with a few conditions."

"Anything." She wants to hug him.

He holds up a finger. "You will never tell anyone about my involvement. Not your friends, not anyone."

"I promise."

He holds up a second finger. "I will not transport it for you. You'll have to get someone to pick it up."

She's less sure about this requirement, but she agrees anyway. If they want alcohol, that group will find a way to get it. Then she has an idea. "What if you pick it up and then leave it in the car. Then I can drive the car to the party?"

He shakes his head. "Not a chance. You're not driving around with a trunk full of alcohol."

"Fine," she says. She'll figure it out. "What's the third

thing?"

"Mom and Dad can never know about this. They can't know about me, but they can't know about you either. It would break their hearts."

She nods. She hadn't been planning on revealing her involvement anyway. And it's not that she likes deceiving their parents, but she also doesn't mind having something connecting her to Matt again. At one time, they'd been so close, but he's been distant and disconnected since he moved back home.

"If anyone ever asks, I will deny everything," he continues.

That seems to go without saying.

"And five." He holds up his palm with all five fingers displayed. "You need to realize something, Chloe. These people—despite how much you want it to be true—are not your friends. They're using you, and you're letting them do it. You understand that, right?"

Here, she hesitates. They're not using her. She agreed to this. In fact, she's volunteered for this. She sets her mouth in a straight line.

"Right?" he prompts again.

The front door opens, and their mother yells, "Hello!" in her musical tone.

Matt gives her a meaningful look.

"Fine," Chloe finally says.

"Say it."

Their mother calls, "Anybody home?"

Chloe stares at Matt.

He moves to close his door on her, and she hisses, "They're using me," under her breath. But she doesn't believe it.

He cocks his head at her. "You'll see."

Their mother comes around the corner and gives a little

noise of surprise to see them talking together. "Well, look at this! My two angels."

"Leave the money in my room before you go to bed, and I'll go tomorrow. Everything will be in the car, and I'll leave it unlocked in the driveway."

"What are you two whispering about?"

Matt responds first. "I was just telling Chloe that I hope you're going to be making that chicken and Swiss cheese casserole with the croutons."

She claps her hands together and comes toward them. "Oh, your dad just loves that, too." She beams at her children. "I'm so blessed to have you both here."

Chloe gives her mother a half smile and quickly moves away, saying, "I have some homework to do." She heads to her room and shuts the door behind her. From her top right dresser drawer, she counts out two hundred and fifty dollars, wondering if this price will be enough to purchase her popularity. Matt's words echo in her head.

When she exits her room, her mother is already in the kitchen humming audibly as she prepares dinner. Matt's door is shut again. Chloe slides the stack of bills under the door and hears his footsteps approach. There's no going back now.

CHAPTER 7

SUTTON-THEN

Megan slowly reverses out of her assigned spot in the back parking lot of Conway High School. The silver Corolla inches backward at a snail's pace while Megan checks all of her mirrors and then twists around to look out the rear window.

Sutton groans. She wishes Megan would hurry up. She's so damn cautious about everything. Megan ignores her, and Sutton says, "Come *on*," just as Dan Armstrong, in his loud red hatchback, speeds past them. Megan brakes hard, and Sutton lurches forward.

Megan glances over and arches a brow as if to say, *I told you so.* Then she glances down at Sutton's chest. "Seatbelt."

"He's an idiot," Sutton mutters. Megan doesn't move, and Sutton sighs dramatically. She pulls the harness across her body.

Finally, Megan continues backing out, and they eventually shift into drive and move forward through the parking lot.

Megan doesn't respond to Sutton's quip about Dan because Megan doesn't say anything bad about anyone. Frankly, it's starting to piss Sutton off.

She and Megan have been best friends since kindergarten. That relationship has continued even after their personalities morphed and it seemed as if they would go their separate ways. Sutton isn't sure why Megan keeps hanging out with her. For Sutton, it feels as if she's stuck like a magnet to Megan's side. Even when she's tried her hardest to pull herself away.

Sutton gazes out the window as they drive out of the parking lot and onto the road, which is flooded with student and bus traffic. It is one of those beautiful late spring days. The sky is a clear blue, and the trees are vibrant yellow-green, preening in their new growth.

It's one of those days that gives you hope that things will be okay.

"So, I have a secret," Megan says, and when Sutton looks over, she finds Megan's face flushed and her eyes shining.

Sutton doesn't ask what it is. She doesn't want to know, but she knows that Megan will tell her anyway.

"I just found out last period that I have been officially named valedictorian of the class of 2004. They'll announce it during the scholarship assembly next week."

The weight of Sutton's jealousy drags her down into a dark pit inside her stomach, which twists and lurches. The brilliant blues and greens outside the car window feel like a cruel illusion.

She doesn't respond and instead twists the knob of the radio, then scans the stations until she finds a song she likes. A breathy female voice sings about being toxic, and Sutton can relate.

Megan doesn't even seem to notice Sutton's lack of response. She continues to go on about the college scholarship; the fact that her parents won't have to pay much of anything for her tuition. Then she starts talking about the graduation speech she'll have to give.

Sutton tries to listen to the lyrics of the song, but Megan's words keep interrupting the music. She dreads the thought of listing to Megan deliver a speech about how great she is, reminding Sutton just how inadequate *Sutton* is by comparison.

Megan's phone, perched in the console cupholder, makes a chirping sound. Sutton pulls her attention from Megan and the music and looks at the solid silver cube.

Sutton does not have a mobile phone because Sutton's parents don't think it's a necessary accessory for a high school student. Maybe, they said, if she were responsible enough to get good grades like Megan. Maybe, they said, if she were ambitious enough to get a job like Megan. Maybe, they said, if she had college plans like Megan. But since she has none of those things, a cell phone remains nothing more than a luxury to be coveted.

Megan gives the chirping object the briefest of glances.

Sutton continues looking at it. "Aren't you going to answer it?"

"Not while I'm driving."

Sutton picks it up, flips it open, and says, "Hello?" as she holds the object to her ear.

Megan begins to protest, and Sutton smiles at her friend whose lips have transformed into a hard slash across her face.

A familiar male voice asks tentatively, "Megan?"

"Oh, Joe," Sutton coos back, drawing out the *o* in his name.

Megan's eyes go wide. "Put the phone down, please," she whispers.

This flirtation between Joe and Megan has been going on for a while, and Sutton thinks it's dumb. They'll both be going to different universities at summer's end, so what's the point? Besides, Megan had promised that she'd hang out with Sutton this summer when she wasn't working at her part-time job at the animal hospital or on the farm.

Megan has been accepted to a college in the city, and even though it's less than two hours away, Sutton knows that Megan won't stay in touch like she says she will. Megan will make new friends and Sutton will be left alone in Conway, trying to figure out what she's supposed to be doing with her life.

Into the phone, she says, "It's Sutton, actually."

She hears the shift in his voice. "Well, hey there." He talks to Megan like she's a princess. He talks to Sutton like she's a temptress. And he is tempted. She can tell by the way he looks at her when Megan isn't looking back.

Her glance slides to Megan; she feels the familiar combination of love, guilt, inadequacy, and jealousy. Megan has everything. There never seems to be anything left over for Sutton. It's not fair.

"Megan is driving. Is there a message?" she asks Joe.

"Just, uh, ask her to give me a call later."

"Sure will," Sutton says in her sugary voice.

There is a pause, and Sutton waits. In addition to all of her other wonderful qualities, Megan is also virtuous, which is a characteristic that a boy like Joe might not find quite as appealing as her other characteristics.

"My, uh, parents are out of town," he says.

Sutton's heart beats just a bit faster. "Mm-hmm. The party tomorrow," she reminds him.

"They're out of town tonight, too."

Heat rises in her face. She is both disgusted by him and excited by the prospect of being with him. She is defensive for her friend and jealous of her competition. She is proud of her own power while knowing that it's only her body Joe wants. It's the one thing she has.

She says, "Sounds good," and infuses the words with as much meaning as possible.

"So…maybe I'll see you later then."

"Sure will," she repeats.

She hears the low chuckle and ends the call. Her face still feels hot as she drops Megan's phone back into the cupholder.

Megan glances over at her. She's still annoyed, Sutton can tell. "What did he say?"

"He wants you to call him later."

"That was it?"

"That was it," Sutton confirms.

"The conversation seemed longer than that."

Sutton shrugs and looks out the window. Megan gets everything she wants. Why shouldn't Sutton get something that *she* wants. Even if she has to take it from Megan. Maybe *because* she has to take it from Megan. She's not sure. She just knows that she feels sick and exhilarated at the same time.

Maybe Megan has continued to hang out with Sutton for all these years because she feels sorry for her. Feels sorry for all of the mistakes Sutton has made. The bad choices in boys, the decisions that could have altered her life forever.

Well, she doesn't need Megan's pity. She doesn't need Megan at all, actually. Megan can give her stupid graduation speech and then go off to college and date as many boys as she wants. She can become a *doctor* and earn boatloads of money. She can get married and have her two-point-five kids in a big house with a white picket fence. She can do whatever she wants, and Sutton will be just fine.

"Sutton?" Megan asks, and Sutton realizes that Megan has asked her a question.

"What?"

"I asked if you wanted to do something tonight after I get off work." Megan works three evenings a week and four hours on Saturdays answering phones at Dr. Kimble's Animal Clinic.

Sutton shakes her head.

Megan's annoyance about the phone call seems to have lifted. "You have plans with someone I don't know about?"

Sutton's pulse quickens again, but Megan is smiling, and Sutton realizes that she doesn't suspect that her plans might be with Joe.

What is she doing? She is a terrible friend and an even worse person.

Then Megan says, "What do you think I should wear to Joe's party tomorrow?" She continues before waiting for an answer. "I was thinking maybe those really low jeans and that one red flowy top that I have. You know, the one that kind of comes off my shoulder."

Sutton studies Megan with her long wavy hair the color of a burnt chestnut and perfectly formed features. Megan rarely wears makeup because she doesn't need it. She is tall and slim, but not willowy. She has weight in all the right places.

Sutton is shorter and skinnier, and her ugly brown hair is dyed a platinum blond. Her skin is not perfect, so she wears a lot of foundation. Her eyes are too small, so she wears a lot of eyeliner. Her lips are too pale, so she wears deep red lipstick.

"That sounds fine," Sutton says indifferently.

"What are you going to wear?"

Sutton shrugs. "I haven't thought that far ahead."

"Since when?" Megan asks, laughing. "Maybe a bandanna for a top?"

"What's that supposed to mean?" But Sutton knows exactly what Megan means.

"Nothing. I mean—You know. That's usually how you dress."

"Are you saying I'm a slut?"

"God, Sutton. No. I was just joking around with you.

What's your deal all of a sudden?"

Something in Sutton snaps, and all of those words that have been rattling around in her head for all of these years gather at the filter of her mind and burst through her mouth, like a dam has broken. "Maybe my deal is that I'm sick of you always acting like you're so much better than me. I'm never good enough when you're around. Not pretty enough, smart enough, nice enough, rich enough. And I don't know if you've ever stopped to notice, but not all of us have parents that will buy us whatever we want. Not all of us can be as perfect as the almighty Megan Richards."

Megan stares at Sutton for a second, and then she shifts her gaze straight ahead and glares through the windshield, her brow furrowed as they continue to drive through town. Megan takes a right onto Poplar Street toward the west side of town where Sutton lives with her parents. They are both silent for a moment. Finally, Megan says, "I don't think I'm better than you."

"Of course you do, Megan. Because you *are*." And then Sutton says something that surprises even her. "Look, I don't think we should be friends anymore, okay?"

"Are you serious right now?"

Sutton doesn't answer. Part of her wants to take it all back, but she doesn't. Instead, she stares out the passenger side window and focuses very hard on the scenery that is passing her by. "Just take me home."

"Did I do something to upset you?" Megan's voice is wobbly, and Sutton shuts her eyes. She doesn't want to see Megan's tears.

They drive in silence, and after a few minutes, Megan pulls up to Sutton's house—the modest brick home where she's lived since she was a baby. Her mom's car is in the driveway, but she has to work this evening, so Sutton knows that she won't be home for long. Sutton is glad. She opens the car door, and Megan says, "Can we talk about this? I can call you later, when I'm done with work?"

Sutton pauses, but she doesn't turn around. "There's really nothing to talk about," she mumbles, not sure if Megan has even heard her.

"I just… I don't understand."

Sutton closes the door behind her and walks away. She can feel Megan staring at her, but she doesn't look back. Sutton can't help her understand. Because Sutton is certain that she doesn't understand it either. It's just the way it has to be.

CHAPTER 8

JOE-NOW

Joe parks in the lot across the street from Beesonstown General Hospital and gazes at the sprawling healthcare complex. Above the building's signage is another placard for a familiar and reputable research hospital. Joe assumes that Beesonstown General Hospital must be under the ownership of this prestigious institution, and this makes him feel slightly better after having driven through the rundown and largely abandoned main-street business corridor of the city. *Business corridor*, he thinks with amusement. He's fairly certain the two dingy-looking men he'd passed just off the primary thoroughfare were exchanging more than just a handshake in the shadow of the alleyway.

Joe locks his luxury sedan three times before he walks across the street. More than once, he looks over his shoulder at his car—expensive and out of place in the visitors' lot.

He'd wanted to climb out of his skin as he'd driven through Conway and toward Beesonstown. The journey has summoned long-suppressed sentiments, like those recalled through the ghost of a forgotten song or the scent of a past cologne. He can feel his younger self clawing forth, trying to reinhabit his body.

He takes a few breaths and attempts to regulate himself.

The automatic doors of the hospital slide open, and he shifts over slightly as an elderly patient in a wheelchair is maneuvered out by a male orderly in a white uniform. The orderly looks professional enough, if a bit overweight and shaggy. The patient doesn't glance in Joe's direction, but the orderly meets his eye, as if he might recognize Joe.

Joe quickly shifts his gaze away, discouraging any conversation.

He's about to approach the reception desk to ask for his father's room number when he catches sight of Paige coming through a set of doors to the right. She's carrying two Styrofoam cups.

"Paige," he calls, and she startles. Coffee streams down one of her wrists.

He hears her swear under her breath as he approaches.

"Sorry. Napkins?" he asks.

She hitches her chin behind her. "Can you grab some from the café?"

Joe jogs through the doors and finds a condiment station where he grabs a handful of paper towels from a dispenser. He glances around. The building has been completely remodeled since the last time he was in the place nearly twenty-five years ago when he broke his arm playing soccer in middle school. It still has that antiseptic smell of a hospital combined with the heavy scent of overcooked food and burnt coffee.

He jogs back toward Paige, swapping the napkins for the coffee. She wipes her hands and the floor before tossing the paper into a garbage can. From a nearby disinfectant dispenser affixed to a doorway, she covers her hands and wrists liberally with the medicinal foam.

"I didn't think you'd get here this quickly," she says, eyeing him as if he's done something suspicious.

"I left immediately. Viv is tying up loose ends at the dealership and making arrangements for the girls."

"Vivian is coming?" Paige asks as they walk toward the

bank of elevators at the end of the hallway.

"Is that a problem?"

She raises her eyebrows, pulls her lips together, and shakes her head. Clearly, she has something to say.

His sister presses the button for the elevator, and the doors slide open. She hits the button for the fifth floor.

"How's Dad?" he asks as the car rises.

"He's…okay. Stable." She stares at the numbers as they tick their way up.

They continue their ride in silence, but when they exit onto the fifth floor, Paige pauses. "When was the last time you saw Dad?" she asks.

He is immediately defensive. "Look, Paige, we're all busy, so I don't want to hear it. I seem to remember you'd gone years—"

She shakes her head and interrupts him. "That's not what I meant." She runs her hands through her shoulder-length brown bob, looking very tired and older than her thirty-four years. "When was the last time that you laid eyes on him?"

"Christmas, I guess." He hates to admit that it's been that long, but Paige looks thoughtful rather than judgmental.

"He's lost a lot of weight since then. I just want you to be prepared when you see him."

"I mean, he's needed to lose a few pounds for the past couple of years," he reasons.

She doesn't respond, and Joe feels a pit forming in his stomach. A bad feeling. His dad is still young. Not even seventy. Surely whatever malady he has is temporary. An anomaly. His dad has always been larger than life. A powerhouse. A fixer.

They walk down the hall, past a nurses' station, and Paige enters a door to the right. She glances back at him, and there's something in her eyes. Something he can't quite read. A warning, maybe? Pity?

As she turns forward, she fixes her face with a wide smile and says too brightly, "Look who I picked up in the lobby!"

Joe sees his mother first—her drawn face free of makeup, her disheveled hair and clothes. She comes toward him, and he offers her one of the coffee cups still in his hands. She hugs him with one arm, then pats his shoulder briskly.

Paige takes the other coffee from him as Joe looks at the man in the bed covered by the thin white sheet. His eyes are shut, and there is a faint resemblance to the man Joe knows as his father. But this man is far, far thinner, paler, sicker, older.

Joe looks from the man to his mother. "What is going on, Mom?"

Her face crumples, but just for a minute. She sets down the coffee and vigorously rubs the sockets of her eyes. "It's acute myeloid leukemia." He waits for additional information, but none is offered.

Paige sits down in a seat that has been pulled next to the side of the bed and gazes at their dad.

Joe shakes his head. How had they not told him? "Leukemia is treatable, though, isn't it?" he finally asks. "Surely there is chemo, radiation, steroids—something the doctors can do."

"We've done all of that," his mother says. Sandra Wright hitches her chin up a notch. "I know you hate it here—in Beesonstown—but he's had excellent care."

"How long has this been going on?"

He watches Paige's gaze flutter to their mother and then back to the inert form of their father.

Sandra shifts from one foot to the other. "He was diagnosed just a little over a year ago. He had been responding relatively well to treatment up until right after the holidays. It was like his body just started giving up."

"And you didn't tell me?" Joe's voice is raised, but he can't help it.

His mom makes a smoothing motion with her hands and lowers her voice to a whisper, as if to counteract Joe's volume. "Your dad didn't want to worry you and distract from the business and your family. And you know him." She gives a soft smile. "He thought he was going to beat this thing."

Joe stares at her. What is she saying? Then he looks at his dad. "Is he…unconscious?"

"No, no. He's just soundly sleeping. They've given him something for the pain."

"A lot of something," Paige adds.

Joe looks from his mother to his sister, still mystified that they could have kept this from him for over a year. And Paige has known their father's condition the entire time, but *he* hadn't? Paige, the person who couldn't even be responsible for bringing a dessert to a dinner. Paige, who had moved out of and then back into their parents' house so many times that she didn't even bother to pack up her clothes. Paige, who at thirty-four had been married three times and been in at least that many *serious* relationships.

He feels like a fool and a jerk. But he also knows there's no use in arguing with them. Not now. They would need to have that conversation later. Now was the time for solving the issue at hand.

"Okay," Joe says as he shifts mental gears. "What is our next move? What does the next round of treatment look like?" He rubs his hands together, ready to get down to business. "I want to talk to his doctor."

That look flickers again between his mother and sister,

and it pisses Joe off. It's as if they're talking about him without saying a word.

"Joe," his mother says softly and puts a hand on his arm. She's always had the most elegant hands. The clear diamond of her ring glints in the afternoon light shining in from the window. "There is no next round. This is it."

"This is *what*, exactly?" He steps to the side, and her hand falls away.

"The end of the line. Treatment is no longer effective. The next step is hospice care."

"No," he says firmly. "Hospice care is for people who are about to die."

A long, heavy silence hangs in the air. It's so thick that Joe rubs at the back of his neck. God, he hates it here. "I want to talk to his doctor," he finally says again. "His— what's it called?" The word flashes into his brain. *Oncologist.* "I want to talk to his oncologist."

"Okay, Joe." His mother's voice is placating, a little bit condescending. "You can talk to Dr. Burman in the morning. He wants to keep an eye on your dad overnight."

"Well, he can't come home at all in the shape he's in now," Joe says, gesturing toward his dad.

His mother's lips are pressed together. "He'll be coming home tomorrow. We've arranged for care."

"How is he going to get medical care at home? What if there's an emergency?"

"They'll send a nurse to help us out a few times a day. But the focus of home care is comfort, Joe. It's what your dad wants. He'll tell you that himself when he wakes up."

There is a pressure on Joe's chest, and he's having a hard time breathing. He tugs at his shirt collar. He takes a few deep breaths, but he can't get enough oxygen.

"Are you okay?" Paige asks, half standing.

Joe waves her back and bends over with his hands on

his knees. His mother is next to him, her hand on his back. He swats her hand away. "Just let me… Just let me catch my breath."

He isn't sure how long he stands like that, taking breaths that are too big and too quick. He only knows that he's starting to feel worse rather than better. And just when he thinks he might pass out, another pair of hands is on him, soft and cool. "Joe?" Vivian's voice says in his ear. She places a soothing hand on his cheek. "Come." She leads him to another chair and directs him to put his head between his knees.

"I'll get a nurse," he hears his mother say through his foggy brain. But Vivian says, "No, Sandra. That won't be necessary."

Vivian magically appears back at his side with a small paper cup of water. She presses it against his lips, and he lifts his hand to take it from her. His wife is an angel.

After he drinks the contents of the cup, she looks levelly into his eyes. She seems to be transferring strength from herself to him. And by God, if it doesn't work. She nods once, and he nods back.

He stands, waits for a wave of dizziness to pass, and breathes through it. He moves to the side of his dad's bed, and Vivian stands off to one side. She'd entered in the midst of a crisis, and after it passed, it was too late for everyone to offer proper greetings.

Joe places a hand on his dad's shoulder. His bones are prominent through a thin layer of skin. "How long will he be asleep?"

Paige speaks this time. "He was in a lot of pain. They gave him a pretty big dose of opiates to try to get it under control."

"They'll try to regulate his medication overnight so that his pain is more manageable with the proper dosage," his mother adds when she sees him about to react to the word "opiates." "He'll be awake tomorrow. In the meantime, we should go home, eat, and get some rest." His mother pushes her hair back from her face and smooths her hands over her pale pink blouse. "It's been a long day, and tomorrow will be longer."

Paige stands, then leans down to kiss their father on the cheek. "See you later, alligator," she says. The usual response doesn't come. She presses her lips together and pats his hand.

Their mother walks over and lays a hand on her husband's forehead. She doesn't say anything before quickly moving away.

"I'm going to stay here for a bit," Joe says, and his mother and sister just nod and walk out of the room.

When they're gone, he looks over at Vivian. "They didn't tell me."

His wife doesn't say anything, and he looks down at his dad. They stand together in silence for a long while.

Finally, Joe draws himself up. "They said the next step is hospice care."

Vivian reaches out and places her hand over the hand of his father. Then she slides it into Joe's. "Come on," she says. "There's nothing more you can do here today."

Joe wishes he could talk to his father, whose breathing is deep and regular. He waits another few seconds, then he turns with his wife and walks out the door and down the hall.

As they step out of the elevator, they pause at the end of the hallway for a passing hospital orderly pushing an old woman in a wheelchair. The woman has limp, greasy blond hair and her left arm is encased in a black sling, resting limply by her side. Dark bruises mar her face, and one eye is almost swollen shut. Joe stares at the ugly red marks circling her throat like a grotesque necklace. Her jaw has a collapsed and sunken look, as if she might not have any teeth. He feels a mix of pity, disgust, and curiosity.

Before he can look away, she turns and stares directly at him, then she does a double take. Her eyes grow wide and haunted. "Joe Wright," she says, her voice barely more than a whisper. His name is not a question.

He frowns, wondering if perhaps she recognizes him from the commercials for the dealership. He would certainly remember if he'd met this woman in person.

The orderly looks between the parties awkwardly, but keeps pushing the woman forward. And although the speed of the wheelchair has slowed, the old woman turns around to stare back at Joe.

"Sutton," she says in a raspy and graveled voice. "Sutton Schultz."

Joe stops dead in his tracks.

Vivian has taken a few steps before she realizes he is not beside her, then she too stops and looks back at him, a question in her eyes.

The wheelchair keeps moving, and Joe looks at the ground so that he doesn't have to see the face of the old woman. A ghost from his past.

Sutton Schultz. It's a name he has pushed far, far down into the recesses of his memory. Hearing it vocalized is like a punch to the gut, but he can't reconcile the name with the old woman—a junkie, it appears—who had spoken it. Sutton would be thirty-eight, the same age as Joe. There was no way in hell that woman had been any younger than sixty.

Vivian glances at the retreating figure who has turned back around in the wheelchair. "Do you know her?"

"No, I don't think so."

"Sutton Schultz," his wife says thoughtfully, and Joe winces inwardly. "Interesting name." She looks around.

"Interesting place."

Joe lingers. He doesn't want to encounter the woman again. When Vivian starts to walk forward, he grabs her hand and heads toward the hospital café. "Let's get a coffee before we go. I'm not sure I'm ready to face what's waiting for us."

It's out of character for him, but Vivian goes along with it. As they walk in the opposite direction, he says as lightly as he can, "Now can you understand why I don't like to come back here?"

"It's got a certain backwater charm, I suppose." She pauses. "But please don't tell me you slept with the woman in the wheelchair." Vivian winks up at him, clearly joking, and he does his best to smile.

But the blood rushes to his head. Because not only did he sleep with that woman, he'd done something much, much worse.

And his wife can never know.

CHAPTER 9

DAN-NOW

The door to the side entrance of Bud's Sports Bar is far heavier than it needs to be. Dan yanks it open before brushing past a rowdy family of five waiting for a table. There are no hostesses here; just harried, weathered servers who might direct you to an empty table if they decided it was worth their time. There was also no "first-come, first-served" rule. Like the rest of Conway, at Bud's it was every person for themselves.

The space is warm and humid, and it smells of beer, oregano, fried food, and stale cigarette smoke.

Dan surveys the crowded front dining room and sees a few people he recognizes. Ryan Tolbert, now the principal at the high school, sits with a dark-haired woman who looks vaguely familiar. Holly Griffin, Dan remembers. She'd been a bubbly, compact cheerleader once upon a time. With them is a young girl who looks to be about Sam's age.

Ryan glances up and catches Dan's eye. He opens his mouth as if he's about to call out, and Dan quickly looks away.

He angles his body so that a server can pass. She balances a tray piled high with plates on a slim shoulder and does not acknowledge his accommodation.

Dan makes his way into another area of the restaurant. This section is furnished with a large center bar that takes up most of the space in the room. Nearly all of the bar stools are occupied on a Friday night, and around the room, various live and pre-recorded sporting events blare from flat-screen televisions mounted to the walls. The diners and drinkers talk loudly so that they can be heard over the televisions and each other, resulting in a thunderous din.

Around the room's perimeter, a few smaller tables are pushed against the walls. Dan searches for Crystal in the sea of faces, but Rob Jankowski, with whom Dan had worked a few construction side jobs nearly five years ago, waves him over before he locates his cousin. Rob claps him on the back as he approaches. "How's it going, man?" he asks. "Haven't seen you around in a while. Can I buy you a beer?"

Dan shakes his head. "I'm meeting someone."

"How are Amber and the kids? I heard you were working on Teddy's car."

Dan appreciates the fact that he is not expected to answer many of Rob's questions. "Yeah, got it in the garage now."

"Old man good?"

"Dad's still kicking," he answers, even though he hasn't spoken with his father in months.

Rob makes another comment, or asks another question, but Dan's phone buzzes and he glances down at the text. Crystal's name flashes up at him. *In the corner when you're ready.*

He looks around and spots her at a low table against one of the walls. She waves.

Rob makes a noise at the back of his throat. "Time has not been kind to that one."

"What's that?" Dan asks, glancing back at Rob.

Rob angles his head toward Dan's cousin. "Crystal Karlik. She used to be a knockout, remember? What I wouldn't have given to hit that about fifteen years ago." He shakes his head mournfully. "But not now. And she's married to old Frank Neumann. That guy's been on disability for years, sucking the system dry."

Dan assumes that Rob doesn't know about Dan's family connection to Crystal, but he's irritated anyway. He says, "Look, I'll see you around," and heads over to Crystal's table. By the time Dan reaches the table and glances back, Rob is laughing at something with the guy on the stool next to him, Dan and Crystal the furthest thing from his mind.

Crystal stands, and Dan gives her half a hug. Rob's right, though, time has not been kind to Crystal.

"How are things?" he asks.

"Can't complain." She smiles. "Well, I *could*, but it wouldn't matter." She sits back down and takes a sip of gold-colored beer from a smudged and streaked glass. An orange slice dangles precariously from the rim's edge.

A young server approaches to take Dan's order. He asks for a bottle of Yuengling, hold the glass.

Crystal eyes him closely. "How are *you* doing?"

Maybe he imagines it, but it seems like her words are infused with meaning. "I'm okay. Like you, won't complain." He smiles, but she just keeps watching him. "Boys are growing up fast," he offers.

"And how's Amber?"

At his wife's name, his heart squeezes a little bit. They'd left things in a bad place, and he feels guilty. That isn't anything new, but he's not proud. And Amber had seemed much more upset than she normally was when they argued. Her words echo in his mind, and he pushes them away.

Crystal doesn't need to know all of that.

"Amber's okay," he says.

The server brings his beer, and he tips the bottle back toward his lips. Crystal seems content with sitting in silence, and he is grateful. When they'd been kids, she had been like a sister to him. Hell, they'd grown up together. She probably knows him better than anyone else. After his own mother had left all those years ago, Crystal's mom Brenda had just about raised both of them. She's been gone for nearly two decades, and Dan still misses the woman with her throaty laugh and tough love.

He glances up at the television closest to them where a basketball game is happening between two teams Dan doesn't know. He's never followed basketball. Some of the crowd in the room, however, seem interested in the outcome.

Crystal clears her throat and says over the noise, "You know, Dan, I'm working for Munson, Munson, and Temple now."

He makes a face. "That guy's a dick."

Crystal looks confused. "Who?"

"Temple."

"You know him?"

"He worked for the district attorney's office back when—" He stops the flow of words. "Well, you know," he finishes. He doesn't want to talk about the past.

There is a pause, this time uneasy, and Crystal chews on her lip.

"I thought you were working up at the quarry," Dan says. "A secretary up there or something?"

She still looks worried as she waves a hand in front of her. "That was ages ago. They laid me off. Hired the superintendent's niece, who apparently was much more qualified than I ever was."

"So how long have you been with the lawyers?"

"Just a few months. I was working in Beesonstown for the redevelopment authority for a while, but they had cuts. So did the community action agency before that, and the career placement agency before *that*." She shakes her head.

"It's a jungle out there."

Dan doesn't say anything. They used to be so close, and he should know all of this stuff about her. He feels like an ass.

"Work is good for you?" she asks distractedly. She seems like she has something else on her mind.

"It pays the bills."

She nods and traces a finger down her cloudy glass.

He tilts the bottle to his lips and drains the beer. He looks around for the server to signal for another.

"Hey," Crystal says. "You know the firm—Munson, Munson, and Temple—they handle all sorts of cases."

Dan catches the server's eye and tilts his bottle toward her. She raises her chin in acknowledgment. Then he turns back to Crystal. "That's good, I guess. Probably interesting work."

"It can be."

The server brings him a second beer, and he takes a long swallow.

"They handle a lot of real estate transactions, and also some criminal defense cases. Every once in a while, they'll take on a *divorce case*." She emphasizes the words, and Dan looks at her. She stares hard at him. "Sometimes, people will call asking for a lawyer." She speaks very slowly.

He sets the beer bottle down and leans forward. When Amber had said earlier that she wanted a divorce, he assumed that she had just been frustrated. And he had understood. There was no way he'd want to be cooped up in that house with the kids all day. He hadn't argued with her. In fact, he hadn't said a word. He'd given her the space she clearly needed and had turned and walked away, brushing past Henry on his way out the door.

He'd worked on the Mustang until Crystal called, and then he'd gone back in the house and dressed, giving Amber a wide berth. "Are you telling me that Amber had an appointment with a lawyer?" he asks, confused. There hadn't been time for that. Had there?

Crystal shakes her head. "I'm not telling you anything," she says.

"Then what's this all about?"

"Dan. I'm not *allowed* to tell you anything. I could lose my job."

He narrows his eyes, trying to puzzle out what she is trying to communicate.

"I can confirm," Crystal says slowly, "that a call came in late this afternoon asking for a lawyer. Because two of our partners are at a conference, Temple, who normally doesn't take on divorce cases, may or may not have returned this person's call." She takes a small sip of her beer. "And that's all I can tell you. I just want you to…take care of yourself."

Dan stares at the table. He isn't typically prone to self-pity, but he does allow himself just a moment to visualize how this might play out for him. A divorce from Amber, who'd never worked outside the home, and an order for child support for four kids under the age of eighteen would leave him penniless. Not to mention the potential loss of access to his kids and his wife, who, despite all of the obstacles, were his life. He wonders if the universe or God or whatever higher power existed would, for the rest of his days, just continue to punish him for what he'd done twenty years ago.

He takes a ragged breath. "What should I do?"

Crystal gives him a sad smile. "I'm not sure I'm the best person to ask. Have you talked to her?"

He shakes his head.

"That might be a good place to start."

Thinking back, Amber had seemed so resigned when she'd last spoken in the kitchen. He knows that she's been unhappy for a while. But hell…who hasn't? "What would I even say?"

"You could tell her that you love her."

He sits back. When was the last time he'd said those words to her? When was the last time she'd said them to *him*? Maybe she didn't love him anymore. And maybe he didn't love her, either.

"Look, Dan. I can't tell you what to do about your marriage. But I do know that divorce can get really nasty really quickly. So, if you don't want to put in the work to save your marriage, you had better look into getting yourself a lawyer. Try to keep it as amicable as possible while you protect yourself. Not only for you, but for your kids. They need their dad."

They need Amber more. He's not sure any of them would even notice if he disappeared.

He's still staring at the table when Crystal says, "Shit," under her breath.

Dan looks up and follows the direction of her gaze to the other side of the room where an older couple has just walked through the door. Paul and Renee Richards are grayer than the last time he'd seen them, but, when they spot him, their expressions are the same as they were twenty years ago. Blame, sadness, anger, reproach. He doesn't blame them one bit.

Why hadn't it been him who'd died that night? That question is his mantra, and it plays on a constant loop in his mind.

Renee slows down as they pass on the other side of the bar. She stares at Dan. But Paul takes her by the elbow and guides her through the room.

Dan swears time slows as they pass. He swears the noise of the televisions meld together, and the voices in the room lower an octave, taking on an underwater quality. He can hear the blood rushing in his ears. Renee's lips move. They seem to be forming a word. He can't make out what she's saying.

"Dan…Dan!" Crystal's voice is urgent and loud, and it breaks through the thickness of the atmosphere.

If the bar's occupants noticed the encounter, they gave no indication. Time normalizes, sounds regulate, and the Richards pass from the room like ghosts.

"Why don't we get out of here?" she asks.

He doesn't answer, but he also doesn't object as Crystal moves to the bar to settle up the tab. She takes her time, and he sits alone, feeling like a fool.

As they walk to the front entrance of the restaurant, Dan does not see the Richards, but he once again catches sight of Ryan Tolbert, who is also leaving with his family. He spots Dan and then says something to Holly, who glances back at him before taking the hand of their daughter and heading out the door.

"Dan?" he asks when Dan puts his head down. He thrusts his hand out. "Ryan Tolbert. We went to high school together."

Reluctantly, Dan takes the outstretched hand. "I remember."

Ryan looks at Crystal. "I know you…" His words trail off.

"Crystal Neumann," she responds. "I was Karlik back then."

He nods in recognition. "Right." He turns back to Dan. "I, uh, just saw the Richards walk through, and it reminded me that I wanted to talk to you." He glances around. "Let's step outside."

Dan casts a wary glance at Crystal. He has absolutely nothing to say to this man.

Outside, the sky is clear, and the setting sun has colored

the clouds pink and orange over the outline of the rundown brick buildings of the town. There is still a slight chill in the air, and the earthy smell from the Mitsin River is mingled with the smell of exhaust from the highway running to the west of town.

Ryan smiles at them. It is a practiced smile. Too wide, too bright. He spreads his hands out in front of him. "As you know, this year marks the twentieth anniversary of the accident out on Falgan Road." The words are as practiced as the smile.

Dan doesn't react, but he can feel the blood drain from his face. In his periphery, Crystal shifts her weight from one foot to the other.

Ryan clears his throat and continues. "We're planning to hold an assembly at the high school to talk about the accident. The Richards have agreed to come and speak, along with some of the emergency responders who were there that day. I'm just letting you know because..." He pauses, swallows. "Well, your son is a freshman this year, and the entire school will be invited to join. I'm sure you've already spoken to him about...what happened. But I just don't want anyone to be blindsided. You know...in case you want to have a conversation with him."

"And you're planning to talk about *me* during this sideshow?"

"It's an assembly," Ryan says calmly. "About the students' making good choices before their upcoming graduation. It's an opportunity to learn and reflect. And no, we're not planning to talk about you as an individual, but obviously what happened is public record. I'm sure some of the kids and their parents know the families of those involved, so it's not out of the realm of possibility that your name may come up, if not in the assembly itself, in conversations afterward. I just want Henry to be prepared for any…comments."

It takes Dan a moment to process this information. In that moment, the sounds are of traffic from the nearby highway. A tractor-trailer jake-breaking down the hill that leads into the river valley. The roar of an engine revving too loudly. The short blast of a horn.

Crystal has placed a tentative hand on Dan's arm.

Then Dan says slowly, "You're telling me that you are knowingly subjecting my son—one of your students—to potential ridicule so that you can make yourself feel better in your self-righteous crusade." He shakes his head as the man in front of him gears up for his retort. But Dan is not done. "You were there, too. You know what happened. Are you trying to make yourself feel better?"

Ryan looks off into the distance before returning his gaze to Dan's. "Yep, I was there. I wasn't the one driving the car, but I sure was at that party." It was a clear dig, but Dan doesn't flinch. "I'm not doing this for any other reason than it's been twenty years, and if I can use that experience to save the life of just one of my kids, then I'm going to do it."

"What a hero," Dan responds, his tone sarcastic. "You deserve all the accolades, Mr. Tolbert."

"Think what you want. I'm certainly not looking for your approval. And you're welcome to join and talk about how the experience shaped your life. It might do everyone some good. Even you."

Dan feels the pressure of Crystal's hand increase, trying to urge him away. But Dan is not going to hit Ryan Tolbert. He wouldn't waste his energy. The guy always had been a hanger-on. A leech. Someone who made no decisions for himself but rode in the wake of the successes and failures of others.

Dan sucks his teeth and looks back at the principal. "I think I'll pass on that. But I hope you accomplish whatever it is you're setting out to do. I'll be keeping my son home from school that week." He doesn't wait for Ryan's response. He breaks contact with Crystal and crosses the parking lot to his truck, climbs in, and drives home. He realizes that he's left Crystal high and dry, but he knows that she'll understand.

When he walks in the front door to his house, he's met by Amber who is descending the stairs. At the same time that he says, "We need to talk about Henry," she says, "What are you doing here?"

They stare at each other in a standoff. But she has the advantage, standing three stairs up, looking down at him, while he is caught in the entryway of the house. He reacts first. "Where else would I be?"

"I want you out. Gone."

There is a shadow at the top of the stairs. At least one of the boys is listening. "Amber, we need to talk about this."

She sees the direction of his gaze. "I've already talked to the boys. They know."

"You talked to them without me?" A wave of anger rises, and he does his best to quell it, but it is strong and heavy in his chest.

"You're never *here*, Dan. And even when you're physically present, you're not here mentally, emotionally. You don't think they know that? You don't think they can feel that?" She stares at him, almost pleading. He doesn't know what to say.

When he doesn't respond, she continues. "I've had enough. If I have to be alone, it's going to be on my own terms. And my terms are, I want you out."

He thinks that she might relent if he stands there long enough, but after a minute, he just nods. "I'll need to get some clothes," he says quietly.

She shifts her body to let him pass.

When he reaches the top of the stairs, the hallway is empty. Whoever had been listening had scurried back to his bedroom.

Dan throws some clothes and toiletry items into a suitcase without really paying attention to what he's doing. When he's finished, he looks around the room. Everything is Amber. The pictures on the walls, the school portraits of the kids atop the chest of drawers in the corner, the jewelry box that he'd bought for his wife on one of their early anniversaries. Even the powdery floral scent in the room is Amber.

The house is silent. He waits another minute, half convinced that she'll rush in and tell him to stay.

When she doesn't, he grabs the suitcase and walks down the stairs. She's moved to the doorway leading into their small living room. Her arms are folded over her chest, and she stares resolutely into the distance.

He hesitates, but she doesn't move.

He opens the door, and still, she doesn't look at him. And she is silent as he pulls the door shut behind him.

He has not even crossed the small front porch before he hears the deadbolt slide into place. As he walks toward his truck, he pulls his phone out of his pocket and presses a button.

Crystal picks up on the second ring, her voice gentle. "You good, Dan?"

His voice nearly breaks when he asks, "Do you mind if I stay with you for a few days?"

CHAPTER 10

SUTTON-NOW

Sutton's entire body aches as if she's been hit by a truck. But the pain is nothing compared to the churning inside her.

She is lying in her childhood bed of her childhood bedroom, wearing an unfamiliar nightgown—her mother's probably. The sun has risen, and she's tangled in white sheets—the ones she'd recently been daydreaming about. Her arm is throbbing; she's shivering and sweating simultaneously. And she is remembering the day before.

She never knew what might trigger Tommy's violent outbursts, and even though she is used to it—the watching, the waiting, the reacting—she still feels the same fear and confusion every time he lashes out at her. Even when she remembers that she deserves it.

She hadn't wanted to go to the hospital, but when she came to, the pain in her arm was so intense it had caused her to vomit over the side of the bed. Because Tommy was nowhere to be found, she'd begged for the help of a grudging neighbor to provide her a ride the short distance to the hospital in Beesonstown. The neighbor—an old woman whose name Sutton doesn't even know—had dropped her off in front of the emergency room doors without a backwards glance.

The hospital visit had been as difficult and needlessly

stressful as she had feared. After her arm had been set, she'd been evaluated for a concussion, though she threatened to leave if they tried to force her to have a CT scan. Her head was fine.

Then came the questioning about her injuries—first, perfunctory, by a doctor, then by an underpaid and overworked social worker. Despite Sutton's claims of a minor car accident and that the bruises on her neck had been caused by the tightening of a seatbelt, the woman with the uneven haircut who gave off a waft of mildew when she moved had encouraged Sutton to call the police.

Sutton would not be getting the police involved. The doctor knew it and the social worker knew it. So, they had mercifully discharged her to free up a bed and the time for someone who needed it more than she did. She was a lost cause. A throwaway. They all knew *that*, too.

With the rapidly diminishing charge she had left on her cell phone, Sutton had called a woman she knew from the mobile home community to pick her up from the hospital. Tara was not a friend, exactly, but she lived in a trailer one row over. When they'd met not long after Sutton had moved in, the women had recognized something in each other. They'd exchanged numbers but rarely used them, except in the event of an emergency. They'd both had their fair share of emergencies, and Tara had had her own string of "minor car accidents."

And then to have seen Joe Wright of all people… At first, she'd thought he was an apparition. But she'd said his name and he had responded. He hadn't known who she was, of course. But she had known him.

And all of those memories had come flooding back before she could stuff them far, far down, back into the small box in the corner of her belly where they burned like an ember threatening an inferno at any moment.

She'd needed a fix. Just something to take the edge off and tamp down that burgeoning ember.

When Sutton had arrived back at the trailer park, she'd found the front door off its hinges and Tommy gone, along with her car, furniture, dishes, bedding, and clothes. He'd even taken the vomit-covered mattress from the bed. Most of the windows had been smashed and the carpet ripped up and destroyed. She'd desperately searched the empty cupboards and cabinets for her grandmother's small trinket box where she'd kept her extra cash and, more importantly, her supply.

It was gone.

Then she had started to feel the familiar shaky, restless feeling. The increase of her pulse and the cold sweat that collected between her breasts. The first pangs of withdrawal, which she desperately needed to avoid.

She'd called Andre but received no answer. He was Tommy's dealer, too.

She'd begun knocking on doors, but the members of the Happy Horizon Park mobile home community were not as friendly as the name might suggest. She'd ended up back at Tara's trailer, where Tara's boyfriend had answered the door and then immediately slammed it in her face.

Sutton had felt like her heart might beat out of her chest. The scraping in her brain had started. Sitting on the concrete steps that led to her uninhabitable mobile home, she'd vomited twice, unlocked her phone, which had less than a five percent charge left, and called her mom.

Now, in the small twin bed, a weak shaft of grayish-light coming in through the window, she again feels like she needs to throw up, but she is empty. She vomited all of the yellow bile in her stomach into the garbage can next to the bed throughout the night. She's turned herself inside out. There is nothing else left in her except for that horrible itch.

That intense desperation.

In one of her fever dreams, Megan Richards had been sitting at the foot of her bed, rubbing Sutton's leg. Sutton had wanted Megan to yell at her, laugh at her, say awful things about her.

But even in death, Megan is better than Sutton.

Sutton is spent and exhausted but also jumpy and restless. She stares up at the ceiling for a long, long time. Hours maybe. Days even.

Finally, the door opens and her mother walks in. Angela Schultz has thin, limp gray-brown hair that molds to her skull. It is held back from her temples with brown bobby pins. She's wearing pink medical scrubs patterned with hundreds of bright pink, yellow, and purple flower petals. The colors hurt Sutton's eyes.

"I brought you something to drink," her mother says and sets a bottle of a pale blue sports drink on the bedside table along with two painkillers.

Sutton wants to laugh, but her face hurts. Those measly painkillers won't do a damn thing for her.

When Sutton gives a small shake of her head, her mother says, "You need to drink to replenish your fluids." She stands next to the bed until it becomes clear that she is not leaving.

Sutton manages to push herself into a sitting position. She tries to twist the plastic cap off the bottle, but she doesn't have full use of her left arm, and her hands won't stop shaking.

Her mother grabs the bottle, opens it, then hands it back.

Sutton takes a small sip, and her stomach immediately roils. She fights to keep the liquid down and takes three deep, deep breaths. She leaves the painkillers where they are.

Angela's expression is grim, her mouth a straight slash

across her face. Sutton remembers very little conversation from the car ride yesterday evening. Her mother had been firing questions at her, but Sutton had been more intent on simply holding herself together. As usual, her father had been silent.

Angela looks down at Sutton's arm in its cast. "You want to tell me what happened? The truth this time."

She doesn't meet her mother's eyes. She doesn't want to answer at all, but she knows Angela won't leave until she does. Sutton is jumpy. "I fell," she finally answers.

Angela forces out a laugh. "First a car accident and now a fall." She shakes her head. "That's how you got the black eye and bruises on your neck, too? A *fall*."

Sutton would do anything for her mother to leave her alone right now. She glances at the nightstand and spots her phone. She needs a charger. There must be a charger somewhere in this house.

Angela's hands are cemented tightly on her hips, elbows out.

"Do you need to call Dr. Richards to tell him you won't be at work today?" Her voice is high and clipped.

It takes Sutton more than a moment to figure out what her mother is talking about, and in those moments all Sutton can think about, again, is Megan. When she remembers her lie from the day before—the stupid lie about the job—she looks down at the lilac-colored bedspread. It has been switched out since the rose-patterned blanket of her childhood. She doesn't answer. Her heart is thrumming a tattoo in her chest.

They are suspended in silence and remain that way until Angela breaks down first. Her voice loosens and wobbles. "Oh, Sutton. How has this happened? How could you have let this happen to yourself?" She gestures up and down at Sutton's form, as if she's a disaster. Worse than a disaster.

As if she's trash.

"I need to get you into a rehabilitation facility," her mother mumbles more to herself than to Sutton.

"It's just the flu, Mom," Sutton says. Like the worst flu anyone could ever imagine, multiplied a million times over.

Angela seems to wilt as she sits down at the foot of the bed. She looks around the room. "After you moved out, I used to sit in here. Just sit and think about all of the things I would have done differently when you were growing up. I would have—" Her voice cracks, and she sucks in a shaky breath. "I would have tried harder to have another child— given you a brother or sister to keep you company. I would have worked less. I would have paid more attention." She shakes her head. "I would have tried harder to understand your pain after your best friend died. That affected you so very deeply."

Sutton wants to scream. After all these years, it's still all about Megan.

She just needs a hit. Just something to take the edge off. If she can just make herself feel better, maybe she'll be strong enough to fight against it the next time.

Her mother slumps forward, her head in her hands.

"Your dad thinks we can sell the trailer, at least get some money out of it."

Sutton pays attention to that. "You can't do that," she says. "Where will we live?"

Her mother goes very still before she looks over. "You can't be serious."

But Sutton *is* serious. Despite everything, Tommy loves her. And he takes care of her. He may have a temper, but he just lets his emotions get the better of him. She needs to be more careful about what she says and how she says it. She knows what sets him off; sometimes she just…forgets. He's got his faults, but who doesn't? If she can just get herself cleaned up, get a job—for real, this time—he won't have any reason to be so angry with her.

She knows he'll be back. He always comes back.

"Look at what he's *done* to you," her mother says.

"I told you—I fell."

Another wave of nausea passes over Sutton, and she leans over the side of the bed and dry heaves into the can with its plastic store bag liner.

Angela moves beside Sutton, smoothing her daughter's dirty, stringy hair back from the bruised face.

When the nausea has subsided, Sutton leans back against the pillows.

Her mother takes a deep breath while she picks up the trash can and stares down at Sutton, as if she's weighing some decision. Finally, she says, "I need to see a patient today just to get the family set up." Her mother, a hospice nurse, had been on call and often required to work at odd hours for as long as Sutton can remember. "I won't be gone long. I've left a notepad with important phone numbers on the counter in the kitchen. Your dad is at the factory, so he won't answer. But if you need anything, call me, and I'll do my best to pick up."

That had always been the way. Her father worked long hours in his factory job, manufacturing food cans on the south side of town, and didn't have much to say to Sutton or anyone else. And her mom dealt with Sutton on her own.

"I don't have a phone charger to be able to call you," Sutton says.

"You can use the house phone."

Sutton doesn't argue.

"I'll only be gone a few hours."

After a lingering glance at Sutton, her mother leaves the room, and the sounds of the house resume. Water runs, a toilet flushes, cabinets open and shut. The hinges of the dishwasher creak and the dishes clink before the door closes again.

Then the front door opens and shuts, and Sutton recognizes the sound of the engine of her mother's small car as it engages. The tires make a crunching sound on the gravel of the parking space as she backs out.

There is silence.

Sutton shuts her eyes for a few minutes. Her mouth is dry and tastes terrible. Her fingers tingle. She has a splitting headache. She may pass out. She forces herself out of bed and goes in search of a phone charger.

She needs to call first Andre, and then Tommy.

As she moves down the hallway, she supports herself against the wood paneling and enters the small kitchen that is still decorated as it was when she was a kid. A paper border of red roosters rings the yellow walls, and the cheery valance over the window above the sink is dusty and printed with farm animals.

She rummages through every drawer in the kitchen. Although she finds no cords, she discovers forty dollars folded in between the pages of a user manual for the microwave that must be at least thirty years old. She stuffs the bills into her sling. Then she moves into the living room and the dining room, pawing through random items and then shoving things haphazardly back into the drawers.

Her parents' bedroom is more promising. She finds two cords, neither of which are compatible with her model of phone. But in the drawer of the small table next to her father's side of the bed, she finds a small tin box with at least five hundred dollars inside.

Every fiber of her being aches to take the entire tin, but she settles on two fifty-dollar bills and five twenties and replaces the rest. She can always come back for more. Her mood lifts just a bit as her nose starts to run. She wipes it on the neckline of the nightgown.

Giving up on the quest for a compatible cord, she paws through bedroom drawers and closets, trying to locate something else to wear.

Sutton has no idea what has happened to her own clothes. And Angela, while not a large woman, is taller and much heavier than Sutton is now. The hospital's scale the day before had indicated that she weighed just over one hundred pounds.

Sutton locates a pair of her mother's old drawstring pants that drag over her feet when she awkwardly pulls them up, and a small black t-shirt with the name of some medical device company printed across the front. She fumbles as she tries to unclasp the sling holding her arm in place, then maneuvers out of the nightclothes and into the fresh shirt. She swears and sweats for the ten minutes it takes her to accomplish the task. She feels like she might pass out.

She attempts to replace the sling but gives up after a minute. Her arm hurts, but the pain is infinitely more manageable than her need for the drug.

She smells awful, but there's no time to wash. She shoves her stash of money deep into the pocket of the sweatpants.

Her dirty white running shoes are neatly positioned near the front door. She stuffs her feet into them and grabs a gray windbreaker—her father's—from the coat tree that has been standing in the same corner for as long as she can remember. The jacket hangs nearly to her knees and the sleeves flap below her hands. But the cast fits easily inside, and when she raises the hood, it hides her hair and most of her face.

She pulls the door shut behind her, and keeping her head down, she heads along the road toward the river.

In high school, there had been an abandoned warehouse close to the bridge that carried the highway over the Mitsin. She'd visited the location on more than one occasion to pick up the occasional dime bag of weed. She was banking on the fact that things didn't change much in Conway.

It is mid-morning on a Saturday, and there isn't much traffic on the residential streets of Conway's west side. The sky is the color of ash, and it's not quite raining, but the threat is there in fast, low clouds. There is a chill in the morning air, and Sutton's teeth chatter. She is glad for the jacket.

She keeps her broken arm angled into her body and peers out from under the hood that falls nearly to her eyes. She has very little field of vision in her periphery. When her eyes dart from side to side, all she can see is the material of the windbreaker.

The muffled sound of a vehicle approaching causes her to straighten and look forward. The car slows as it passes, and she glances sideways. It's a black and gold Conway cop car. She lowers her gaze and picks up her pace. The cop drives next to her for a few seconds, and perspiration beads on her forehead. Sweat trickles down her back despite the chill. She prays.

Then the car accelerates and makes a left turn at the next street. She lets out a breath, but her senses are heightened.

At the end of the street, she looks around. No one seems to be in the vicinity, and she veers off the road, taking a worn footpath through the weeds that leads under the bridge. A few kids play at a park near the river's edge, but Sutton is far enough away that even if those kids see her, they wouldn't be able to identify anything but a small figure in baggy clothes.

Sutton walks parallel with the river, keeping close to the

bridge's huge stone abutment. Rounding the structure, she finds herself on a gravel roadway that is only accessible from a nearly hidden and dead-end street. The abandoned warehouse building still stands, though it's more derelict now than it was twenty years ago. A slim tree, green with new growth, has found its way through a section of partially collapsed roof, and the windows have long been broken out. Even the graffiti has worn off the side of the brick.

Sutton carefully picks her way around the building, careful of the broken glass and debris that litter what was once the building's entrance. The place looks completely devoid of life, and her heart sinks. Then she spies a needle in the dirt near some weeds.

She finds a door, and pushes it open. It swings inward on rusty broken hinges.

The interior is dark and smells of earth and mold. It takes her eyes a minute to adjust. She kicks an unidentified object, and it skitters across the floor littered with dirt, rubble, and leaves.

A heap of fabric is piled in one corner. It could be discarded clothing or a body.

She steps cautiously over forgotten objects; damp wooden beams and concrete blocks. An abandoned shopping cart sits alone against a wall.

Sutton walks through a doorway toward the far end of the building. Here, there are signs of recent human activity. The remnants of a fire, random articles of clothing strewn about, discarded food packaging. Broken glass crunches beneath her sneakers.

When she attempts to turn, something tight grips her right arm and something sharp pokes into the side of her neck.

From behind her, the hot, putrid smell of rotting breath. A low male voice whispers close in her ear, "What the fuck are you doing in here?"

She struggles to disengage herself from the grasp, but it squeezes, and the sharp object digs into the skin near her throat. "I'm just looking to buy," she stammers.

The guy forces her around and peers into her face. "I thought you were one of those stupid kids," he says. His expression is still filled with suspicion.

Sutton doesn't answer.

"Buy what?" The object still lingers near her neck.

"Just some fairy dust. I'm good for it."

He relaxes his grip on her arm. "How much you got?"

She hesitates. "Twenty."

Finally, the guy steps away and continues to study her in the dim light coming through the window. He is scruffy and dirty, and so young. Much younger than she is. "I can hook you up," he says.

Huddling away from him, she reaches under her coat and into the pocket of the sweatpants. She pulls out one of the bills and squints at it. Is it a fifty or a twenty?

The man snatches it away, and from his bark of laughter, she assumes it's the higher denomination. "Stupid bitch, don't even know what you got." But from his own pocket, he produces a small baggie.

Sutton doesn't care about his insults. She snatches the bag from him. "You got anything to cook with?"

She doesn't want to use dirty instruments, but she'd rather not snort the stuff, and there's no way she's going to cook it at her parents' house. Besides, she needs the fix right now.

He leads her through another door, where two other figures—men, she thinks—sit inert on the dirty floor. There are more windows in this room and a filthy table or desk, as if the room had been an office at one time. On the desktop are some needles, a few spoons, a half-empty bottle of water, and a lighter. The guy motions toward the paraphernalia, and Sutton glances at the men on the floor before leaning over the desk.

If she were at home, she'd inject it into her foot, but she doesn't want to take her shoe off here. Besides, there's no more time.

Working with one hand, she awkwardly taps the powder into the spoon and mixes it with some of the water. It's nearly impossible to flick the lighter and hold the spoon with her arm in a cast, and the guy who sold her the drugs takes some pity on her and helps. When it bubbles, she manages to work up the sleeve of her coat with one hand, and he prepares the needle for her.

She tries to stay calm, but the sight of the needle makes her tremble salivate.

There is no way she can shoot up with her useless left arm, so she looks at her new friend. "Can you—?"

He shrugs and runs one dirty finger over the crook of her arm. It's dark, and he doesn't spend much time trying to find a vein. She doesn't care. But he must hit something because after just a minute, she feels the familiar rush of bliss take over her body. Her arms and legs grow heavy, and she sinks down against the wall behind the desk. She looks up into the face of her friend. He's leering at her. "There's plenty more where that came from, honey," he says.

Sutton shuts her eyes. As long as he keeps making her feel like this—as long as he makes it easy for her to forget who she is—she doesn't really care what else he does to her.

CHAPTER 11

CHLOE-NOW

Chloe is unloading the dishwasher when her phone on the counter lights up and vibrates. Her ex-husband's name pops up on the screen. She frowns and contemplates letting the call go to voicemail. But that means she'll just have to call him back later and potentially ruin her day. With an audible sigh, she abandons the dishes and presses accept.

"Jason." Her greeting is one word and to the point. She hopes that it encourages him to communicate his purpose quickly. But recognizing that the prompt is probably too subtle, she quickly adds, "What can I do for you?"

"Hi, Chloe."

"What can I do for you?" she repeats, slowing the words down for her impossibly literal ex-husband.

In the pause that follows, she can hear voices in the background. A child bellows and then a female voice responds. She pictures Jason and his family at breakfast and glances at the clock on the stovetop in her own kitchen. It's after ten in the morning. It's no surprise to her that Jason Lawrence and his family would eat a mid-morning breakfast on Saturday, destroying any sense of routine for the rest of the week. They had probably eaten a meal laden with carbs and fat, too. Bacon, eggs, and pancakes with plenty of sodium and lots of processed syrup. Or maybe it had been something devoid of nutritional value altogether—sugary cereal and insubstantial pre-packaged oatmeal with dehydrated fruit.

Chloe and Emma had eaten their egg-white omelets and fresh fruit nearly three hours ago. Now, her daughter is getting ready for a golf lesson after reading a chapter in her biology textbook. After golf, they'll visit the art museum, which is featuring an exhibit on Japanese printmakers.

"I was hoping we might be able to meet for lunch today," Jason says, and that gives Chloe a start.

Despite the spark of curiosity, and because she has just run through her own day's agenda in her mind, she immediately responds, "Impossible."

"Okay, then." Jason's drawl is slow, deliberate, infuriating. "Tomorrow?"

Chloe exhales. Sunday is Emma's free day, when her daughter is able to decide what educational pursuit she would prefer. Impromptu activities like lunch with Jason are difficult with a schedule as busy as theirs. He doesn't understand the need for structure. He never has.

Chloe says as much to Jason, then adds, "Anything that you need to tell me at lunch, you can tell me right now during this phone call. I have a few minutes before we need to leave for golf."

She hears the reluctance in Jason's silence and tries to be patient. Jason is a cautious man. Every thought, every word, every decision must be considered, weighed, and reconsidered. And then the process must be repeated in his mind before communication can take place.

Chloe had tried so very hard when they were married to understand this. But it had used up vast reserves of her goodwill until she inevitably just ran out of everything.

Chloe is the type of person who needs to keep moving. If you act with intention there is less time for self-reflection and second-guessing. Looking backward, to the past, is what keeps you from moving forward. She knows this better than anyone.

Through the receiver, she notes fading of the background noises, then the click of a door closing. Jason has presumably moved somewhere more private.

"We need to talk about Emma," he finally says.

"What about her?"

"She called me last night."

Chloe frowns. Emma must have called him using the landline. Emma is surprised that she hadn't heard her daughter retrieving the handset, which is located outside Chloe's first-floor bedroom.

When Jason doesn't immediately elaborate, she prompts, "Okay…so?"

Jason stews over his next words, and she taps a finger on the counter, thinking. She would use the drivetime in the car today with Emma to reinforce the rules for the phone. As Emma well knows, the house line is for emergencies only. Calling her father at night when her mother sleeps just feet away is most certainly *not* an emergency.

Still, Chloe won't be too hard on her daughter. She remembers those confusing pre-teen years. She wishes *she'd* had a few more rules and a lot more structure to help her better navigate the terrible things to come.

Jason's voice pulls Chloe out of her own thoughts.

"It's just that there are some things we need to discuss," he finally says. "About Emma. About how she feels."

"That's what we're doing, Jason. We're discussing. Right now. On this phone call."

"Chloe, she's not happy."

Chloe hesitates but recovers quickly. "Well, of course she's not *happy*. She's twelve. What twelve-year-old girl do you know that's happy? It's a tough time."

"This goes beyond hormones." He pauses, then plunges. "She's not happy with you."

Chloe is silent. She tries to decide if she's furious, hurt, or amused.

"Chloe?" Jason asks. "Are you there?"

"I'm...here." She walks from the kitchen to her office and shuts the door softly behind her. "This unhappiness is something that you deduced from your conversation with her?"

"There wasn't a lot of deduction necessary."

"Well, what exactly did she say?"

"She said a lot," he says after a pause, then clears his throat softly.

Even though she's alone in her office, she rolls her eyes at his lack of detail. "What *exactly* did she say?" she repeats.

"Chloe, don't do this."

"Do what? Ask you for information?"

"This isn't one of your psychological experiments. This is our daughter. And she swore me to secrecy."

"Why are you calling me then?" she asks, raising her voice slightly. She ignores the crack about a psychological experiment. She has no idea what that even means. But she continues, "A twelve-year-old child swore you to secrecy, and without any additional information, I'm just supposed to take you at your word that she's unhappy with me. What is it that you would like me to *do* exactly?" She is being caustic, and that's not fair. But in what world can one parent not talk to the other about concerns regarding their child, even when that discussion is uncomfortable? Sometimes Chloe can't believe that she'd been married to a man as underdeveloped as Jason.

And yet here *she* is, trying to goad him into saying more by making him angry. It is sick and manipulative. Unfortunately, it happens to be how the two of them had communicated throughout their entire marriage. Which is why the marriage no longer exists.

He doesn't respond to her angry questions.

"If you can't tell me what she said, then I'm afraid this conversation is over, Jason. I will not speak in vague generalizations with you about *my* daughter." This is a shitty thing to say. But there are other shitty things about the situation, too. It's shitty that Jason remarried less than a year after they divorced. As if he'd just been waiting for her to leave so that he could finally make himself happy with his new wife and start a new family.

It's shitty that she does all of the hard work of parenting, and yet Jason feels as if he has some right to swoop in and act the hero the minute Emma decides she doesn't like how things are going at any given moment. As if it's never occurred to either Jason or Emma that it's *Chloe* who is the one always trying to raise Emma, to protect Emma. Chloe's not asking to be recognized. She's simply asking to be acknowledged, respected. She can forgive that of Emma, who is just a child. But Jason? She finds it unconscionable.

She's about to end the call when he blurts, "She said that she hated you and that if she had to live with you for one more second, she was going to—" His words end abruptly.

A pause. Chloe's blood chills and her fingers tingle. "Going to what?" she asks, her voice a whisper. But she knows what the next words are. She doesn't need Jason to say them. An image of her brother—that horrible scene that *she* discovered—flashes into her brain, and she squeezes her eyes shut.

"She didn't mean it, Chloe. I'm positive of that."

It suddenly occurs to Chloe that she hasn't seen Emma since breakfast. Emma is supposed to be reading and dressing for her golf lesson, but who's to say that's what she's been doing.

Chloe forgets Jason and bounds up the stairs, vaguely aware of Jason's tinny voice coming through the speaker of the cell phone still in her hand.

She throws open the door to Emma's bedroom and finds Emma half undressed next to her closet.

"What are you doing?" her daughter screeches, covering the top part of her body with a white shirt clutched in her fists. Her face quickly morphs from surprise to outrage.

"I'm—I'm sorry," Chloe stammers. "I just wanted to make sure you were getting ready."

Emma glares at Chloe, who backs out of the room and shuts the door behind her.

Her pulse thrums, and she breathes quickly. When she remembers Jason on the other end of the phone, she looks down and finds that she's still connected. She shifts the phone to her ear. He can likely hear her breathing.

"You okay?" he asks.

She nods before realizing he can't see her. "Yeah," she says breathlessly. She slowly walks back down the stairs.

Jason says softly, "Emma's not Matt."

Chloe shuts her eyes again. Very few people even know that she once had a brother. Of those who do, even fewer know what actually happened to him. Chloe had even kept his cause of death from Emma.

"Look," he continues. "I didn't tell you to scare you—"

"Well, it *did* scare me, Jason."

"Suicide doesn't run in families."

Emma knows that Jason's proclamation is not true, but she doesn't argue with him. "I'm not saying Emma is suicidal. But we never would have believed that Matt was either."

Her brother had never been diagnosed with a psychiatric disorder. Looking back, Chloe suspects that he was depressed, socially awkward, and questioning. He may have even been bi-polar or schizophrenic. But there had never been any indication that he might harm himself.

It was the unforgivable actions of Chloe, prompted by the wicked actions of others, which had tipped him over the edge. Even her ex-husband doesn't know the full extent for which she is responsible for her brother's death.

"I'm trying so hard to protect her," Chloe says, more to herself than to Jason.

"And you are. But in protecting her, there can be the danger of…smothering her a bit."

Chloe's bites her tongue.

"She mentioned her friend Tori," Jason continues.

"Tori's a bad influence." Chloe knows all about bad influences. She knows the pressure to fit in, the temptation to act like someone you're not in order to impress people who don't deserve your energy or your time.

"Tori's thirteen and her parents are both doctors. I'm not sure how Emma spending a Friday night watching movies would be a negative influence on her burgeoning psyche."

"Talk to me when you're a twelve-year-old girl."

Jason breathes into the phone. "Chloe, I think there might be some other options we can explore here. I've been discussing it with Becky, and we have a proposal."

Chloe cringes at the mention of Jason's wife, sure she will not be a fan of any forthcoming suggestion. But she waits.

"Now, this is just a suggestion," Jason says.

Chloe responses through clenched jaw, "Just spit it out, Jason."

"What if—" He hesitates. "How would you feel about Chloe spending the summer with us?"

Chloe is shocked into a brief silence. Then she chuckles. The longer she chuckles, the harder she laughs, until tears are streaming down her face and she's not sure if she's laughing or sobbing.

When she finally regains some composure, Jason's voice is tense. "What is so funny?"

"You moved back to Conway."

"And?"

"When we got married, we both agreed that we would never go back there. We both agreed that we would never raise our children there." It isn't lost on her that Jason has since had more children with someone else, and they were, indeed, raising those children in Conway. But hell would freeze over before Chloe agrees to the same thing.

"I'm not saying that Emma would have to be raised here. But maybe it would be good for her to have a break."

"A break from me."

"A break from life," he clarifies. "Emma has a sister and two brothers here. She could get to know them a little bit. We wouldn't be taking anything away from the school curriculum you've…instituted. It would simply be a change of scenery with her family."

Her family. Chloe shakes her head. Jason hasn't been around for months, and now he's Emma's *family*. A family that doesn't include Chloe.

But what's more, if the conversation with Jason has highlighted anything, it's that Chloe needs to keep a closer eye on Emma. Her daughter will not become like Matt, whose inner voices were louder than the external solutions. And she will not become what Chloe had once been—a sad, pitiful girl whose desperation to be noticed led to the downfall of people she cared about.

Instead, Chloe will give Emma the tools she needs to navigate any challenge that life throws at her. And she will do that far, far away from the pain and suffering in Conway.

To Jason, she simply says, "No."

A silence. "You're making a mistake, Chloe," he says softly.

Chloe ends the call. She doesn't care what Jason thinks. The only thing she's done that that *hasn't* been a mistake is loving her daughter fiercely. And the only possible solution for this current hiccup is reaffirming her commitment to give everything of herself to Emma. Because no one had known how to do that for her.

CHAPTER 12

JOE-THEN

Joe ends the call and stares down at his phone as he and Ryan inch behind a yellow school bus on Crawford Avenue, the main thoroughfare through Conway.

Ryan isn't paying much attention, as he sits behind the wheel of his brand-new Silverado pickup in the color blue mist. Joe knows the exact shade because Ryan and his dad bought the truck from Joe's dad. And because it came from Wright Automotive Group, Ryan has told Joe every detail about the vehicle.

Ryan is more than happy to be stuck behind the school transport. Not only might every student notice them from the back of the bus, but at every forced stop, there is a longer opportunity for bystanders and other motorists to admire Ryan's shiny and expensive early graduation present.

Ryan gives a mini salute to a middle-aged man standing on the sidewalk outside Vera's Corner Market. Finally, he glances over at Joe. "Is she coming over?"

Ryan is referring to Megan, but Joe shakes his head. "That wasn't Megan. It was Sutton."

Ryan scrunches up his face. "I thought you called Megan."

"I did. Sutton answered Megan's phone."

The bus lurches forward in front of them and Ryan follows close behind. Through the back window, a freshman flips them off. Both Joe and Ryan pretend like they don't see the kid.

"Sutton didn't give her the message?" Ryan asks, trying to work out the conversation.

Joe's trying to work it out, too. He's not sure if Sutton had been serious about coming to his house that night, but it sure sounded that way. Then again, it could have been a joke. She'd answered Megan's phone with Megan sitting right beside her.

Joe had been joking, too. Or maybe flirting. But it had been harmless, hadn't it?

After Joe relays the conversation to Ryan, Ryan says, "If you're taking Sutton, I'd be more than happy to take Megan off your hands."

Joe rolls his eyes. Ryan is all talk. He only has eyes for Holly Griffin right now.

And Megan is one of those girls who has always been cute, but she's also nice and smart and kind and hardworking. In other words, invisible. Or maybe "shrouded" is a better word. It isn't that the boys hadn't been interested in dating her, exactly. But she'd seemed far too evolved and unattainable to them. Joe himself only recently considered Megan as a potential romantic partner. It was as if a lightbulb had flashed above his head. Suddenly, she was just there—illuminated—in front of him.

The connection is new—they've only recently begun to talk outside of school. And Joe is cautious. He isn't sure he wants to become involved with someone his last summer before college. Especially with a girl who has the potential to take up all the space in his head and then break his heart. Not that he'd admit that to Ryan. Or out loud to anyone for that matter. He's barely admitted it to himself.

"Seriously, though," Ryan continues. "Please don't tell me you're thinking of ditching Megan for Sutton."

Where the situation with Megan is volatile, Sutton, on the other hand, is completely predictable. Sutton is tiny and birdlike with thin, sharp features, assets too big for her small body, and a magnetic sexual pull to her. One sideways glance from those black-rimmed eyes, and you *know* she's done things. But there's no danger of developing feelings for her. She is expendable.

"Didn't you sleep with Sutton after homecoming?" Joe asks Ryan, and Ryan shudders but doesn't answer the question.

Instead, he says, "Seriously, dude. She's gross. If Megan is interested in you, you'd be a moron to go for Sutton instead."

Joe looks out the passenger window as they roll down the hill toward the memorial bridge over the Mitsin. The river is still cold and rushing fast from the melting snow and spring rains. Soon, though, the summer heat will rise and many of their days will be spent floating down the river toward the campground—through rapids and past the abandoned railroad tracks and distillery a few miles outside of town.

He tries to picture which girl might be beside him, but the face keeps switching between Sutton's sly smile and Megan's lively eyes and open laughter.

The school bus finally turns right down Pittman Street, and Ryan speeds up as he continues over the bridge and west out of town toward the countryside where they both live. "Besides," Ryan continues, "Sutton and Megan are friends. Do you know how messed up it is that Sutton would consider coming over when she knows you're talking to Megan?"

"Yeah, *talking*." Joe emphasizes the word. "It's not like I've pledged my undying love to her."

Something in Joe's voice triggers Ryan, who stares over

at him open-mouthed. Ryan lets out a guffaw. "Wow. You're really into her." He slaps the steering wheel lightly. "Who would have thought that Megan Richards would be the one to bring you to your knees. The wild Joe Wright, godlike object of every Conway High School girl's dream, finally tamed by studious, quiet Megan Richards."

"Stop it," Joe grumbles as Ryan continues to laugh.

Joe can't be into her. He just can't. Not now. He attempts to shift the conversation. "And what about you? Aren't you into Holly?" Ryan has been dating Holly since Christmas, and from where Joe sits, it doesn't seem as though Ryan has any intentions of breaking up with her.

Ryan lifts a shoulder. "Yeah, she's all right."

But Ryan's nonchalance is affected. He'd been the biggest player in their group for the past three years. He'd slept with half the senior class and probably most of the junior class.

"I'm just saying," Ryan continues, reverting back to the prior subject, "Megan is pretty cool, and this year she's really blossomed, if you know what I mean. I don't know why any of us didn't notice her before."

Joe does. She's too good for them all.

"I can't even begin to understand how she's friends with Sutton."

But Joe understands that too. Sutton is a stray. To Megan, someone like Sutton would have been a project. A lifelong project, maybe.

He feels what's becoming a familiar tug in his chest when he remembers Megan. He's got to stop. To distract himself, he says, "Tell me what Sutton is like."

"You know what she's like. Nasty."

"Nasty how?"

Ryan looks over at him. "No, I'm not gonna do that, man. It was once, and I'd had too much to drink."

Joe raises his eyebrows.

"Hey, if you want my sloppy seconds, I won't stop you. But I will think you're a complete idiot."

"You're breaking my heart," he mutters as Ryan pulls into the drive-through line at the burger place at the edge of town.

After they order their food, their conversation shifts from girls to tomorrow's party and the fact that Chloe Nicholson is bringing the booze.

Ryan takes a big bite of his burger and mumbles around the sandwich, "You think she'll pull it off?"

Joe picks the pickles off his burger. He always forgets to tell them no pickles. "I don't know," he says.

"Should we have a backup plan? I'm sure I can find someone else to supplement."

Joe peers into his burger, and satisfied that he won't feel the out-of-place crunching between his teeth, he takes a bite, chews, then swallows before he responds. "I told you guys—I don't care what you do. I'm supplying the location only. If my dad finds out about this party, he'll be mad, but if he finds out I had something to do with the alcohol, he'll kill me. He's weird about stuff like that."

"Well, you don't want to have a lame party," Ryan says.

Joe won't admit this to Ryan, but he doesn't care if the party is lame. He just wants to be with his friends one last time before they graduate. Sure, they'll all hang out over the summer, but there's something a little bit exhilarating and also a little bit sad about the fact that their graduation marks the end of a slice of their lives. Most of his friends are excited about it and can't wait to graduate, but Joe is going to miss it. Even thinking about it now causes a hard lump to form at the back of his throat, and that makes him feel like an idiot. He chokes down another bite of burger and swallows hard.

When they finish eating, they continue their journey onto Falgan Road before turning right and winding higher until they reach Joe's hulking brick home on Mitsin Ridge. Ryan doesn't come in because he promised his grandfather that he'd help him with a remodeling project that evening.

Joe wishes Ryan would have stayed for a little while, though. He feels restless. The baseball team had not made it to the quarterfinals this year, and without any sports or homework, no after-school job, and his family, including Paige, gone for the rest of the week at one of Paige's equestrian shows, Joe isn't sure what to do with himself.

The cleaning people had been in the house that day, and the interior is gleaming and spotless. There is a lemony scent in the air made more noticeable by the fact that he's the only one in the space. It makes him fidgety. He wanders through the empty kitchen, which also smells like lemon when it should smell like his mother's elaborate and inventive cooking.

Joe opens the polished silver refrigerator and peruses the well-stocked contents. He eyes his father's collection of craft beers on their dedicated shelf. He doesn't love the taste of beer, but it's a lightly warm, sunny day, and he takes an IPA with a cartoon label and uses a bottle opener to pop off the cap. He'll only have one; otherwise, his dad will notice.

He heads through the sliding glass door and to the back deck that overlooks the river valley. He loves this house and this view, and he'll miss it when he leaves for school in just a few short months. He'll miss his whole family, in fact. Even his annoying little sister.

He switches on the outdoor stereo system and finds an alternative rock station. The Killers blast from the speakers, and Joe sinks back into a cushioned outdoor chair. He tips the beer bottle to his lips. The IPA is bitter, but after a few swigs, he adjusts to the taste. He surveys the tops of the trees and the snaking river below.

From deep within the gorge, he can hear the echo of voices—someone calling to a friend or a riding partner on the Great Allegheny Passage trail—part of the network of old railway that has been converted to a hiking and biking path that runs along the Mitsin. Joe is at least a mile above them.

A Modest Mouse song comes on, and Joe finishes his beer. He sets the bottle on the side table and watches as the sun hangs lower and lower in the sky. After a few minutes, his eyes start to droop to the sounds of "Float On."

Images of his friends play through his mind, and as he drifts into sleep, he dreams of playing baseball that looks like soccer, of gilded hallways and classrooms, of the boys and girls he's known his entire life. Blink-182 is playing a concert in the gymnasium, and Nate is the band's frontman. Everyone cheers for Nate, but instead of street clothes, Nate is suddenly dressed in fatigues, and someone starts shooting at the stage. There is screaming, and the crowd collectively falls to the floor. Joe crawls in circles. He can't find Nate. And then Megan is there, right in front of him. Her face is close to his, and she's smiling. Her lips are stretched wide as "Somewhere Only We Know" plays in the dark, and all of the people are gone. It's only Joe and Megan. She holds out her hand and says, *Joe.* He smiles at her. *Joe?* she says again.

He wants to kiss her. He says her name.

He feels breath on his face, and something is wrong. Who is in front of him?

He opens his eyes with a start, and he's back on his deck. The sun is low in the sky, and there is a chill in the late springtime air.

Sutton Schultz is leaning over him. "Joe?" she asks.

He blinks at her, confused, trying to get his bearings.

She smiles. Her teeth are small, white, and pointed.

They remind him of the incisors of a small animal. Her lips are painted a dark cherry color. The color looks flat and dry and nearly black. Like dried blood.

"There you are," she says when he recognizes her.

She is drinking one of his dad's beers, and he must look confused because she raises her eyebrows. "I hope you don't mind. I got it from the refrigerator."

"It's okay." But it's not okay. She's just walked into his house. He'd left it unlocked, but he feels violated. He tries not to let it show.

"This is a really nice house."

He mumbles a thank you.

Maroon 5 is playing on the radio. "I love this song," Sutton coos. She shuts her eyes and sways to the beat, mouths the words.

Joe straightens. He'd talked a good game with Ryan, but now that Sutton is here, he can't decide how he feels. "I didn't think you'd actually show up."

She keeps swaying to the beat and starts singing the chorus. She's wearing a pair of tight black jeans and a spandex tank top that's squeezing her breasts into high creamy mounds above the fabric. An oversized blue denim shirt is thrown on over the tank top, but Joe barely notices the extra clothing.

She sings the lyrics louder, and even though Sutton has a nice clear voice, Joe hates this song and its depressing lyrics set to an overly jazzy rhythm. There's something staged and awkward about the whole scene. Joe is embarrassed for her.

"I didn't think you'd come," he repeats, louder this time over the song.

"I said I would." She sounds annoyed.

"I thought maybe you'd bring Megan with you."

She rolls her eyes and stops moving to the music. "You

know she's not really into you, right?"

He doesn't say anything and looks out at the tops of the trees and their bright green leaves. He can feel her staring at him, studying the side of his face.

"I'm sorry," she says, and when he looks over, her eyes are wide. "Did you think she actually liked you?" She laughs lightly, a cruel sound.

He's not sure what she's talking about, and he doesn't want to ask. He doesn't want her to know that his heart is squeezing in his chest right now.

"That came out wrong. Of course she *likes* you. But she's been dating a kid from college—where she's going in the fall. She met him last year when she visited, and they've been talking online. I think he might be a sophomore or something."

He feels a black pit open in his stomach.

"You know Megan. She's just so…nice. She wasn't sure how to tell you."

He manages to lift a shoulder. "It's not like we were dating or anything," he says. He can hear the tight defensiveness in his own voice. He'd really wanted to date her, he admits to himself. He'd really wanted to see where it might have gone. To Sutton, he says, "And she knows you're here?"

Sutton makes a pouty face. "Do you really think I'd show up here without her knowing about it?"

Joe remembers the tentative phone calls he'd shared with Megan, the innocent notes passed in class, forging a connection. He remembers the looks that they'd exchanged that had promised so much more. It's true that he'd initiated much of that interaction, but she had responded.

To find out now that she is just too nice to tell him how she really feels is a disappointment. A devastating disappointment. But to know that Megan is absolutely fine with her promiscuous friend being alone with him… And she must know what they might be doing. What Sutton had been planning. That hurts most of all. Maybe Megan had even sent Sutton here. Maybe she was trying to make it easy on him. It makes him sick to his stomach. It makes him angry.

Sutton finishes the beer, stands, and puts the bottle next to his on the table. When she leans down, her breasts are at his eye level. He looks at her body, and when he looks up at her face, she's staring at him intently. She moves closer and puts a hand on his thigh.

He doesn't want to react to her touch, but he can't help it. Her fingers with their sharp red nails make small massaging motions on his leg.

"Do you, like, want to go inside or something?" Her fingers inch upward from his thigh, and he sucks in a breath. "It's getting cold," she whispers. "I could warm you up."

Before her hand can go any further, he grabs her wrist. Her expression falters, but he smiles at her, though it feels more like he's baring his teeth. If Megan is okay with the situation between him and her best friend, who is he to resist?

He leads Sutton to a chaise lounge that is covered in the same thick cushion as the chair. "Out here is good," he says, and they both squeeze onto the narrow piece of furniture.

There are hands, lips, teeth, hot skin, and cold air. Sutton's mouth is warm and wet, her body soft and willing where he is hard and urgent. She tastes like beer and smells fruity and sweet. When her teeth catch his earlobe, they are as sharp as he thought they'd be.

There is a rapid acceleration followed by the sharp thrill of pleasure.

Then it's over. Quick and hollow. The silence from the

river valley is deafening.

Joe stands and sorts out his clothing. Sutton doesn't bother, and her breasts are exposed in the chilly night air. He wants to tell her to cover up. Instead, he looks away. "I should, uh, get inside."

"I can come in if you want. My parents are at work."

He shakes his head. "I probably shouldn't press my luck. You know…since I'm having the party here tomorrow night."

She looks hurt, but she doesn't argue. She straightens her clothing in the awkward silence that follows.

He glances at her empty beer bottle. "Are you okay to drive?" The question fills the space between them.

"I walked."

"Don't you live on the west side of town?"

She nods.

"That's, like, five miles from here." And it isn't a straight five miles. Over a mile of that distance is along Falgan Road, where people drive way too fast around the twists and turns. He lets out a quiet breath. "I'll take you home."

"You don't have to," she says. "I don't mind walking."

"Well, *I* mind you walking." He ignores the wide smile on her face. He knows he's opening something up that he should instead be closing. "I'll grab my keys."

He wants her to stay outside, but she follows him in, through the kitchen and to the front of the house where he'd set his keys in the bowl on the entryway table next to his phone. Sutton looks around the main living room to the left. She wanders over to the fireplace and studies the photos on the mantel. "Your mother is beautiful," she remarks.

He feels weird saying thank you to that, so he doesn't say anything.

"How old is your sister?"

"She's in middle school," he responds. He's not sure

why he doesn't want Sutton to know basic information about him or his family. It feels too intimate. It occurs to him that he and Megan have already shared much of this information about themselves. It had felt natural. He'd rushed to get all of the details about himself out to her, and he'd listened, greedy for information about her family and her life.

The irony of the discrepancy also occurs to him.

He feels like such a jerk after what has just happened with Sutton. So, he offers, "Paige and my parents are at a horse show in Ohio."

His phone trills, and Sutton looks over as if she's trying to see the details of the call from the distance between them. He takes a breath and walks into the dining room on the other side of the house.

"Hey, Dad."

"Hiya," his dad says too loudly into his mouthpiece. "Can you hear me?" he yells over the crackle of static.

"Kind of." Joe raises his voice as if that might help his dad make out the words through the interference.

"We're all set up out here in the camper. Just calling to check in on you."

"All good here."

"Any issues at the house?"

Joe feels movement behind him and turns around to find Sutton standing in the doorway. The dining room is dimly lit, and Sutton's blond hair catches the light from the streetlamp outside. He can't see her face in the shadow.

"Nope, no issues. Just going to grab something to eat and watch some television before bed."

"Okay, son." There is a pause. "Remember, no company this weekend." His dad means parties, and Joe cringes inwardly.

"Roger that."

"All right. We'll check in tomorrow."

He ends the call, and Sutton moves to stand close to him. "It's nice that your parents care about you." She walks her fingers up his arm, and he shivers.

His body responds when she touches his neck with her cool fingertips. It would be easy to let her stay for a while.

But he steps away abruptly. "Come on," he says, more roughly than he means to. He softens his voice when he continues, "Your parents will wonder where you are, too."

She looks like she might argue, but she follows him when he walks out of the house. He opens the passenger door of his maroon Blazer for her. She climbs in, giving him a smile that has transitioned from sly and cunning to shy and hesitant. The expression makes him think of Megan, and desperation and guilt fill his chest.

He wishes it were Megan in that seat.

He is an idiot.

They don't talk much as he travels through the rural streets to Falgan Road. Once they pass the stoplights in town, Sutton navigates him to her house. It only takes them a few minutes.

In front of her house, she leans over and kisses his cheek before climbing out. It is a poignant gesture, and Joe is embarrassed for her. For them both. He waits for her to open her front door and walk in, but he doesn't look over even when he can see her waiting for him to wave before he drives away.

After retracing the route to his house in the opposite direction, he pulls his car into the garage and locks all of the doors before he heads to his bedroom. His phone rings. He flips open the device, and Megan's name is illuminated on the screen. His heart thumps in his chest, and he nearly accepts the call.

But instead, he presses the red X icon.

She's already made enough of a fool of him. He won't let her embarrass him again.

CHAPTER 13

JOE-NOW

When Joe opens his eyes, the sun is streaming through the window. He is alone in an unfamiliar space that smells like flowers and vanilla with just a hint of dust. Because the full-sized bed in his childhood room is much too small for two adults, he and Vivian slept in the guest room with the king-sized bed. He feels the crick in his back from the impossibly soft pillow-top mattress.

A faint hum of voices reaches him from the first floor, and he shuts his eyes again.

He had dreamt of Sutton Schultz. The young version of her—lithe and blonde and full of temptation. He blinks away both the dream and the memory of the old woman he'd seen in the wheelchair yesterday, still not quite believing it could have been the same person.

When they'd returned from the hospital last evening, Viv had mercifully asked no more questions about the woman, and equally as mercifully, no one else felt much like talking either. The family had eaten, mostly in silence, the greasy pizza that Paige had ordered. The scant dialogue between them was excruciatingly polite, and Vivian did her best to cut through the strain and navigate potential conversation pitfalls where she could. Joe was glad for her presence.

Today, they will find out more about the plan for hospice care, but Joe will no longer remain silent. He is prepared to insert himself into the process and decision-making. It's not that he doesn't trust his mother and sister to make the right decisions; it's just that they have never dealt with anything like this. Admittedly, neither has he. But he's confident in his ability to make decisions that aren't wholly based on emotion.

He opens his eyes again and looks around the bright white room with its pale-yellow walls and rose-colored curtains. It's strange being back here—sleeping here—after being away for so many years. Vivian had been respectful of his need for silence last night even when they'd been alone. But soon she would have questions, and he would owe her answers.

He checks his phone that's plugged into the outlet near the nightstand. It's nearly eight in the morning, which is late for him.

He skims two new emails about a minor issue at one of the offices. The issue isn't anything the general manager won't be able to handle. Then he checks the social media pages for each of the dealerships. Mackenzie, the bubbly part-time marketing intern, has already posted the scheduled content on the main channels and has responded to a few new comments about inventory. She has a lot of ideas for content on some of the newer video-based channels that are less familiar to Joe, but Vivian is working with the young woman on that initiative.

Social media makes him nervous. It makes him feel so…exposed, putting himself out there for the whole world to see; opening himself up to unsolicited judgment and commentary. He knows that the medium is necessary for business growth and brand management. But he doesn't have to like it. And he doesn't have to participate in it personally.

Vivian, on the other hand, has developed an active social media presence, partly because of her earlier years as a minor public figure. Now, she shares posts about the dealership and her role as a successful businesswoman, wife, and mother. She doesn't share much content that features Joe and the girls—Natalie and Ava—specifically, but he knows that photos have been posted in the past. Some of his old acquaintances from Conway and their wives follow Vivian. He hates it, but there's not much he can do about it without seeming controlling, out-of-touch, and petty.

Joe rises, brushes his teeth, and throws on a pair of jeans and a t-shirt before padding down the stairs in his bare feet, something he never does at home. In his childhood house, he's regressed.

When he enters the kitchen, Vivian and Paige are drinking coffee at the granite-topped island. The soft murmur of his mother's voice reaches him from his dad's old office on the other side of the living room.

Vivian pours him a cup of black coffee, and he smiles his thanks. "Sleep okay?" he asks. He takes a sip of the strong, bitter liquid.

Vivian arches an eyebrow at him in response to his question, and he smiles in commiseration and understanding.

From the stool where she is perched, Paige says, "Mom is on the phone with the social services liaison at the hospital about hospice setup. She's already talked to the nurses, and Dad did well last night. Once Dr. Burman makes his rounds, he should sign off on home care." She has appointed herself as the deliverer of the news. She has a purpose.

Joe can't help thinking that she seems very pleased and self-important regarding her new role. "I want to talk to the doctor before that happens," says Joe.

Paige sets her jaw, but she doesn't respond.

Vivian, who likely saw his sister's expression and wants to keep the peace, changes the subject, and not necessarily to a more appealing one. "Paige was telling me what it was like growing up here."

"Not much to tell. There was nothing to do," Joe says flatly.

"Yeah, Joseph couldn't wait to get out, especially after his senior year," Paige agrees, and Joe winces. He doesn't look at his sister. Paige has often struggled with the gift of discretion, unlike the rest of the family. She's never minded who knew their business, and Joe could never be sure when she might share something private with the exact wrong audience.

Vivian isn't paying attention. She walks to the sliding door that opens onto the back deck. There is a mist rising in the cool morning from the river valley. It looks like they are sitting atop a wispy cloud. And technically they are.

"It's beautiful here," Viv murmurs. "Peaceful."

"There's as much to do here as anywhere else," Paige says. She wants to pick an argument with him.

But Joe doesn't bother engaging because her retort is not remotely true. And his attention is on his wife. He doesn't like the faraway look on her beautiful face as she gazes at the forest surrounding them.

"We should bring the girls here more often," his wife says just as his mother walks into the room.

"I've been saying that since Natalie was born." There is mild censure in Sandra Wright's tone.

"What did the doctor say?" Joe asks.

"Social services liaison," Paige corrects.

"Once Dr. Burman sees your father, he will sign the paperwork, and then he'll be released for home care. They'll arrange for ambulance transport. In the meantime, a team of technicians and a nurse will visit to set up for him here. The nurse will be assigned to us throughout the care." His mother is perfectly coiffed and made-up, but her voice is strained and there are carefully concealed pouches under her eyes. "Joe and Vivian, if you don't mind, you can stay here and direct the hospice team. Paige, you come with me. You can drive my car back, and I'll ride in the ambulance with Dad."

Joe holds up his hands and presses forward against the air, as if to stop any momentum. "I need to talk to this Dr. Burman before we agree to anything."

"Your father and I have already agreed to this." Sandra's tone is measured and controlled, but Joe knows she's annoyed with him.

He's annoyed, too. "I understand that. But as someone who's been kept in the dark about the situation for over a year, you'll forgive me if I'd like to find some of my own peace of mind."

Paige starts to say something, but their mother gives Joe's sister a small shake of her head. "It's fine. Paige can stay here with Vivian, and Joe can come with me."

Joe nearly argues that the nurse and technicians may not be necessary at all if his conversation with the doctor changes the plan, but he decides to keep his mouth shut. Better to pick his battles.

They all eat a quick breakfast of toast and cereal before the group disperses to dress for the day. Within an hour, Joe is in the passenger seat of his mother's posh SUV, and they are driving off Mitsin Ridge.

As they turn onto Falgan Road, Joe keeps his eyes averted from the tree around the slight bend in the road. It is adorned with the familiar cross and colorful flowers. A collection of shiny Mylar balloons has been affixed at its base.

His mother also keeps her jaw set and her eyes straight ahead.

After they have traveled through Conway and onto the highway leading toward Beesonstown, Joe feels like he can breathe again. His mother, sensing the easing of tension, relaxes her hands on the wheel. "Vivian is looking well," she says. "Beautiful as always."

He murmurs his agreement.

"And Ava and Natalie? How are they doing? It's been so long since we've seen them."

Joe breathes through his defensiveness. He knows it's been too long, and he wants to deflect some of the blame onto his parents. It's true that he and Vivian have been busy with the dealership, but his parents could have reached out, too. And if he had known the seriousness of his dad's condition, he would have visited with the girls.

To his mother, he says simply, "They're doing great. Getting big. They would love to see you."

There is a taut pull in the tendons of her neck, and she purses her lips. She switches on the radio to a soft rock station. A pop song from the nineties fills the space between them even as the singer is lamenting being torn. Joe knows the feeling.

When they finally reach the hospital, the building is bustling with patients and visitors on a Saturday morning. Joe and Sandra squeeze into the elevator with a number of people who don't feel the least bit uncomfortable continuing their conversation about Uncle Randy's advanced gout, spinal arthritis, and the accompanying gory details. They don't even seem to notice Joe and his mother; the family talks right over their heads without a glance. Joe is equal parts appalled and fascinated.

When they exit the elevator, a short dark-skinned man is standing at the nurses' station. He glances up and says,

"Mrs. Wright, I'm glad we intersected. I've just signed off on your husband's care plan, and the social services team can help finalize the transport and at-home arrangements."

His mother smiles. "Thank you, Dr. Burman. And how did you find him today?"

"He's much better than he was yesterday. Stable, awake, and comfortable. That's our goal." He pats her arm and turns to walk away.

"Excuse me," Joe interjects. "I'm Joseph Wright. The...son."

The doctor turns back. He looks impatient and indifferent, but he nods. "Nice to meet you."

"I'd like to talk about my father's treatment."

His mother says, "I'm just going to say good morning." She exchanges a look with the doctor then ducks away.

Dr. Burman tucks a file under his arm and turns to face Joe with his full attention. "What would you like to know?"

"Why isn't more being done for him?"

He gives Joe a long, steady look. "I'm not at liberty to discuss the exact treatment plan with you because I haven't discussed that with the patient—"

"He's my father," Joe interrupts.

Dr. Burman's demeanor remains calm. "I can tell you that typical treatment for acute myeloid leukemia involves chemotherapy, demethylating agents, and the use of cytarabine. If treatment using those methods proves ineffectual, then end-of-life care is the next best option. Your parents are well aware of the treatments and their chances of effectiveness. They are also quite informed and certain of next steps."

"I was not a part of any of these conversations."

The doctor looks as if he's going to say something and then stops himself. With a glance at the woman in white scrubs sitting at the desk next to them, he leads Joe a few steps away. "Sometimes, parents keep things from their children in an effort to protect them. I'm not saying that's what is happening here, because I don't know your particular situation. I have two grown daughters—Elora and Marisa. I would do nearly anything to allow them to avoid pain and suffering. Do you have children, Joe?"

Joe nods, but he resents the mollification. He knows what the doctor is trying to do.

Dr. Burman waits.

"Natalie and Ava," he finally offers.

"Ah, two girls. Same as me. I imagine you would do anything you could to protect them, too."

Of course the answer is yes. It does not mean, however, that Joe would ever keep his children in the dark about something so grave as illness or death.

"We as parents are imperfect," Dr. Burman continues. "And we do the best we can with the tools we have, but we have to get comfortable in the knowledge that we will make mistakes. Sometimes, we may make decisions that turn out to be wrong, but we make them for the right reasons."

Dr. Burman's words remind Joe of the decisions his parents made twenty years ago, and his mind wanders to the reaction to that party, the response to the accident, the choices that were made in the aftermath of the entire incident. If those decisions—no matter how questionable— had not been made, what would Joe's life be like right now?

Dr. Burman is still talking, and though Joe's mind has wandered, he pulls his attention back to the man in front of him.

"I'm not telling you what to do. But if it were me, I would talk to my parents honestly. But make sure you give them grace. As parents, someday we will ask that of our own children."

Joe nearly caves to the sentimentality of the little speech.

But he's not that naive. "I think we should get a second opinion."

"That is certainly your father's prerogative. In fact, I've proposed that option to both of your parents throughout his treatment and care. My professional opinion is that any of my esteemed colleagues will provide identical medical advice. But I support any decision that your parents make." He emphasizes the word *parents*.

The doctor stares at him a beat longer. His calm, fatherly manner disappears, replaced by the brisk impatience that Joe had sensed initially. When Joe offers no further response, the doctor gives a curt nod and walks away, presumably to continue his rounds. Joe feels dismissed and impotent. And that makes him angry. He takes a few deep breaths and tries to cover up his frustration, then walks down the hall to his father's room.

His mother is sitting beside the bed with both of her hands covering one of his father's. Her eyes are shut. If Joe hadn't known better, he might think his mother is praying. But Sandra Wright has never been a religious or even spiritual woman.

His father sees him first. "Hey, Joe." There is an attempt at cheerfulness, but all Joe can hear is the weakness in the man's voice. It takes his breath away.

"Hey, Dad," he responds, attempting to match his father's forced optimism. He feels the strain in his own voice and hopes that his father doesn't pick up on it. "Not feeling so well?"

"I've been better." There is an effort at a chuckle, but it turns into a cough.

"I just talked to your doctor, and he tells me that you might be able to get a second opinion."

His mother shakes her head. "Joe, we've been through this—"

"Sandy." His dad's voice is low but surprisingly firm. "I appreciate that, Joe. But this has been a long road, and I think I'm just about out of gas."

"I'll bet you have enough fuel for one more trip," Joe says.

His dad smiles, but there is exhaustion in his face and eyes. There's something else there, too. A rigidity that hadn't been there before. Joe wonders if it's pain.

"Well, we'll see what happens." His dad pats the top of his mother's hand. "But whatever that is, it's not going to happen in this hospital bed. I'm ready to go home."

There are tears in his mother's eyes, and Joe can't abide any of this. "I wish you'd told me earlier," he says, trying to keep the emotion out of his voice.

"Maybe we should have told you," his dad agrees. "But you have so much going on with your work and your family. I know exactly how that is."

"Work doesn't matter, and you're my family, too."

His dad nods. "You're right." He glances at his wife. "The truth is, I kind of thought I was invincible. When it turned out that I wasn't—well, here we are."

Here we are, Joe thinks. He rubs his hands together, stands a little straighter, takes a breath. "I know a few people in the city. I'll make some phone calls this afternoon. See if we can't get you fixed up."

With that, his mom stands. "I'm going to see if I can find our social worker." She leaves her husband and Joe alone in the room.

His father has shut his eyes, and his breathing levels out. Joe goes to the seat his mother just vacated and sits quietly.

"I'm not sleeping," his dad says. "Just resting."

"We can rest together."

"Didn't sleep well in your old room?"

"Viv and I slept in the guest room. The bed's bigger."

His dad opens one eye at that and shoots Joe a lecherous look. Joe laughs harder than he should because it's a relief to know that the old man hasn't lost his sense of humor.

They fall again into silence, and Joe listens to the faraway beeping of monitors elsewhere on the floor. It's surprisingly peaceful in the room. He again thinks his father has fallen asleep, but then the man says suddenly, "Go easy on your mom."

"What's that?" Joe asks.

"For not telling you. That was all me."

Joe is quiet for a beat. "I would have come."

"I know you would have. But Paige has been here, and God knows she needed something to do with her time."

Joe chuckles softly.

"Maybe it was selfishness. Or ego, or pride. I don't know. No one wants their kids to see them wasting away."

"Is that what you think of me?"

"Of course not. That's what I think of *me*."

"I just wish there were more time."

"We've got some time," his dad says. "Not much, but some."

Another silence.

"I always felt like we should have talked more about what happened back then. You know, the…accident, when you were graduating, and what happened afterward."

Joe's heart jumps at that, partly because this was a taboo subject in their house. Those few weeks are never mentioned. The existence of them has been so deeply repressed that there are times Joe believes his parents have forgotten they actually happened.

Joe is also anxious because his dad's words closely mirror his thoughts of just a few minutes earlier. He so rarely comes home, and when he does, all of those memories tend to deepen and blossom. He's painfully aware of the fact that it's been twenty years. Twenty years ago, many lives changed forever; not just his.

And Megan Richards had lost hers. If she had survived, where would she be? Successful, no doubt. Would Joe have married her? Probably not, but maybe. Who knows…

Because unlike the story Sutton Schultz had told him that night, there had been no college-aged boyfriend. There had only been her crush on him. Who was to say what the future would have held, had she survived?

Even if he and Megan had never spoken again, she'd likely be married with a few kids of her own by now. She would have contributed positively to the world. He'd ruined that. He'd ruined her. He'd ruined everything.

"We don't need to talk about that, Dad."

His mother re-enters the room with a cheerful-looking middle-aged woman with a halo of short brown curls. "Hello, Mr. Wright," she says too loudly. "Are you ready to go home?"

His father just smiles and nods, and Joe is pushed to the background as the process begins.

CHAPTER 14

DAN-THEN

"Are you fucking stupid?" Greg Armstrong throws his hands up in the air and glares at Dan, who is on the other side of the massive bay of the garage.

His dad is not a large man, but he's stocky and he's mean. Covered in oil and grease, he looks stronger than he probably is.

It's been at least two years since Greg has physically struck Dan, and Dan doesn't think his dad would dare try it now that Dan is at least six inches taller than the older man. But the words now might be harsher than the fists used to be.

Dan had been under a truck at the far end of the garage, but he stands to find out what mistake he's made this time.

"You're a goddamn moron," the man continues, and throws a wrench. It skitters across the floor.

Dan hesitates and then approaches cautiously. "What did I do?" he asks.

"There's oil pouring from this thing!" His dad gestures wildly at the 2003 Volkswagen that Dan had worked on earlier that morning. Dan can see the puddle of dark liquid pooling under the car.

He stands there lamely as his dad hits the hood and pulls up the engine cover.

"You didn't tighten the housing down all the way.

There's goddamn oil all underneath the engine compartment."

Dan moves forward. "I'll clean it out."

"No, idiot. You've done enough already. Just...go away."

Dan starts walking back toward the truck he'd been working on, and his dad yells, "Hey, dumbass. I said go away. Away. Out of here. I don't want to see your worthless face."

"But I'm almost done—"

Another wrench sails toward him, and Dan sidesteps the heavy metal just in time. It clatters off the wall and falls to the floor.

He doesn't ask any more questions; he just ducks his head and walks quickly from the garage and into the house, which is a semi-modern version of a log cabin—long and narrow and deep in the wooded community of Highland Rocks on the side of the Chestnut Ridge. Even though there are over a hundred homes in their community, the community itself consists of thousands of acres. Greg Armstrong's house is on three wooded acres. The enormous garage had been a later addition, built after Greg was fired from his job as a mechanic about a decade earlier and then went into business for himself.

Dan tries to stay out of Greg's way, and mostly he succeeds, even when he's doing work for the man. Dan is a decent mechanic. It's just that he makes careless, stupid mistakes sometimes, and that makes his father angry. He knows he can be an idiot, but sometimes—like today—his father's criticism cuts deeper than it does other days.

Part of his sensitivity probably has to do with his upcoming graduation from high school. Dan has no life plans other than to keep working with his dad. He doesn't know how long he can do that. The man's temper seems to be getting worse.

He supposes that's why his mother, Sheila Armstrong, had left them twelve years earlier, but he wishes he knew for sure. Aunt Brenda has done what she could, even going as far as trying to get custody of Dan. For some reason, his dad fought that with all his might. Aunt Brenda says it's a control thing, but Dan isn't sure. At least Greg has never prevented Dan from spending time with Brenda and Crystal. That may have killed him.

There's no point in going to school. It's a Friday, and yesterday had been the last day of his vocational mechanic program. If he shows up at the high school now, he'll have to sit in unfamiliar classrooms with kids he hasn't talked to in the three years since his program started. He has nothing in common with them. He'd rather work if he could. But now that he's been thrown out of the garage, he has absolutely nothing to do.

From the house phone, he calls Crystal, who is two years older than he is but currently unemployed. She has her cosmetology license, but she says that doing other people's hair just isn't her thing. Crystal is pretty enough to be a model herself, but they live too far from the city for any opportunities for that type of work. He half expects her to just be gone one day like his mom. But unlike his mom, he doesn't think she'll leave without a word. She loves her family too much to do that to them.

He doesn't expect her to pick up but is relieved when he hears her voice on the other end of the line.

"Hey, Danny," she says. "Everything okay?"

At the sound of her soft voice, he feels his resolve weaken. A hard lump forms in the back of his throat, and tears spring to his eyes. He dashes them away with the back of his hand and swallows down on the painful pressure. "Yeah," he manages.

She doesn't believe him. "What did he do?"

"He didn't do anything."

"Bullshit. Fucker," she says under her breath. "Did he hit you?"

"No. He just—" Dan stops, considers what he wants to say and then decides he doesn't want to talk about it. "You know how he is. Look, are you going to be around?"

"For a while. Mom has an appointment in a bit. She still can't shake that cough."

"Can I come by?"

"Of course. Would you mind stopping to pick up a loaf of bread and a half gallon of milk on your way? I haven't had a chance to get out yet today."

"Sure," Dan says, thinking of the meager amount of money in his wallet. His dad owes him a few hundred bucks, but Dan hasn't found the right time to ask for it.

He's glad his Civic is parked near the house rather than outside the garage. He can drift out of the driveway without making too much noise, and by the time he needs to engage the engine, he'll be far enough away that Greg Armstrong won't hear a thing.

He stops at a mini-mart at the bottom of the mountain and spends most of the money he has left on the staple items for Crystal and Aunt Brenda. When he walks in their front door and heads to the kitchen to deposit the groceries, he can hear his aunt's rasping cough from the second floor. Crystal is in the kitchen of the small house that sits not far off the highway, just outside of town. "Thanks, Danny," Crystal says, taking the items. "Did that asshole say anything else to you?"

Dan shakes his head.

"You're eighteen now. You can leave, you know."

"Where would I go?"

"You can move in here."

But the house only has two bedrooms, and Dan doesn't want to impose.

Aunt Brenda comes into the room, wearing a long pink nightgown that hangs from her slight frame. Dan is struck by how thin she looks. Her coloring is also gray, and her face is puffy. She squeezes his arm lightly, slightly out of breath. "There's my boy," she says in her low husky voice. She grabs a cigarette and lighter from a bowl on the counter.

Crystal frowns but doesn't comment. Dan says, "Aunt B, do you think you should be smoking with your cough?"

She just smiles at him. "Something's gonna get us all, Danny. I'll not be changing my ways now." She laughs and it's low and throaty, then lights the acrid-smelling cigarette, the familiar menthol fragrance wafting into the air. "Besides, Crystal is taking me to the doctor today. They'll fix me right up."

"Well, I hope so."

She lowers herself onto one of the vinyl-covered kitchen chairs. "So, why aren't you in school?"

He explains his predicament, and she nods, inhaling then blowing out a stream of smoke. "But you'll be graduating in two weeks, right? I want to make sure I get to watch you walk across that stage. For your mom."

Dan gets the same pit in his stomach every time someone mentions his mom. And this time, it's particularly deep and hollow. For as long as he can remember, he thought if she was ever going to show up anywhere, it might be for his graduation. Now that it's almost here, he wants it so badly that he's terrified he'll push it away. He nearly asks Aunt Brenda if it might be possible. But he can't let anyone know how much he's been praying for it.

He has daydreamed about what he'll say. In some of the daydreams, he's angry, and he yells. Tells her he didn't need her then and he doesn't need her now. But those daydreams make him anxious, angry, and sad. The ones that make him happy are when he folds her into his arms—because in his dreams, he remembers her as a small laughing woman with blond-brown hair who kissed the top of his head and read him bedtime stories. In the best daydreams, she tells him how much she loves him and that she didn't want to leave him, but she had to go to keep them both safe.

It's stupid, he knows. And it makes him feel like a pathetic little kid.

"I'll walk across the stage for you, Aunt Brenda," he says, and he means it, because without Aunt Brenda, where would he be?

The woman pats his arm. She asks, "Your dad treating you okay?"

Dan shrugs and casts a sidelong look at Crystal, who meets his eye. He can trust Crystal with his life. She never tells his secrets.

"She wouldn't have left you if she felt like she had another choice." His aunt rarely omits that reminder from any of their conversations. And Dan responds like he always does.

"I know, Aunt B."

But Sheila Armstrong hadn't told anyone she was leaving or where she was going, including Brenda, her older sister. And as much as Dan wanted her back—as quickly as he'd forgive her if she walked through the door—he can't help but feel that she just hadn't wanted him enough to take him with her.

Crystal says, "Mom, you need to get dressed if we're going to get to your appointment on time."

Aunt Brenda waves her cigarette around in front of her face. "As soon as I'm done with this." She puts it to her lips and inhales so that the tip glows red. Her exhale turns into a rasping cough that goes on and on and on. It sounds bad, and Crystal fills a glass tumbler with water from the tap and sets it in front of her mother. Aunt B tamps out the cigarette after that. With some effort, she pushes herself up from the chair and walks out of the room, hacking as she goes.

Crystal watches her mother and says, "I don't think it's good."

Dan doesn't know how to respond, so he says nothing.

Crystal looks back at him. "You're welcome to come with us, or stay here, if you want."

He shrugs. "It's okay. I'll figure it out." He's got a few friends who are in school right now, and some older friends he knows who are probably working.

"I heard there's going to be a party tonight," Crystal says. "At Joe Wright's house up on Mitsin Ridge. His dad owns the car dealership heading toward Beesonstown."

Even though Crystal has been out of school for two years, somehow, she knows more than Dan does about the kids in his class and their plans. "I know him," Dan says. But that's a stretch. If Joe and Dan passed each other in the hallway, neither would say hello to the other, though Joe probably knows Dan's name, too. They'd been in the same classes in middle school.

"You should go."

Dan makes a face. The last thing he wants to do is go to a party at that guy's house. Joe's an entitled rich boy who thinks he's better than everyone else, especially someone like Dan.

"Oh, come on," Crystal says. "It would be good for you to be around people your own age. When's the last time you hung out with someone who isn't a thirty-year-old mechanic?"

"I hung out with my friend C.J. last week. He's my age. I know him from tech school."

"What did you do?"

"We worked on his car."

She rolls her eyes. "Aren't there any girls you're interested in?"

There actually *is* a girl he's had a crush on since elementary school. He doesn't get to see her much anymore, but when he does run into her, she smiles brightly and says hello. She is pretty; she is smart; she is kind. She is way out of his league.

"Ah, so there *is* someone."

Sometimes, he hates that she can see into his head. "Not anyone who would want to have anything to do with me."

"You'll never know if you don't go."

"Not going to happen."

"Come on, Danny. One night of fun."

He picks up a discarded pen and taps it on the table. "I won't know anybody there."

"Don't you go to school with them?"

"Yeah, but I don't hang out with them. They don't even know who I am anymore. I'm just a trashy kid from the tech school."

"Don't you dare say that," Crystal says, and her tone is surprisingly vehement. "Don't you dare sell yourself short like that. You're brilliant. You got that?"

He was going to laugh at her, but she is frowning at him so deeply he just says, "Okay," a little bit cowed.

She pauses. "How about this. How about if I go with you?"

"Why would you want to go to a high school party?"

"I'm not *that* old. Besides, I still talk to a few of the girls from the cosmetology program. We'll just go and say hello. If it's lame, we'll leave."

It will undoubtedly be lame, but there is no way he is driving with Crystal. Crystal likes to talk. A lot. And besides that, the high school boys will definitely be trying to hit on her. That's not to say she'll be interested in any of them, but she won't turn away the attention either. He has no plans of getting stuck at Joe Wright's house while Crystal flirts her way through his graduating class.

"Fine," he says. "I'll go for one hour. It'll be terrible, and then I'll leave. But I'm only going to get you off my back, and I'll be driving myself."

Aunt Brenda comes back into the room wearing a pale blue blouse and high-waisted jeans with the belt cinched tight around her thin waist. "Going where?" she asks.

"To a party up on Mitsin Ridge."

She raises her eyebrows. "Fancy." To Crystal, she says, "Come on, I'm ready. Let's get this over with."

Crystal tousles Dan's hair like she did when he was a kid. "It's going to be fun, Danny. You'll see. You won't regret it."

CHAPTER 15

DAN-NOW

Dan sits at the kitchen table and sips his coffee while Crystal moves around the small space, scrambling eggs and frying bacon. The coffee is weak and milky, but Crystal had set it in front of him, and he will drink it in return for her hospitality.

He has enough seniority built up in his job at the railroad that he's rarely scheduled to work on the weekends, but he wishes that he'd been able to work today so that he isn't completely imposing on his cousin and her husband during their weekend time together.

Crystal doesn't seem to mind his presence. She hums an old R&B song from the 1970s that must have been released a decade before she was born.

Frank lumbers into the kitchen and Crystal turns around. "Good morning," she says in her sing-song voice.

Frank had once been a muscular man, but most of the bulk is now just extra weight. He limps toward the table and makes a noise when he lowers himself into the chair. "Morning, Dan," he says, slightly out of breath.

"Morning, Frank."

Crystal sets a cup of coffee in front of her husband and kisses the top of his head.

Dan has never understood Crystal, who is kind and joyful and smart. When she'd been young and beautiful, she had the whole world at her fingertips. Yet she's chosen to stay in Conway, working whatever odd job came her way. She's dated other local men over the years, but Frank, fifteen years her senior and twice divorced, is the first man she's married. Dan's never asked Crystal why she stayed or why she never had children of her own.

Despite the scarcity of her life, living in this dumpy little house on the west side of town, she remains full of life and joy. Dan loves her more than he's ever loved anyone besides his own children.

As Crystal turns back to the stove, Frank slurps his coffee noisily. "How you doin' today?" he asks.

Dan shrugs. "I've been better."

"Yeah. I've been in your shoes. It's not a great place to be. You're welcome to stay here just as long as you need." Frank nods his head once, and the matter is settled. He is a man of few words. Dan nods back his thanks, and that is all that will be communicated on the subject.

Crystal sets down two plates in front of each of the men while she eats at the counter.

The scrambled eggs are undercooked, the bacon is overcooked, and the toast is burnt. Like his watery coffee, Dan downs it all.

After they've finished eating, Dan clears the dishes from the table. "Unless anyone objects, I'd be happy to grill some steaks this evening." He'd seen the old barbeque in the corner of the back porch and figures it's the least he can do.

Crystal starts to protest, but Frank speaks first. "That would be great, Dan. Been a while since I've been able to get out and cook a proper steak."

"You don't have to do that," Crystal says. "We're happy to have you here."

Dan bumps Crystal with his shoulder and helps her scrape the dishes and load the dishwasher.

Frank drinks another cup of coffee at the table. "Crystal and I are heading over to Julie's this afternoon for little Bella's birthday party," he announces, referring to one of his daughters and granddaughter.

"You're welcome to come along," Crystal adds.

Dan shakes his head. "I'll probably head back to the house to work on Teddy's car."

Crystal furrows her brow. "Do you think that's a good idea?"

"Why wouldn't it be?"

"Amber asked you to leave."

"Yeah. Well, it's still my house, and I'm working on her *brother's* car."

"I'm just suggesting that you may want to give her some time."

Dan shuts the dishwasher door with a bang. "It's not like I'm going to barge into the house and force her to talk to me. But I have every right to be there. I'm the one paying the mortgage."

Frank stands and shuffles from the room.

"I didn't say you should forfeit your right to the house." Crystal's voice is low and soothing. Dan remembers that placating voice. It's the same voice Crystal's mother used to use on him when he was a child. "I just think that you should give her a little time, that's all."

"Does that mean I can't see my kids either?"

"Of course not." Crystal smooths her hair back from her face. "Look, I've never been through this. I'm just trying to put myself in Amber's shoes and imagine how I'd feel. As a woman."

Dan rolls his eyes, and Crystal cocks her head. "That's exactly the type of attitude that's going to get you in trouble."

"I don't even know what I did," Dan says, aware that his

voice is close to a whine. "Shouldn't I at least get some explanation?"

"Maybe it wasn't just one thing, but a whole lot of small things. Think about this from Amber's perspective. She's home with four kids all day long. You come home and work on a car or do a project in the yard, have a few beers. She cooks and cleans. She doesn't get a break. When was the last time you took her out to dinner?"

"Took Amber out to dinner?" he asks.

"Yes, Dan." Crystal sounds exasperated. "When was the last time you took your wife to dinner?"

"Where would we go? And who would watch the kids?"

Crystal throws up her hands. "I don't know—the Crawford Inn," she says, naming the only decent place in town. "And, hell, I'd watch the kids if you asked me."

He blinks at her. "She didn't demand that I leave because I didn't take her to dinner."

"But the effort might go a long way in showing some appreciation." Crystal tosses her dishtowel on the counter.

Dan knows she's frustrated, and he doesn't want *her* mad at him, too. "Okay, fine," he says. "I won't go home today. Should I call her?"

Crystal bites her lip. "Give her a few days and then ask her to talk. That might give her some space and distance."

Dan's not sure what a few days is going to do when this issue clearly took years to form, but he nods anyway.

"In the meantime, you might want to do some research on a good divorce attorney."

"But I don't want a divorce." He's said it without thinking, and he realizes that he means it. His marriage isn't perfect, but it's familiar and comfortable.

"I know you don't, Danny. But it might not be up to you."

Dan wants to argue with her. And he wants her to tell

him that everything's going to be okay.

He doesn't like the way she looks at him with that pitying expression on her face. He knows what she's thinking. What the whole town is thinking. *There goes pathetic Dan Armstrong. His mom abandoned him. He killed that girl and went to jail. Now his wife doesn't even want him, and he's going to lose his kids.* Serves him right.

Dan feels a deep rage start to build up in him. None of it has been fair.

He stalks out the back door before he says something to Crystal that he might regret.

He stands on the narrow back porch. As he takes a few breaths to cool his temper, he surveys the surroundings.

Crystal's yard backs up to a narrow alley. The neighbors to the left have installed a tall brown fence, and there is an empty lot to the right. A few hundred yards behind the house and across a gravel alley sits an old, abandoned warehouse surrounded by a rusty chain-link fence that isn't keeping anything in *or* out. Dan frowns at the decrepit building that looks as though it might house unsavory characters. He will install some fencing around the yard over the next few weeks.

He turns. The stainless-steel grail sits in the corner of the porch, behind some outdoor furniture that has seen better days. A rusty propane tank is affixed to its bottom. Dan moves the furniture and moldy cushions enough to wiggle the grill through the space. He opens the hood gingerly, not sure what he might find, living or dead. Luckily, he only uncovers dirt, old grease, and a few leaves.

He locates a bucket and wire brush on the stand next to the propane tank and enters the house to fill the bucket with hot water and some dish soap. The kitchen is empty.

When Crystal finds him on the porch thirty minutes

later, he's still scrubbing.

"Sorry about that," she says. "I don't think I did a good job of cleaning it after last summer."

He shrugs. "It'll still work."

"I don't think the tank has anything in it."

"I have to run to the grocery store to get the steaks anyway," he responds.

She watches him scrub for a little while longer. "You're sure you don't want to join us at Julie's? Might keep your mind off things."

He shakes his head. "I'll be fine."

"You have my number if you need it."

He puts his weight into a particularly grimy spot on the top rack of the grill.

"It's going to be okay, Danny," Crystal says before she walks back through the door.

Despite the fact that he'd been waiting for her to say those words, he doesn't believe them for a second.

Not long after he hears the tires of Crystal's car crunch on the gravel of the driveway, he gives up on his task. The grill is as clean as it's going to get. He wipes it with some paper towels and props the hood open to dry out. Then he dumps the dirty water into the long grass behind the porch and heads inside to grab his keys and wallet.

As he walks out to his truck, a Conway police cruiser drives slowly down the road. It comes to a stop in front of the house. The window lowers and Nate Kasinski's face appears.

"Hey, Dan," Nate says.

Dan raises a hand. Dan and Nate aren't friends, but they are friendly. By the time Nate returned from his deployments and took a job with the police department, Dan had married Amber and was a father to two children. Nate is now chief of police, and after living in the same town together for as long as they have, they acknowledge each other when the occasion arises.

"What are you doing over here?" Nate asks.

Dan hesitates. There's no way Nate can possibly know what's going on in his marriage. Not yet. Still, the question gets his hackles up. "Just helping Crystal out with some things around the house."

Nate nods. "I expect she needs it, with Frank in the condition that he's in."

Dan doesn't respond.

"How's Crystal doing these days?"

"She's getting along okay." Nate isn't married, and it occurs to Dan that Nate would have been a more suitable match for Crystal than Frank ever was. But it's not his place to judge.

"Heard she's working for the Munsons and Temple."

"For a few months now," Dan confirms, even though he's just learned this news himself.

Nate nods. He's put on some weight in the past few years, and while his face looks nearly the same as it had in high school, there are now fleshy pouches under his eyes, and his uniform pulls across his belly.

"You might want to keep an eye out. There are some seedy characters hanging out down this way. I haven't gotten any calls this past week, but we try to keep our patrols regular over here with the few men we have."

As the older population has slowly faded away, small pockets of Conway have seen the rise of a more questionable element. It's kept Nate and his department busy, and Dan knows he's had a hard time keeping officers in town. As soon as Nate trains them up, they leave for a bigger city with better pay.

"I plan on installing a fence in the back."

"Good idea. We've had a bunch of transients who have

traveled into town on the trail," Nate said, referring to the Great Allegheny Passage. "Hard to keep up with them, and we can only hold them for so long before we have to let them back on the street. We just don't have the space."

It's a county-wide problem and one that Nate and the town of Conway have no solution for.

"I'll keep an eye out," Dan responds.

Nate nods. "Have yourself a good one," he says and rolls slowly away.

Dan climbs into his own truck and heads to the Save-A-Lot. There, he picks up the groceries and on his way out, purchases a new propane tank.

When he returns to the house, he refrigerates the food and moves back to the porch to install the tank to the grill. He's only outside for a few minutes before he sees a figure in a faded, red-hooded sweatshirt and a pair of filthy jeans walking fast down the alleyway toward the house.

The man keeps his head down and his hands in his pockets, but Dan makes out a scruffy beard under the hood.

Dan eyes him as he comes closer. He fully expects the figure to keep walking when he sees Dan watching him, but instead he stops.

"You live here?" he calls. His voice is high and slightly panicked.

"What's it to you?"

The guy shuffles from side to side. His hands are out of his pockets, and he pulls at his fingers compulsively. "There's a woman." He gestures behind him but doesn't elaborate further.

Dan squints, realizing the transient is less of a man and more of a boy. "What woman?"

He gestures behind him again. "Back there." There's nothing but the old warehouse in the direction he's pointing.

"There's a woman in the warehouse?"

The kid nods.

"Is she okay?"

"I'm not sure. She won't—" He looks from side to side, twitchy and agitated. "She wouldn't wake up."

Dan's pulse quickens. "Is she breathing?"

"I think so. I don't know."

"Do you know her?"

The kid shakes his head. "Never seen her before."

"Did she take anything?"

His gaze slides away, and Dan knows the answer to the question without having to press for it. "Where in the building?" Dan is already heading that way, and he pulls his cell phone from his pocket as he jogs.

When the kid sees the phone, he starts to walk fast in the opposite direction. Within seconds, he's running away.

Dan calls the local police line instead of 911. When the dispatcher answers, he asks to be connected to Nate. The woman asks his name, and he gives it to her.

There is a brief pause before Nate's voice comes over the line. "Dan?"

Dan is at the busted door at the front of the warehouse. He relays to Nate the conversation he's just had with the drifter.

Nate says, "On my way. I'm out at the old library, so it'll take me a few minutes to get there. Did you call 911 for an ambulance?"

Dan says that he hasn't, and Nate says, "I'll get them here."

The library is across the river on the other side of town, headed up the gentle slope of the foot of the mountain. It'll take Nate at least ten minutes to make his way back down to the west side of town. Maybe longer.

Dan doesn't wait. He pushes his way through the door

into the dim, shadowy interior of the old building. The place stinks like dirt, piss, and body odor. He isn't sure why the town doesn't tear this place down.

He moves through the building carefully, looking closely at piles of old papers and clothes in the corners for what could be the shape of a human body. In the farthest room at the back, he doesn't have to look closely at all. A woman is slumped forward behind a broken old table. Long blond hair spills out of the side of a gray hood, and blood runs in a thin trickle from her arm, exposed where the sleeve has been pushed up. A needle, spoon, and lighter are lying on top of the desk.

Dan crouches down beside her. "Hey," he calls, shaking her shoulder. "Are you okay?"

Her head rolls limply with the movement. She doesn't seem to be breathing.

Dan reaches beneath the hood and her dirty hair to touch her neck. After a few seconds, he's able to detect just the flutter of a pulse beneath his fingertips. It's faint but definitely there.

In the distance, he hears the wail of a siren, and then Nate's voice calls, "Dan, you in here?"

"Back here," he answers, and Nate comes running into the room. "She's alive."

As Nate approaches, he glances at the paraphernalia on top of the desk. He swears and pulls from his pocket a small bottle with a nozzle at the top. Dan moves away and gives Nate room to dispense the spray into the woman's nose. After he administers the treatment, he checks for breath and a pulse, deciding whether he needs to start CPR.

But it's less than a minute before the woman comes to, and by that time, the sirens are just outside the building and two emergency technicians rush into the space. They fire questions at the woman whose eyes are now wide. Her chin starts to quiver. "Can you tell us your name?" one of the men asks her as he bandages up the wound that is source of the blood.

She doesn't answer, and he affixes a blood-pressure cuff to her bicep.

The second technician pulls at her other arm still in the coat, and the woman yelps in pain.

"Your arm is in a cast?" he asks.

She nods, and the man shines a small flashlight in her eyes. Dan can see that she has a swollen and black eye and there is a ring of bruises around her throat.

She looks at Nate. "Are you going to arrest me?" Her voice sounds more resigned than frightened.

"Do you have a place to go?" he asks, and she nods.

"My parents live down the street. Not far from here."

"What's your name?"

"Sutton. Sutton Schultz."

Dan's eyes meet Nate's, then both men quickly look away, each for their own reasons.

CHAPTER 16

CHLOE-NOW

Chloe gives her daughter a sideways glance as she drives. She can only see part of the side of Emma's smooth round face because her daughter stares resolutely out of the passenger side window. It's as if the passing scenery in North Fairhaven is the most interesting thing Emma has ever seen.

Chloe takes a breath. "I was thinking we could go out for a late lunch after your golf lesson this afternoon."

Emma lifts a shoulder but doesn't answer.

"There's a new place called The Oasis Café that supposedly has a Mediterranean menu. Would you like that?"

"Whatever," Emma says.

Chloe's instinct is to keep talking, asking questions, probing until Emma answers her, but during her last session with Elaine, her therapist cautioned Chloe to give Emma space as she navigates through the complex feelings of her early teenage years.

When Chloe was a teenager, no one seemed to care how she'd been feeling. Looking back, she wished someone had taken the time to ask her a question or two. It wasn't that her parents hadn't loved her. They'd loved her more than anything. It was just that they had very little idea what kind of love a young girl needed.

They continue the drive in silence.

When they arrive at the Fairhaven Country Club, Emma stomps off to her lesson with a golf pro named Chad without a backward glance, and Chloe heads to the café, where she sits at a corner table and opens her laptop. She responds to a few emails from her staff, but it's hard to keep her attention on work. Mostly, she's thinking about her conversation with Jason.

She'd been perplexed when Jason had moved back to Conway. After all of their talk of getting out of the place, she didn't understand how he could have possibly wanted to go back. Even if it had been with a younger, nicer wife and improved family. Oh, he'd given her plenty of reasons. His parents weren't getting any younger; his sister and her husband had moved south after their kids had started families of their own; there was less commotion than there was closer to the city. Blah, blah, blah. But Chloe knows the real reason—Jason is weak. And he couldn't hack making a home anywhere he felt slightly uncomfortable. Chloe had always pushed him far outside of his comfort zone.

There is certainly nothing for Chloe in Conway. Her parents have been gone for years. After Matt's death twenty years ago, her mom and dad—already older than the rest of her classmates' parents—had aged rapidly. Chloe had still been in college when they'd passed away, one right after the other, as if neither of them could bear to go on without Matt or each other.

Which left Chloe all alone.

The fact that Jason has suggested Emma spend the summer in Conway is still quite laughable. It's also slightly demented and insulting. And Jason wonders why she treats him with barely concealed contempt.

Not only is Chloe fiercely protective of her daughter, but she's also self-aware enough to admit that she cannot stand the thought of being left alone again. And she certainly isn't going to be abandoned for Conway—that godforsaken place with its awful regressive population and terrible memories.

A male server approaches her to ask if she'd like anything to eat. She orders a cup of tea, but no food. She'll save those calories for her lunch with Emma.

She's impatient as she waits. Agitated, even. She lightly thrums her fingertips on the white tablecloth and glances up at the television screen in the corner of the room for the distraction. The sound is muted, but the captions scroll across the bottom of the screen, transcribing the voices of the PGA Championship announcers. Chloe doesn't recognize the athletes. She does not know how to golf and has never cared to learn. But it will be a skill that Emma might find useful in her own future.

The television cuts to a commercial, and an advertisement for a car dealership she knows well appears. A dashing man in an expensive-looking polo shirt and tailored pants is staring at her from the screen, his hair perfect and smile dazzling. He's standing next to a football player in his full black and gold uniform. Chloe doesn't know who the player is, but she sure as hell knows Joe Wright when she sees him.

She rarely watches television at home, but when she does, she masochistically drinks every drop of Wright Automotive Group advertisements.

Now, at her corner table, she devours the commercial, taking it all in. *Everything is just going his way, isn't it?* she thinks bitterly.

Chloe is a regular visitor to Joe's wife's public social media feeds. She'd recognize Joe, his drop-dead gorgeous spouse, and their perfect children anywhere.

Joe, the man, is incredibly handsome. Even better looking than he'd been in high school, when he'd still been young and dumb. Now, he has the same wavy dark hair.

Those intense, piercing blue eyes. But he also wears an air of sophistication. An elegance that hadn't existed when they'd been teenagers. And while most of the men that she currently knows in their late thirties are starting to show signs of middle-age—a puffy softness and a glimpse into the old men they would soon become—Joe looks fit and solid. She swears she can see abs beneath the pale-yellow shirt tucked into those dark pants.

Despite his looks, Chloe hadn't been attracted to him in high school, and she isn't attracted to him now. He's too perfect, too confident, too charming.

He's also manipulative, cowardly, and downright evil.

It had been Joe who pointed the finger at Chloe after that party twenty years ago. It had been Joe who had told the police and his lawyers that she'd been the one to supply the alcohol. It had been Joe who had forced Chloe to implicate her brother. Everything had been Joe's fault.

On the screen, Joe's gorgeous wife appears with him, her red hair long, shiny, and flowing over alabaster shoulders and a form-fitting gold dress. He puts an arm around her, and they dazzle together, radiating success and money.

If you buy a car from Wright Automotive Group, you too can be as successful and beautiful as Joe and Vivian Wright.

Chloe's upper lip lifts in a sneer.

Joe had simply waltzed off into the sunset after high school, to some ivy league school on the other side of the state where he'd played sports, studied business, and married the stunning and accomplished Miss Pennsylvania. His life has always been charmed, and Chloe's has always been shit.

She's had to lift herself from the mud—pay for her own education, bury her brother and her parents, start a business, raise her daughter—all on her own. She had no beautiful partner to take care of her, and no rich family to fund her lifestyle or pick up the broken pieces of herself.

It's hardly fair.

She hates Joe Wright with every fiber of her being.

The commercial ends just as the server appears with her tea. He is staring at her with a concerned look on his face. "Is…everything all right, ma'am?"

Chloe looks up at him and realizes that she is clutching the knife from her place setting in her fist as if she were preparing to stab someone.

She tries to laugh it off and makes an inane self-deprecating comment, but she can sense the server's discomfort as he sets the small carafe of hot water and a black tea packet in front of her.

When he hurries away, she prepares her tea and sips it as she attempts to shift her attention back to her work on the laptop screen, but her mind and heart aren't in it.

Joe Wright has distracted her with memories and now those memories are linked with her earlier conversation with Jason, which she keeps replaying in her mind.

There's much Emma is too young to know and understand. But beyond that, Chloe can't believe her daughter would want to leave what she has in North Fairhaven—the activities, the restaurants, her friends—to spend the summer in dumpy, rundown Conway, with her half siblings, where there is nothing to do and no privacy.

She remembers Conway, the beauty of its lush green hills and rushing river juxtaposed with its rundown houses and abandoned buildings. For Chloe, the place is a wasteland of bad memories and lost hope. No matter how much splendor there might have been in the sloping hills on the north side of the Chestnut Ridge or the meandering flow of the Mitsin River, she can't think of anything that would entice her to return.

Elaine has told Chloe on more than one occasion that the town of Conway represents Chloe's own sense of fear and loss, and that's why she has such a negative impression of her hometown. She supposes that's true. Joe Wright may have ultimately been to blame for much of her pain, but it is Conway that provided the backdrop for the drama.

Elaine has encouraged Chloe to visit Conway to confront those feelings head-on. But Chloe hasn't been able to bring herself to return. Nor does she believe it will help. If anything, reliving those memories may do more harm than good. She can confront her feelings and do the work on her shadow self without making the hour-long drive southeast to her hometown.

But as she sits alone at this table, she has the uncomfortable realization that perhaps Elaine is right. Maybe she needs to return in order to neutralize the power the place seems to hold over her. At the same time, she has the opportunity to show Emma just how awful it is there and how awful it might be with her father.

Her heartbeat quickens, and a flutter kicks up in her belly—a combination of anxiety, anticipation, and dread.

Without overthinking her uncharacteristic spontaneity, she dials Jason's number. He answers on the fifth ring, just as she thinks the call might go to voicemail. "Chloe," he says by way of greeting. He sounds breathless.

She doesn't bother with pleasantries. "I was thinking that we might come for dinner tonight."

There is a pause. "What?"

"Dinner," she repeats. "Emma and I could come for dinner."

"Here? To the house?"

"If it wouldn't be too much trouble."

Another pause.

"Why?" Suspicion is heavy in his voice.

Chloe looks around the café at the golfers who are starting to gather at the tables for lunch. Emma will be finished with her lesson soon.

She clears her throat. "Well," she says into the phone. "On our call earlier, you suggested that Emma might come and stay with you this summer. Naturally, I haven't talked to her about that, but I was thinking that if we were to explore that idea…" Her words trail off, and she feels just the slightest twinge of guilt. She has no intention of exploring anything of the sort with her daughter. "It would be good for Emma to have some idea of what it might be like," she finishes.

She can feel Jason considering her suggestion with nothing but the most positive of intent. The man doesn't have a manipulative bone in his body. And even though Chloe really does want Emma to get a small taste of what life would be like living with a stepmother and three small children, she's betting on the fact that Jason's life is just complete chaos right now. Emma has spent twelve years as an only child. She will not be interested in the confusion, noise, and drama of a large young family.

Jason's tone is hopeful when he says, "I think that sounds like a great idea. Let me just check with Becky."

She holds on the line, waiting for her ex-husband to consult with his wife.

A group of four men who appear to be a few years older than Chloe look over at her as if they're discussing her. She angles her body away.

When Jason finally returns, it sounds as if he drops his phone. Chloe winces and holds her own phone away from her ear.

After some rustling, he mumbles, "Sorry. Becky has suggested that we meet at the Crawford Inn instead."

Chloe had been hoping to get the full chaotic experience of their home. She pitches the idea of visiting the house again with an assurance that she does not care about its state of dishevelment. Of course she remembers the chaos of those toddler years, assuming that this is Becky's concern.

But Chloe's home has never been in a state of anything but pristine order.

Jason checks again, but Becky doesn't budge, so Chloe and Jason agree that his family will meet Chloe and Emma at five o'clock at the Crawford Inn, which had always been the best restaurant in Conway.

When Chloe disconnects, she feels calmer and more centered than she has all day. She is back in control of the situation. She signals for the server to bring the check, and as she looks away, one of the men in the foursome catches her eye again. She frowns. He doesn't look remotely familiar. To her dismay, she realizes that he is heading in her direction.

He is tall and lean with a slow gait and a deep tan, despite the fact that it's only May. He looks like he probably travels to sunnier locations to play golf over the winter months, too.

"Excuse me," he says as Chloe rummages in her purse for a few dollars to pay the bill. She comes up with a five and hands it to the server.

"Keep the change," she instructs.

She tries to ignore the man, but he just waits, looking patient and amused. Finally, she says "Yes?" her voice clipped. She adds, "I'm in a hurry. I need to pick up my daughter."

He smiles. The expression is as easy as his walk. "I don't want to keep you from your daughter. I just wanted to say that I've seen you here before, and every time I do, I promise myself I'm going to say hello to you. Then I chicken out. Today, I decided I wouldn't chicken out. So, hello," he says.

She is momentarily speechless. Is this man hitting on her?

"I'm Tim, by the way."

When she recovers, she says, "I'm Chloe."

"Nice to meet you, Chloe." He holds out a hand. His fingers are long and warm. "This time of the year, I'm here most Saturdays when I'm not on call." He seems to be waiting for a response, but she's not sure what to say.

He smiles again. "Have a good day with your daughter."

As he walks away, Chloe belatedly murmurs a weak, "Thank you."

She blinks after him.

"Who's that?" Emma's question comes from behind her, and the unexpected voice causes her to jump.

Chloe turns quickly. "There you are," she says, ignoring the question, which has no good answer. She puts Tim out of her mind. "Change of plans today."

Emma looks at her sideways. "I'm not going for a walk."

"I was thinking that maybe we could take a drive out to Conway and poke around a bit before meeting your dad, Becky, and the kids for dinner."

Her daughter is immediately as suspicious as her ex-husband had been. "Why?"

"I just thought it might be a nice change. And you so rarely get out that way to see your other family."

"He told you I called him." Emma's voice is thick with betrayal.

"He did, but it's okay. It's good that you talked." Chloe knows it's awful, but she silently revels in the fact that Emma is upset with her dad for once. So often, he is the hero of the stories in her daughter's head, and she is the villain.

"Did he tell you what we talked about?"

Chloe nods, and Emma's face falls. "But that's okay, too," she assures her daughter. "I'm not trying to invalidate your feelings. But I *do* want to show you some things that might make you understand a little bit why I'm the way that I am, and why I want you to be successful, too. Is that okay?"

Emma's gaze slides to the floor. She shrugs but she doesn't argue.

Chloe pats Emma's arm. "Come on. Let's get out of here."

She slings her handbag over her shoulder, and as she does, she sneaks a quick glance behind her. Tim is watching. He gives her a small grin and lifts a hand.

She turns away, following her daughter to the door. She does not look back.

CHAPTER 17

JOE-NOW

Sandra Wright's car smells like her spicy, expensive perfume even when she's not in it. It's the same scent she's worn for as long as Joe can remember. Every time he's caught a hint of a similar fragrance over the years, he feels a slight pain in his heart.

Now, driving her car, he is overpowered by a sense of failure and languishing brought on by the cologne. He powers down the window in an effort to cleanse his nostrils and clear his mind.

He drives behind the ambulance, and every so often he catches a glimpse of his mother's silver-blond hair glinting in the vehicle's artificial light through the back window. He imagines her bent over the wasted figure of his father, holding his hand.

He easily imagines Vivian doing the same for him. So what is it about his mother that makes him feel so lost and resentful?

The traffic is light on the highway but heavier on the narrow streets of Conway as visitors gather at the river park for weekend bike rides and hikes on the trail toward the mountains. Though the sky is a colorless gray, the air has warmed, and the rain has held off.

On Falgan Road, Joe thinks he sees a figure in the distance bent over the vestiges at the adorned tree. Again, he keeps his eyes averted, though he can't help but wonder who might be saying a prayer at that altar. Megan's mother perhaps? An old friend? One of their classmates?

He wills himself not to look, but he can't stop himself from thinking about the ghosts of the past as he continues the rest of the journey to Mitsin Ridge.

When he slows in front of the house, there is a medical supply company van parked in the driveway, along with an older silver vehicle that is badly in need of a wash. Joe parks off the road in the front yard as the ambulance backs into the driveway. Paige stands outside smoking a cigarette. She stamps it out before she thinks anyone may have seen her.

But Joe has seen.

The next half an hour is a flurry of activity. Paige and Vivian direct the ambulance crew into the house, and his mother talks with an older woman with thin, lank hair whose eyes keep flitting to Joe.

The medical technicians have rearranged the living room so that his father's hospital bed is in a sunny corner spot with easy access to the first-floor toilet and kitchen and a view of the television screen mounted on the wall. They've also left a walker, a wheelchair, and a portable toilet that Joe's father swears he will never use.

Once Bill Wright is settled, they take their leave. The ambulance crew departs shortly thereafter, and the family is together with the tired-looking nurse who reviews his father's medication schedule. Joe should be paying attention, but he wanders away, leaving his mother and Paige to listen and take notes.

Vivian walks over and rubs his arm. "How are you holding up?"

He shrugs. "This feels like it's all a done deal." He gestures around the room. "We're just bringing him home to die, I suppose."

"Come on, Joe. Don't be so morose. They're doing the best they can."

"Everyone keeps saying that to me. But if they were doing the *best they can*," he says, emphasizing the words, "then I wouldn't have just found out about this yesterday."

From across the room, Paige hears him and shoots him a look of disgust.

Vivian steers Joe into the kitchen. "I know you're upset." She pulls out a sparkling water from the refrigerator and hands it to him. "But you need to let go of the bitterness and try to be positive for your dad's sake."

"He could have called me himself," Joe grumbles.

Vivian looks at him levelly. "We are well past playing the 'could have, should have, would have' game. The focus now should be on ensuring the time your father has left is filled with love and peace."

His wife is right, but he doesn't respond. Memories in the Wright household were never characterized by love and peace. More like silence and tension. Secrets and suppression. Restraint and regret.

He takes a long swallow of the carbonated liquid and hiccups. "We can't stay here indefinitely. What about the girls?"

"I've already talked to Bonnie," says Vivian. "She can stay with them for as long as we need her. And I can stay here as long as you need me."

"I always need you," he says.

"I know. But your family needs you more right now, and I'm an outsider."

He opens his mouth to protest, and she puts up a hand.

"I'm starting to understand how your family works. Finally, after twelve years of our own marriage, I'll add, which speaks volumes in itself." She is clearly referring to Joe's own reticent nature. "But I think you all have some discussions that need to take place."

He places the bottle on the kitchen island and narrows his eyes. "What did Paige tell you while I was gone?"

"See there?" she asks. "The fact that you feel the need to ask that question, and in that accusatory tone. She didn't tell me *anything*. That's the point, Joe. Even the most basic curiosities were met with a…" She hesitates. "A caginess that's just weird. And it occurred to me—I really don't know much about you before our marriage. Sure, I've met your fraternity brothers and I've heard all of the college stories. But how you grew up, who you dated in high school, what you did for fun here? Nothing at all."

"This is it," he says tightly. "What you see is what you get."

She gives him a look that indicates that she doesn't believe him for a second.

Paige appears from around the corner. "The nurse would like to talk to you." She addresses Joe, but Vivian follows along as well.

As he walks through the living room, Joe glances at his father, who appears to be comfortably settled in his corner bed. His eyes are shut, and his mouth is slack. He looks nothing like the man Joe remembers.

They all gather in the office at the back of the house. Sandra Wright's face is set in a look of fierce determination, and she doesn't glance in Joe's direction as he enters the room.

The nurse turns to Joe. "I'm Angela," she says and sticks out a hand. She's wearing a bright pink set of scrubs with a pattern that looks like rose petals, but upon closer inspection, Joe realizes that the petals are actually the wings of butterflies. Angela has a firm, capable handshake.

"Joe," he responds, and she nods.

"As I was telling your mother and sister, I will be your

father's primary nurse, but there are two backup nurses on your dad's team—Madison and Gillian." She hands him a card. "One of us will be by twice a day—ten in the morning and six in the evening—but you can call the answering service at any time if you need additional help. My personal number is also on the card; feel free to reach out to me directly." She waits for an acknowledgment, and he nods. "I understand you'll be staying here throughout this process."

Process. What a detached word.

He glances at Vivian, who raises her eyebrows at him. "Yes," he agrees.

Angela continues to talk directly to Joe, presumably because she's already shared this information with the other women. "I want you to be aware," she says, "this will not be an easy experience. Your mom is going to need your full support."

"Of course." He glances at his mother whose eyes are fixed on some unknown object in the distance. He looks back at Angela. "I talked with Dr. Burman this morning and let him know that I have some contacts in the medical community in the city. We can take him for a second opinion."

A pregnant silence follows, and Vivian speaks first. "I think that's something we can discuss later," she says softly.

He's annoyed at the interruption, and doubly so when he notices Paige smile gratefully at Vivian.

Ignoring Joe, Paige asks, "How long do we have? With Dad?" she adds.

Joe becomes even more exasperated with his sister. Why would she be asking about the timeframe when they haven't even explored all of the options?

Angela lifts a hand. "Days…Weeks. Honestly, it's up to your dad. But there will be signs when the time is near."

Angela opens her mouth to elaborate, but Joe cuts her

off. "Has anyone told Dad that we haven't yet explored all the options?"

"Oh, for God's sake, Joe," his mother erupts. "There are no more options. This is it. This is where it ends. You're just going to have to accept that." With each statement, her voice has increased in volume, and the last sentence is a demand.

There is a collective stunned silence, and his mother clears her throat softly. "I'm sorry. I shouldn't have lost my temper like that." The quiet apology is to the nurse.

Angela is dispassionate. "It won't be the last time emotions get the better of you. All of you. Try to give each other, and yourselves, grace." She looks around at the group and asks if they have any last questions. When no one responds, she rubs her hands together. They make a dry sound, like autumn leaves skittering across an asphalt street. "I'll just look in on Bill once more, and then I'll be back this evening."

Before Angela finishes her sentence, her cell phone chirps, and she retrieves it from one of her oversized pockets. "Excuse me," she says faintly, frowning at the display. "Angela Schultz," she says, and her name is a question. She takes a few steps away, but she is still within earshot. And while they're all trying to give her some privacy, they are also waiting for her.

"Yes, it is. Sutton is my daughter."

Schultz. The sudden recognition of Angela's last name hits him in the chest. *Sutton Schultz.* The woman from the hospital. The girl he used to know.

Vivian recognizes the name, too. "Sutton," she whispers. "Isn't that the woman we saw yesterday?" she asks, but Joe is listening to Angela.

"Oh my God." Angela sucks in a breath. "Is she—" Her voice breaks and there is a pause. Her hand is on her throat while she listens to the voice on the other end of the phone call. Paige and Sandra hover in the doorway.

Angela exhales the breath she'd been holding. Her thin body seems to deflate. "Did they take her to the hospital?" Another pause. "Why not? She needs treatment."

Joe feels his mother's eyes on him, and even though he is determined not to look at her, he glances over anyway. He doesn't know what she's thinking, but he wishes that his parents had moved far away from this godforsaken place where he'd grown up.

Angela's back is to them, but her position does nothing to dampen the words. "So, you're telling me you just left her alone?" That question is quickly followed by a demand: "*Who?*" Then a curt, "No, it's fine. I'm on my way."

She hangs up the phone, and her face is pinched and taut. "I apologize," she says, her voice breathless. "There is an emergency, and I need to go."

Sandra's hands are pressed together in front of her stomach. "Is there anything we can do?"

Angela shakes her head, flustered. "I—I'll be back this evening. If you need anything in the meantime, please call the answering service." She rushes to the door, and a few seconds later, they hear her car accelerating out of the driveway, its small engine whining with the surge of power.

Vivian is the first to speak. "That poor woman. I don't want to speculate, but when we saw her daughter yesterday, she looked like she may have been in desperate need of a rehab facility."

Sandra's tone is high-pitched with shock when she asks, "You saw Sutton yesterday?" The question is directed at Joe.

Joe wishes Vivian would stop speaking. "She was being wheeled out of the hospital. I didn't even recognize her," he says.

"You all know her?" Vivian asks. "Why didn't you say

anything to Angela? Maybe we can help."

"You know nothing about the situation. We can't help them," Sandra snaps.

Vivian's eyes widen, then flash with anger.

Joe should defuse the tension, but he's not sure how.

It's Paige who says, "Mom, go sit with Dad. Joe, why don't you and Vivian take a break upstairs. I'll stay down here." She fixes Joe with a stare, and if he ever had a question as to whether his sister had known what happened between him and Sutton twenty years earlier, there is no question now.

Vivian turns and stomps away, and Paige wraps her arm around their mother's shoulders and leads her into the living room, leaving Joe alone and helpless.

With a sigh, he runs a hand through his hair and climbs the stairs to the guest room. Vivian is throwing her clothes into her small valise.

"What are you doing?" he asks.

She glares at him. "I don't know what's going on, but I'll be damned if I'm going to slide into the bizarre passive-aggressive dance that's happening in this house." She folds a pair of jeans furiously then tosses them carelessly into the suitcase on top of two balled-up blouses.

Joe approaches cautiously and puts his hands on her arms. She stiffens, but she stills. "Please don't go," he says.

"Why would I stay, Joe? The three of you are walking around on eggshells with your knowing looks and your secrets. I'm on the outside looking in, and there's a deadbolt on the door."

He presses against her from behind. "I'm sorry," he says. "I know this is hard for you, too."

She is quiet for a moment and then she turns in his arms. "I'm not trying to make this about me. I just feel so…useless."

"Join the club," he quips. Then he says, "You are not useless. I need you more than you can possibly know."

She rests her face in the crook of his neck, and he runs a hand down her long red hair. It's thick and there's a slight electrical charge in it. It crackles under his fingers, like fire. "How about if we go out to dinner tonight?" he asks. "There's one decent place in town. We can get a nice meal, have a glass of wine." Joe assumes the Crawford Inn is still in operation. By city standards, the place might rate at a five on a ten-point scale. But in Conway, it's the closest they would get to an elegant dining experience.

"And you'll tell me about your childhood?" she asks. "You'll tell me who Joe Wright was as a boy and a young man?"

Joe nods, his chin brushing against her temple. "I'll tell you anything you want to know."

"You'll tell me about Sutton Schultz?"

He hesitates before answering, "Yes." He'll tell Vivian a story about Sutton Schultz. But he won't tell her the whole truth, which was buried twenty years ago along with so many other people, words, and lives. He needs Vivian to love him just as he is. He will not risk his future by dredging up his past.

CHAPTER 18

SUTTON-NOW

Sutton rushes back into consciousness, her heart thumping against her breastbone. She is terrified, especially when she sees the cop. Still, she would rather go to jail than to the hospital. In jail, they will not call anyone; they'll release her quickly if she's not a danger to anyone but herself. Small police departments don't have the resources to hold addicts for long periods of time. Nor do they have the manpower to pursue charges for every overdose. To them, she is nothing more than a nuisance. A statistic. Better off dead.

She agrees.

The emergency techs try to convince her to allow them to transport her to the hospital, but she shakes her head furiously and begs them to let her go. If they transport her to a hospital, they will attempt to admit her to a rehab facility, which means they will call her parents.

She tells them her name. She tells them she has a place to stay. They don't argue with her for long. To them, too, she's just a junkie. Not worth their energy.

The cop who had given her the Narcan stares at her for a long while. He consults with the emergency responders and another man and finally tells her she can go home. He offers to drive her.

The other man tells the cop he'll stay with her, and the

cop nods and gives him some of the Narcan, just in case. He tells him what to do if she slips backward after the initial dosage has worn off.

She doesn't know these men, and she doesn't trust them, especially not the cop. But it's possible the other guy—the one dressed in jeans and a flannel shirt who offers to stay with her—might know where she can get some smack for later. To take the edge off. Something safer than what she'd gotten in in this hellhole.

The man's stare is guarded and framed with deep lines around his eyes, like he might have seen some stuff. There's a tough, lean, knowing look about him.

She watches the activity around her—watches as they discuss her like she's not even there.

The cop talks to the emergency techs, and they ask him to sign some papers, which he does. Then he and the other guy bundle her up between them and guide her to the police car. They help her into the back, and once inside, she shuts her eyes.

She can hear their voices outside the car, but she can't hear what they're saying. She feels jumpy and agitated, and completely exhausted and depleted at the same time. She silently curses the guy who had given her the dope. It was definitely cut with something. Fentanyl probably. She's lucky to be alive.

She amends that. She would have been luckier if she'd died.

Who would miss her if she'd floated into the abyss in the dirty warehouse? Her parents probably, but there would be a small part of them that would have been relieved. No more worrying, wondering, waiting.

Tommy might miss her, wherever he is now. Word would reach him eventually, and he might be sad for a minute or two. Then he would carry on with his own life, and she would be forgotten.

That's it, she thinks. That is the extent of people in her life who might care whether she lives or dies.

She rolls her head to the right and looks out the window at the two men deep in conversation. Something snags in her brain, and she blinks. She can't quite latch onto the thread of memory that flutters in her mind.

Instead, she thinks about Joe Wright. What would have happened if things had worked out differently? If all those years ago, she'd fought against him and his parents and made a different decision?

She had convinced herself that the decision had been for the best. But in that moment, she wonders… At the very least, she would have had someone to love her, to depend on her. She burns for that now. She longs for an anchor.

The two men break apart and enter the car. They don't look at her, don't speak to her.

As the car pulls away, she feels a familiar queasiness. She has very little in her stomach except for the blue Gatorade.

She leans forward and vomits on the floor of the police cruiser.

"Shit," she hears quietly from the front seat.

"Won't be the last time," the other voice says.

Both of the men laugh. At her.

Then they are at her parents' house, and they help her inside, even though she doesn't need any help.

She immediately goes to her bedroom and sinks down on the bed, wishing she had faded away forever.

CHAPTER 19

DAN-NOW

Dan and Nate both look down at Sutton, her hair hanging in ropy strings on the purple blanket. She stares up at the ceiling, conscious and alert. Maybe she is ignoring their presence. Maybe she doesn't see them at all.

As they walk from the room, Nate mutters, "Wonder who did that to her?"

He's referring to the black eye, bruised neck, and the broken arm, but Dan's mind immediately considers where Sutton has ended up as a person. Twenty years ago, she'd been tiny, pretty, and edgy, with a furtive energy. She'd run with the popular crowd, but Dan isn't sure she'd ever fit in with that group. She'd been too desperate. Too willing to sacrifice herself for a crumb of attention. The attention she got was likely not the attention she had sought.

She'd also been best friends with Megan Richards, which had made no sense to him or anyone else.

Megan had been special. She'd been an angel.

Sutton had been caught up in all of it, way back when. At the party, she'd been all over Joe, and Joe had allowed it. But thinking back now, Dan isn't sure Joe had been into it.

Even then, Dan had been convinced Joe was trying to make Megan jealous by messing around with her best friend. Which was how Megan ended up in Dan's car that night.

He and Nate stand in the outdated wood-paneled living room with the muted brown and orange floral sofa and dim lighting. On the mantel above a non-working fireplace, Sutton's posed high-school portrait stares back at him.

Nate's words shake Dan out of his contemplation. Most of the time, he successfully avoids thinking too deeply about the past. Lately, though, the memories seem to be showing up at the most inopportune of moments.

"Sutton hasn't lived around here for years. Last I heard, she'd moved to Beesonstown," Nate says.

"Maybe her injuries prompted the move back."

"Could be." Nate shakes his head. "Man, what happened to us?"

Dan doesn't answer. He shifts his gaze around the outdated room.

"Twenty years," Nate continues, not noticing Dan's discomfort. "Twenty years, and we're still here, not two steps from where we were back then. I was gone for eight years—all over this world—and came right back to Conway, like there was never any doubt in my mind where I'd end up."

Dan feels the same way to a point. While the military certainly isn't the same as prison, as soon as Dan had been released, Conway pulled him back like a magnet.

Part of that was Amber, but they could have relocated as a family. Started over. It had never been a conversation. *Why not?* he wonders.

"At least you have a family," Nate continues, oblivious. "Amber is a hell of a woman, and you have great kids." He shakes his head again. "Despite everything, you're the one who did it right. I'm here alone, getting older every single day."

Dan glances sideways at Nate. The man is envious of *Dan*? If Nate only knew.

An unbidden errant thought worms its way into his consciousness. What if Amber divorces Dan and marries Nate? He could easily envision Nate moving into his home, his bed. Helping Amber with meals and housework. He can picture Nate playing ball with Sam, coaching Mason's soccer games someday. Hell, he can see him standing with Amber for Henry's senior night, and cheering Luke on during his baseball games. He can see it all so clearly that there's a part of him that wants to preemptively punch Nate in the face.

He's being ridiculous. Amber and Nate don't know each other. If the two of them have ever met, Dan is unaware of the introduction.

But Dan also realizes that Nate would make a better husband and father than he is, and that makes him die just a little bit more inside.

The two-way radio on Nate's hip crackles, and the woman from dispatch alerts Nate to a non-emergency incident at a gas station along the highway.

Nate grabs the radio and affirms the assignment.

He turns to Dan. "I'll alert the mother of what happened, tell her she needs to get home. You mind sticking around for a bit?"

"You sure this won't be a problem?" Dan asks. "Me staying here?"

They both survey their surroundings.

Nate lifts a shoulder. "None of this is protocol. It would have been protocol to take her to jail after she'd refused medical treatment." He exhales, weighing his decision. "I'd rather someone be here with her. If the mother complains, I'll take the heat."

Dan nods. "I'll just look in on her and then wait outside." He doesn't think he should be alone in the house with Sutton.

Nate offers his hand, and Dan shakes it.

"Thanks for everything, man. You saved her life."

How ironic. He looks in the direction of Sutton's bedroom. "I'm not sure she wanted to be saved."

"That might be true of a lot of us."

The two of them might have been friends had their lives turned out differently. But in the end, Nate is a cop and Dan is still a felon. Those labels are hard to shake. So, there will be no easy meetups for a beer at Bud's. There will be no relationship beyond a nod of the head when they pass each other in the hardware store.

After Nate leaves, Dan looks in on Sutton, making sure the woman is still conscious. He's pretty sure she knows he's there, but she again doesn't acknowledge him, and he doesn't speak to her. Then he heads to the porch and sits on the stairs, waiting.

A short time later, a small SUV steers fast down the road and whips into the gravel parking space at the side of the house. An older woman slams the car door behind her and does a fast shuffle up the sidewalk. She wears scrubs, and her gray hair flutters around her head in the breeze.

Dan stands when she approaches.

"Where is she?" she demands as she charges up the steps. She passes in a scented cloud of medicinal soap and fabric softener.

"In the bedroom," Dan says. "I checked on her a few minutes ago."

"She could have relapsed in a few minutes," the woman shoots back as the door slams behind her.

He's not sure if he should follow, wait, or just head back to Crystal's house, only two streets away. He glances at his phone and decides to linger for five minutes, just in case. He can at least explain what happened, if she's interested.

An old wooden porch swing at the far end of the house drifts lightly on the gentle wind. Dan sits carefully, and its rusty chains whine with his weight and the unexpected movement.

Ten minutes later, the woman returns. Gone is the harried energy. She seems smaller, diminished.

There is a long silence before she speaks. "Officer Kasinski said that you know Sutton." She doesn't look at him.

"I wouldn't say that." But Dan isn't sure how to describe the non-relationship with the woman's daughter.

She seems to understand. "You knew her once."

"I knew her once," he agrees.

She turns toward him and studies him closely. "You're the one who was driving the car."

Anyone who remembers the accident may have seen the news coverage of the scene, the arrest, the trial. Twenty years later, many people wouldn't have remembered his name or even his face. Unless they had been connected to the people involved. Sutton is connected.

He doesn't think a response is necessary.

The woman breathes deeply. "It feels like yesterday."

For Dan, it feels like forever ago and, at the same time, he can close his eyes and relive every single second, as if it is all still happening to him.

"Sutton has never recovered from that night, you know." An edge inserts itself in her voice. A sharpness.

The skin on the back of Dan's neck prickles.

"They were best friends. It's hard to lose your best friend like that, so suddenly." The woman's arms are folded across her chest. She stares at him sideways, waiting for him to react.

Dan doesn't know what happened between Sutton and Megan, but *that* night, they were not best friends. He remembers Megan staring at Sutton with Joe. He remembers her obvious distress. He remembers Sutton running after them as they left, and Megan's harsh words in return.

He doesn't say any of this out loud.

"What were you doing in that crack house, anyway?"

"I'm sorry?" he asks, confused by the shift in topic and the sudden demand of the question.

"Officer Kasinski said you found her in that abandoned warehouse by the river. Is that not true?"

"A man in the alleyway"—he gestures vaguely in the direction of Crystal's house—"told me that a woman was in trouble. I ran over and called the police."

Sutton's mother stares down at Dan as he still sits on the swing. He should have stood up. Now, he's the one who feels small and powerless with her above him, accusation flashing in her eyes.

"Maybe it was you who gave her the drugs. Maybe it's you who is her dealer. Did you do anything else to her while you were unattended in my home?"

Now, Dan does stand. He does his best to remain calm. "Ma'am, I was just trying to help."

"Like you helped Megan by driving her into a tree? Like you helped Sutton by traumatizing her and causing the events that got her addicted to drugs?" Her voice has risen considerably in pitch.

Dan doesn't bother defending himself. He walks off the porch, past her as she sneers at him.

"It's all your fault, you know. You've ruined so many lives. And what did you get—two years in prison? Two years for murder? You should have gotten life for everything you've taken from those kids. You should be ashamed of yourself," she yells after him.

A neighbor has emerged from his house to eye Dan suspiciously and cast his own judgements.

Hunched forward, Dan hurries quickly down the street, his hands shoved deep into his pockets.

"I hope you rot in hell," is the last thing he clearly hears her say.

When he arrives at Crystal's house, his heart is pounding, and he is shaking. It's been years since he's been publicly attacked. But it reminds him of what a worthless piece of shit he really is, and not just in his own perception. The world hates him just as much as he hates himself.

In Crystal's refrigerator, he spots a six-pack of light beer. He needs something stronger. He throws open kitchen cupboards and slams them shut again until he finds a cubby with a number of half empty bottles of amber-colored liquid.

He chooses an Irish whiskey, pours a tall tumbler, and drinks it down fast. The relief starts to flow through him, but not quickly enough. He pours another. Then he goes to the shabby living room with its brown sculptured shag carpeting and green Berber sofa. It's not unlike the outdated décor in the home of Sutton's mother.

Dan sinks down on the worn sofa and closes his eyes.

You should be ashamed of yourself. The old woman's words ring in his ears.

Yes. He is ashamed of himself. He's ashamed that he's the one who survived when it should have been the beautiful girl with the bright future.

To whatever source, God, or higher power that might have been listening, he slurs hotly, "You fucked up. You took the wrong one."

CHAPTER 20

CRYSTAL-NOW

Crystal enters through the front door before Frank has made his way up the front sidewalk. Dan's truck is parked in the driveway, but the house is silent. There is no scent of grilling steak, no sound of dishes clattering from the kitchen, no movement from the back porch.

"Dan?" she calls. In the kitchen, she notices the plastic bags from the Save-A-Lot on the counter. When she pulls open the refrigerator, she finds a package of thick ribeye steaks.

"Crystal!" Frank calls.

She follows the sound of her husband's voice to the living room.

Frank is staring down at Dan passed out on the living room sofa. Saliva trickles down his chin and makes a darker color stain on the front of his flannel shirt. An empty bottle of whiskey and glass tumbler sit on the coffee table in front of him.

Frank gives her a long, level look. "You said he was sober."

"He *was*," Crystal responds, immediately defensive. But she remembers the way he'd swallowed down those beers at Bud's—one right after the other. "He's had a lot going on."

Frank's chest heaves with a mighty exhale. "We agreed that he could stay here if he were sober, Crystal. That was the deal."

Crystal doesn't look at her husband. He is a good, kind, and decent man. But an agreement has been broken. "We can't kick him out on the street."

"He can stay with his dad."

"No." The word is fast and firm. "I'll take care of it. I'll talk to him."

Frank shakes his head slowly, but he doesn't say anything else. He pulls himself up the narrow stairs to the second floor of the house, moving deliberately and with effort. Not only is Frank's speed decreasing as he ages, but his range of motion is less and less. Eventually, Crystal knows he won't be able to climb those stairs at all.

She runs her hands through her hair. She can't think about Frank's declining health right now. She can only concentrate on one problem in her relationships at a time. She waits until she hears Frank moving around in the bedroom and then she sinks down next to Dan on the sofa.

She shakes him gently. "Dan?" Her mouth is close to his ear. His head lolls to one side, but he doesn't respond.

She shakes him again, harder. This time, he sucks in a quick breath, then settles and mumbles something, his head falling against the other shoulder.

On the cushion next to him, Dan's phone begins to buzz. Amber's name lights up on the screen. Before thinking better of it, Crystal picks it up and presses accept, walking away from the inert form of her cousin. "Hello?" She keeps her voice quiet so that Frank doesn't hear.

There is a pause, and then a tentative, biting, "Uh, who is this?"

"It's Crystal," she answers quickly. "Crystal Neumann, Dan's cousin."

A pause. "I'm trying to reach Dan. I've been calling."

"Yes, he's here." She spots the bags on the counter and

thinks fast. "He's actually outside right now, getting the grill ready to cook some steaks. He's staying here for a few days while—" She stops herself. "Well, you know."

"Would you mind getting him?"

Crystal looks around, panicked. "Actually, I don't see him on the porch. He might have run back to the store for something he forgot."

"Without his phone?"

Crystal's heart skips a beat as she reaches for her next excuse.

But Amber says, annoyed, "Can you just have him call me please when he gets back? It's about Henry."

"Sure, I'll let him know." She opens her mouth to ask Amber how she's doing, try to gather some information from the other woman. But Amber has already disconnected.

Crystal marches back to the living room. "Dan." She shakes him hard until he stirs and blinks up at her.

His eyes are unfocused and bleary as he looks around the dim room. It's late afternoon, but the sun hadn't quite made a full appearance that day, so the room is dusky and filled with shadows. "What time is it?" he slurs.

Instead of answering, she looks pointedly at the empty whiskey bottle.

He pushes himself up into a sitting position, then immediately braces his elbows on his knees and rests his forehead in his hands.

"Amber called." She holds out his phone, and he looks over at it, confused. When he seems to recognize that the device is his, he takes it and scrolls through a string of unanswered text messages. He swears under his breath.

When Dan doesn't elaborate, she says, "Everything okay?"

Amber had indicated that the call was about Henry, but

Crystal had been so focused on Dan, she hadn't thought to worry about Dan's son.

"You know the assembly at the high school Tolbert told us about last night?"

Crystal nods.

"Apparently Henry now knows about it. He also knows that my name will be mentioned."

Crystal sits down next to her cousin. There isn't a lot that she can say, so she rubs his back like she used to when he was a kid and crying about something his dad had said or done to him. Dan is the closest thing she has to a sibling. Or a child, for that matter. "What can I do?"

He shakes his head. "Nothing. You've done more than enough for me." He leans over and kisses her on the cheek. "I'm going to splash some water on my face and then give Amber a call." He walks to the kitchen, and she calls after him, "Drink some water."

The water runs for a long while, then she hears the back door bang shut.

Frank lumbers back down the stairs. "Did you talk with him?"

"He's dealing with another crisis." She grabs the whiskey bottle and the glass and walks past Frank.

He follows her into the kitchen. "You're an enabler, Crystal. You know that?"

She frowns at her husband. But she's not angry; she's hurt. His words are not true. And to think—it's Frank of all people telling her that *she* is an enabler of Dan. If anything, she's enabling *him*.

"I'm just trying to help," she snaps. "It's so much more than most people do."

"It's just that you always go above and beyond to try to help everyone you know. Rushing in like some kind of hero. Or savior." He sighs deeply. "Look...I know you think you're helping, but you're making things worse."

Crystal is well aware of the effect some of her actions have had on the lives of others. If she hadn't been so insistent on helping Dan all of those years ago, the accident would never have happened. Megan Richards would still be alive, and Dan would not have gone to prison. He might have had the chance for a normal, happy life. She's thought about that every single day for the past twenty years.

To Frank, she says, "Is that what I'm doing for you? Making things worse?" She can't stop her voice from wobbling.

Frank isn't moved by her tears. "Honestly, I have no idea what you're doing with me. I'm glad you're here. I truly am. But you're a beautiful young woman, and I'm a broken old man. You have this incessant need to fix things, me included. I have to tell you, sweetheart. Not everything, or everyone, can be fixed."

The back door squeaks on its hinges as it opens, and Crystal turns away from Frank. Dan walks in and removes the package of meat from the refrigerator. The chemical odor of the propane wafts inside.

No one speaks, and after a moment, Frank scoffs and hobbles from the room. A few minutes later, Crystal hears the drone of the television set.

She turns to her cousin. "Everything okay?"

Dan looks like hell. His eyes are red, and she's sure he's still slightly drunk. He clumsily tears open the package of steaks and places them on a plate. "I'll talk to Henry tomorrow. I'm taking him to breakfast at ten. He should have heard this all from me a long time ago."

"It's a hard story to tell." Crystal's voice is soft. While Dan had taken the brunt of the punishment, there were others involved. Joe Wright, for example, who got off scot-free even though he'd been the person hosting the party.

And poor Chloe Nicholson, who had paid a high price for her own actions that night.

Dan bangs cabinets open and shut, and Crystal walks over, reaching for the plastic shakers of seasoning. She hands them to him, and he shakes the seasoning over the cuts of meat.

"But it's my story, isn't it?" asks Dan. He rubs his forehead with the heel of a palm. "And I can't seem to turn the page."

Crystal isn't sure that he's ever even tried to move on to the next chapter.

Dan begins washing the potatoes as the steaks rest.

"I can do that," Crystal offers, approaching the counter.

He waves her away. His movements are slow and measured, like he's concentrating on the simple task of preparing the food. But his hands are steady enough.

"Do you know what happened today?" he asks, not waiting for a reply. "A junkie came up the alley and told me there was an overdose in that abandoned building." He gestures in the direction of the old warehouse by the river. "I called Nate Kasinski, and I ran in there," Dan continues.

"Why would you do that?" Crystal asks, alarmed. The unmistakable odor of weed and woodfire often drifts from the nuisance building, and Crystal has called the cops to check the location on more than one occasion. She's fairly certain indigent people may have been living there over the winter.

"I wasn't going to let someone just die in there." He looks at her, then quickly averts his gaze. She knows that his mind has just gone to Megan.

"You know who it was?" he continues, again not expecting an answer. He dries the potatoes with a paper towel and begins pricking holes in them with a fork. "Sutton Schultz. Can you believe that shit?"

Crystal frowns. The name is vaguely familiar, but she can't quite place it.

"The best friend," Dan offers, waiting for Crystal's memory to catch up.

When the recollection of the small blonde girl clicks, Crystal's mouth falls open. "She's a junkie?"

"Yep," Dan says.

"Is she—" Crystal abruptly stops herself before she utters the word. "Is she okay?" she amends.

Dan returns to his potato preparation, wrapping the small round tubers in aluminum foil. "She's fine for now. I waited at her parents' house for her mother to come home. And when her mother returned, the woman told me that Sutton's problems are my fault. In fact, everything that happened is my fault. And you know what? She's right."

"Oh, Danny," Crystal says, and she wants to fold him into her arms like she used to when he was a kid healing from the purple-green bruises of Greg's fists. "We're all responsible for our own actions. That girl could have made a thousand other choices over the past twenty years. Her decision to get high is not a result of anything that you did."

"I'm the catalyst, Crystal. Without me, all of those lives would have gone on uninterrupted." He gathers up his plate of steaks and wrapped potatoes. "I should have never been born. My mother must have known it. My dad sure as hell knew it." He walks toward the door, his jaw set. "Now I've ruined everything for Amber, and I'm about to ruin everything for Henry." He stops. Looks at her. "How many more lives am I going to screw up?"

He doesn't wait for a response before shouldering the back door open and letting it close behind him.

Crystal puts her hands to her face. She knows what Frank has just told her—that not everything can be fixed.

But doesn't she owe it to the little boy—the child that Dan had once been—to try?

CHAPTER 21

CHLOE-NOW

Chloe takes the turnpike to the highway that leads straight to Conway. Even though it's a simple route, it takes them almost an hour of traveling south on roads that are in poor condition—past deteriorating buildings, shuttered businesses, and unkempt houses—to make it into the town where she'd grown up.

Emma has visited Conway in the past. Jason's parents have lived just outside of town for their entire lives, and after Jason moved back with Becky, Emma has been a guest in their home. But those visits have been short and limited. She's not sure Emma has had time or occasion to notice her surroundings.

As usual, Emma stares out the window with a faraway look on her face, and Chloe keeps the radio tuned to a pop-rock station where a breathy female voice sings about the summer being cruel. Chloe can relate.

When they pass an exit for the neighboring town of Pleasanton, Chloe says, "That's where your grandmother was born."

"Grandma Lawrence?" Emma asks with a note of interest. She refers to Jason's mother, a bright and bubbly woman who always has a smile and a kind word.

"Your Grandma Nicholson. She died before you were born."

Emma frowns and looks back out the window again.

Chloe has rarely spoken about her parents, so she shouldn't be surprised or hurt by Emma's indifference.

She glances at her daughter and then turns her attention back to the scenery passing them by. She hasn't driven this road for years, but the route is familiar to her. The state has reconfigured many of the exit ramps, and a few new buildings and commercial developments have emerged, but the landscape itself remains unchanged.

Chloe feels a tug—a pressure—in her chest and the odd sense that she is going back in time.

To counteract the sensation, she talks. "Your Grandfather Nicholson was born in West Virginia but came to the area to work with his uncle who ran a lumber company in the mountains. Then, when the quarry operations started in the 1960s, he took a position as a laborer. Your grandmother was a few years younger than he was, and he married her straight out of high school."

Chloe's parents hadn't talked often about their childhood, how they'd met, or their courtship, but Chloe had once stumbled across a shoebox filled with sepia photographs and had asked enough questions to piece the stories together. It hadn't been a particularly remarkable or romantic story, but it was *her* story, and she had cherished it.

Chloe quickly recognizes that telling a story about her past to counteract the sensation of traveling backward through time has the opposite effect; the heaviness of the past sinks deeper in her limbs. She is quiet as they pass a patch of overgrown farmland bordered by a large building that had once held a robust manufacturing presence. Weeds and trees now twist their way through the remaining concrete of a ruined parking lot.

"How did they meet?" Emma asks, still gazing out the

window.

Chloe is surprised and pleased by the question. She wets her lips.

"My mother's family owned a small diner in Pleasanton. As a teenager, she waitressed there. My father stopped in one Saturday when she was serving coffee. He came every weekend after that until she noticed him, and he kept coming in until he worked up the courage to say hello. It took about a year of weekend coffees before they had an actual conversation." Chloe laughs softly. "Dating is so much different today."

Even when Chloe had been in high school, things were so much different than they were today. She hadn't invested in a cell phone until she'd been a college student. In an isolated location like Conway two decades ago, only kids whose families had an abundance of discretionary income had their own phones. Only kids like Joe Wright, she thinks, the irritation of seeing his face on the television screen still fresh in her mind.

Back then, the lack of constant connection had required a level of personal interaction that does not currently exist. If Chloe wanted to, she could run her entire business remotely, without ever meeting a client face-to-face. While there might be convenience in that option, there is a real sense of loneliness as well. And it is why she works so hard to ensure that her homeschooled daughter participates in plenty of outside activities.

"Was she pretty?" Emma asks.

It takes Chloe a moment to process the question. Maybe because she had just been stewing on her hatred for Joe Wright and ruminating on the past, her mind leaps to Megan Richards. But Emma couldn't possibly know anything about Megan. "Who?" Chloe asks.

"Grandma Nicholson."

Chloe considers that for a minute. Even when she'd been young, Maggie Nicholson would not have been called conventionally pretty. She'd been sturdily built with a long face and a strong jaw. But she had a quick smile, and was kind and caring. She'd loved her children above everything.

Her parents had tried for years to have children, and after Matt and Chloe had finally come along, their mother had been a bit more careful and timid than maybe she should have been with her children.

While Chloe hadn't understood it back then, now she recognizes that the years of trying to conceive had made her mother handle her children as if they might disappear at any moment. Maggie Nicholson had always been careful not to upset her children; denying them was done with the most tentative of dissent.

Where that indulgence may have made some children spoiled and likely to take advantage, it'd had the opposite effect on Matt and Chloe, who became equally as careful with their parents. The result was a quiet reverence on both sides. Unfortunately, it had also meant that no conversations took place that had the potential to cause any discomfit.

Chloe remembers Emma's original question: *Was she pretty?* She responds, "Your grandmother was beautiful."

"What about my grandfather?"

Walter Nicholson had been so gentle and patient. "He would have loved you so much," Chloe says.

Emma is silent again as they continue the drive and finally turn off the highway and into the city of Conway.

It feels surreal to be back, and Chloe wonders for the thousandth time what she's actually doing here.

Her hands are slick on the steering wheel as they travel up a steep street toward the high school. She feels like the car is driving on autopilot.

The last time Chloe laid eyes on the school building itself had been during her high school graduation ceremony—that sad, somber event that was more memorial than a new beginning. Her parents had insisted she attend, despite everything else that had happened the two weeks prior to graduation day.

The car crests the hill, and the high school complex is laid out before them. It looks much the same as it had when Chloe attended. She notices an unfamiliar building to one side, and the football field seems newer, fresher.

She idles at the stop sign and stares at the building's pale concrete facade, the painted blue windows, the unassuming front entrance with its brown roof and blue and white marquee. Chloe feels no sense of evil. The building is just a building.

A car behind them taps its horn—a friendly alert.

Emma says, "Mom," in an accusatory tone.

Chloe blinks and moves forward, slowly drifting closer to the building and traveling well under the posted speed limit. The car behind her honks again, longer and more aggressive this time.

She ignores it and continues her cautious journey. Finally, she turns into the school's long driveway, and the car speeds past, the driver laying on the horn. A middle finger is aimed in Chloe's direction, but she barely notices.

Emma sinks down in the seat.

Chloe pulls in front of the building and stares up, not speaking.

"Mom, what are we doing here?"

"I went to school here." She is aware of the faraway tone of her voice. She is aware of Emma beside her. But she is also aware of the ghost of her past self, her old classmates walking through these doors.

"But what are *we* doing here?" Emma asks again.

"Just remembering."

"Remembering what?"

Before she can answer, she catches sight of a black Chevy with the bold Conway police department lettering painted yellow on the side. It pulls in behind her, and Chloe watches in her side mirror as a uniformed officer climbs out of the driver's seat.

Emma covers her face with her hands.

Chloe powers down her window, more annoyed than concerned by the interruption. She's wearing her big designer sunglasses that cover half of her face and doesn't give in to the immediate impulse to remove them when the cop approaches.

The masculine face peering in at her is familiar. It's rounder than she remembers, and there are lines around the eyes and a thickness to the jaw that hadn't existed the last time she'd seen it. But Nate Kasinski is unmistakable.

She hadn't known him well in high school. He'd been a popular athlete who'd gotten decent grades and left for the Army immediately after graduation. She's surprised he ended up back in Conway.

He studies Emma and then turns his attention back to Chloe. "Everything all right here?"

"Everything is fine, officer," Chloe answers, a fake brightness in her tone. "Just doing some sightseeing." She wants him to go away.

"Sightseeing," he repeats. She can tell that he's trying to examine her eyes behind the lenses. "You new to the area? I watched you driving pretty slowly through town a few minutes ago."

"You could say that." She gives a little laugh.

He doesn't react. "I'm more interested in what *you* could say."

"I could say a lot of things," Chloe responds, her smile

fading. "I could say I'm doing absolutely nothing wrong while I show my daughter the high school. I could say that we're minding our own business. I could say that your interrogation borders on harassment."

"Mom," Emma breathes quietly beside her.

Nate Kasinski sucks on his teeth. Then he says, "Well, you—being new to town—wouldn't know this, but we've had an influx of illegal drug activity around here." He gives her expensive SUV a once-over. "Anytime I see a nice car like yours driving slowly through our community and then casing the high school, I have a duty to investigate. Surely you understand that, Ms...." He stares at her, and she stares back. "I don't think I caught your name."

She needs to learn to keep her mouth shut. She could refuse to answer, but she really doesn't want to get into a legal argument with a townie cop. Finally, she responds, "Lawrence," using Jason's last name—her former married surname.

She can feel Emma staring at her in horror. She'd been extremely vocal about reverting to her maiden name after her divorce. More times than she could count, Chloe had preached the unquestionable essentiality of maintaining one's own identity as a woman.

The officer studies her more closely, and she prays that he does not ask for her license and registration.

He looks across at Emma again. "And what's your name?" He asks the question as if Emma is a much younger child. His unnatural, high-pitched voice makes Chloe think this man does not have children of his own.

"Emma," she responds quietly.

"What do you think of the school?"

She lifts a shoulder. "It's okay."

He glances back at the building. "I went to school here a long time ago."

Chloe shuts her eyes behind her sunglasses. Emma is not one to chat up a stranger, especially a police officer, and she hopes this is not the day that Emma will decide it's in her best interest to overshare. But her daughter just makes a noncommittal noise in response to the officer's comment.

"You'll be attending this place in a few years, I take it?"

Emma looks at Chloe, clearly bewildered. Chloe answers instead. "Emma is homeschooled."

He nods, as if that makes sense. But then he leans forward, nearly into the car, and asks, "So what are you doing up here then—at the high school?"

Chloe realizes she's backed herself into a corner. She stammers, "I—well, we—we were passing through, and Emma—" She glances over at her daughter's confusion. She looks back over at Nate Kasinski. Then she runs out of steam and energy. Suddenly, she feels very tired. "I was just showing Emma where I'd gone to school." She hopes that this shuts him up and he asks no more questions.

No such luck.

"You graduated from Conway? What year?" he asks.

Her brain does not work fast enough to come up with a plausible lie. "2004," she responds.

He looks shocked by this pronouncement. "What was your name back then?"

There is no way out of answering this question, and she sighs. "Chloe Nicholson."

The silence that follows is heavy with recognition. Nate Kasinski was there when Chloe announced that she would bring the alcohol to the party on Mitsin Ridge. In fact, Nate had been the one to transport that alcohol to the party for her. Nate had been friends with Megan. He would have remembered Chloe's role in the accident. He would have remembered the aftermath. She can feel him trying to decide what to do with this information.

Finally, he says, "You probably don't remember me. I'm Nate Kasinski." He taps the name badge on his chest.

When she looks up at him, she sees something in his eyes. Sorrow, maybe. Regret. She looks away again. "We really need to be going."

"Sure." He hesitates. "Sorry to keep you for so long."

She is about to shift into drive when Nate leans back down. "Hey, for what it's worth, I was really sorry about what happened to Matt. I left for basic training before I had the chance to offer my sympathies." He opens his mouth, then shuts it again. He takes a breath. "It should have never happened that way. He didn't deserve it." He swallows. "Neither did you."

Chloe shuts her eyes and blows out a steady, quiet stream of air, then inhales. Once again, she pastes on her brightest smile and looks up at him. "It was a long time ago."

He nods. "Maybe I'll see you around."

She pulls away, her limbs going numb and limp as she turns onto the main road.

"You know him?" Emma finally asks. Her daughter has been staring at the side of Chloe's face, and Chloe has been trying to ignore the questioning look.

"A little. It was a really long time ago."

"Does Dad know him?"

Chloe shrugs. "Probably not." Jason is two years younger than Chloe. While her ex-husband certainly knew what happened her senior year, there would have been no reason for Jason to have any contact with Nate Kasinski.

"What did he mean when he said you didn't deserve it?"

"He was just talking about…something that happened a long time ago."

"The Matt he was talking about… Is that your brother?" Emma asks. "My uncle?"

Chloe swallows. Emma has seen old photos with Matt in them. Chloe has told Emma about Matt and the fact that he died. But she's never felt it necessary to explain the circumstances around Matt's death. For many, many reasons. "Yes, he was talking about your uncle."

"What happened to him?"

"He died," Chloe responds. "When I was eighteen."

"Yes, but how? You've never told me how."

"It was an accident." She's being vague, but she doesn't know how to tell Emma, in pieces, the story of that night and its consequences. She doesn't know how to separate what happened to Matt from her role in the greater tragedy. Because there is no separation.

Elaine has been gently insistent that Chloe must relay these events to Emma someday, but Chloe disagrees.

"A car accident?" Emma prods, much more interested in this particular subject than she's been in anything else Chloe has to say.

"It was—an accident at home." She shudders because even ambiguous references remind her of that horrific day. Of what met Chloe when she'd pushed her way into Matt's room after that terrible loud popping sound. Of that panicked, incoherent 911 call. Of her mother's scream then loss of consciousness. Of the arrival of the ambulance and police, and the questions. Of Matt's lifeless body being hauled out on a stretcher covered with a blood-soaked sheet.

Chloe realizes that she's shaking, and the car has stopped.

"Where are we?" Emma asks.

Chloe is shocked to find that she's parked in the driveway of her childhood home. The small one-story house with its brick facade and small windows. She stares up at it. Where the high school had been just a building, this place hurts her heart.

"This was my house," Chloe responds.

"The accident was here?"

"Yes," she says. She wonders how many others have lived in this house since she moved out. Following her parents' deaths two years after Matt passed, the residence had sat vacant and for sale until someone who didn't know or care about its history made an offer. It had been a lowball offer, but Chloe had accepted it to be rid of the place, which was an albatross around her young neck.

She'd used the proceeds to pay off the debt she'd incurred from the unexpected funerals of her sibling and both parents. The rest, she'd invested in starting her own business after college.

"What kind of accident was it?" Emma asks slowly, as if she's no longer certain she wants to hear the answer.

Chloe looks at her daughter and makes a decision. She's not sure it's the right one. "Your Uncle Matt had some mental health issues," she says gently. "They were exacerbated by some…other things that happened—things that shouldn't have happened. Someday, I'll tell you about them, but not today." Chloe gazes up at the window on the far right of the house. The window is dark, but she swears that she sees movement there, maybe Matt's quirky face smiling at her crookedly. Chloe smiles back just in case it really is him in the window.

Then she looks back at Emma, taking his appearance as a sign of encouragement, even if it had been a figment of her imagination. "He took his own life, honey, because he decided that this world is an unfair place to live."

Tears spring into Emma's eyes, and Chloe gathers her close, softly crying herself for the first time in years. As the tears flow, something that had rusted tight in Chloe's chest loosens just a bit, and she can finally breathe.

CHAPTER 22

CHLOE-THEN

Chloe descends the short staircase of the bus and emerges on the street in front of her house. Matt's light blue hatchback is in the driveway, and she gives the vehicle a long look. There is a break in the rain that has been falling most of the day, and she lingers in the humid air.

The bus lurches away, and she looks around. The street is deserted, but it's likely that one of the nosy old neighbors is peeking out at her from behind curtains.

She ambles to Matt's car, trying to look casual and relaxed, even though her heart is beating a tattoo inside her chest.

The back seat is filled with brown paper grocery bags, and a blanket conceals what looks like cases of pop. But she knows the cases contain something else.

With another quick look around, Chloe moves to the back of the car and feels for the trunk latch. She lifts it a few inches and peers into the dark space. Two half kegs of beer lie sideways with towels shoved between them for support.

Chloe breathes out. She shuts the trunk and turns to walk to the house to wait.

Nate Kasinski had been elected to collect the alcohol, though he hadn't been happy about it. But he drives a truck that belongs to him; he has no siblings that might ask questions; and his uncle is a Conway cop, so he's the least likely of the group to be pulled over for any minor infractions.

Chloe had told Nate to arrive at her house directly after school, before her mother returned from work.

She glances at her watch as she walks toward the door. They've got half an hour, tops.

"Hi, Chloe," Ralph, the old man from across the street, calls to her. He sets down his small dog, Lemon, who immediately starts barking at some invisible threat in the yard.

"Hi, Ralph," she says and continues toward the door.

"Nice day, isn't it?"

It isn't a nice day, but she calls back, "Yeah." She's nearly there. Her hand is on the doorknob, and she just needs to walk into the entryway.

"You ready for graduation?"

She shifts her backpack on her shoulder. "I guess so."

He lets out an unnatural sounding laugh. "You've gotten so pretty over the past year. I imagine you'll have all the boys chasing after you in college."

She doesn't respond to that creepy comment.

She pushes open the door, and Ralph calls, "Saw your brother today. I hadn't seen him in a while."

"Oh, he's been here," she answers and looks to the sky, contemplating just walking into the house and slamming the door behind her. But if she does that, Ralph will no doubt tell her parents that she'd been rude.

"His car is usually parked right there, but he hardly ever leaves the house. Would have thought he might have a job by now."

When Chloe doesn't answer, Ralph continues, "You tell him that I have some work he can do around my house, if he's interested."

"Okay, Ralph. I'll tell him."

Just as she steps over the threshold, she hears the rumble of a loud engine accelerating up the street. She recognizes this engine from the school parking lot and turns to watch Nate's big white truck roll up behind her brother's car.

Ralph doesn't even pretend to be discreet. He picks up Lemon, who is barking furiously at the intruding vehicle, and openly stares at Nate.

Nate steps down from the truck and lifts a hand to Chloe. She beckons him toward the house. He looks confused. "No, I'm just here to pick up the stuff," he says, and she hurries toward him.

"My neighbor is watching," she hisses, and Nate turns around, makes eye contact.

"Hi, there!" Ralph calls, Lemon tucked under his arm and wriggling to escape.

Chloe grabs Nate's arm and pulls him toward the front door. He follows without further resistance. Even though he doesn't protest, she knows he'd rather be doing anything else than walking through Doughy Chloe's front door.

She hears Matt moving around in the kitchen. And then he is in the doorway. "Hey…" His mouth is open to say something else, but he catches sight of Nate. "Oh," he says instead.

Nate is tall with perfect posture and a military style haircut. Chloe assumes that these traits are in line with his post-graduation plans. He's not particularly good-looking, but he is solid and clean-cut. "Look, I'm just here to pick up the stuff," he says and holds up his hands.

Matt shoots a questioning glance at Chloe.

"Ralph is outside," she says in response.

Her brother nods in understanding.

Chloe peers out the small window next to the front door and groans quietly in frustration. Lemon is again running up and down the yard, yapping, and Ralph is watching the dog, his hands clasped behind his back.

"Can't we just tell him I'm picking up some stuff from you?" Nate asks. Even though his voice is even, Chloe can tell that he's irritated.

"He'll ask what it is."

"We don't have to tell him."

"He'll walk over to see for himself," Matt says. "Don't you have neighbors?"

Nate looks perplexed. "I don't *talk* to them."

Ralph looks up at the sky and claps for Lemon.

"He'll go inside in a minute," Chloe says. "It's starting to rain."

Nate groans. "So much for a fire tonight."

Chloe looks back at Matt. "Do you think he'll say anything to Mom and Dad? He's already made a comment about you leaving the house today."

"I don't think they pay much attention to what Ralph has to say." But Matt looks unsure.

Nate bounces from one foot to the other. "I don't have all day."

Chloe looks back out and watches as Ralph climbs his front steps with Lemon in his arms. She waits until the door bangs shut behind him before she says, "Okay, let's go."

There's still the risk that he will watch them from his window, but he likely won't be able to see clearly what they're transferring from Matt's car to Nate's truck. At the very least, with the rain, he'll avoid coming outside to ask questions.

Nate follows Chloe through the now steady downpour. "If we'd done this when I got here, we'd be dry," he points out.

She ignores the comment and hands him the bags from the back seat, which he quickly places into the cab of the truck. Then she attempts to keep the cases hidden with the blanket and struggles to lift the lot of them at one time.

Nate gently nudges her out of the way. "I got it," he says, easily and discreetly transferring the bulky packages.

The kegs are heavier, and Nate strains to transfer the bulky weight alone.

"Do you want me to ask Matt to help?" she asks as he manages to lift the barrel into the back seat.

He moves his head from side to side and rolls his broad shoulders. "It's just a bit awkward. I'll manage."

To Chloe's surprise, Matt emerges without being asked, and he helps Nate transfer the second barrel. They are all soaked by the time the task is over.

Other than a quick lift of his hand, Nate doesn't exchange any pleasantries, and Chloe and Matt return to the house in silence.

Matt shakes himself off like a dog, and the musty scent of unwashed clothes and body odor drifts toward her. "Does that guy even know your name?"

Chloe pulls her wet hair away from her face. She's fairly certain Nate knows her name. They've been in classes together, and her rhyming nickname has likely stuck with him, even if she's not as doughy as she'd once been. It's telling, though, that she can't answer her brother's question with absolute certainty.

Matt looks at her, and Chloe says defensively, "What difference does it make?"

"It's like I said yesterday. You're taking a lot of risk just to get these people to like you."

"Then why did you agree to help me?"

"I don't know. Maybe because I'm such a loser. The least I can do is help you to be as unlike me as possible."

"You're not a loser."

He continues as if he hadn't heard her. "That guy out

there," he says, talking about Nate. "He doesn't worry what people think about him or if they like him or not. You can tell. And the whole time he was here, I kept thinking about how I needed to be more like him. I'm six years older than that kid. I should be doing something with my life. Instead, I spend my days in my bedroom, playing video games on my computer and messing around with the guitar."

"Then why don't you do something?" Chloe asks. "You have a college degree. Why don't you get a job?"

He shakes his head. "You don't get it."

"Don't get what?"

"There's something wrong with me, Chloe."

Chloe lowers her eyes. Matt's always been a little bit different. He's overweight, socially awkward, moody, distant. But then, so is she. The only difference between them is that she's been trying to work on her shortcomings, and Matt has remained stagnant. "You just need to get out of the house more—" she starts to say.

Matt holds up a hand. "You sound like Mom. And that's not what I need." He taps his temple with a finger. "There's something wrong up here, Chloe. That's what I'm trying to tell you. That's what I've been trying to tell *them*. No one will listen to me."

"But…you're not crazy, Matt. Maybe you're just, like, lonely or something."

He throws up his hands. "You all want to take the easy way out of this conversation." He stares right into her eyes. "But this isn't an easy issue. And don't say I didn't try to tell you that."

A chill travels up Chloe's spine and spreads across the back of her neck. But she breaks eye contact and walks away. "I need to get ready," she mumbles, rushing to her bedroom, away from Matt and his unsettling words.

In her bedroom, she lays her outfit out on the bed—a

pair of new slim jeans and a soft blue top that is much lower-cut than she'd ever worn in public before. She adds a zip-up sweatshirt because the night air might be chilly.

She hears the garage door open followed by the engine of her mother's car as it pulls into the space beneath her bedroom. From Matt's room next door, the faint pinging sounds of some game on his computer travel through the wall.

Chloe reflects on her brother's words, and she walks to the kitchen where her mother has hauled in a few brown paper bags from the grocery store.

"Hey there, honey," she says when she notices Chloe standing in the doorway. She takes in Chloe's still-damp hair. "Did you get caught in the rain?"

Chloe nods. It wasn't technically a lie.

Her mother smiles sympathetically then says, "Meatloaf and mashed potatoes for dinner, okay?" Before Chloe can answer, she continues, "I thought I'd bake some Kolaczki this evening." She's referring to the traditional jam-filled Polish cookies that her mother's own grandmother had taught her to bake as a child.

"I'm going to a party, remember?"

"Oh, that's right. At the Wright house." She raises her eyebrows and sucks in her cheeks. "Very fancy. Do you need a ride? Maybe Matt can take you."

Her friend Scott, who she's known since elementary school, has agreed to pick her up, and she lets her mother know. Like Chloe, Scott's just glad to have a reason for an invitation to Joe Wright's party.

"Oh, little Scotty Dolan. I haven't seen him in so long." Maggie Nicholson beams at Chloe, and it makes Chloe feel awful. "Well, if dinner isn't ready by the time you leave, I'll make you a sandwich. I just bought a pound of chipped ham."

Chloe has learned not to argue, but it's been a struggle to lose weight in a house where food seems to be everyone's preferred communication method.

Her mother moves around the kitchen, humming tunelessly. Maggie is not a tall woman, but now nearly sixty years old, her body is generous, and her face shows its age. It's a good face. Kind, trusting, and loving. Even when life may not have been kind to her mother, the woman hasn't lost her optimistic nature.

Chloe hesitates for a minute then says, "Have you talked to Matt recently?"

"Well, of course I've talked to him. I talk to him every day."

"I mean, like, have you had a conversation with him about his plans and his future?"

Maggie pulls a massive package of wrapped ground beef out of one of the bags and sets it on the counter. "Matty just needs some time to figure out what it is he wants to do. He's a late bloomer, probably because it took so long for the good Lord to bless me with him. I'm happy to have him as long as he wants to be here." Her tone is ever so slightly defensive, and Chloe tries again.

"What I mean is, have you thought maybe there's something else going on with him. Maybe there's some…mental health issues."

Despite her attempt to be as gentle as possible, Chloe's mother spins around. "Chloe," she scolds. "There is absolutely nothing wrong with your brother. For goodness' sake. What has gotten into you?" She turns back to the groceries. "You get invited to this party with your fancy new friends and then become a little too big for your britches."

"I'm not saying it to be mean, Mom. I just—I think it might be good for someone to have a conversation with him."

"I did not ask your opinion on how to raise my own son, young lady, thank you very much. Matthew is just fine."

Her mother continues putting the groceries into their place in cupboards and on shelves. But the humming has stopped, replaced by the banging of doors against wood.

Effectively dismissed, Chloe walks back down the hallway. She can no longer hear the electronic notes of the video game. There is no sound at all coming from Matt's room, and Chloe debates whether she should knock on the door. She decides against it, and showers instead.

By the time she has shimmied into her clothes, dried her wavy hair, and fastened a few strategic pieces of hair in a clip above her ears, she's nearly forgotten about Matt. She carefully applies more eye makeup than she normally wears for school and smudges the black eyeliner and brown eyeshadow across her lids. She applies two coats of black mascara and coats her lips with a nude-colored gloss.

When she's finished, she studies herself in the mirror with a critical eye. The end effect is definitely passable, and while she'll never be as graceful and beautiful as Megan Richards or as thin and edgy as Sutton Schultz, she feels…okay. She thinks she might even look pretty.

She hears her father's small pickup truck pull into the driveway next to Matt's car, and when she finally leaves the room to wait for Scott to pick her up, her dad is in the kitchen, which smells like beef and onions. Walter Nicholson is still in his dusty work clothes. He glances over at Chloe, then does an honest-to-goodness double take. "Glow Worm," he exclaims. "Is that you?"

She smiles at him.

Her mother is cutting up cucumbers for a salad. She glances over at Chloe, too, but she doesn't smile.

"You're a knockout, sweetheart."

"It's pretty crazy what a little makeup can do," she says, and shifts from one foot to the other.

"Don't sell yourself short. You've really come out of your shell this year. Just in time for college and the next part of your life." He pops a cherry tomato into his mouth. "We need to transfer some of your newfound confidence to Matt."

Her mother's knife clatters onto the cutting board. "Will you both just lay off Matt, please?" She stomps to the refrigerator and pulls out some carrots which she then scrubs furiously in the sink.

Her father frowns and looks at Chloe, who glances away.

He doesn't seem to be overly bothered by his wife's mood, and he turns his attention back to Chloe. "So, this party you're headed to… It's at the Wright house?"

Chloe nods.

"Bought a car once from Bill Wright. I assume the parents will be there?"

Chloe's heart sinks. Up to this point, no one has asked for any details about the party, and she doesn't want to lie to her dad. "I don't think Joe would have people over without his parents at home," she says, hoping that her response would be enough to sidestep the question.

"I suppose not," her dad says, frowning. "So, no alcohol then."

It was more of a statement than a question, but Chloe can feel the heat climb up her throat. She doesn't answer.

"You know to refuse if someone offers you alcohol, right? Nothing good can come from a high school party where drinking is involved."

Her mother sighs noisily and turns on her husband. "Walter, Chloe isn't going to drink. We didn't raise delinquents."

It isn't until this very moment that Chloe wonders what had possessed her to tell her parents the truth about her destination that evening. She could have told them that she was watching movies at Jessica's house or going out for dinner with Katie and her family. She'd been friends with Jessica and Katie since elementary school. Her parents wouldn't have questioned those plans at all.

But neither Jessica nor Katie had been invited to tonight's party, and they were both barely speaking to her these days. Like her mother, they thought she'd gotten a bit too big for her britches. And maybe a part of Chloe *did* think she had outgrown her old friends, if she were being honest with herself.

"What time do you think you'll be home?" her dad asks.

"She's eighteen, Walter."

"Nothing good happens after midnight, Maggie."

"I'll be home by midnight," Chloe says, hiding the trepidation in her voice the best she could.

"Well, if you need anything, call the house phone. We'll wait up."

Her mother must have decided she was no longer quite as angry with Chloe because she turns from the prepared salad and says, "Do you want me to make you a ham sandwich with some potato chips?"

Chloe shakes her head just as a horn honks outside the house. "I'm sure there will be pizza and snacks." She has no idea if this is true. "Scott's here. I'll see you both later."

Her dad kisses her cheek, and her mom gives her a wave. "Make good choices," she says. It's an off-the-cuff comment more than it is a demand. But it makes Chloe pause with her hand on the doorknob.

It's far too late for that.

CHAPTER 23

JOE-NOW

Joe sits by his dad's side and watches him sleep. He tries to reconcile this diminished figure with the man who used to intimidate him when he was a kid. Not because William Wright had been especially large, menacing, or angry, but because the man had been so damn sure of himself at all times. Joe has tried to mimic that confidence, but he usually just comes off as arrogant. He worries that the arrogant part of his personality has stuck without the substance that his father had.

The nurse—Angela—had warned them that Dad would sleep a lot because of the number and high doses of pain medication he was taking. Opioids, anticonvulsants, corticosteroids, antidepressants, anesthetics. Joe had been shocked at the amount of pills that were doled out in a day.

Paige walks into the room and stands beside him. She smells slightly spicy from her flavored cigarettes that their mother makes her smoke on the back deck. "How are you doing?" she asks softly.

He watches the steady rise and fall of his dad's chest. There is a slight rattle coming from his lungs. Faint, but he can hear the gurgling. After a moment, he glances up at his sister. He doesn't answer her question but asks, "How are *you*?"

She nods. "I'm okay. You know. It's tough for all of us."

He's not sure if their dad can hear them. He'd heard that people who were in comas or unconscious could be affected by the conversations around them. His dad is only sleeping as a result of being drugged out of his mind, but Joe figures they'd better be mindful of their words. Just in case.

"Where's Vivian?" Paige asks.

"She's dressing for dinner. We're going to take a break, have dinner at the Crawford Inn." It occurs to him that his sister has been dealing with a lot. More than he has and for much longer. "You're welcome to join us."

"Thanks, but I'll pass. I bought some steaks and wine. Mom and I are bingeing a new show."

"You and Mom have gotten close." He remembers some of the knock-down, drag-out fights that Paige had had with their mother when she'd been a young teenager.

"That's what happens when you screw up your life so badly that you're forced to move home with your tail between your legs." She says this with a wry smile, but Joe can hear the wound beneath the words. "Can't all be perfect like Joe." This, too, is said lightly.

He studies her. Is there envy there? Resentment?

"It's been helpful for me to be here. I'm sure Mom would have managed just fine on her own, but this…" Paige waves her hand around. "This has been harder on her than she'll let on."

"I still don't understand why no one called me."

"That was all Dad." She taps their father's hand lightly with her fingertip. The skin is translucent and loose and bruised.

Joe remembers his strong, firm handshake.

"He didn't want to worry or distract you."

Joe wants to be angry, but all of that fire has been extinguished, at least for today.

Paige removes her hand and cracks her knuckles. "I had

some reservations when Vivian showed up, but I'm glad she's here," Paige says. "She's different than I thought."

"You've met her before."

"Sure, at holiday dinners, family weddings. Before this morning, I'm not sure I've ever had an entire conversation with her."

This is Joe's fault. He's succeeded beautifully in staying away. "What did you two talk about this morning?"

"Nothing important. What it was like growing up here. What kind of father Dad was. She asked about my marriages, and I gave her the Cliffs Notes version. She wanted to know what little Joey Wright was like." Paige bumps her shoulder into his. "I told her that I was much too young for a report on little Joey, but I could give her a report on teenage Joseph."

"And what did you tell her?"

"That you were a jerk then, just like you're a jerk now." Paige laughs, but Joe does not. Her laughter fades and she says, "I just told her you were a typical older brother. You know. Played sports, hung out with your friends. It's not like we were exactly close enough that I had much information to share."

"You didn't tell her about that night?"

"What night?"

Joe looks over at her to see if she's being coy or flip. But she looks genuinely bemused.

He hesitates. "The night of the party."

"Jesus, Joe. No. Why would I do that?"

He doesn't remind her that she'd mentioned the accident in Vivian's presence that very morning. And why *would* she do that? Paige wasn't at the house that night. Maybe she didn't even know about all of the aftereffects of the party. The investigation, the accusations, the other more personal ramifications.

"She did ask about Sutton, though," Paige says carefully. "She said you'd seen her at the hospital."

Joe stiffens.

"Pretty coincidental that Sutton's mother is Dad's nurse. Given…everything else."

"What is that supposed to mean?"

"I mean, you know. The rumors about you and Sutton after graduation."

Joe wishes he could erase the entire thing from his past—what happened between them. If he could take any of it away, Megan Richards would still be alive. "I can't believe she told you any of that," Joe says, half under his breath, furious.

"Who?"

"Who do you think? Mom."

Paige shakes her head. "Mom didn't tell me anything. She's never said a word about any of that."

Joe's blood runs cold as the meaning of her words sinks in. "Then who told you?"

"They were rumors, Joe. It was a long time ago."

"Who told you?" he repeats, raising his voice.

"Joe, I honestly don't remember. Keep your voice down." Paige glances at their father.

"So, you're telling me that someone just casually mentioned this speculation about your brother in passing when you were fourteen years old, and you don't remember who it was?"

"It wasn't when I was fourteen. It was years later. You were long gone by the time I heard the story."

"And what *is* the story you heard?"

"Can we not do this in front of Dad?"

Joe stands and stalks to the other side of the room, furious and embarrassed, of all things. For all these years, he's assumed that no one, except for his parents and Ryan

Tolbert, had ever known about him and Sutton. Sure, everyone had seen them together that night, but after the accident, he'd only had one more direct conversation with her. It hadn't gone well, but eventually, the situation had worked itself out the way it should have.

Paige follows slowly, her arms crossed tightly over her chest. She's wearing an athletic shirt with a logo from a college she did not attend. "I don't know why you're making such a big deal out of this," she says. "It was twenty years ago."

"Because it's my life, Paige. And it's private."

"Nothing is ever private in Conway."

It's why he hates this place so goddamn much. "Can you just tell me what you heard?"

She sighs, resigned. "That you slept with Sutton, got her pregnant, and then paid her to have an abortion."

Joe stares out the window, at the breeze gently swaying the branches of the trees back and forth. It looks so calm and peaceful out there. All of nature in harmony; everything in unity. He tries to breathe in some of that serenity while his heart is pounding furiously in his chest.

He does his best to keep his voice calm and measured. "And you never thought to question this? Ask yourself if it was true?"

"Of course I did, Joe. I assumed it was a rumor. Most people assumed it was a story. Just townie gossip."

"You never asked me about it."

She scoffs. "Right, because we've always been so close," she says sarcastically. "I was just going to call you up while you were away at grad school or wherever." She flings her arms in front of her. "Oh, hey, Joe," she says in a falsely chipper voice. "I know I haven't talked to you in four years, but can you tell me if you knocked up a random girl in high school and then forced her to abort her baby?"

"You don't believe it then?"

Paige rolls her eyes. "You seem to have this weird belief that everyone's thoughts and opinions are centered on you. Like, nothing can move forward unless everyone considers what Joe Wright might possibly be doing or what opinions he has. Let me tell you, no one cares about what you're doing even a quarter as much as you think they do. I honestly could not have cared any less about what happened between you and Sutton Schultz when you were in high school. When I heard the rumor, it was a four-year-old story. And as much as I didn't really care then, I care even less now."

He tolerates her diatribe because he doesn't have a choice. But he'd barely listened to a word she'd said. "You didn't answer my question."

She sucks in a breath and lets it out through clenched teeth. "Fine," she finally says. "Up until ten minutes ago, I didn't really believe the rumor, as little as I've thought about it over the years. But now...I might."

He glares at her, and she tilts her chin up. "People who are innocent in a situation don't act the way that you're acting. But whether it's true or not, it was twenty years ago. You were young and stupid. You made a mistake. Get over yourself." Her voice has gotten progressively louder.

Vivian comes down the stairs and rushes into the room. "Hey," she says glancing at the sleeping figure of Joe's father as she approaches. "What's going on?"

Paige pokes a finger toward Joe. "Your husband really is an asshole." She turns and storms out of the room.

Vivian turns her attention to Joe. "What happened?"

He shakes his head. "She's a brat, just like she's always been."

His wife gives him a reproachful look. "You two need to try to get along. Your dad doesn't need this negative energy, and neither does your mom." She places a calming hand on his arm. "Let's just get out of this house for a little while and try to relax. Okay?"

Joe's temper immediately begins to rise all over again. Ever since the girls had come along—maybe even before— Vivian has fallen into the habit of mothering Joe like she did her daughters. It's insulting and condescending, and he certainly doesn't need that right now on top of everything else. But he bites his tongue.

He doesn't feel like going out to dinner. What he'd like to do is go home. To *his* home. He nearly tells Vivian that he's not up for a night out. The words are on the tip of his tongue.

And then it occurs to him that if he doesn't take the opportunity to get away, he will be stuck here. Even if he rejects his wife and decides to take a drive alone to cool off, there isn't anywhere for him to go.

Vivian is waiting for a response, and he is pouting. He's not any better than his sister.

Joe grumbles an agreement and trudges upstairs to shower and dress for dinner. He takes his time in the bathroom, alternating between seething, stewing, and breathing in deep calming breaths. He half expects Vivian to be in the bedroom when he emerges, but the room is empty. Vivian is giving him a wide berth, for which he is simultaneously grateful and resentful.

He's acting like such a child.

After he dresses, he plods back down the stairs. His wife is standing in front of the fireplace mantel, studying the family photos displayed there. Some of his petulance disappears at the sight of her.

She looks beautiful, as usual, in a seafoam-colored cashmere sweater and a pair of light brown leggings with well-made fawn-colored boots. While many men may not notice how their wives dress, Joe always appreciates Vivian's efforts to accentuate her appearance in the most understated way. The irony of it is that she could be wearing a brown paper sack; she would look just as stylish and beautiful as she does in the most high-end clothing and jewelry. Beyond her looks, she is intelligent, kind, caring, and an amazing mother. She is nearly perfect.

Despite his earlier frustration with her coddling, his anger has abated, but his brooding has not. He does not deserve Vivian. Being back in his parents' home—in his hometown—continues to make that abundantly clear.

On the far side of the room, his mother is sitting next to his dad, who is propped up against his pillows, eyes open. Joe attempts to quell his moodiness. He walks over and puts a hand on Bill's shoulder. "Glad to see you're awake."

Sandra holds a small can of ginger ale in her hand. A bendable straw wobbles precariously from the silver top, and she steadies the straw and holds it to her husband's lips.

"How are you feeling?" Joe asks.

"Never been better." The response is quick, and even though the voice is weak, Joe can't help but smile.

"You've been sleeping so much."

"That's the medicine," his mother answers for her husband. She's still a bit standoffish with Joe. Her responses to him are short, her expression tight. But Joe knows that this is the extent of the acknowledgement of any conflict. The tension will simply seep away, leaving tender emotions to eventually scab over and scar.

"I can hear what you're saying," his father says mildly, and this gives Joe pause. Was he referencing his wife's tendency to respond on his behalf or the earlier conversation between Paige and Joe?

Joe doesn't ask the question aloud, and instead addresses his mother. "Is the nurse coming back?"

She nods. "Between six and seven."

Joe pulls his phone from his pocket and glances at it. It's only five. With any luck, by the time he and Vivian return from dinner, Angela Schultz will be gone.

"Do you want us to bring you anything back or pick anything up on the way home?"

"Vivian has already offered, and I told her that I'd let her know." She doesn't look at Joe when she answers.

Joe lingers a second longer then gives his dad's shoulder a squeeze. Bill gives him a half smile and a weak wave of his hand.

The ride into town with his wife is quiet. Vivian seems pensive, but Joe doesn't question it. He needs to remember that this situation must be overwhelming for her, too. While his family is pleasant enough, they're not much more than strangers to her. And he knows how hard it is for her to be without her daughters. He needs to be more patient with her. More generous.

As Joe steers onto Falgan Road toward town, as always, he steadfastly ignores the tree with its shiny balloons and wilting flowers. When the anniversary occurs, he supposes members of Megan's family will once again adorn the tree with trinkets and other symbols of remembrance. With the date fast approaching, Joe would prefer to be far away from Conway.

"What happened there?" Vivian asks, pointing toward the tree.

Something in her voice makes him think she already knows. He considers lying or simply shrugging her question away. But his uncertainty of the extent of her knowledge causes him to respond instead, "A girl died in a car accident a long time ago."

"Did you know her?"

He keeps his eyes on the road in front of him, and the

glint of a flattened Mylar balloon reflects in his side mirror, despite the dreariness of the day. "I knew her."

He braces for more questions, but none come. Instead, Vivian looks out the window and doesn't speak again until they arrive at the restaurant.

The Crawford Inn is located in a dated standalone structure along the town's main street. On the side of the building, facing a paved parking lot, a slightly faded mural depicts a scene of well-dressed men and women boarding a train at a station marked *Conway*. Based on the figures' clothing, Joe assumes the time period to be the late nineteenth century, when the coal town and transportation hub was in its prime. While the elaborate painting must have been commissioned years ago, Joe hasn't been in town to see it.

As Vivian climbs out of the car, she stares up at the mural, which Joe has to admit is impressive and a bit more culturally significant than he would have given the city officials credit for commissioning.

Inside the rustic interior of the establishment, a young, professional-looking girl wearing an all-black uniform greets them at a wooden podium. She asks if they have reservations, and when Joe answers, "No," she arches an eyebrow, and says, "You're lucky you arrived early." She gives them a small smile and shows them to a table in the corner of the dining room.

The tablecloths are pressed and white, and the silverware is arranged precisely on linen napkins.

"This is lovely," Vivian says after a server brings them a bottle of sparkling water and two menus in thick burgundy portfolios embossed with gold lettering.

Joe nods, distracted. He doesn't remember the place being upscale. But it's been over twenty years since he dined here with his parents, and the restaurant likely has changed management more than once.

When their server, a young man wearing the same black outfit and a white waist apron, returns, he lists the specials—fresh trout with pan-roasted fingerling potatoes and a porcini-crusted filet mignon with eggplant caponata—which would rival any restaurant in the city. Vivian orders a glass of very good sauvignon blanc, and Joe requests a locally brewed craft beer before the server nods crisply and leaves them alone to peruse the dinner menus and make their decisions.

They have the place mostly to themselves, though a few other older couples are scattered about the large dining room.

When the server returns with their drinks and takes their order, Joe decides on the filet and Vivian chooses the trout. After the man commits their orders to memory, nods his approval, and hastens away, Joe takes a long drink of the bottled beer, eschewing the chilled glass. He shuts his eyes and stretches his neck to his right and then to his left. For the first time since yesterday morning, he feels somewhat normal.

When he opens his eyes again, he catches Vivian watching him carefully as she sips her wine. "What?" he asks.

She lifts a shoulder. "You're just…different, that's all."

"Different how?"

"I don't know." She seems to be concentrating on choosing her words correctly. "Tense. On edge. I know the situation is difficult, but it's more than that."

"I haven't been back in a while," he responds.

"I don't go home often either, and when I do, I may feel a vague pull of nostalgia. But you…" She pauses, assessing him. She doesn't appear to like what she sees. "You seem almost at war with yourself. With this place. I don't understand it."

Joe remembers Paige's earlier comment—that others aren't thinking about him nearly as much as he is thinking about himself. And maybe that's true. But he can't shake the feeling that Conway is pulsing with some ancient evil, and he is at the center of it. He doesn't say any of this to Vivian. Instead, he quips, "My dad is dying, Vivian. That's putting a bit of a damper on my mood."

It is the first time he's said those words out loud, and despite the sarcasm, he is shocked at the emotional gut-punch they deliver. He feels a hard lump form in the back of his throat, and he stands quickly. "Excuse me."

He registers her saying, "Joe," as he hurries away, but he doesn't turn back around.

The restroom smells of lemon and bleach, and Joe stands at the sink with the water running over his hands. An adult contemporary song from the eighties is playing over the speaker. It had probably been playing in the dining room, too, but the high ceilings and voices of the diners and servers had swallowed up the melody. The vocalist lyrically laments a fight between the present and the past while bitterly sacrificing the future to conflict.

Joe doesn't want to admit that the words are dangerously close to his current feelings, so he covers the music with the static of the high-powered hand dryer and takes a few deep breaths before heading back to Vivian.

To the right of their table, a group of three adults and four children—all of whom seem to be sullen and restless—are just settling into their seats, jostling for position. Joe wonders what would possess the parents to bring two babies and a toddler to a restaurant like this one. He is aware that the adults seem to be looking at him, and he studiously avoids eye contact. Again, Paige's words echo in his mind—*No one cares about what you're doing even a quarter as much as you think they do.*

He turns his attention to his wife. On the table in front of her, a basket of bread has been served. It remains untouched, and Vivian purposefully avoids eye contact with him.

"I'm sorry," Joe says as he sits down. "I'm just…not dealing with any of this well."

"I'm not your enemy," she responds, her chin raised, and her eyes focused on a spot on the wall to her side. "I'm your wife. And you're shutting me out."

He is about to apologize yet again with a promise to open up more to her when a deep voice sings out across the room. "Oh. My. God. Could that possibly be the elusive Joe Wright gracing us with his presence?"

Joe blinks, and when he opens his eyes, he sees a man who looks very much like an aged version of his old friend Ryan Tolbert walking toward him. Joe is mildly surprised to find that he's happy to see this face from his past. Ryan had been one of the few people he considered a close friend once upon a time. Though they haven't stayed in touch, he has mostly fond memories of Ryan.

Joe introduces Ryan to Vivian, and Ryan says all of the appropriate and charming things to his wife without insulting Joe.

"So, you still live here?" Joe asks.

"Yeah, I live behind the library, up on Kensington. Started out teaching at the high school, and now I'm the principal."

"No kidding," Joe says with a laugh. "I bet Mr. Wandel wouldn't be so thrilled with that development," he says, referring to their own high school principal.

Ryan cocks his head. "You know, we grow up; get wiser. Mr. Wandel and I keep in touch these days." Ryan gestures between Joe and Vivian. "And you two seem like you're killing it with your dealerships. A partnership with Keith

Jenkins? That's huge, man."

"That's all Joe," Vivian says. "I'm just in the background for moral support."

Joe shoots his wife a look filled with both gratitude and accusation. Her words aren't even remotely true, and she knows it.

"Just like his old man," Ryan responds. "Speaking of which, how's he doing? I imagine it's been a little tough since his diagnosis. Probably hard on your mom."

Two children at the neighboring table start to wail loudly, and all three of them look over. Joe catches the older of the two women at the table staring back at him with blatant hostility on her face, which he finds ironic. It's her family that's ruining the atmosphere for everyone else.

Joe quickly looks back at his old friend. "His diagnosis?"

"Leukemia, isn't it? Holly's aunt—" He stops himself. "You remember Holly Griffin? Well, Holly Tolbert now." He gestures behind him, and a pretty, plump woman waves gregariously back. "Anyway, Holly's aunt was diagnosed with the same thing a few years ago. It was hard on everyone."

Joe is confused. How is it possible that Ryan knows about his dad's diagnosis—has known for some time, apparently—and Joe has just found out? It's clear that not only is he the last in the family to find out about his dad, but he may also well be the last in Conway to know what's been going on with his own family.

"If you need anything, I'm sure Holly would be happy to talk with you or your mom about the experience."

"Uh…thanks," Joe says, and all of the joy he'd felt for this reunion with his old friend fades away. He can feel Vivian's sympathy emanating from her, and he doesn't want that either.

The server is heading their way with a tray of food, and

Ryan moves out of the way to let him pass. "I'll let you enjoy your dinner," he says and turns to walk away. But before he gets five feet from them, he turns back around. "Oh, but before I go, in case we don't get a chance to talk before you leave. It's coming up on the twentieth anniversary of—" He pauses. "Well, you know," he finishes. "Megan Richards."

Joe's world tilts slightly.

"I'm having an assembly at the high school a few weeks before this year's graduation ceremony about the dangers of drinking and driving. Megan's parents have agreed to speak, and a few of the emergency responders from that night. I've invited Dan Armstrong to say a few words, too, but I doubt he'll show up. I can't blame him."

If Ryan notices the horror on Joe's face, he doesn't let on.

He holds out his hands and continues enthusiastically. "If you're going to be in town, you're welcome to come and talk about how you got to know Megan; what a great girl she was. You're a local celebrity around here, so your words would mean something." Ryan gives him a lopsided smile. "You can also talk about the party if you want, but I know that might be sticky with how everything went down afterward." He waves his hand in front of him. "That's beside the point, anyway. What we really want to do is pay tribute to Megan and remind these kids that our dumb decisions can have real-life consequences. We all know that better than anyone. Am I right?"

The server has delivered their meals and disappeared discreetly. But all Joe can see is Ryan looking exceedingly pleased with himself. Joe is speechless.

Ryan seems to be waiting for some kind of reaction, but when none comes, he says, "You don't need to give me an answer right now. I'll get your number before you leave." With a wave he starts back to his own table, only to be distracted by the family of seven next to them. "Oh, hey, Becky," Joe hears Ryan say. And then he hears nothing else. Because when he looks up at his wife, her head is cocked, and her eyes are narrowed. The plate of trout is cooling in front of her.

"Joe," she says slowly. "Who is Megan Richards?"

CHAPTER 24

CHLOE-NOW

Joe Wright is walking toward her. In the flesh and blood. Chloe had thought the woman at the table next to the crew of them looked familiar, but out of context and at the Crawford Inn, it hadn't occurred to her that she could possibly be the beautiful woman from the commercial she'd seen just hours earlier. The woman whose social media she regularly stalks. Vivian Wright, in her light green sweater, is just as gorgeous as the woman from social media, but much more understated and refined as she sips her wine quietly, looking up at her approaching husband with a slight frown marring her pretty face.

One of Jason's twin boys, a petulant look on his face, throws a soggy cracker on the floor. Across from her, Becky leans forward to pick it up. The other twin grabs his mother's hair with a slobbery hand. "Liam, stop," Becky says. Jason makes movements as if he might do something, grab something, say something. But in the end, he does nothing but reach into the air.

Chloe has been watching Jason and his new family with a mystified sort of bemusement, but after she catches sight of Joe, she can't keep her eyes off him. His gaze passes right over her, though she swears that there is disgust in his eyes as he notices the commotion surrounding the children.

Once an arrogant ass, always an arrogant ass.

In the way their tables are positioned, Chloe has a view of both Joe and his wife. He leans forward and says something to her. Chloe wishes she could hear the words, but the three-year-old shrieks when the crayon she's been using to color the tablecloth snaps in half.

Chloe tries to read the lips of the beautiful couple, but in profile, she can't make out the formation of the words. If she has to guess, though, the wife is upset with Joe.

And then a masculine voice cuts through all the noise of the restaurant, and a man approaches Joe's table, fawning over him as if he's a beloved celebrity—the town's prodigal son.

Becky's head whips around, and she says with something akin to worship, "Oh, it's Principal Tolbert."

Chloe looks at her ex-husband's wife. "Ryan Tolbert?"

"Do you know him?" Becky breathes, her eyes wide.

"Not really." But Chloe certainly remembers Ryan. He and Joe had been best friends once upon a time. Apparently, they aren't anymore. "Do *you* know him?" she asks Becky.

Becky nods. "I've been substitute-teaching at the high school a few days a week since Christmas. Keeps me from going crazy." As if on cue, one of the boys smacks a chubby hand against the other boy's cheek, and they both start wailing.

If there had been any hope of overhearing the conversation, it is lost now. Joe Wright looks over and catches Chloe's eye. She forces herself to stare right back at him. Again, there's no recognition there. It's funny that ruining someone's life doesn't obligate the recollection of said ruined person in the future. She feels foolish. All of these years she's spent so much energy hating Joe Wright, and the man doesn't even know she exists.

Jason's daughter, Harper, has calmed down thanks to Emma, who has somehow produced a paper placemat.

Tears still hover at the edges of the young girl's eyelashes, but Emma and Harper are now peacefully coloring at the other end of the table. At least two of Jason's children are composed. Chloe is pleased that it is the girls.

As Becky pacifies the twins, Chloe thinks she hears Ryan Tolbert say something about a diagnosis. Is that the reason Joe might be in town? She knows she shouldn't take pleasure in someone else's misfortune, but there is a very small, shameful part of her that wishes Joe the same kind of pain that she's experienced.

She lifts her glass to take a drink of water.

A server delivers meals to Joe and his wife, and Ryan Tolbert turns to walk away before turning back around. There is a lull in the general conversation and noise of the restaurant. As Ryan turns back toward Joe's table, Chloe hears, clear as a bell, "It's coming up on the twentieth anniversary of…well, you know. Megan Richards."

Her water glass nearly slips from her fingers. Chloe hasn't been able to fully move on from what happened in high school, but she'd thought the town might have forgotten. Apparently not.

The din in the dining room picks up again, and next to her, Becky is talking loudly to Jason. Chloe loses the thread of the conversation across from them, but judging by the look on Joe's face, he is as surprised and displeased with the topic as Chloe is. And then Ryan walks away from Joe, and Becky seizes the opportunity to call out, "Principal Tolbert! Hello."

He turns. "Oh, hey, Becky," he says. He looks around the table. "Out with the family I see." He gives Chloe a wan smile. Just like Joe Wright and Nate Kasinski, he clearly does not recognize her.

Becky says, "This is my husband Jason, and his ex-wife Chloe."

Chloe sees a flash of recognition, but it's gone as quickly as it had appeared. He just nods a greeting to them both.

"I heard you saying something about an assembly," Becky says. "I have a pretty full schedule already for the rest of the school year, but I'm happy to help out if you need an extra set of hands."

Ryan appears slightly taken aback. "I was just telling Joe Wright about it." He gestures behind him at Joe's table. "He used to live around here. And I appreciate the offer, but I think we're all covered. It's going to be a conversation with Megan Richards' parents about the dangers of drinking and driving."

At Becky's blank look, Ryan continues, "She's a girl that Joe and I graduated with. We'd all attended a party a few weeks before graduation, and Megan got in the wrong car with the wrong person." He shakes his head. "It was…tragic. I not only want to continue to honor Megan's memory, but I also want our kids to know what can happen when you drink and drive. I want them to realize the consequences. The lives that can be affected."

Jason catches Chloe's eye.

Becky, however, is oblivious, and says, "That's just awful. And you said that was twenty years ago?"

He nods once, solemnly.

Something seems to click in Becky's brain. "Oh, the marker out on Falgan Road. Jason, that's the girl that Chloe knew?" She looks at Chloe. "The one from the party you went to?" Becky makes a face that Chloe assumes is meant to indicate her sympathy, but the woman's expression manifests as a grimace. "So sad."

Chloe stares at her ex-husband.

Jason stammers, "I—I may have, uh, mentioned it to Becky."

Ryan's gaze has now landed on Chloe, and he cocks his

head. "Chloe," he says slowly, recognition dawning. "Chloe Nicholson."

By this time, Emma is listening with interest from the other end of the table.

"Oh, wow," Ryan says. "Yeah, of course. I didn't realize you still lived around here."

"I don't," she says tightly.

"It was terrible, what happened after. With your brother…" His words trail off. She stares at the man until he shifts uncomfortably. "You're welcome to join the assembly as well, if you'd like."

"I would not," she says, her words clipped, decisive.

He purses his lips. "Right."

One of the twins chokes on a cracker and starts coughing violently. Becky and Jason immediately abandon the conversation to tend to the child, while two servers appear with their dinners. Ryan walks away, and Becky is the only one who acknowledges his departure. "See you Monday, Principal," she calls.

Jason says softly, "I'm sorry, Clo. I couldn't have known that they'd all be here."

"You told her about all of it? Even Matt?" It's a quiet question, filled with accusation and betrayal. Jason has always known that Chloe does not like to talk about that period in her life, and while she knows she can't expect that Jason won't say things to Becky… Well, she was once his wife, too.

"I never thought it would come up like this."

"I'm his *wife*," Becky says. The words are more defensive than they are territorial. "Besides, I didn't say anything about you bringing the alcohol."

Chloe stares at Jason, open-mouthed. "You told her that, too?" she whispers furiously. "Jesus, Jason."

As the other twin starts to gear up for a full-blown

meltdown, Emma approaches Becky from the other side of the table. "Can I hold him?"

Becky nods weakly, and Chloe says, "Emma, you need to eat something." But no one objects when the girl lifts the squirming baby from the highchair and takes him to sit on her lap.

Chloe's attention wanders to Joe Wright and his wife. They are barely touching their food and appear to be engaged in a heated discussion. Chloe is fairly certain they're arguing over the subject of Ryan's visit to their table. The woman had appeared serene and dreamy, if a bit distracted, before their dinner arrived. Now her face is clouded, as if she might cry.

Chloe picks at her own dinner—she'd opted for the scallops with marcona almonds—but she barely tastes the food.

Jason's voice breaks into her thoughts. "Chloe?"

He says her name as a question, so she knows he's been trying to get her attention in his quiet, unobtrusive way. She's still furious with him, but she's not going to make a scene in the restaurant in front of Becky and Emma. Or Joe Wright. "What?"

"I thought maybe we could discuss the subject that came up when we spoke on the phone earlier."

When she doesn't respond, he says tentatively, "The possibility of Emma spending the summer with us."

Chloe takes a breath. Returning to Conway had brought back all of the awful memories and intersected her with all of the awful people who had been oblivious to her existence then and continued to be just as unaware of her now. Why Jason thinks she'd want to expose Emma to any of this is beyond her.

Then she looks over at Emma with one of the twins on her lap. She has no idea if it's Gavin or Liam. The baby is belly laughing at the faces Emma makes. Harper is alternating between chewing on her chicken nuggets and chattering at Emma about something.

Becky digs in her bag for a toy to distract the other moody twin babbling next to her, only half participating in the adult portion of the dinner because her children consume nearly all of her time and energy.

Chloe looks back at Jason, who is waiting expectantly for her answer. She simply says, "No."

His brows knit together, and he sets his mouth in a thin straight line, but he says nothing.

Becky looks up and opens her mouth, but Jason gives a little shake of his head, and she snaps it shut again.

There is a small part of Chloe that feels guilty, but the bigger part of her knows that she's doing the right thing for Emma. And based on what has happened at the table this evening, Chloe suspects that, should Emma accept the invitation, she will just end up as free childcare for the overwhelmed Becky while distracted Jason wanders around oblivious, like he always has.

Then Jason does speak up. "You know, Chloe, I've always been kind of in awe of you and your ability to take a shit situation and spin gold out of it through sheer willpower and brute force. When you decide something is going to happen, by God, it happens. But you also have the most infuriating ability to shut out anything that displeases you." He glances at his wife. "Becky is the best thing that's ever happened to me, so I'm glad things worked out between us the way they did, but, Chloe, you just discarded me. Threw me out of your existence and awareness. And it hurt."

Emma has stopped playing with the baby and is listening attentively.

"Jason, now isn't the time."

"Because it's never the right time for you, Chloe. And only *you* seem to get to decide what's the right time for everyone around you. Well, I'm not doing that anymore. You have removed me—" He gestures around the table. "Actually, you have removed *us* from your life, and you've tried to completely discount that Conway even exists. I know that bad things happened to you here, Chloe. I know that in your mind, Matt's death is inextricably linked with this place and that party and those people." He points at Joe and his wife, who look over at them.

"Jason, stop," Chloe orders through clenched teeth.

"I will not be silenced. Because as much as you wish it isn't the case, Emma is my daughter, too, and I love her just as much as I love Harper, Gavin, and Liam. I want to *know* her, Chloe. I want her to know her sister and brothers, and I want her to know this place. It's part of her. It's part of you, too. In one moment, twenty years ago, you got stuck in a whirlpool of regret and blame and guilt and shame. And as much as you want to pretend otherwise, this town is always there, looming in the back of your mind, and you just keep on running from it. I've gotta say—the harder and faster you run, the closer the pain is to you. If you don't come to terms with the past, you're going to spend the rest of your life running in place from a town and people who don't even know *you* exist."

When the speech is over, Jason is slightly out of breath. His voice had not been raised, but he'd spoken with an intensity that Chloe had never experienced—not once—in their marriage. She doesn't agree with anything he's said, and beyond that, she is embarrassed. He has embarrassed her publicly in front of half the town of Conway, in front of his wife, in front of her daughter. And what's worse, he's reduced Matt's death to a moment in time. He's diminished it to a memory, and he's taken away any fault for it, even if the ultimate blame lies with Chloe. There must be a reason for Matt's death; otherwise, nothing holds any meaning at all.

She very deliberately folds the napkin from her lap and sets it on the table beside her. She says to Emma, "I think it's time for us to go."

Emma's eyes are still wide, and she does not protest. She kisses each of the children on the forehead and gives her father a small smile and a weak, "Bye."

No one tries to stop them.

Once in the car, they are both quiet. Chloe can't stop playing Jason's words in her mind. She can't stop thinking about the surprised eyes of Joe Wright at the next table; the look of what could have been recognition that passed across his face. She can't stop thinking of her brother, and how twenty years has passed so quickly. How so much, yet so little, has changed.

They are nearly halfway home when Emma finally looks over and says, "Mom?"

"Hmm," she answers, loath to get into a long discussion right now. She is exhausted.

"I'm the one who asked to stay with Dad this summer."

Chloe takes two breaths through her nose before she reacts. "You want to live with your father?" She's not angry. She's just...numb.

"It's not that I want to live with him forever. It's just like Dad said—I have a whole family that I don't even know."

Chloe has often thought about Emma's position as an only child. She had assumed that her daughter liked being the center of attention, but perhaps she's been fooling herself. "We can visit more often, if you'd like. You can spend more weekends that don't interfere with your activities."

Emma makes a noise that sounds like a laugh. "The

activities are for you, and you know it."

"What on earth are you talking about?"

"The only reason I'm in so many things is so that you can say that I am. So you can prove your program works and that your child is the best of all the children. You want me to be the smartest, thinnest, most accomplished child so that you can brag about it to your work people."

"Emma, that's not true—"

"Yes, it is, Mom. You say that it's because you want me to be well-rounded, whatever *that* means. But you don't care about me. You don't care how I feel about anything."

Chloe eases the car to the side of the highway and shifts into park. As traffic whizzes past them, she turns and faces her daughter, whose face is mottled with anger in the slowly sinking daylight. Her hair needs a good brushing. "I do care about you. I care about you so much." She exhales. "Look," she says, resting her hands lightly on the steering wheel. "When I was a girl, my parents were amazing people, but they didn't have much money, and they didn't have much time. They were a lot older than the other parents, and they were just…out of touch."

Emma is staring straight ahead, but Chloe can tell she's listening.

"I loved them very much, and they did the best they could." Chloe chooses her next words carefully. "Emma, I made some decisions back then that changed the course of my future. Those decisions also changed the course of the future for others. I'm not blaming my parents for that. At all. But if they had been just a little bit more…attentive, things would have turned out much differently for me. *I* would have turned out much differently." She looks at her daughter. "I'm not saying that I make all of the right decisions now, for you, but I'm just trying to protect you from having to go through what I went through."

"Are you talking about your brother?" Emma asks after a second.

Chloe takes a chance and smooths Emma's hair away from her flushed face. "Partly, yes. But there were a lot of things leading up to that, too."

Emma's eyes are still angry, but some of the temper has fled. "What was the accident that Dad was talking about?"

Chloe wishes for what feels like the millionth time in their relationship that Jason had been a bit more cognizant of his surroundings. But she answers Chloe's question. "Right before I graduated from high school, I was invited to go to a party." She wets her lips. "I was not one of the beautiful, popular kids. I was a little overweight and a lot awkward."

"Like me," Emma interrupts.

"It's a totally different situation." Which is true. It's also true that Emma *is* a lot like Chloe was as a child. The difference is that Chloe is paying attention. "But I had worked really hard to lose weight and get in shape, and by the end of my last year in high school, I finally looked how I wanted to look. But I still felt like I was just pretending to belong. It wasn't enough that I had been invited to the party. I felt like I had to prove that I was worthy enough to be there. So…" She pauses and chooses her words. "I offered to bring all of the beer and the other alcohol."

"I thought you had to be twenty-one to drink alcohol."

Chloe nods. "You're supposed to be. You're also supposed to be twenty-one to *buy* alcohol."

"How did you get it then?"

"Your uncle Matt bought it for me."

"But he was older than you, wasn't he? He was older than twenty-one?"

"He was twenty-four."

"So, it was okay."

Chloe shakes her head. "It was okay for him to buy it for himself or for other adults, but it was against the law for him to buy it for a bunch of underaged teenagers. It wouldn't have been a big deal. No one ever would have known. Except a girl named Megan Richards, who was popular, beautiful, sweet, and kind—a girl everyone liked and wanted to be like—died in a car accident after leaving that party. The boy whose family owned the house where the party took place—they had a lot of money, a lot of power, and a lot of connections, so he didn't get in trouble. He pointed the police to me because I brought the alcohol. I had to tell them how I'd gotten it. And my brother—he wasn't equipped to deal with something like that. After the police came to question him, a few days later… That's when I found him in his room."

Chloe realizes that tears are streaming down her face as soon as she's stopped talking. She tries to dash them away with the back of her hand because she's telling her twelve-year-old this awful story. No child that young needs to hear something like this, let alone from her hysterical mother. "I'm sorry," she says in a wobbly voice, and then she realizes that Emma is crying too, and Chloe pulls her close, murmuring an apology over and over again.

Eventually, Emma asks, "Did you go to jail?" Her voice is muffled by Chloe's shoulder.

Chloe releases her daughter and sucks in a deep breath through her nose. She wipes her face and clears her throat. "No. After Matt died, Megan's family insisted that no charges be filed. The district attorney could have come after me, but he didn't. Still, all of it was too much for your grandmother and grandfather. They blamed themselves, and they both died within a few years."

"Did anyone go to jail?"

"The boy who was driving the car did."

"What happened to him?"

"I have no idea," Chloe says. She realizes that she hasn't thought about Dan Armstrong in ages even though she's thought about the party every day for the past twenty years. She's been too busy obsessing over Joe Wright.

Emma puts her hand in Chloe's like she used to when she was a child. "Do you think Matt would forgive you?"

Chloe thinks about that. She remembers the conversation with him the day of the party, when he'd tried to tell her there was something wrong with him. "Yes," she finally says. "I think he would."

"Do you think that Megan Richards would forgive you?"

Chloe smiles. She doesn't think Megan would have even blamed her in the first place. "I think so," she says to her daughter.

"Then maybe it's time that you forgave yourself."

Chloe looks at Emma and starts crying all over again.

CHAPTER 25

DAN-NOW

Dan groans as he opens one eye. The sun is streaming through the window of the back bedroom of Crystal's house. A drum pounds in his head, and he squeezes his eye shut again. His mouth is foul and dry, and he presses the heels of his hands into his eye sockets and kicks out of the tangle of sheets twisted around his bare legs in the twin bed. As the sheets fall to the floor, he hears the clink of a glass bottle toppling on its side.

He sits up too quickly, and the room tilts. But he manages to grab the bottle, which is empty. He sets it back down, right side up.

Now on the edge of the bed, he leans forward with elbows resting on knees and his forehead cradled in his palms.

After dinner last night, Crystal had insisted on tidying the kitchen, and Dan had gone out under the guise of grabbing more trash bags for his cousin. He'd bought the trash bags, along with a liter and a half of spiced rum. He'd drunk it alone in his room, and it had gone down easy.

He feels anything but easy now.

His phone lies on the floor next to him, and he picks it up. It's nine forty-five in the morning.

He's supposed to pick up Henry at ten.

He swears again and throws on the clothes he had worn

the day before. Before heading into the bathroom to brush his teeth and wash his face, he plugs his phone into the charger. When he stands, Crystal is in the doorway.

She eyes the empty bottle, but she doesn't say anything. "Heading out?" she asks instead.

"Picking up Henry for breakfast," he responds, squeezing past her. He is going to be late.

When he comes out of the bathroom, she is standing in the same place. "Dan, we need to talk."

"Can it wait until I get back?" He sits on the edge of the rumpled bed and stuffs his feet into his two-day-old socks. He will need to grab more clothes from the house, if Amber will let him inside.

He hears Crystal exhale and looks up. His cousin is biting her lip, and her brow is furrowed.

"What's wrong?" he asks.

She holds her hands out in front of her. "I don't want to hold you up. It's just that—" Her hands drop in front of her. She pauses.

"What?" he asks, annoyed. Crystal is an amazing person, but she's always had a hard time just saying what she means. There's usually hemming and hawing and roundabout discussions before she eventually, finally, and only sometimes gets to her point.

"The drinking," she says. She avoids looking at the bottle on the floor, but Dan glances at it.

"What about it?"

"Look, I know you're having a hard time lately. I understand…"

Dan rolls his eyes, and the movement hurts his head. He picks up the empty bottle of spiced rum and stands, sucking in a quick breath as he does so. His whole body hurts. "I've got to go," he mumbles and moves past her again.

She follows him down the stairs.

Frank is in the living room, staring at the television screen. The sound seems to be turned to the highest volume, and the narrator drones on about evidence of gold and silver in some sort of ancient pit. Frank doesn't look at Dan as he walks past.

Dan throws the empty bottle into the kitchen trash can, and looks in the refrigerator for a bottle of water.

"You still smell like booze," Crystal says from the other side of the room.

"Do you have any ibuprofen?"

She stares at him, as if she is debating whether or not to indulge him with the medication. Then she makes a noise and reaches into a high cabinet next to the refrigerator. She hands him the bottle of painkillers.

He shakes four pills into his hand and pops them into his mouth, chasing them with gulps of the cold water. His stomach roils, and he takes some steadying breaths.

"Dan, I'm worried about you."

"You can save it, Crystal. I'm fine. I just needed something to take the edge off."

"Is this why Amber kicked you out? Because of the drinking?"

"You know there's more to it than that."

"I don't actually. I don't know anything."

He shakes his head and heads for the back door, then realizes he's forgotten his keys. He hurries back up to the bedroom and grabs the keys and his phone, which he'd also forgotten.

When he comes back down, Crystal is wiping the spotless countertop furiously with a paper towel. She doesn't look at him, and guilt gets the better of him. "We'll talk when I get back, okay? I won't be gone long." He places his hand on the doorknob.

At the counter, Crystal hangs her head. "The last thing I

want to do is make things harder for you. But if the drinking doesn't stop, you can't stay here."

Dan goes still, then he turns around. "Are you serious?"

She shrugs helplessly. "I'm sorry, Dan. Frank doesn't want—"

"Frank," he scoffs, not caring that Frank is in the next room. He doubts the old man is able to hear him over the blaring television now spewing nonsense about the Knights Templar. "Frank told you that I can't stay here? After all you've done for him? Can he even wipe his own ass?"

"Dan," Crystal says sharply. Then she lowers her voice. "This isn't all Frank. I—I don't want to enable your behavior."

"I don't have a drinking problem, and you know it. What I do have is a problem with people treating me like I'm less than a piece of dog shit on the bottom of their shoe. My wife, my kids, Nate Kasinski, Sutton Schultz's mother. Everyone thinks I'm trash, Crystal. And now you're jumping on the bandwagon?" He has started yelling and his head is pounding. He might vomit.

But then Frank lumbers into the kitchen, moving faster than Dan knew he could. "What's going on?" he roars, looking at Crystal who has started to cry. He turns on Dan. "How dare you drag your drunk ass into my house and then make my wife cry. All she's ever done is try to help you. Not sure why. It seems like you're beyond help, if you ask me."

"Nobody asked you, Frank," Dan yells.

"Get out," Frank yells back, and Crystal shrieks, "Stop it! Both of you."

They do.

She takes two deep breaths as if to steady herself. "Dan, go see your son. Frank, go watch your show." She turns to Dan. "We'll talk about this when you get back."

Frank crosses his arms. "I don't want him back here."

"Don't worry," Dan says, yanking the door open. "I'll be out of your hair tonight." He slams the door shut behind him, half expecting Crystal to rush out after him. She doesn't.

He glances at his phone. It's now after ten and there's a missed call from Amber.

He doesn't both calling back. He takes the roads in town faster than he should and thanks heaven for light Sunday morning traffic. It only takes five minutes to drive from the west side of town to the south side, but he knows his wife will be furious and his son will be disappointed.

He pulls into the driveway with a spray of gravel, walks to the front door and knocks. No one answers. He knocks again, louder. Again, no answer. He'd pulled into the driveway behind Amber's minivan, so she's definitely home. From behind the closed door, he can hear Mason squealing either in delight or frustration. He can't tell which.

"This is ridiculous," he mumbles under his breath, and he pulls open the storm door then cautiously enters the house.

"Hello?" he calls.

Amber's voice comes from somewhere on the second floor, but it's the commotion from the kitchen that draws his attention. He hears Sam yelp, then Luke bellow, "Seriously, how stupid can you possibly be?"

When Dan walks into the room, an entire gallon of milk is pouring from an overturned plastic jug onto the floor, and both boys watch it glug out of its container. Dan's first instinct is to yell, but he swallows that down and instead snatches up the carton, trying to avoid stepping on the puddle that has begun to spread across the linoleum floor.

"Go get a towel," he instructs Luke as Sam's face crumples. "Make it two towels," he calls to Luke's retreating back, and he rubs his younger son's shoulder before throwing the nearly empty carton into the sink. "It's fine," he says. "Just a bit of milk. No use in crying over it." He smiles at his own joke, but Sam doesn't smile back.

The boy dashes away tears from his eyes. "What are you doing here?" his son demands instead.

Dan attempts to hide the hurt that comes with the question and keeps his voice as neutral as possible when he answers, "I came to pick up Henry."

Luke comes back into the kitchen with the towels, and Dan soaks up most of the milk before Amber walks into the room with a red-faced Mason on her hip. She sighs when she sees the mess, then she gathers a visibly upset Sam beneath her free arm as Dan moves the towels around the floor.

He feels her studying him and when he looks up, she says, "You look like shit."

For a minute, he considers lying. He thinks about telling her he's doing just great, having a fantastic time with Crystal and Frank. She'd know he was lying, but it was the principle of the situation. In the end, he's too tired to lie. "Yeah, well, I feel like shit."

The older boys have fled the room, leaving Dan alone with Amber, Mason babbling but calm for a change. She also looks tired and strained. He hasn't been the best husband, but she couldn't say that he didn't pitch in when he was home. He's always helped with breakfast on the weekends and taken care of the older kids' needs while she was busy with the baby.

She leans down and picks up the sopping towels with her left hand and wrinkles her nose as she comes close to him. "You smell like booze." Then she looks away, disgusted, before walking behind the kitchen to the small mud room that Dan had converted into a first-floor laundry years ago.

When she returns, she slides Mason into his highchair next to the kitchen table. The baby pounds the plastic tray with his fists and burbles some noises that sound like, "Dadadadada!"

"What are you doing in here, Dan?" she asks.

He had wondered if she'd ask that question. He wants to tell her that this is his house too. He wants to tell her that these are his children, and he has a right to see them and be a part of their lives. But that might be something his dad would have said.

But, no, he corrects himself. His dad would have said something much, much worse. And he has to assume that's why his wife—Dan's mother—had left them.

To Amber, Dan says, "I heard the boys arguing."

"They were fine. I would have taken care of it."

He can't help but quip, "Always just fine on your own, aren't you?"

"Haven't had much of a choice, have I?"

It's a rhetorical question, but even if she'd expected an answer, Dan wouldn't have had one. He looks around the room at the dishwasher that hasn't been emptied, the mound of dirty dishes piled high in the sink, the cereal box left open on the counter, the sticky kitchen table littered with crumbs. "Is Henry ready yet?"

She places her hands on her hips and shakes her head. "You want to tell me about this assembly before you talk to Henry?"

"There isn't anything to tell. I ran into Ryan on Friday at Bud's, and he mentioned it. The Richards will be speaking, apparently. And that's all I know."

"Well, is your name going to be mentioned?" she asks.

He spreads his hands in front of him. "No idea."

"You didn't ask?"

He shrugs.

"Dan, you've paid your debt to society. Your name doesn't need to continue to be dragged through the mud. Your children don't need to be involved in this. Don't you want to fight for them?"

While Dan doesn't want his kids caught up in his mess from two decades ago, he isn't sure what he can possibly do to stop the Richards from telling their story. It is their life that had been irrevocably altered by his actions. If they choose to talk about it, there isn't a damn thing he can do about it.

"You know what I think?" Amber asks.

Dan knows that she's going to tell him whether or not he answers that question. And she does.

"I think there's a part of you that likes this. You crave the continued attention on the subject."

"Don't be ridiculous."

"Is it ridiculous, Dan? What happened was a long time ago, and you do nothing to defend yourself when it comes up. You just sit back and take it, like you're a punching bag. Like you *deserve* it. And in a weird, toxic way, you invite it. This assembly is exactly what you want on the twenty-year anniversary. It's what makes you relevant."

It's this last sentence that causes the blood to rise to his face. "Stop it, Amber." His voice is a low growl.

"It's true, isn't it? Without Megan Richards, your entire identity just disappears. Isn't that why we stayed here? Isn't that why you refused to even talk about moving out of this town? You're obsessed with her."

"Amber, stop it!" This time his voice is raised. There is a throbbing behind his eyes, and his heart thrums in his chest.

"You've let it ruin your life. You've let it ruin my life. And now it's going to ruin your children. If you let that happen, you're as sorry an excuse for a father as you are for a husband."

The throbbing behind his eyes becomes a white-hot poker of pain as the hot blood becomes rage. For just a second, his vision goes black. He's afraid of his actions, of what he might do next. Through his haze of fury, he is dimly aware of Mason still pounding on the tray, of Amber's pretty face screwed up, mean and taunting, in his line of vision. His fists are balled tight at his sides. He can't breathe.

He moves toward her, then past her, through the doorway, and bangs out the front door of the house, where he bends at the waist and gulps in the cool morning air.

A few minutes later, he hears Henry's voice. "Dad?"

Dan straightens and does his best to smile. "Hey, bud," he says and holds out an arm. Henry's voice has deepened. It's not quite a man's voice, but it's lost the timbre of a child—a combination of adolescent uncertainty and innocence, like he's still trying to find his footing in the world.

He does not accept Dan's outstretched arm, and Dan wonders how much of his exchange with Amber Henry may have heard.

"Where are we going?"

He takes a few more slow breaths. "Hometown Diner okay?"

Henry shrugs in what Dan assumes is acceptance and heads for the truck. Dan wishes he knew what Amber had told the boys about his absence. He should have thought to ask. He wonders if he should say something about it to Henry. But when he climbs into the truck, Henry hunches forward and stares at his phone, shutting out the possibility of conversation.

Dan winds his way through the mostly deserted streets. As they cross the Memorial Bridge traversing the Mitsin River, they crawl past a group of serious-looking cyclists in full spandex and shiny helmets on expensive bikes. The group must be staying in one of the town's newer bed and breakfasts that have begun popping up since Conway became known as an outdoor enthusiast's travel destination.

Dan isn't sure how he feels about this new crop of people who have begun to invade their space. While the town certainly could use an economic boost, one of the appeals of living here is the familiarity of the people and the slow pace. A new demographic will not only change the way the town functions, it will shift how it feel to exist in the space. He's heard people say that visiting Conway is like stepping back in time fifty years. He wants to keep it that way.

The thought reminds him of Amber's allegations that he wants to continue living in the past. Which isn't true.

Is it?

He turns off the main thoroughfare and pulls into the parking lot of the diner, which at the end of a rundown strip of shops—a discount store, a pizza parlor, a walk-up bank branch, and a beer distributor.

Next to the truck, a group of teenagers tumbles out of a small shiny red car. The vehicle is new and has a Wright Automotive sticker on the back bumper. The girls all have long shiny blond-brown hair, and the boys sport the same shaggy haircut. They laugh loudly and yell incomprehensibly, jostling against each other.

Henry groans, his hand frozen on the handle.

Dan looks from the teenagers to Henry. "You know them?"

Henry just looks down. Dan knows Henry doesn't want to be noticed by this particular group at all, let alone with his dad. Let alone with *Dan,* he clarifies to himself. It's not out of the question that even kids as young as these would know who he is. He recalls the whispered glances in grocery stores, pharmacies, and restaurants over the years. Conway has not yet forgotten him.

The only other option for breakfast is a franchised chain that serves watery omelets, half-cooked hashbrowns, tough pancakes, and canned corned beef hash. Though his oily stomach protests, he says, "We'll try another place," to Henry.

They travel a short distance before crossing traffic into a poorly maintained parking lot filled with crumbling asphalt and potholes. Dan maneuvers slowly around the disintegrating roadway and backs into a spot marked with faded yellow paint. Though they are later for breakfast than they'd originally planned, they've managed to beat the church crowd and are seated quickly in a corner booth.

A short, thin woman of about sixty strides over and asks, "Something to drink?" in a nicotine whiskey voice. Her frosted pink lipstick has already settled into the lines around her lips, and her teal-green eyeshadow is the hue of a bygone era. Her hair is teased high on her head and frosted so blond that it is likely close to the gray color that it would have been naturally. Her name tag reads *Laura*.

Dan orders a water and a coffee. Henry asks for a chocolate milk, which makes Dan smile. At fifteen, Henry is still much more of a boy than Dan had been at the same age. At fifteen, Dan had been drag-racing at midnight, smoking cigarettes, and drinking beer. At fifteen, he had passed for twenty-one. Or at least the local bartenders hadn't bothered to card him before they served him. He's glad that Henry has retained some of Amber's optimistic innocence.

When Laura brings the coffee, Dan gulps the hot liquid down black, scalding his tongue. It prompts Laura to refill his mug before she asks what they'll have to eat. Henry opts for a full breakfast of bacon, eggs, and hashbrowns, while Dan sticks with a short stack of pancakes. He hopes that the batter is bland.

After they've ordered, Dan looks at Henry who seems to

find the swirls of his chocolate milk mighty interesting.

"So," Dan starts slowly, hesitantly.

Henry doesn't look up.

"Your mom tells me you have some questions about this…thing at school."

Henry lifts a thin shoulder. The boy is wiry, fast, and slippery on the soccer field. He's just starting to get some peach fuzz on his upper lip, but it's so light, it's nearly invisible.

Dan takes a sip of water, and when it becomes clear that Henry isn't going to speak, he says, "Why don't you start by telling me what you've heard?"

"Not much." Henry picks up the paper wrapper from his straw and twists it between his fingers. "The principal announced an assembly next week, and some kid told me it was about you. About how you'd—" He stops abruptly. "About what happened to some girl."

Dan scratches the side of his face. "What did he say happened to this girl?"

"That you were…drunk and drove into a tree. And she…" Henry's words trail off and he looks as if he wants to cry. Or crawl under the table. Maybe both.

A flood of incoming customers enters the restaurant, and in the lull in conversation, Dan watches as a table of senior citizens are seated in the booth across from them. They glance in Dan's direction and smile. Just a nice father and son having breakfast. Talking about how he'd committed murder.

"It didn't happen exactly like that," Dan says. "I guess I thought I'd have more time to tell you all of this."

Henry stares at the table, and Dan really wishes he hadn't had that bottle of rum the night before. Or better yet, that he had some rum to get through this conversation. He takes another gulp of coffee. It's watery and weak.

"Her name was Megan." As Dan says that sentence, something threatens to break apart in him. To his horror, he hears his voice crack. He swallows down the words. Stops. Takes a sip of water.

Henry looks up in horror and then quickly looks back down again.

"Sorry," Dan says when he's composed himself. He takes two breaths, and when he trusts himself to speak again, he says, "Her name was Megan Richards." The words feel so heavy as they tumble from his mouth. He clears his throat, and he wonders if he's said her name out loud since that night. He's not sure that he has. He thinks about what he should say next. There is no script for talking to your son about this sort of thing. "I didn't know her well."

And then Dan tells Henry about that night…

CHAPTER 26

DAN-THEN

Dan isn't sure where to go when he leaves Crystal's house. He doesn't have many close friends, and those that he does have are either in school or at work. He could go hang out with Hodge, the old man who fixes transmissions and carburetors for his dad sometimes when Greg Armstrong has too much work to do, but he doesn't feel like doing that, either. He drives around for a while, shifting his modified Civic fast until he finds himself traveling up the mountain roads. He passes the quarry where so many of the guys in town end up working. Dan won't work there. He'll probably just work with his dad fixing cars. The thought depresses him, and he wishes his dad weren't such an asshole.

The spring leaves have filled out, but Dan can still see gaps where they haven't completely grown in on the mountain. The foliage is the bright green color of new growth and the optimism of summer. With all of the rain that has been falling, it'll soon be a thick, lush canopy covering the hills.

At the top of the mountain, the road levels off and the quarry dump truck traffic subsides. He passes a few lumber trucks and some early weekend travelers, but the gray morning has kept many of the weekenders away, at least so far. Many of them will drive up the mountain roads from the city later, after their office jobs, with their kayaks, bicycles, and camping gear affixed to F.J. Cruisers and Jeeps.

Dan slows and steers into the small town of Ferncliff that borders the Ferncliff Falls state park. The waterfalls rush fast and ferociously on the Mitsin River—the same river that travels through deep gorges in the mountain and into the town of Conway. The Great Allegheny Passage trail follows the river, and if you were so inclined, you could bike or hike the seventeen miles from Conway to Ferncliff. Dan had never been so inclined.

He parks in one of the half-empty lots along the river, roams down to the water's edge, and sits on a bench where he watches the white frothy water roil and churn before tumbling over the steep cliff in the river.

Below this set of falls, the rapids continue to seethe for at least a mile until the river levels out and finally flows peacefully down the mountainside. Outdoor adventurers travel from all over the country to ride these rapids, and a few people lose their lives each year here.

Dan has never been into whitewater rafting, but he does like staring into the angry waters. It comforts him to know that nature can be as furious and unpredictable as he feels most of the time.

A woman with a black Labrador stops on the bank next to him. She must be close to forty with dark hair pulled back into a lank ponytail, wearing a puffy vest over a white top and jeans. Dan studies her out of the corner of his eye. As the dog snuffles at the ground next to her, she stares out at the water.

"You ever think about jumping in?" she asks suddenly, speaking loudly over the rush of the falls.

Dan glances around, but he's the only other human in the vicinity. "Huh?" he asks. He's pretty sure he's heard her correctly, but he asks anyway, maybe to buy himself some time.

She looks at him. Her eyes are dark and blank. "Jumping into the falls," she repeats. "Do you ever think about it?"

He looks back at the water. If you jumped in right here, the water would thrash and pummel you before pitching you over the edge of the waterfall, where you'd likely get trapped by the force and probably drown while the water beat your body against the boulders hidden below.

Yes, he's thought about it.

But to this strange woman, he says, "Not really."

"I have." She looks back at the river. Her dog squats to pee in the grass and then sits down and sniffs the air.

Dan isn't sure if he's supposed to say anything. He doesn't normally invite conversations with strangers. "Why?" he asks, genuinely curious.

She holds the dog leash loosely in her hands and moves closer to him, but not too close. Dan thinks she could probably drop the leash and the dog would stay right where it was.

"How old are you?"

"Eighteen."

Her gaze shifts between the water and him. "It seems like yesterday that I was eighteen. I had my entire life ahead of me. Now half of it is behind me." She pats the dog's head, and it licks her wrist and pants happily. "See, I'm just an old woman rambling about nothing to you, aren't I?" She laughs a humorless little laugh when she looks at his stricken expression. "It's okay," she says. "I get it. Like I said—just yesterday, I was you."

Dan regrets this interaction. The dog wanders over to him, and he strokes the wiry fur on its head and scratches it behind the ears.

"Some days, she's the only thing that keeps me from jumping." The woman leans down to pat the dog lightly on his haunch. The dog twists around and noses her hand. "But in a few years, she'll die and break my heart all over again."

Dan desperately wants to get out of this conversation. His reluctance to be rude vanishes and he stands.

The woman doesn't look particularly surprised or offended by his departure. But before he turns to walk away, she says, "You think you have your whole life ahead of you, too. But it's all an illusion. Time will chew you up and spit you out, just like that water down there. And maybe you'll come out the other side, all alone, wondering what happened, what it was all for. The answer is nothing. It was all for nothing. All the relationships, the sacrifices, the heartache, the pain. It means nothing in the end."

Dan hesitates then, wondering if he should leave her, or if she really might just throw herself into the river.

But as quickly as she'd appeared, she pulls the leash taut and starts to walk away from him, away from the river, the dog trotting obediently beside her. "Take care of yourself," she says over her shoulder. His eyes meet her empty ones, and he shivers, even though he's not particularly cold.

Where the angry river had seemed comforting before— a kindred spirit—now it seems foreboding. He walks away, too, in the opposite direction.

As mid-afternoon approaches, the parking lot begins to fill with people. The sky remains gray, and Dan dodges raindrops as he walks across the road to the sidewalk lined with bicycle rental shops, cafés, and ice cream parlors. A low log building houses the white water rafting rental company and offices, and Dan walks to a small restaurant next door that sells cold drinks, coffee, and sandwiches.

He orders a bottle of water and a hot dog, spending the last of his cash, and eats at a table next to four guys in their twenties who seem to have just arrived. They are all well-dressed and tan even though there hasn't been much sun yet this spring. The men's sunglasses, clothes, and shoes all look like they cost more than Dan's car, which admittedly had not cost all that much when he'd bought it two years ago.

They are talking about their jobs and girlfriends and vacations. They are laughing and joking with each other. They are not looking at Dan. And it is such a contrast to the strange woman next to the river. But Dan feels much more connected to the woman, as if he has everything in common with her, even though these men are only a few years older than he is.

He finishes his hot dog and walks in the rain back to his car. He drives on the winding mountain roads to his house in Highland Rocks on the other side of the mountain. His father is still in the garage when he pulls up the drive. He parks close to the house and doesn't go near the garage, instead entering the house and heading straight to his bedroom. He told Crystal that he'd go to the party at Joe Wright's house, but he's wavering. He's nearly out of gas, and he has no money. If his dad won't pay him, then he won't be able to go anyway, and that will make the decision for him.

He lies down on the bed for just a second and shuts his eyes. The next thing he knows, the front door screeches open then bangs shut, and the clock on his nightstand reads five in its bright red block letters. He swears and stands, smoothing out his bed as he hears footsteps thudding down the hallway. He has just straightened when his father twists open the door and narrows his eyes. "What are you doing? Sleeping?"

"No," Dan says, and his father shakes his head.

"No good piece of shit." Greg Armstrong starts to close the door again.

"Hey," Dan says, and the man stops, glares back over his shoulder. "Uh—I was wondering. You—" He stops, then continues hesitantly. "I haven't been paid for the past few months' work I've done."

There is a pause. Then his father says, "Yeah?" It's a challenge rather than a question.

"Well, I was wondering if I could get some money."

"What makes you think your work is worth a flying fuck?"

Dan feels the blood start to creep up his chest into his neck. The hatred he feels for this man is so strong, it must be oozing from his pores. But there's nothing he can do. His father is thicker, stronger, and meaner than Dan. He doesn't think his dad would hesitate to kill him if he'd ever worked up enough balls to challenge him physically.

But to his surprise, his dad pulls his wallet from his back pocket and throws four twenty-dollar bills onto the foot of the bed. "I'll have to get you the rest next week."

"Okay," Dan says, snatching up the bills. Maybe his dad realized that his cheap labor is a lot better than what he'd be able to get from anyone else.

"I'm going up to the club tonight."

Dan looks up. His dad rarely shares his plans with him.

"So, uh, you're on your own for dinner."

Dan nods. Usually someone will throw something frozen into the oven—chicken or pizza. Occasionally one of them will boil some noodles and sauce for spaghetti or grill some steaks and leave a serving for the other. But there is never conversation about dinner plans.

"I'm going out tonight," Dan responds, and his dad knocks the doorframe lightly with his fist. He looks like he might say something else, but he just walks away, leaving Dan's door wide open.

They don't talk again, or even see each other, for the rest of the evening. Dan pours himself a bowl of cereal, showers, and dresses before he calls Crystal.

Aunt Brenda picks up. "Hello?" she asks in her raspy voice.

"Hey, Aunt B."

"I thought you were going to that party with Crystal."

"I was calling to see if she wanted me to pick her up." He had sworn he wouldn't ride with Crystal to the party, but now that thinks about it, he really doesn't want to walk into the party alone.

"She already left. Went to pick up that girl—what's her face. Poppy?"

Poppy King, Dan assumes. She is in the cosmetology program at the tech school but is one of the few students to span both groups—the academics and the tech-ers.

"Oh," Dan says, and his disappointment must be noticeable because Aunt B says, "I'm sure she'll catch up with you there."

"Yeah."

He is about to hang up, but his aunt says, "Dan?"

He says, "Yeah?" again.

"Hey, I—I got some news from the doctor today."

All Dan can think about is the cough and the cigarettes. He knows what the news is, but he waits, thinking about his mother. Aunt B is going to leave him, too. He can feel it.

"Why don't you come around this weekend and we'll talk?"

She sucks in heavily and then exhales. Dan can nearly smell the acrid stream of smoke through the phone.

"Yeah, okay, Aunt B."

"Have fun tonight, Danny. Try to enjoy yourself. You take yourself too seriously. We only get a little bit of time on this earth."

He hangs up and remembers the woman with the dead eyes and black dog and a chill runs through him. She seems like a warning or something. What was the other word for a symbol of bad things to come? An omen. A terrible omen. He knows he's being stupid, dramatic. She was just a woman looking at the river. Same as him.

He makes the drive back down the mountain and stops for gas along the highway leading from the north into the town of Conway. At the very least, it's stopped raining. The roads are still wet, but the sky has opened up into a clear blue, the sinking sun forgiving and mellow.

Dan has no idea what time this party is supposed to start, no idea if Crystal and Poppy have stopped somewhere to get a bit to eat or if they've arrived at Joe Wright's house, so he takes his time at the gas station and lingers inside the small convenience store until the cashier nearly accuses him of trying to shoplift and tells him to leave.

Dan pays for his gas and gets on his way. He detours through town, driving way slower than normal, before finally turning onto Falgan Road, and winding his way up the rural street toward Mitsin Ridge.

When he arrives at the Wright house, the driveway is already filled with cars, and more vehicles are lined along the street. Dan backs his Honda into a spot on the grass at the end of the driveway, wondering if Joe's parents know about this party. If they don't, he's going to have a hard time denying it happened with all of the tracks and divots the cars and trucks have left in the rain-soaked, manicured lawn.

Dan shoves his hands in his pockets and hunches forward as he heads toward the massive house. Another car pulls in haphazardly behind him, and he glances back. He does not want to get stuck here.

He is momentarily distracted by the sight of Megan Richards who has unfolded herself from the front seat of the arriving vehicle. Her long auburn hair hangs wavy and thick down her back, and she is tall and beautiful. But she does not smile. She does not look happy to be here. She's with a girl named Holly that Dan remembers from elementary school. A bubbly, friendly, inconsequential person who never stops talking about everything and nothing. Beside Megan, Holly is chattering, but Megan doesn't seem to be listening, and Holly doesn't seem to notice.

Megan is staring at the Wright house as if she's walking toward her doom.

He moves slowly, hoping that they catch up to him, hoping that she says something. But she doesn't see him at all, and they pass by. He follows them into the house, filled with people. Music plays from somewhere. It's a thick, steady beat, but over the voices, Dan can't hear the melody.

He looks around, moving from room to room. He recognizes these people, but he doesn't really know them. Some of them look at him as if he's a bad pun—with amusement and just a touch of derision. He feels them whispering behind his back: *What's* he *doing here?*

He ignores them, pushing and pivoting through the throng of bodies until he finally finds Crystal and Poppy in a kitchen that is four times the size of the one in the cabin that Dan shares with his dad. Poppy has a red cup in her hand, but Crystal is drinking beer from a bottle with a fancy label.

"Danny," Crystal says. "You made it. Isn't this place wild?"

Poppy says hello, before becoming distracted by another conversation. She wanders off.

As suspected, Crystal is one of the best-looking girls here, and a number of disconnected boys circle around her, trying to figure out something to say—a topic that might catch and keep her attention. She ignores them to put a hand on Dan's arm. "You doing okay?"

"What's going on with your mom?"

Crystal gives his arm a little rub and then goes to the counter and pours him a beer from one of the kegs. She hands it to him. "Let's not talk about that tonight."

He takes the cup, but he doesn't drink. "She's sick, isn't she?"

Her eyes don't quite fill with tears, but they do shine. "There's nothing we can do about it right this second. Let's just have a good time tonight. Yeah?"

She takes a sip of the beer, and Dan glances around the room at these dumb kids, laughing about dumb things, talking about dumb subjects. He knocks back the beer in three swallows.

Crystal stays close, but she doesn't babysit him. She talks to people who she knows and some who she doesn't, and she keeps an eye on Dan as he drinks another beer standing alone in a corner.

After a while, Joe Wright enters the kitchen from a sliding glass door leading to the back of the house. Dan can see the tops of trees and knows that the view from the yard is of the Mitsin River flowing below. It's the same river he'd sat beside that morning, just from a different location and vantage point.

Joe looks around. He seems to lock eyes with Dan, but maybe it's Dan's imagination. Then he leans over and says something to the guy next to him. Dan can't remember his name. Nate? Ryan? They're interchangeable to him. Two different versions of the same guy.

Sutton Schultz is attached to Joe's elbow. Now Sutton, he knows. Tiny and thin, she has a pointy face and slightly protruding teeth. Dan has always thought she looked like an opossum. Her blond hair is straight and frayed on the ends, and she wears so much dark black eye makeup that he can barely see the whites of her eyes. The eyeliner gives her a harsh, inhuman look. Her lips are painted a bright red, but the rest of her skin is very pale. She keeps touching Joe, and he doesn't stop her, but he also doesn't seem to be paying much attention to her.

Joe claps his hands, shaking free of Sutton's grasp, and he tries to yell above the din of voices. His voice carries, and though he has to try a few times, eventually the voices in the room quiet enough for him to be heard.

In the lull, the beat of the music blossoms into an R&B song where a man is singing about not wanting to know that he's being fooled by a woman. His words are accompanied by a mystical, minor harmony.

"Listen," Joe yells over the music. "We got the fire going in the yard, and we're going to move this party outside. No one should be in the house except to use the bathroom. Got it?"

There are some murmurs, and Joe says, "If people don't get outside, then the party is over." There is panic in his voice, and Dan realizes that this gathering may have spiraled out of Joe's control.

The mob starts moving, slow and amoeba-like, toward the sliding doors. Joe stands by, overseeing the progress, his face tense.

Crystal has been swallowed up by the exiting bodies, and Dan hangs back watching Joe from the sidelines. Joe is a really good-looking guy, and he'd been a really good-looking kid. Smart, athletic, rich, cocky. How was it that someone could be born into such a perfect life without having to try for any of it? How was it that he got anything he wanted, even things that he hadn't asked for, just because of who he was?

Dan doesn't know anything about Joe's family—his parents or his siblings. But he's fairly sure Joe's mom didn't abandon Joe when he was just a child, barely old enough to remember.

It wasn't fair.

As the crowd thins, Dan notices Megan Richards standing back on the opposite side of the room. Joe glances at her, and Sutton clings more tightly to his arm.

Megan says something, and Dan can't quite hear all of the words. Something about calling her and hanging out.

Joe's response is low and absorbed by the beat of the song, but the tone is abrupt and dismissive. Dan watches a slow, sly grin spread across Sutton's face.

"This was you," Megan says to Sutton, to which Sutton replies, "What's the matter, Megan? Finally didn't get something you wanted? That you thought you deserved? That's just awful." Sutton says this last part in a high-pitched, sing-song voice, like a child.

Joe gently forces Sutton back and says, "I know you're seeing some college kid, Megan."

"That's not—" Megan tries to interject, but Joe interrupts, "Save it for someone who cares. It's not like I don't have other options." And then he turns, with Sutton on his arm, leaving Megan standing shocked, her mouth hanging open.

Joe notices Dan watching them. "What are *you* looking at?" he spits out. "What are you even doing here? You weren't invited."

Dan doesn't answer. He knows that over half of these other people weren't invited either. He turns to find Megan, but she's vanished from the room. He knocks back the rest of his beer, now warm, and pours himself another from the keg.

Joe's question to him is valid. What the hell *is* he doing here?

CHAPTER 27

Sutton has spent the night again going through the typical withdrawal symptoms—agitation, rapid heartbeat, fever, nausea, and chills. Now, her mouth is dry, and she has a headache. She vaguely recalls her mother being with her throughout the night, appearing and disappearing like an apparition. There is an itch in her brain and under her skin. The need for the rush of relief, the antidote for her symptoms, the cure for her life.

She can hear her parents moving around outside of the bedroom, talking in low murmurs, probably discussing what to do about her.

The light in the room makes her eyes hurt, and she feels like her head has been squeezed in a vice. She would give anything to be in her own place with Tommy, who would take care of her. He always takes care of her when she's at rock bottom. And right now, she doesn't think she could get much lower.

Where is *Tommy?* she wonders with a sudden grip of panic. He always comes back. But he doesn't always clean out their belongings. She aches to call him and lets out a soft moan.

When she inhales, she can smell herself—the sweet decay of vomit and the acrid scent of her own body. The thought of trying to stand in the heat of a shower is too much.

She thinks about food, testing herself out to see if she might be hungry. Even though the thought of eating makes her want to throw up, there is a hollow ache in her stomach. An animal instinct drives her to crave sustenance even as the rest of her wants to reject it.

She folds herself on her side and stares at the wall instead of the ceiling.

She doesn't remember much after entering the abandoned building the day before. She recalls the man and the drugs, the dirty spoon and needle, then the sweet relief and release when the dope hit her system. What she wouldn't give for that oblivion now…

She had floated away until something sharp and violent had brought her back. Then chaos—rough hands pulling and gripping. Men touching her, holding her—their big hands raw against her skin. There was thrashing and fighting, followed by a restless, drowning sensation, like being held just below the surface of the water, until she was too exhausted to fight or even move.

Then the hell had come. The sickness. If only they'd given her one fix. Just a hit to take the edge off. Everything would have been fine.

Instead, her body had twisted inside out, her clothes damp with sweat, her hair tangled around her, her eyes crazed and staring. She'd clawed and scratched, not sure if she had been trying to stay above the surface or bury herself deeper in the darkness.

Sutton is calm now, at least outwardly, but she knows that her parents will never let her out of this prison of her childhood. It's ironic. As a girl, how many nights had she prayed to get out of this room? As an adult, how many more had she prayed to get back here, to rest here?

She hadn't realized that this place was a demented limbo between life and death, madness and sanity, innocence and depravity. She recalls the familiar image of a child from a horror movie, floating above her bed, thrashing and squirming, as the child's family looks on in terror.

Sutton is that child.

Her mother opens the door, and Sutton can see the play of emotions on the woman's face. There is disappointment and relief, angst and hope.

Sutton wants to tell her that it is useless. She is a lost cause, a bet not worth taking. But she just closes her eyes before her mother realizes that she's awake.

Angela Schultz moves closer; Sutton can hear the soft shuffle of the carpet and the gentle creak of the floorboards. Then she can smell the powdery fabric softener of her mother's clothes. Sutton silently prays that she'll go away.

"Honey?" The voice is soft and tremulous.

It breaks Sutton's heart.

"Sutton?"

She can't seem to stop her eyeballs from shifting under her thin eyelids.

"Sutton, are you awake?" There is a gentle hand on her shoulder, and Sutton can't stand the merciful prodding.

She opens her eyes. Her mother is an old woman. Older than she was even the day before.

She hears an exhale of breath. Relief? Regret?

"I know you're probably not hungry, but you need to eat."

Sutton's head is pounding, but she manages to give a shake of her head. "Can't eat," she says. Her voice is hoarse and weak.

"Well, you're going to get some food in you," her mother responds. She sits down on the edge of the bed and places a hand on Sutton's shin.

Her skin hurts. She wants to move her leg away, but she

doesn't have the strength.

"Sutton, you need help. More help than your dad and I can give you. We can see that now."

Sutton is vaguely aware that this will be the rehab conversation. The one where her mother begs her to get help, and Sutton promises that she'll clean herself up. There have been many iterations of this dialogue, all dependent on her mother's level of awareness of her situation. But this is the first one where her drug use has been so apparent to her parents.

"I'll get help," Sutton says, her mouth dry and her throat sore. She is lying.

"We found a place. It's not close, but it has everything you need—residency, intervention, detox. They'll have a bed for you in a week. I wish it could be sooner. In the meantime, one of us will be here with you. We're working with a counselor who can help us to make this transition less painful. He's suggested methadone therapy. We'll take you to Beesonstown today."

Sutton had tried methadone therapy a few years earlier, but it had been too difficult to make it to the clinic each day. She hadn't had a regular ride, and it was so much easier just to get the dope from whoever happened to have it on the street. Besides, standing in line for the diluted smack had been a demeaning experience. She hadn't been like those other junkies who were standing waist deep in their graves. She'd been normal.

Except now she knows she is exactly like those junkies. And looking at her mother's sad, determined face, she has no chance of talking her way out of this situation.

Sutton just nods, and her mother looks like she's going to say something, ask something. Instead, Angela stands and waits. Sutton had expected her to leave the room, but when it becomes clear that she isn't going anywhere, Sutton feels like she has no choice but to pull herself out of the bed. Her head pounds and a wave of dizziness nearly knocks her back on the bed. Her mother steadies her with a strong grasp.

They move to the bathroom where Sutton undresses carefully, aware of her mother's silent tears when she sees her emaciated body. Most of the bruises on Sutton's arms and thigh have faded to a yellow-green color.

They wrap the cast on her arm with two plastic bags and secure the barrier with a rubber band. Her mother twists the shower knobs, and after a minute, Sutton steps under the lukewarm spray. She lets the water hit her face, and she shuts her eyes.

Angela doesn't leave the room but allows Sutton to wash her own hair and body. It is an awkward process, but in the end, her body is cleaner than it had been.

After she steps out of the shower and wraps herself in a towel, her mother hands her a small pile of clothing—a white lace bra, pink t-shirt, and jeans. Something clicks in her mind. "Where did you get these?"

"They're yours. God knows why I saved the clothes you'd left here when you moved out, but I won't complain about that now."

Sutton runs a finger down the warn pink material, the soft denim. She'd worn these in high school. A bubble of something—memory, grief, wistfulness—catches in her chest and threatens to emerge as a sob. She breathes back the emotion and pulls on the clothes, looser than they were when she was eighteen. She remembers wearing this very outfit to class. Remembers smiling and laughing. Remembers what it had felt like to have hope.

Her mother helps her blow-dry her hair, and Sutton stares at her sunken, aged face in the mirror. She barely recognizes that face.

After her hair is dried, her mother stares with her at the

reflection. "We're going to fix this," she whispers.

Sutton does not share her mother's optimism, but she admits to herself that she feels a bit better. Slightly less like a piece of garbage, and almost human.

"Your dad has some toast and juice for you in the kitchen." Her mother is picking up her discarded clothes and holding them between her fingers as if they are contaminated.

As Sutton moves to leave the room, her mother says, "I wanted to ask you something."

Sutton turns back around.

"How do you know Dan Armstrong?"

The name, like the appearance of the old clothes, is a punch to her gut, but this one threatens to bring her to her knees. Dan had been driving the car in the crash that killed Megan. For so many years, Sutton had spent time hating him with a passion. She'd gradually admitted to herself that he hadn't been the only one responsible for Megan's death. Still, he remains the symbol of both Megan's mortality and her martyrdom, and Sutton despises him. It should have been him who died that night.

"Why would you ask me that?"

"He's the one who found you yesterday. He was here—outside—when I got home. I told him to get out, and I called that cop, Nate Kasinski, and gave him a piece of my mind." She rubs Sutton's shoulder. "I know how painful that still is for you, with the anniversary coming up." Angela shakes her head. "All of this started with him."

Sutton's head swims with this new information. "Nate Kasinski?" she asks as another flash of recognition explodes in her mind. She hasn't heard that name in years.

"The police chief," Sutton's mother clarifies, oblivious.

Police chief, Sutton thinks.

"You know, it's funny. All of these connections..."

Angela's words trail off. "I actually met Joe Wright yesterday, too."

When her mother says the name, Sutton feels a sharp pain in her stomach, and she doubles over.

"Honey, are you okay?" She leans over with Sutton and helps her walk to the bedroom. She sits Sutton on the edge of the bed and calls for her dad. They fuss over her until Sutton assures them that the pain has passed.

"Maybe it's hunger," her mother says, and they bundle her between them and help her to the kitchen where they make her eat a piece of dry toast that tastes like cardboard and sits like a rock in the pit of her stomach. She chews and swallows deliberately and breathes slowly, trying to keep the nausea at bay.

They brew her a weak tea and tell her to sip the warm liquid. It helps a little bit.

She looks between her parents. They should be enjoying retirement. They deserve to be happy and unconcerned. They deserve Sunday dinners and grandchildren. Not the train wreck they'd gotten with Sutton.

After she's finished swallowing what she can, they look at her hopefully, as if eating a few bites is a major accomplishment. Maybe it is.

The morning is cool and damp, and her dad gives her a jacket to wear. Her mother helps her into the front seat of the SUV and climbs into the back seat, while her dad is at the wheel. His face is grim as he backs out of the parking space. He has always been a quiet man, and Sutton can feel the emotion—resignation and disappointment—coming off him in waves.

Angela is trying harder to hide her distress. She's doing it as much for her husband's sake as she is for Sutton's. She chatters from the back seat, attempting to make everything normal. She comments on the weather, on the promise of the clear day and the beginning of summer.

Sutton can tell that her dad wishes his wife would stop talking, but he doesn't say anything.

Her mother is buckled into the middle seat behind them, but she leans forward so that her head and shoulders are nearly in line with their shoulders in the front. "You know, I was thinking," she says. "After seeing the Wrights yesterday, Sutton, maybe it would do you some good to reconnect with some of your old friends. After we get you through this rough patch," she adds.

Sutton leans her head back against the headrest of the seat.

Angela continues, "I know you are in completely different places now, but you were friends with Joe once. You can be friends again." There is a slight pause. "He's extremely good-looking. Was he that good-looking when you were in high school?"

Sutton stares out the window. She is exhausted.

"His wife is also very nice. She was some kind of pageant winner."

"Miss Pennsylvania," her dad answers unexpectedly, and when her mom stares at him with a question on her face, he says, "I remember from the commercials."

"Right," her mom responds. "Sutton, do you think that might be something that you'd want to do?"

Sutton forces her mind back to the conversation. "What?" she asks.

"Spend time with some of your old friends."

"They weren't my friends, Mom."

"Well, I know they weren't close friends like..." Her words trail off, and she starts again. "I know they weren't your best friends, but I'm sure they'd be happy to hear from you. The Wrights are going through their own tough times, and I'm sure Joe would be happy to know—"

"Stop talking about him," Sutton interrupts.

"It's just that you could use some normal—"

"Please, Mom."

Angela stops for a few seconds, then says, "I don't see what harm—"

"Do you know what happened with Joe when I was in high school?" Sutton interrupts, though she knows her mother definitely does *not* know.

But her mother tries to answer anyway. "I know the party had been at his house."

That damn party really was the center of everything, wasn't it? Sutton will never be able to escape it. "No, Mom. Not the party. Joe Wright—I dated him for a while." But that wasn't right, and she'd been lying to her parents for so long. Maybe she'd been lying to herself, too. "Megan was talking to him. She really liked him, and he really liked her."

Her mother grows quiet and still. Sutton doesn't think she's uttered Megan's name out loud since that night.

She exhales. "I told Joe that Megan was dating someone else. Someone in college. And then—" She swallows. "We slept together. It was all so stupid. And it should have just been one of those dumb things that happens when you're a kid. But then, that party…" The silence in the car is deafening, but Sutton keeps going. "It's the reason she got in the car with Dan Armstrong. She didn't even know him. She wouldn't have even been talking to him if it hadn't been for me." Sutton's gaze shifts to her dad, whose gray eyebrows are knitted and rough jaw is clenched.

"But…why would you do that?" Her mother's voice is quiet. "She was your friend."

"Didn't you ever wonder why someone like Megan was friends with someone like me?"

Her mother doesn't answer.

"It was so she could feel better about herself."

"Oh, Sutton. That's not true."

"Yeah, Mom. It is. Do you know how much I hated knowing that? Hated feeling so inferior to her all the time when she was so beautiful and smart and perfect? I could never live up to that." Sutton's head is pounding.

"You were beautiful and smart, too."

She laughs. "No, Mom. I was hanging on by a thread, even back then." She wonders if she should keep talking. But she needs them to know how awful she is. She needs them to understand. "After I slept with Joe, I made sure she knew. I didn't care who else knew, as long as *she* did."

"Stop it," her dad says.

Sutton does stop for a minute. She considers swallowing down all of her words and tucking them away deep in her stomach, where they've stayed quiet and hidden all these years.

But they burble there like a sickness, churning and roiling until they come spewing out of her mouth.

"When she died, I was glad," she says, and her mother inhales sharply.

Sutton is exaggerating for effect, but it's true that a part of her hadn't been completely devastated about Megan's death. "But if I'd thought being Megan's friend when she was alive was bad, it was a million times worse after she died. When she became a glorious, untouchable angel. If she had outshone me in life, well, I was just about goddamn invisible in the shadow of her death."

"Stop it," her dad says again, louder this time.

She keeps going. "After a few weeks, after all the vigils and the funeral and the charade of a graduation ceremony, I took a pregnancy test."

"Oh, Sutton," her mother sighs from the back seat.

"And I thought, 'This is finally my chance to be relevant. To matter.' But when I told the almighty Joe Wright, he was mortified. He begged me to have an abortion. When I refused, his parents—they gave me money. A lot of money. I didn't want to take it, but then I realized I was about to have a baby no one would want or acknowledge. Joe wouldn't even look at me." A noise emerges from the back of her throat. A combination of a laugh and a sob. "It would have just been a constant reminder of…everything. So, I took the money. Had the abortion. Killed the baby. But I've never stopped thinking about it."

She can't see her mother, but the silence from the back seat is full of disappointment and judgment. The stillness is a living thing—breathing, beating, growing.

When her mother finally speaks, her voice is tight. "We would have helped you. It would have been…hard. But we would have gotten through it. It would have been better than this slow death you've been dying ever since."

It's easy for Angela to say those words now. But Sutton knows how her parents would have reacted back then. She had done the right thing.

No one speaks the rest of the drive to Beesonstown. Sutton had thought unburdening herself might help, but, if possible, she feels worse than she had before. She feels trashier, dirtier. And why wouldn't she? She had just confirmed to her parents what they'd known all along. She is human trash. Scum.

She senses their realization as they stand in the line at the clinic with the others whose stories probably mirror her own.

CHAPTER 28

JOE-THEN

This is going to be a terrible night. Joe surveys the interior of his parents' house through the sliding glass doors from the patio.

Most of the people invading the normally pristine space are random classmates, but there are also a healthy number of strangers milling through the kitchen, and probably the living room and dining room. He doesn't even want to think about what might be happening on the second floor. He's not sure exactly what he was expecting, but he realizes that he has no idea who has been informed of this gathering. From the looks of it, the entire county has been notified. There is no way that his dad isn't going to find out.

Somehow Chloe Nicholson has managed to procure two half kegs in addition to a bunch of bottles of flavored malt beverages and hard liquor. At least there is no danger of running out of booze anytime soon.

He's shocked to walk past Crystal Karlik who had graduated years earlier, but when he hears Dan Armstrong's obnoxious red car revving its way into his driveway, Joe realizes that the gathering has officially spiraled out of control. All he can hope to do now is contain any damage to the house and try to figure out a way to keep his parents from finding out immediately.

Cars are parked in both the driveway and the yard.

Muddy tracks are going to be left where tires have sunk into the wet earth. His parents won't return from Paige's equestrian competition until Sunday afternoon, so he'll have all day tomorrow to try to rake the grass and repair the landscaping. If worse comes to worse, he can say that Nate got his truck stuck as he attempted to back down the driveway and tore up the yard spinning his way up the sloping hillside.

He runs a hand through his hair. This is a disaster.

At least it has stopped raining. Ryan and Nate have been trying to get a fire going outside with the damp wood, and as soon as they are successful—*if* they are successful—he needs to steer people from the inside of the house to the outside.

His neighbors are far enough away that he doesn't think they'll call the police or his parents, but he'll need to keep an eye on the road to make sure no one is blocking the right-of-way. As relatively unpopulated as Mitsin Ridge is, people still drive up here on a regular basis.

He walks from the back patio through the sliding glass door to the kitchen. Sutton Schultz holds on to his arm as if they're a couple. He can feel her small fingers clutching into the flesh of his bicep. She's been by his side all day, and he doesn't want to be an ass, especially after what happened last night, but he needs to find a way to gently end whatever she thinks is going on between them.

He tries to shake her off, but she is glued to him, smiling up with her black-rimmed eyes.

Joe looks at the collection of people in his kitchen. Crystal Karlik is drinking one of his dad's craft beers, and Joe hangs his head slightly. But she winks at him and all he can do is give her a weak smile. Sutton's arm makes its way around his, like a snake winding itself around a limb.

Ryan walks in behind him. "Nate managed to get the

fire started."

Joe lets out a breath. Thank God for small miracles. "Hey, do me a favor. Can you move the kegs and all of the alcohol into the garage? I want to keep as many people as possible out of the house."

Ryan nods and looks around the room. "What's Armstrong doing here?" he asks, hitching his chin toward the doorway where Dan stands, looking uncertain.

Joe rolls his eyes. "What are *any* of these people doing here?"

He turns away from Ryan and disentangles himself from Sutton, lifting his hands over his head. The music is playing loudly from the speakers in the family room, and Joe has to yell to be heard. "Listen! We got the fire started, and we're going to move this party outside. No one should be in the house except to use the bathroom. Got it?"

There are some murmurs, and Joe continues, "If people don't get outside, then the party is over." He does his best to keep his voice calm and authoritative, but he is frustrated and a little bit scared. He didn't agree to host this kind of house party, and he has no one to blame but himself.

To his relief, people start to move and slowly trickle out of the kitchen through the glass doors. They pass by with their red cups in their hands, unaware of his angst. They're only here to have a good time. Chloe Nicholson struggles to move one of the half kegs, and he's about to tell her that Ryan will take care of hauling the keg to the garage. But when the crowd has thinned, he finds Megan Richards watching him.

He hates the immediate breathlessness and shock of electricity that shoots through him when he looks back at her.

Sutton's hand returns to his arm and squeezes tight. For the first time, he squeezes back. At that moment, Sutton proves useful. He knows he shouldn't manipulate the girl's clear affection for him, but when Megan looks at him like that—like he has a chance with her—he can't seem to help himself.

Megan appears to be shocked by the contact that he has with Sutton. Ignoring Sutton, she says to Joe, "Hey."

He wets his lips but doesn't respond to that softly spoken greeting. The words of the song that is blasting through the speakers—*I don't want to know*—seems oddly reflective of his thoughts.

"I thought you were going to call yesterday," she says over the music. "I waited then I tried to call you later..." Her words trail off. She looks from Joe to Sutton, then back again to Joe.

She cocks her head to the side, and he can see the pieces clicking together. Finally, understanding dawns.

She looks directly at Sutton. "This was you."

Joe's eyes remain on Megan's face, which has flushed with emotion, but there is a smile and a taunt in Sutton's response when she speaks.

"What's the matter, Megan? Finally didn't get something you wanted? That you thought you deserved? That's just awful." She draws out the word "awful," as if she's pouting herself.

Joe doesn't like the sing-song tone of Sutton's voice or the implication of her words. Like he is an object or a prize that they're fighting over. It makes him question Sutton's motives, and he doesn't want to do that. This needs to be about Megan's actions, not Sutton's reaction. He steps in front of Sutton and says, "I know you're seeing some college kid, Megan."

Instead of guilt, shame, or regret, there is confusion on her face.

Is it possible that she doesn't know what he's talking

about? Is it possible that it's not true at all?

Megan begins to speak. "That's not—"

But Joe isn't in the mood to hear her excuses, and he certainly doesn't want to think those excuses might be the truth. "Save it for someone who cares. It's not like I don't have other options." He turns away from the hurt on Megan's face and catches sight of the triumphant smile on Sutton's. He knows he should question this entire situation, but he doesn't. He can't. Not now. He's slept with this girl for God's sake. Regret floods through him, but he doubles down on his actions, because in that moment, he's not sure what else he should do.

Dan Armstrong is watching them. Joe doesn't know Dan well. He's not sure he's ever even spoken to him. But Dan has clearly overheard the entire exchange. Misplaced rage bubbles up in his chest. "What are *you* looking at?" he says to Dan. "What are you even doing here? You weren't invited."

Dan doesn't respond, and Joe reaches for Sutton's hand. With her by his side, he practically drags her out of the kitchen.

He decides to give up on the rest of it—policing the house, ensuring everything is in order. This entire situation—Sutton, the party, the alcohol, Megan—has been one giant mistake that he'll unravel some other time. This evening, though, when everything else has spiraled out of control, the least he can do is try to enjoy himself. This is supposed to be the last gathering. The last hurrah. One of the nights that they would take with them and remember forever before the next part starts.

Chairs have been arranged in a large circle around the fire, which is struggling to consume the damp wood. Nate is piling kindling onto the pyre, which seems to be helping, and he has split some of the larger logs into smaller pieces.

There is a chill in the still damp air, but the clouds have moved out and the sky is clear.

Joe sits, and Sutton pulls her chair close to his. He notices the curious glances in their direction. He is embarrassed. He needs to tell Sutton that this will never turn into a relationship. That he isn't interested in dating someone during his last summer before college. He knows this will piss her off and maybe hurt her, since it had been obvious that he'd been interested in dating Megan under the exact same circumstances. But with Megan, he'd daydreamed about continuing that relationship even when they were at their respective schools—her in the city and him across the state. His emotions had gotten way ahead of his logic.

He is an idiot.

Ryan brings him a plastic cup nearly overflowing with beer and leans down close. "What are you doing?" he asks. Joe knows he's talking about Sutton.

He feigns innocence and takes the beer. "What?"

Ryan shakes his head. "What is with you today? Megan is right inside. Alone."

"She has a boyfriend, apparently."

"Since when?"

"Some college kid. She met him on her fall visit, and they've been talking ever since."

Ryan frowns. "I don't know, man. Holly and Megan are pretty good friends, and she's never said anything about it. Where'd you hear that?"

Joe's heart sinks even further and he doesn't respond.

Ryan looks past him to Sutton. They can tell she's listening, and Ryan just shakes his head. "Dumb, my man. Dumb, dumb, dumb."

As if to cement Ryan's words, Joe pulls Sutton closer to him, and she giggles in response.

CHAPTER 29

JOE-NOW

The crushed limestone of the Great Allegheny Passage is damp and soft under Joe's feet, and the air is cool as the mist rises above the Mitsin. He breathes in and out deeply and steadily on every third footfall. He's running at an aggressive pace, as if he's outrunning his past. It's cliché, he knows. It's also true.

It's been years since he's run this path—since high school, training for cross-country meets and conditioning for baseball. Although the river is obscured by its blanket of fog, he remembers float trips in huge rafts with his friends over the easy rapids—music blaring, laughing, talking, acting like the rowdy teenagers they were.

The earth smells sweet, like new growth and promise, and the river still retains the scent of winter and melted snow from the mountain. He runs past the same benches, some of them refinished, the same sporadic houses collected along the Mitsin's banks. Some newer construction has taken place along what was once a flat meadow, and the lawns of the sturdy houses are filled with swing sets, trampolines, and dog kennels enclosed in split wood fences. The next generation. *His* generation.

Last night, when he and his wife had returned from their ill-fated dinner at the Crawford Inn, Vivian listened to Joe tell the entire sordid story of those last days of high school. She'd furrowed her delicate brow but hadn't spoken as the words had poured out of his mouth, from start to finish, from Megan to Sutton and everything in between. And when the words had finally run out, she'd sighed and held his hand.

"But Joe," she'd said. "You were just a kid. You were all just kids."

That should have made him feel better. But the fact that his wife had understood and empathized and *didn't* blame him for his awful choices made him feel worse. As if he were being excused by someone who didn't have the right to absolve him of anything.

He'd also been confused. He expected that Vivian would have also been as concerned about his role in a girl's death and another girl's pregnancy. But she'd seemed unconcerned. Like he had been telling her a story about someone else. And in a way, he supposed he had. The Joe of twenty years ago was a much different person than the Joe of today. Wasn't he?

He had let her hold him in the borrowed bed, had let her kiss him and think that she had helped somehow. But afterward, he had gone to the kitchen and poured himself a glass of the good scotch that his dad always kept in the back of the cabinet in his office. Joe sat in the living room as his dad breathed his steady end-of-life rattle nearby.

He and Vivian had briefly encountered Angela Schultz the evening before when they'd returned, and she had assured him that Sutton was doing well, even though Joe hadn't asked. She'd looked at him hopefully, like she'd been expecting something from him. He didn't think she knew about the pregnancy or his family's role in ending that condition. He doubted that she'd still be around if she did. What she could possibly want from him would remain a mystery. He had no intention of engaging with her any more than was absolutely necessary.

He'd drunk too much of the scotch and gotten too little sleep. He'd tossed and turned and finally rose before the rest of the house, walking down the winding road to the trail where he is now running as if his life depends on it.

He passes the campground that started operations when he'd been in high school. The place now sprawls out along the riverbank, taking up acres of what had been empty wooded property. A small convenience store is open for vacationers, along with an inground pool and hundreds of places for seasonal residents to park their recreational vehicles. Many of the spots are already occupied for the summer months, and the smell of bacon and sausage being cooked over an open flame wafts through the damp morning air. It brings its own kind of nostalgia for a simpler life that Joe has never known.

He passes by the abandoned brick skeleton of a distillery that had been the long-ago haunt of an American industrialist and financier. He runs past overgrown honeysuckle and berry bushes, wildflowers and clover, bedrock and boulders. He passes natural waterfalls spilling over the hillside from hidden streams, and rust-colored water bubbling up from abandoned underground mines.

He runs for miles until he reaches the next town—an old railway community marked with Victorian-style mansions, some of which have fallen into disrepair, and Gothic-looking churches. Then he stands under the rusting beams of a bridge's trestle and breathes hard.

A group of cyclists pass him, each rider raising a hand in acknowledgment as they speed by. He gives them a nod and wishes he would have thought to bring some water with him. Even though he's only run about five miles, he feels depleted from last night's alcohol and lack of sleep. But without his phone or wallet, there's not much he can do but turn around and jog in the direction from which he'd just come.

His return pace is much easier, but some of the mist and cool morning air has burned off, and by the time he finishes his run and climbs back up the winding hill to the house on Mitsin Ridge, he is exhausted and drenched.

The family is in the kitchen, and the interior smells of bacon, though it's not the woody, smoky smell of the campfire breakfast.

Vivian pours him a cup of coffee as he gulps down a bottle of water. She scolds him for failing to take his phone with him.

He scarfs down a plate of eggs, bacon, and toast and gulps the rest of his coffee before heading up to shower.

Vivian intercepts him before he makes it to the bathroom from the bedroom. "Hey," she says softly. "I've been thinking about our conversation last night." She sits on the edge of the bed and pats her hand once beside her.

He has been thinking about it, too, but he doesn't say that. He sits down next to his wife and waits for her to speak, hoping that she won't want to rehash the discussion or ask a lot of questions. He doesn't think he's in the right frame of mind to have that dialogue.

"I think it might be time for me to go home."

Of all the things he expects she might say, this is not one of them. "If that's what you think is best. I'm sure Ava and Natalie will be glad to have you there."

"They will," she agrees. "But, Joe..." She wets her lips. "You need to deal with everything that happened when you were younger. I'd always known there was a part of you that was closed off to me, and I didn't try to pry it open. But being here with you and your parents—it feels like part of you got stuck in that situation. Like you've never moved on from it. Any of you."

Joe doesn't agree with her assessment. Instead, he feels as if he's moved on in spite of what happened twenty years ago.

"If you don't find a way to deal with it," she continues, "it's going to keep festering inside you and between you all until someone finally works up the courage to lance the thing." She gestures toward the door, indicating his family downstairs. "I'm not sure how you do that with a group of people loath to talk about anything that causes any discomfort or conflict at all." Her hands flutter in front of her. "In the meantime, my presence here is not helping anyone."

"That's not true," he says quickly. "It's helping me."

She cups the side of his face in her hand. "You're sweet. But I need you back at home, whole. The girls and I need all of the good, the bad, the imperfections, the mistakes. We need the real, vulnerable Joe Wright who's done some amazing things and some questionable things. We need to learn from and love that guy."

"There are a lot of things that you shouldn't love."

She shrugs. "Maybe we won't love the things, but we'll love the man. Until you love him, too, none of us are going to get very far."

"I'm not sure I can love that part of me."

She nods slowly. "How about you just start with trying to forgive yourself?" Then she stands and grabs her suitcase from the closet, packing it with the few outfits she'd brought with her.

Joe watches her while she completes the task. "Maybe I should just come with you. It's not that far of a drive. I can come back here in the evenings to spend time—"

"No." She stops and puts up a hand. "Your mom and Paige need you. Your dad needs you for this transition. Stay. For them and for you."

Joe knows that she's right, so he doesn't argue. And by the time he's showered and dressed for the day, Vivian has already said her goodbyes to his mother and Paige and is sitting with his dad, whose eyes are hazy but alert.

She kisses his forehead, and he grasps her hands. To Joe, his father says, "You've got yourself a good one."

Is there subtext in those words? Is his father telling him not to mess this up, too?

With a promise to video call later, Joe kisses his wife and watches as she backs her car out of the driveway and pulls away.

With Vivian gone, the house feels just a little less alive.

Not long afterward, there is a knock on the front door. Joe answers, expecting to see Angela Schultz. But this is a younger nurse who introduces herself as Madison. His mother strides purposefully to the door and leads Madison over to her husband. Joe can hear Bill trying to be social, but he just sounds weak and tired.

His mother and the nurse manage to get his father up and help him to the bathroom. They call Joe over for help with this task. When his dad is settled again, the nurse gives him a rudimentary sponge bath, then, with Joe's mother, plans out his father's medication for the day.

Bill Wright, exhausted by the activity, falls asleep, and Joe, Paige, and Sandra talk with the nurse in the office. Madison appears competent, capable, and no-nonsense. Joe supposes you'd have to have those qualities in order to stay in a job as emotionally taxing as this one.

Madison says, "His vitals are still good, but his muscles are definitely weakening. It might be time to think about a catheter so that the trips to the bathroom aren't so strenuous for him. How did he do yesterday with that?"

His mother holds a hand to her throat. "He didn't need to use the toilet yesterday."

Madison pauses. "Is he eating and drinking?"

"Not much," Paige offers. "Can we put him on an IV or something?"

Madison hesitates for a second and then lists the benefits and drawbacks of intravenous fluids for a patient on hospice care. The young nurse clearly doesn't think it's a good idea.

To Joe, it seems like the easiest decision in the world. "I didn't think hospice was about knowingly killing someone," he quips bitterly.

Madison is not bothered by his reaction. "You're correct. It's about making your loved one feel comfortable and providing an easy transition. But there are no easy answers, and there are no *right* answers. It's about what's best for your dad."

"What would you do?" Sandra asks, and again Madison hesitates. "What I would do is irrelevant in your situation. I will say, though, that there is no physical reason why Bill can't eat and drink, so the fact that he isn't doing that means that there might be an underlying reason."

"I suppose we could ask him what he wants," his mother says, and Joe throws up his hands. But he doesn't say anything else. He is outnumbered in this equation, and now Vivian isn't even here to stand beside him.

Madison watches this interaction and says, "I do think you should ask him. In fact, I think it should be Joe who has that conversation."

"Why?" he asks, his eyes narrowed.

"Because I sense that you have strong feelings about the entire end-of-life situation, and an honest conversation with your dad might be helpful for you both to process what's happening."

Joe snorts, and before he thinks better of it, he says, "This family has never had an honest conversation with each other in our lives."

"Joe!" His mother has always been horrified by the airing of any dirty laundry in front of an outsider, but Madison appears unmoved. "Well, I suggest that you start today then. Before it's too late."

She gathers her equipment in her bag and tells them that her colleague Gillian will take the evening visit. Angela Schultz is taking the day off to deal with some personal matters.

Joe wonders if the personal matters have to do with Sutton. But neither he nor anyone else asks the question. Still, he feels the familiar invisible string connecting him to the woman and wonders again how his wife could be so untroubled by that link. He could have had another child, for God's sake.

But he doesn't. And that is all because of him.

After Madison has gone, the house descends into stony silence. Paige and Sandra huddle in the kitchen, drinking an early glass of wine, and Joe opts to sit with a novel in the living room, somewhat comforted by his dad's regular breathing. The legal thriller that he's picked out from a bookshelf in his dad's office is also comforting. Joe honestly can't remember the last time he's read a novel.

He is well into the rising action when he notes a change in the breathing pattern—an unevenness that hadn't been there before. He lays the book flat on the sofa beside him and looks up, finding his father's eyes open and staring at the ceiling.

Joe walks over and pulls up the chair that has been placed next to the bed. He sits down, laying a hand on the thin, cold arm.

A small can of ginger ale is sitting on a tray nearby, a remnant of the nurse's earlier visit. Joe picks it up. "How about something to drink?"

His dad moves his gaze to Joe's. Was it his imagination or are the movements slower than they had been yesterday?

Bill stares at the can as if trying to work out what it might be, and Joe takes the opportunity to move the straw to his dad's lips. He takes a small sip, though most of the liquid dribbles down his chin. He coughs, a weak, rattling sound.

Joe picks up a napkin from the tray and wipes the clear soda away. "Kind of hard to drink, huh?"

His dad moves his head slightly. "Hurts," he says.

"It hurts to swallow?"

"Everything."

Joe makes a mental note to talk to his mother and the evening nurse about the pain management plan. He remembers the task he's been assigned—to talk to his dad about intravenous fluids. "How about if we get you on an IV to keep up with your nutrition since it's hard to eat and drink?"

He barely gets the words out before his dad answers, "No." The word is firm and final, and it surprises Joe with its intensity.

Joe is quiet for a minute. "Why not?" His aim is not to argue. He only wants to understand.

"I'm tired, Joe. It's almost time to go."

Joe *does* want to argue with that, but instead he sits back and swallows hard.

"I like Vivian." Bill holds up a finger. "You did a good job."

Joe nods, not quite trusting himself to speak. When he feels composed, he says, "I like her, too." His voice breaks, and he clears his throat, covering up the sound.

"You've done a good job with everything—the dealerships, the Wright name. I'm proud of you."

Joe tries to remember if his father has ever told him that before. It means a lot to him, especially right now.

"I should have told you earlier that I was sick." Bill coughs, and the effort is weak. His lungs rattle.

Sandra glides silently into the room and places a damp washcloth on the tray beside Joe. Then she fades back out again without a word. If his dad sensed that his wife had been near, he gives no indication.

"I know how busy you are." He inhales twice, deeply. "I also know how much you hate to come back here."

"That's not true," Joe says. But he is lying, and they both know it.

"That girl—the one who died…"

Joe waits, but his dad doesn't say anything for a long moment. Joe picks up the washcloth and lays it against his dad's forehead.

"I paid off the mortgage on the parents' farm. It couldn't bring her back, but it was something."

Joe goes very still. "You paid them off to assuage your guilt for my actions." A pit has opened up in his stomach and his limbs feel heavy.

"No," his dad answers. "That girl could have been any-one. It could have been you. Could have been your sister. It wasn't guilt I felt. It was grief." There is another long pause. "I had the means, and I wanted to help." His breath is ragged and uneven. He continues, "There are thousands of parties just like that one where nothing happens." He shakes his head slowly. "We should have talked about it then."

When his parents had received the call, after the accident and the police had been to the house, they had raced home, driven through the night, from the equestrian show over three hours away. His father hadn't said a word to Joe, but he'd made discreet calls to parents, ensuring all of the teenagers were safe and lightly encouraging silence and solidarity. He'd talked with the police in low tones, and he'd called a lawyer who had somehow made any culpability on the part of Joe or the Wrights disappear.

His father had worn a thick aura of disappointment, but not a word had been uttered. Not then and not when the situation with Sutton had come to Bill Wright's attention. He'd wielded his checkbook and influence like a weapon.

"Please tell her I'm sorry."

Joe frowns. "Megan?" he asks, confused.

"The other one," he says and pauses. Joe fully expects his father to say *Sutton*, but he doesn't. He says, "Chloe."

Joe reaches deep into his memory and finally pulls up an image of a shy, plump girl. "Chloe Nicholson? Why?"

"I told the district attorney to go after her for the alcohol at the party," he says. "To keep them off your back. Her brother had bought the stuff. After they questioned him, he killed himself."

Joe blinks. Had he known that? He searches for some recollection, but he doesn't pull anything up. That had likely been around the same time that he'd found out Sutton was pregnant, which had taken every ounce of energy he'd had at the time.

This effort of speaking seems to have depleted Bill, and Joe wets his father's lips with the washcloth as he closes his eyes. They sit in silence for so long that he assumes the older man has fallen asleep. Joe starts to rise.

His dad whispers, "You were just a boy, and you were made to bear that burden alone. The burden of a man. Please forgive me."

Joe sits back down and bows his head against the bedside, pressing his father's hand to his forehead.

And he cries quietly. He cries for Megan Richards and for Sutton Schultz. He cries for Chloe Nicholson. He also cries for the young Joe Wright, who should have known better but didn't. Joe has been blaming and shaming that kid for a long, long time.

Maybe that kid deserves a break.

CHAPTER 30

CHLOE-NOW

"Hi." Emma's voice gently fragments Chloe's reverie as she sips her coffee.

"Good morning." Chloe pats the seat of the chair next to her at the kitchen table. "Want some breakfast?"

Emma sinks down, still soft and blurred from sleep. She yawns. "I'm not hungry yet."

Chloe fights the urge to tousle Emma's hair like she used to when her daughter was a young child.

The morning is gray and misty, but sun is in the forecast for the rest of the day. Chloe glances out the bay window in their cozy breakfast nook. It's early, and her usual instinct would have been to plan the day around the weather, making arrangements for an educational and fun outdoor activity. But when she looks into the round face of her daughter, she realizes that before long, that face will transform into a young adult, and then a grown-up. Gone forever will be this child beside her. Without realizing it, Chloe has been accelerating that timeline by filling up every single minute with activities designed to educate, distract, and, though she hates to admit it, control.

She hadn't slept much the night before, thinking about the conversation she'd had with Emma on their way home from Conway. It had been a decidedly adult conversation to have with a child, but in the end, Emma had been the voice of reason. And Chloe hadn't been able to stop thinking about forgiveness.

She considers asking Emma how she feels about the conversation—if she wants to talk about it again or ask any questions. But something seems to have shifted between mother and daughter last night. Emma seems just a little more mature, a little wiser, than the day before.

"Any thoughts on what you'd like to do today?" Chloe asks instead.

Emma stares at Chloe as if her mother has lost her mind. "I have a tennis lesson this morning and a piano lesson this afternoon. Remember?"

"I thought we might cancel those today."

"Why?"

Chloe shrugs. "It might be nice for you to do something that you actually want to do, rather than something you feel like you must do."

Still not fully trusting this scenario, Emma tests the waters. "Well, there's a movie that I thought it might be fun to see."

Chloe waits for an explanation, and Emma starts slowly, explaining the plot of an animated movie about a fat cat who has an emotional journey and great adventure. As Emma talks, her face becomes more animated, her gestures bigger, her voice faster and louder. Then, at the look on Chloe's face, she finishes with, "It's stupid. I know."

"No, it's not stupid. It's just that I used to watch the cartoon that movie is based on. Also, I'm trying to process the plot." Chloe laughs and sits back in her chair. "How about this? You look up the afternoon times; I'll call Tori's parents to see if she can join us, and we'll go out to lunch, then gorge on popcorn while we watch the show. Popcorn may or may not be our dinner." It actually pains Chloe to say that, but one unhealthy afternoon is not going to do anyone any harm. As long as they don't make it a habit.

Again, Emma looks as if she doesn't quite trust what Chloe is saying, and Chloe realizes that she's going to have to work to earn her daughter's trust back. While trying to be involved and invested, she's damaged their relationship.

Finally, Emma says, "Are you sure? It can just be the two of us, if you want."

Luckily, Emma is a highly empathetic and kind soul. Chloe thinks her daughter might also forgive her readily. "I'm positive. It'll be a girls' day. We'll have a blast."

Emma's face brightens with a wide smile. Chloe has not seen that smile in quite some time.

As Emma jumps up to go research movie times, Chloe rinses her coffee cup and starts gathering the ingredients for breakfast. She pulls bacon and eggs from the refrigerator and a bag of frozen hashbrowns from the freezer. She preheats the oven, and as she prepares to bake the strips of bacon, her phone chirps with a new text message.

She glances at the notification. Jason. The text is two words: *I'm sorry.*

One thing about Jason is he never hesitates to admit to his faults. Except this time, she should be the one doing the apologizing.

She is about to text back, but then she pauses and presses the call icon instead. The dial tone trills three times, and she's about to end the connection when Jason picks up. He sounds breathless and slightly annoyed. "Hi, Chloe."

"Did I catch you at a bad time?"

"No, it's fine. Harper's just being…a three-year-old."

It's been a long time since Emma was that age, and though Chloe has often wondered whether they should have had at least one more child, she can't say that she misses those chaotic early years when even one toddler had been a handful.

Chloe had been distracted during the previous night's dinner, so she hadn't fully appreciated the happy disorder that the children had contributed. She'd been too busy being angry, entitled, and judgmental.

"What's up?" Jason asks.

She hesitates, then plunges in. "We walked out pretty abruptly last night. I'm sorry we didn't say a proper goodbye to you, Becky, and the kids."

"The restaurant got a little crowded with memories and emotion. I understand why you left. And I'm sorry for getting caught up in it, too."

"I spent a lot of time thinking about what you said—about running away from Conway—"

Jason starts to apologize for that, and Chloe interrupts him. "No, Jason. You're right. That town has been like a monster that chases me while I run just fast enough so that it doesn't catch up. But I'm always looking over my shoulder. As Emma and I drove around yesterday, I started to realize it wasn't as evil as I had remembered, and I was giving it much more power over me than it deserves. And then when Ryan Tolbert and Joe Wright didn't even remember me, I realized that I was giving them—and what happened twenty years ago—all the power, too."

She can hear Jason's steady breath on the other end of the connection. He's probably thinking about how he should respond.

"I'm going to stop doing that now."

"I think that's a wise decision."

She pauses. "I've also been thinking about the other proposition you made—Emma staying with you for the summer."

"It was just an idea, but we'd all really like it. It doesn't have to be full-time. It can be weekends, or a few weekdays. Whatever you think is best." The words come fast, but they are controlled. He's doing his best to tiptoe around Chloe's sensitivities.

"I've never been without my Emma-bug," she says, and is surprised when a sob threatens to bubble up in her throat. She swallows down on that particular vulnerability and takes a breath. "But you were right; she should know her brothers and sister. And, honestly, it might be good for me to spend some time with myself. It's been a long time since I've done any soul searching." She's also rather shocked when an image of the man at the golf club café pops into her brain. Tim, with the warm, firm hands.

She tries to forget about Tim.

There is excitement in Jason's voice when he says, "Chloe, that's fantastic news. Really. Thank you. Harper will be so excited, and Becky..." His voice trails off. Then he asks carefully, "Are you sure you're okay with this?"

"No. But I will be."

"Well, you're welcome here, too. Anytime."

"You're too generous, Jason. And I mean that sincerely."

He gives a short laugh. They agree to work out the plans over the next week. After the Memorial Day holiday will be enough time to make all of the necessary arrangements for Jason and Becky to prepare space and for Emma and Chloe to finish up schoolwork, pack, and wrap up activities in North Fairhaven.

Chloe is aware that the Tuesday after Memorial Day is the anniversary of the accident, but she will not let that dictate her life. Not anymore.

After she ends the call with Jason, Chloe calls Tori's mother. The woman's greeting is cool, and Chloe wonders what information Emma may have passed along to Tori. She informs Chloe that Tori has other plans that day, and Chloe nearly begs the woman to allow Tori to adjust her schedule to spend the day with Emma. It takes some convincing and some charm—something that Chloe has not practiced much lately—but the woman finally gives in. Chloe agrees to pick Tori up at eleven thirty, in time for lunch.

With those plans made, Chloe returns to breakfast preparations. As she puts the bacon in the oven, scrambles the eggs, and fries the potatoes, she opens up a music app on her phone and hits a playlist. An Australian band sings an upbeat song about a girl's big black boots and long brown hair. Chloe sways her hips in time with the distinctive, quick four beats per measure.

Emma walks into the room and when Chloe looks over, she laughs. Chloe uses a spatula and sings into it like a microphone. She holds out her hand, and Emma comes forward, dancing around the kitchen holding hands with her mother.

By the time they're done, the eggs are slightly scorched, the bacon is overly crisp, and the potatoes are dry. They are out of breath and laughing. It's the best breakfast they've ever had.

And Emma is always going to be Chloe's girl. No matter what.

CHAPTER 31

DAN-NOW

Dan waits in line behind two other couples to pay for breakfast at the diner counter while Henry lingers just outside the door.

Dan tries not to read into it, but he can't help feeling like Henry doesn't want to be associated with him. No one in the restaurant had given any indication of recognizing Dan, which meant that something had shifted for Henry.

Henry had listened quietly as Dan slowly dealt out detail after detail, upping the ante toward a final configuration when he'd laid the cards on the table in front of his son. Dan had held his breath during the reveal.

When Henry had looked at the final hand in front of him, he'd said nothing, his expression unreadable, eyes blank. Dan had expected pain, judgment, or at the very least a question. But during Dan's narrative, all of the emotion had drained from Henry's face. His son had just looked down and finished eating his pancakes, growing stiller by the second. As they'd sat in the lingering silence, Dan had even noticed his son's eyes darting around nervously, as if he'd been watching for signs of recognition on the part of the other diners.

Dan hadn't noticed one person looking in their direction.

That meant that Dan's decision to recount to his son

what had happened that night twenty years ago must have altered Henry's opinion of Dan as a person.

Dan had left his own breakfast mostly untouched. Henry had not spoken as they stood to leave.

Henry is currently scrolling on his phone, doing his best to look casual despite the frequent flicker of his gaze in Dan's direction.

Dan reaches the front of the line and puts the bill and his card down on the counter in front of the young woman at the register. She is young and fresh-faced, with her hair in a high ponytail at the top of her head. "How was everything?" she asks in a bright voice with a wide smile.

Something in her manner and tone reminds Dan of Amber when he'd first met her. Despite his situation, Amber had been so impossibly optimistic that she'd even made Dan believe that everything might just be okay.

What a joke.

To the girl, he says, "Everything was great," impatient to leave. He recognizes that the time spent with Henry had not been meant to make Dan feel better, but rather to help Henry understand. He has no indication that the goal had been achieved, and now Dan just feels like a failure not only as a husband but as a father.

He glances around and notices that Henry has gone to stand on the sidewalk near the parking lot.

The girl hands Dan his card and lays the receipt on the counter for him to sign, which he does with an illegible scribble.

When he hands her back the receipt and the pen, she murmurs, "Armstrong," and Dan looks up. Surely this girl can't possibly know who he is.

"Yeah?" The word is terse and a bit more aggressive than warranted.

Her clear brown eyes widen slightly, and she looks

down, cheeks pink. She hands him his copy of the receipt and manages an obligatory, "Thank you. Have a good day."

He gives her a hard look before taking the slip of paper she's holding between them. She doesn't meet his eyes.

He's about to turn when she blurts out, "Tell Henry that I said hello."

Dan looks back at her and notices the red flush that has crept up her neck. There is no one behind him, so he says, "You know Henry?"

She nods.

He hesitates. "Do you know who I am?"

Her eyes widen again as she looks at him. "Henry's dad?" she asks in a small voice.

He waits, and she shifts, visibly uncomfortable with the interaction. "Sorry," he mumbles. "I will tell Henry you said hello." He nods at the door. "He's right outside."

"I know. I saw you eating." She gestures toward the table where they'd been sitting a few minutes earlier, then she looks down as if she'd admitted something embarrassing. "Well, have a good day," she says, and her voice is loud. She looks mortified, looks down again, and busies herself straightening the stack of receipts in front of the register.

Dan walks out, and Henry falls into step beside him without looking up from his phone.

"Do you know that girl?" Dan asks.

"What girl?" Henry replies, but Dan can tell by the way his son has asked the question that Henry knows exactly who Dan is talking about.

Dan plays along. "The one at the register."

Henry shrugs. "She's in a couple of my classes."

"What's her name?"

It takes Henry a few seconds to respond, but before he climbs into the passenger side of the truck, he says, "Rikki."

Dan climbs into the driver's seat and looks over. "Rikki

said hello."

The shadow of a smile appears on his son's face before he turns toward the passenger window.

It occurs to Dan that Henry may not have been silent because he was mortified by Dan's story but because he had been distracted by the appearance of Rikki in the restaurant. Dan clears his throat and says, "Do you have any questions about what I told you?"

Henry shakes his head. "When I told Mom what was going on, she told me a lot of the same stuff already. But it helps to hear it from you."

"Did your mom say anything else?"

"Not really. Just that if I've ever been drinking that I should call one of you for a ride, no matter what time it is, where I am, who I'm with, what I've been doing, or how embarrassed I am. All that stuff."

"All very true."

"Guess you couldn't call Grandpa, huh."

It's not a question. And though Greg Armstrong has mellowed with age, the boys long ago realized that their grandfather was a curmudgeon, at best. "No, I would not have called him."

"What did he say when you finally did?"

Dan blinks, thinking back. What *had* his dad said? Dan had been in the hospital when he'd first seen Greg after the accident. Dan himself hadn't called the man. Presumably, someone at the hospital had made that contact. Or the police.

Dan is recalling the memory as he speaks to his son. "He told me about Megan," he says, more to himself than to Henry. "That she didn't make it. I think he might have cried." The memory is hazy and new. But his father's actions when Dan was released from the hospital had seemed out of character to Dan even when he'd been a young, scared kid who had no idea what to do next.

Greg Armstrong had not hit, threatened, or yelled at his son. Instead, he'd doubled in on himself, stepped up, spent his savings, and remortgaged his home to pay for Dan's lawyers and fines. For once in his life, he'd done exactly what Dan had needed from him.

Henry interrupts Dan's memory to say, "I'm glad you and Mom are my parents."

Dan smiles over at him, but the smile fades when Henry asks, "Are you guys going to get divorced?"

"I—I think that's up to your mom."

Henry is quiet for a minute, but when Dan turns off the main road to drive toward the house, Henry says, "There are things *you* could do, too."

Dan pulls up to the front curb and notices that Amber's car isn't in the driveway. He remembers that Sam had been invited to a birthday party that afternoon. She would have taken Mason and maybe Luke along, too. Even so, Dan decides against going into the house with Henry. He needs to follow Amber's lead in the situation. But he turns to his son and says, "What other things could I do?"

Henry wavers, torn between saying what's on his mind and sinking back into adolescent silence. In the end, he speaks. "You could help out more around the house. Mom does everything. Even when you're home, you're in the garage working on Uncle Teddy's cars or something."

Dan opens his mouth to defend himself. Then he clamps his lips closed and breathes. "That's fair."

"You could be less moody. I know you have a lot on your mind, but none of us are in there with you."

"Okay," Dan says slowly.

"You could stop thinking so much about what happened in the past. No one cares as much as you think they do."

"Says who?" Dan asks.

Henry shrugs.

Dan doesn't push the issue, but he knows that Megan Richards' parents would not agree with that assessment.

"You could quit drinking."

That hits home. Dan changes the subject. "You don't have to go to that assembly at school if you don't want to."

Henry looks at his dad. "I'm going to go."

"Why?"

"What's the use in running away from it? It's going to happen whether I'm there or not. I'd rather be there and hear what they have to say."

Before Dan can respond to that, Henry thanks him for breakfast and climbs from the truck. His shoulders seem less hunched as he walks into the house and closes the door behind him.

Dan looks at the front door for a minute before driving away, aware that he needs to clear the air with Frank and Crystal after their last interaction. It occurs to him that his fifteen-year-old son is acting like more of an adult than he has been.

He pulls away, but rather than driving in the direction of the west side of town where Frank and Crystal live, he finds himself heading up the winding road that leads to the mountains, retracing the route he used to travel to and from school when he was a teenager.

When he pulls into the gravel driveway of his father's cabin and climbs from the truck, he hears noises coming from the garage his dad had built all those years ago. When he walks inside, he sees his father's filthy denim-clad legs sticking out from beneath an ancient-looking, khaki-colored Chevy C-10 pickup truck. The sound of tools clanging against metal meets his ears. He knows his dad has aged because he doesn't hear the familiar stream of swear words he'd become so used to as a kid.

Dan knocks his fist loudly against the side of the workbench, signaling his presence. The noise under the truck pauses, and Dan yells, "Hey there."

Greg Armstrong rolls himself out from under the truck on the creeper. Dan isn't sure if his father's eyesight is going or if he really doesn't recognize his own son. After a brief blank look, the older man says, "Dan." He awkwardly maneuvers himself off the creeper and stands, wiping oil-covered hands against his grimy jeans. "Something wrong?"

"Nothing at all." Dan nods his head toward the truck. "Yours?"

His father nods. "Picked it up for a good price. Figured I'd do a little work, and maybe sell it and make a few bucks. Some of these trucks go for up to forty grand."

"What's wrong with it?"

"Not much. Clutch needs replaced, so I need to drop the tranny. Pain in the ass is all."

Dan walks around the vehicle and notices some rust on the front fender and the passenger side door. He suspects that there's probably more. "Little bit of wear. Not awful."

His father walks to the small refrigerator in the corner of the garage and pulls out two bottles of beer, holding one out to Dan.

Dan moves forward to take it, and then he steps back. He thinks about Crystal's tears, Frank's furious face, Henry's words.

He thinks about Amber. "Nah," he says. "A little early for that."

His father's shrug says *suit yourself*. Greg places the second beer back into the refrigerator and pops the top off his own, swallows it down.

Dan looks away.

"So, what's going on?"

"Why does something have to be going on? Just haven't been out here in a while. Thought I'd say hello."

His dad barks out a laugh. "You never just stop by."

When Dan doesn't respond, Greg says, "How are Amber and the boys?"

"They're fine." Dan rocks back on his heels. What *is* he doing here, anyway?

"Tell the boys to come see their granddad sometime."

This is a mild censure directed at Dan. The boys are all too young to drive, so it would be up to Dan to transport them. Dan doesn't bother arguing that the phone, and transportation, work both ways.

The older man takes another swig of the beer and squints an eye. It seems as though they're out of things to say to each other. Dan wonders if he should leave. Then, unprompted, unplanned, he says, "Amber kicked me out."

"Did you cheat on her?"

"No!" The word escapes quickly and forcefully.

"Then whatever you did can probably be fixed."

"What makes you think I did anything?"

His father takes another swallow of beer before dangling the bottle by its neck between two fingers. He doesn't answer Dan's question.

"Why did Mom leave?" Dan asks, and that catches his father off guard. It's been thirty-two years since either of them had seen the woman. Dan doesn't recall ever asking his father that question. Maybe because he had been afraid of the answer.

"That was a long time ago, Danny."

"Sure was." But Dan waits for an answer anyway. When no words come, Dan says, "Do you know what happened to her?"

His father sighs. "You really want to do this? Now?"

Dan's heart thumps in his chest. *Does he?* He's not sure

of the answer to that question. But he says, "Yes," anyway.

"Do you remember anything about the time that she left?"

Dan shakes his head. He'd wracked his brains for more hours than he cares to think about trying to remember the last time he saw his mom. But he'd been a child—six years old. All he's ever had is a vague memory of a woman with cool dry hands and a warm smile.

"We'd had a fight. I know you'll be shocked by that," his dad says wryly.

Dan doesn't laugh or acknowledge the quip, and his father clears his throat. "The fight was my fault," he admits, this time without the extra commentary. "The next day, she said she needed some space. She had a cousin in the state of Washington. Michelle or Michaela—something like that. I'd only met her once." He waves his hand, and Dan assumes that his dad has not kept in touch with this woman. "Your mom wanted to take you with her, but I refused. I knew that if I let you go with her, I'd never see either of you again. But she went anyway." He takes another drink from his bottle. "I knew what she was trying to do. She thought she'd establish a life out there and then come back for you."

"That didn't happen," Dan says.

His dad shakes his head. "I gave her the space, and I waited three weeks before I tried to contact her. She didn't leave a number or anything, so I called your aunt Brenda, who hadn't heard from her either. We tracked down Michelle, or whatever her name was. Your mom just disappeared one day without a word. Michelle had come home from work, and Sheila was gone. She said that she figured she might have gone home."

"Nobody called the police?"

He nods. "We called the police. I even flew out there. The cops didn't take the case seriously. Young mother leaves her family, travels across the country, and then disappears. They told me she probably wanted to disappear."

Dan is quiet, processing this new information. "Is that what you think?"

"Hell, no. She would have left me in a heartbeat, but she never would have left you. There's no way."

"Then what happened to her?"

"I wish I knew. There was a serial killer who was arrested in the area about ten years later. I always wondered about that, but there was never any evidence that I knew of. Just something that might explain it."

Dan rubs his temple with his fingertips. "Why didn't you ever tell me any of this?"

"There wasn't anything to tell. All I have is questions and a weak theory."

"But I thought she'd left *me*," Dan says, his voice intense, passionate.

Greg Armstrong looks mystified. "Why would you think that?"

"Because, Dad, I was a little kid. I thought my mom didn't want me."

His father clearly doesn't know what to say to that. He drinks down the rest of his beer.

"Is that why you never dated anyone else?"

"I always thought maybe she'd come walking through the front door," his dad responds with a faraway look in his eyes. "I probably should have been more practical, though. I was a shit dad. And you could have used a mother."

Dan didn't argue with his father's assessment of his own parenting abilities. "I had a mom," Dan mumbles.

His dad continues, lost in his own memories now. "There was a woman once. Kathy. We went out a few times when you were in high school. I liked her a lot. I was going to introduce you, but then everything else happened, and I figured you needed me more than I needed Kathy. After that, a relationship just didn't seem worth the time or complication."

Dan considers this. He will never excuse his father's verbal and physical abuse. But as awful as his father had been, the man had done everything in his power to help Dan when he needed it most. Greg Armstrong had never said *I told you so*, or *You deserved what you had coming to you.*

He had simply emptied his savings and borrowed against everything he owned to help out his son. Some people may have said that it was the least a parent could have done for their child. But for someone like Greg, who had been scraping along the bottom of the parenting responsibilities of food and shelter, it had been a lot.

His father pitches the empty beer bottle into a gray trash can in the corner of the garage. While the garage is cluttered with tools and spare car parts, and it still smells of grease, primer, and putty, the space is much tidier than it had been before his dad mostly retired from full-time work. The repair work the man does now is limited to his own projects and repairs for people around the isolated neighborhood of Highland Rocks.

His father makes a move as if he might go back to work on the truck.

Dan bites the bullet. "Would you mind some company for a while until I figure things out with Amber?"

That slows the older man down. He turns and arches a bushy gray eyebrow. "You want to move back in here?"

"Not permanently. I just need a few days." He spreads his hands in front of him, feeling like such a failure. Here he is, at thirty-eight years old, asking the man that he'd once hated more than anything for a place to stay. It wasn't supposed to work out like this.

Dan prepares for his father to tell him what a disappointment he has turned out to be.

Instead, Greg Armstrong says, "It never ends up the way you thought it would," echoing Dan's exact thoughts. "I never thought I would have ended up a single dad. Never thought I would have ended up on the side of this mountain alone. Never thought I would have ended up nearly exactly like my own father."

Dan doesn't know much about his paternal grandfather; only that his father hadn't spoken to the man for years before he died alone and indigent in an anonymous nursing home in the central part of the state.

"And here you are, Dan, well on your way to continuing the same pattern." His old man shakes his head. "I'd hoped you'd do better with Amber and the boys."

Dan wants to argue. It's not as if he's asked his wife to kick him out of the house. But he keeps his mouth shut, thinking of the comments Henry had made earlier. His son is right. There are things he can do. And he can start by listening.

"You can stay, but only if you promise to fix this, Dan. It's too late for me, but you still have time to make it right."

Dan nods once and turns to leave.

"You know, I always wanted what was best for you, even if I didn't always show it. I at least wanted better for you than I had. I know I failed in my part of the deal." Greg holds up both hands. "No excuses. Just…promise you won't turn into me," he says, and Dan swears that there are tears in the old man's eyes.

This time Greg Armstrong does turn away from his son. He lowers himself back down on the creeper and prepares to roll himself back under the Chevy.

"Dad," Dan says before his father disappears.

The old man looks up at him, his face upside down and contorted like some carnival clown soiled with black greasepaint instead of white powder.

"Thanks. For everything."

Greg grunts and rolls away from Dan, leaving Dan to walk back to his truck alone in the driveway of the house of his youth.

Twenty minutes later, when he pulls into Crystal's driveway, the temperatures are in the upper sixties, and fluffy clouds slide lazily over the blue sky. Crystal is on the small front porch watering two hanging baskets filled with small pink and purple flowers. She stops what she's doing, holding the watering can by its green handle while he climbs the stairs toward her.

"How's Amber?"

"Okay. Pissed…harried. The usual."

The question that Dan knows Crystal really wants to ask remains unspoken. *Did she ask you to come home?*

"How about Henry?"

"Henry's just fine."

"Did you tell him about…everything?"

Dan sighs. Then he asks, "Did you know that my mother had gone out to Washington to stay with a cousin of ours and disappeared?"

"A cousin?" She frowns deeply. "No, I don't think I knew that."

He stares at her for a second, deciding if he believes her. Then again, she is only two years older than him. She also would have been just a child when Sheila Armstrong left her family.

"Where did you hear that?" Crystal asks.

He doesn't answer her question. "Do you know who this cousin would have been?"

She shifts the watering can from one hand to the other

and looks into the distance, concentrating. "My mom occasionally mentioned someone named Melanie and her husband George. But I'm not sure where they lived."

His father had mentioned Michelle or Michaela. Melanie was close enough. "You don't have contact information for them?"

"It might have been in Mom's paperwork, but I got rid of that when I moved in with Frank."

"A last name?" He's grasping at straws.

"Our mothers' maiden name was Porter, but I don't know if Melanie was a Porter." She sets the watering can down. "Where is this coming from?"

"I went to see my dad."

"And he told you all this? Now?" Her voice is filled with scorn.

"Better late than never, I guess."

"What were you doing up on the mountain, anyway?"

He looks at her levelly. "I need someplace to stay, Crys."

She scoffs. "No way. You're not staying with him. I talked to Frank, and he's cooled down. You can stay right here, close to Amber and the boys."

"I appreciate that, Crystal. But I've imposed on you long enough." He didn't just mean the last few days. He's been leaning on Crystal for years.

"Danny, you know you're not an imposition. We are worried for you and frustrated with your behavior. But we can help you. We can fix all of it. Of course you'll stay here." Her voice is smooth, but there's an underlying desperation. "I've cleaned up your room, and I'm roasting a chicken for dinner." It's his favorite meal, and she knows it.

He closes the space between them and enfolds her in a hug. Somewhere along the way, they had become a family that had stopped hugging and touching. Crystal freezes momentarily before she allows herself to soften and lean into him. She smells like earth and vanilla. She smells like a mom. She would have made an amazing mother. Hell, she's been a pretty good stand-in for his own.

"Thanks," he says, and he can feel the relief spread through her bones. "But this is something I need to do. I've been running away from my dad just like I've been running away from everything else. It's time I faced that demon head-on." He doesn't necessarily mean to call his father a demon, but that's one word for him, Dan supposes.

"I worry about you. Especially there."

He lets her go and stands back. "I know you do. You always worry about everyone except yourself."

"That's not true," she protests at the same time as her aged husband bangs out of the front door. Dan doesn't say anything, but he's fairly certain Crystal knows what he's thinking.

"Hey, Dan," Frank says cordially. "About earlier…"

His words trail off as Dan holds up his hand. "All good, Frank," he says. "I'll just grab my stuff and be out of your hair."

Frank repeats Crystal's invitation to stay on at the house, but Dan just thrusts out his hand. Frank looks at it for a minute before he takes it. "Thanks for everything," Dan says. "I won't be a stranger. I promise."

He doesn't look at Crystal before going into the house to gather his scant belongings. He knows she'll be crying. Sure enough, when he comes back downstairs with his suitcase, her eyes are red, and she's rubbing her nose with a tissue.

He kisses the top of her head, and before she can ask him to stay again, he says, "I'll give you a call tomorrow. I promise."

"Remember, Amber has an appointment to meet with her lawyer."

"You're not supposed to know that, and neither am I," he says. The chide is gentle, but Crystal colors anyway. "Amber and I will figure this out, one way or another. But I won't let my boys feel about me the way that I feel about my old man. I'm going to be better with them, whether Amber and I are married or not." He's not sure if he's talking to Crystal or to himself.

Crystal smiles up at that. "I'm glad, Dan."

"I am too. For the first time in a long time, I feel glad for something."

He gives her one last squeeze, then gets in his truck. It's time to confront his past, present, and future before it's too late.

Before Dan returns to his father's house, he needs to make just one more stop. It's a place he's been avoiding for the past twenty years. There is a ghost, or an angel, he needs to face.

CHAPTER 32

SUTTON-NOW

"How are you doing?" Angela Schultz stands in the doorway to the wood-paneled living room, wringing her hands together.

Sutton looks up from the sofa where she's been flipping through an old copy of *Good Housekeeping* that she found in a dusty book rack in the corner. The cover is tacky, and Sutton assumes that, at one point, her mother may have used the magazine in the kitchen to make one of the springtime salad recipes at the back of the issue.

She feels like she's been hit by a truck. The methadone, while staving off the withdrawal symptoms, does not deliver the same effects as the real drugs. Sutton is tired and edgy, and she just wants to go home. To *her* home, where she's free to come and go as she pleases and talk to whoever she wants to. Here, she's basically a prisoner, even if it's for her own good.

The visit to the clinic had gone as she'd predicted. After meeting with a bored and underpaid social worker for whom the novelty of helping addicts had long since worn off, she'd been placed on a thirty-milligram medication regimen. Then they'd sent her on her way after instructing her to return at the same time the next morning.

Her mother had loudly announced within earshot of clinic staff and patient population that Sutton would be checked in to a residency program the following week and that the treatment she was receiving at the clinic was only a stopgap measure. No one had cared or even acknowledged her mother. As much as Angela wants to pretend that Sutton is better than the other addicts in the small squat building at the corner of the strip mall parking lot, Sutton, along with everyone else in the place, knows that she is exactly the same.

"I'm fine." Sutton looks back down at the magazine. She skims an article outlining surefire tips to make your home sparkle.

Her mother sits on the other side of the sofa, and Sutton presses herself further into the corner, tucking her feet under her.

"I was wondering if we could talk about what you said in the car this morning."

Sutton had said a lot of things in the car that morning. So many things that her dad had not been able to look at her. As soon as they'd returned home, he'd changed clothes and gone out. Sutton hasn't seen him since.

"I was just wondering. You mentioned the Wrights paid you money. Are you sure that the parents knew what was going on?"

"What difference does it make?"

"It's just that…well, maybe that boy told you his parents knew. Maybe he just wanted to scare you into staying away."

"They knew."

"Are you sure? Because they seem like good, decent people. I understand Joe making that decision as a kid, but I doubt his parents would have become involved like that—"

"They knew, Mom. Trust me."

"But if you had just been taking his word—"

"Mom," Sutton says sharply. "His dad handed me the money himself. He wasn't a nice person. At least not to me."

She tries not to think about that meeting. It had been embarrassing—mortifying. She'd thought she was going to meet Joe to talk more about the situation. She'd been sure he'd come around and see that the pregnancy was a sign that they should at least try to make a relationship work. Now she knows how delusional that had been. But at the time—especially in the wake of tragedy—she'd thought there'd been no other choice.

Without a car or a ride, she'd walked into town and entered the café that had been attached to the small train museum, neither of which had survived the economic conditions of the past twenty years. Back then, the café had been a cute and cozy place with shabby-chic furniture and plenty of used books.

When Sutton had arrived at ten in the morning, the café was empty except for the elderly woman who owned the place and one lone male customer at a corner table. The door chimes had tinkled, and the woman behind the counter had lifted her chin at the man in the corner. That detail had stuck out; later she believed that everyone had been out to get her.

She moved to sit down at a table on the other side of the room to wait for Joe, but the man had stood, strode across the room, and taken a seat across from her.

She'd been so shocked, she doesn't remember saying anything at all. Back then, Bill Wright had been tall and imposing, with deep-set intense eyes and dark eyebrows slashed across a prominent brow. He'd probably been handsome, but to an eighteen-year-old, he'd been as ancient as her dad and not nearly as friendly. He'd said, "Joe is my son. He won't be coming today."

When Sutton had pushed her chair back, he'd hissed, "Sit down," through clenched teeth.

And so she did.

"Joe is a good kid who's made some mistakes," he had said. For a minute, Sutton thought he was going to talk about mistakes and accidents and how the best things sometimes come from those mistakes.

But instead, he'd continued, "In two months, Joe will be leaving for college. He will major in business and economics, he will join a fraternity, and he will graduate with honors. Someday, he will take over my business. But what he will not do is raise a child with a piece of trash who's tried to trap him into a lifelong commitment."

It had taken her just a second to process his meaning—that *she* was the "piece of trash" to which he had referred.

And then he'd asked, "Do you understand what I'm saying?"

When Sutton didn't respond, he leaned closer across the table.

Frightened, she looked up and the woman behind the counter was watching them with a raised brow. She had not seemed inclined to intervene on Sutton's behalf.

"Let me make this very clear to you," Bill Wright had said. "You will not be having a child with my son."

Then he reached into a briefcase and pulled out a fat envelope. He pushed it across the table. "Five thousand dollars," he'd said. "You will not tell a single soul about this. If I find out that you have, I will tell people that you stole the money from my home office when you visited my son. I will have you prosecuted, and you will spend time behind bars. Do you understand?"

Sutton had stared at the envelope without touching it.

"Take it." The words were a threat.

She hadn't for a second thought that he was bluffing. And after everything else that had happened, no one would believe her version of the story. She did not want to risk going to prison for a crime she didn't commit.

She had pulled the envelope toward her, and Bill Wright had let out an audible breath.

"Tomorrow at eleven, my wife will pick you up at your house. She will drive you to the women's clinic in Beesonstown, and you will eliminate the connection that you have with my son. You will never speak to him again. You will never call him, you will never contact him, and you will never speak of any of this. Is that clear?"

Sutton had looked at the fat envelope under her hands. She'd briefly considered thrusting it back toward him and telling him to go to hell. Looking back, she'd wished she'd done just that. But she'd been a kid, and she'd been terrified.

"Is that clear?" he asked again. His voice was loud, threatening, and mean.

She'd nodded, and he'd looked at her a beat longer and then blown a breath through his nose. She remembers that he'd smelled like stale garlic. Then he'd stood and his chair scraped discordantly against the hardwood floor of the café. He'd walked out with just one more word, muttered almost, but not quite, under his breath. "Slut."

Sutton had felt frozen until the woman behind the counter had said with a sneer, "If you're not going to order something, you need to leave."

Sutton had left.

The next day, at eleven in the morning, Joe's mother, a thin blond woman with a pinched and unsmiling face, had pulled in front of the house while her parents were at work. Without saying a word, the woman drove to a small and nondescript building just outside of Beesonstown. Sutton had ended the pregnancy alone in a cold and sterile room. Then the woman drove her home just as silently.

It had been infinitely worse than the interaction Sutton had had with the woman's husband.

A month later, Sutton used some of the money to buy a

cheap car and rent a small apartment in Beesonstown. She'd gotten a job waitressing at a sports bar in town. Then she had learned to bartend while she'd lived up to her reputation according to Joe Wright's father—the ugly muttered word as he'd left her in that café always ringing in her ears.

"They just seem so kind," Angela murmurs, pulling Sutton out of her memory. "Maybe you misunderstood."

Sutton doesn't respond. It's not worth arguing.

"And what you said about Megan, about being glad that she died…" The word trails off as if her mother realizes what she's saying but can't stop the momentum of the sound. She swallows. "That can't be true. Not really."

Sutton supposes that her mother needs to assure herself that she didn't raise a complete psychopath. Angela will never admit that Sutton is a horrible person.

"I still haven't been able to charge my phone."

Her mother stares at her.

Sutton tries again, appealing to her mother's sense of friendship and connection. "There are probably people who are worried about me."

"What people?" her mother asks.

"I have friends, Mom."

"I've seen your so-called friends on social media. You don't need them in your life. Besides, I've told the ones who have tried to contact you on your page that you're with us and you're safe."

Sutton throws down the magazine. "I at least need to let Tara know where I am," she argues. "Tara doesn't use social media, and she's probably worried." The reason she doesn't use social media is that her boyfriend had forbidden her from using it. And it could be true that Tara is worried about Sutton, even though there's a better chance that Tara hasn't been thinking about Sutton at all.

Her mother looks skeptical, studying the purple bruising on Sutton's face and neck that has begun to turn a putrid yellow-green shade at the edges. "I don't want you calling that good-for-nothing piece of crap."

"I won't call Tommy," she mumbles.

She misses him. Sure, he hits her, and most of the time she's done nothing to deserve it. But she can also be pretty terrible to him, too, and hard to live with. She isn't a great cook or attentive to any sort of housekeeping. She hasn't been able to hold down a job. She's often moody. Some of their screaming matches have been perpetuated by her. Tommy certainly had his moments. She touches her fingertips to the bruise on her neck without thinking. But there are also times when he is sweet and caring.

She remembers the ruined, empty trailer and her heart sinks. What if this time he doesn't come back? Despite her promise to her mother, she knows that she will call him again.

Her mother exhales loudly. "We can get you a charger. But, Sutton, I don't think you're grasping our concerns. If you continue on this way, you will die. And there won't be anything anyone can do to save you."

CHAPTER 33

SUTTON-THEN

Sutton's fingers sink into the warm, firm flesh of Joe's arm. She knows that people are looking at them, marveling at the new development of their relationship. She can hear the jealous whispers behind her back.

How did she *manage to snag Joe Wright?* Sutton imagines them saying. *We've been wrong about her all along.*

Through the glass, Sutton catches sight of Crystal Karlik, who is beautiful and had been homecoming queen two years earlier. She has no doubt that Joe could date Crystal if he really wanted to.

But tonight, he is with her.

Even as she basks in their jealousy, her gaze remains fixed straight ahead. They are right to question it, because Sutton is in the wrong place, with the wrong boy.

She pushes the thought away. For one night, she will enjoy being someone worthy of admiration.

She is already buzzed from the alcohol. Her senses are fuzzy at the edges, softening the world around her.

She follows Joe into the kitchen where people she's known for years, and some she doesn't know at all, mill about. They laugh and sway with the music, swallowing lukewarm beer and sweet, fizzy malt sodas. There is celebration and revelry in the air—in the laughter and dancing happening all around them.

But Joe's muscles are tense under her hand, and the anxiety rolls off him in waves. She wishes that he'd just drink some beer and relax. This is his party—his victory—and he doesn't seem like he's having fun. And if he's not having fun, how can she?

Ryan Tolbert is right behind them, and he says something to Joe that Sutton doesn't catch over the noise. She leans in closer, trying to make out the conversation, but Joe shakes her off suddenly and raises his hands in the air. He yells for everyone to move out of the kitchen—out of the house—and take the party outside. There are a few murmurs, but mostly the crowd obeys, shifting together like a slow-moving swarm of buzzing insects.

Sutton panics for a brief moment as Joe moves away from her, leaving her alone as the crowd flows around her. The crowd thins, and Sutton sees Megan framed in the doorway, her brown eyes wide and shiny, her full lips pursed in a pout. Her hair is a loose auburn cloud around her shoulders and her face is bare. She couldn't be more different from Sutton with her processed and heat-straightened blond hair and black-rimmed eyes.

But Megan isn't looking at her. She's staring at Joe, and he's staring back.

Sutton's panic grows, and she clutches for Joe's arm. *Mine.*

Only when Joe's arm snakes around Sutton's narrow shoulders does Megan look at her, her face wounded. And maybe Sutton would have felt guilty, but she is lost in the thrill of excitement resulting from Joe's returned affection. This is what she'd been craving.

Megan wets her lips and looks away from Sutton, back to Joe. She tells him that she waited for him to call her yesterday. Sutton waits for the rejection as she feels Joe shift. But instead, he pulls her tighter against him. She angles her body so that she is molded against his side. A song hangs in the air between them—something melodramatic and whiny—as Megan looks at Joe and then back at Sutton.

"This was you," Megan says. For once, Megan's voice isn't all sweetness and light. For once, there's some fire there. Some venom.

Sutton bites back. "What's the matter, Megan? Finally didn't get something you wanted? That you thought you deserved?" She opens her eyes as wide as Megan's. "That's just awful." She can feel her lips curving in a grotesque smile, but she can't help it. Joe Wright's arm is around her shoulders. Joe Wright had slept with *her*. Not Megan. Megan could have the looks, the grades, the future. In this moment, Joe is all that Sutton wants. And she doesn't think it's too much to ask.

"I know you're seeing some college kid, Megan," Joe says, and when Megan tries to argue her case, when Sutton gets just a little bit nervous, Joe barks out, "Save it for someone who cares. It's not like I don't have other options."

Sutton's smile falters. *Other options.* That's what she is. She's an option. A flip side. A cheaper alternative. She forces herself to smile wider to hide her shame.

"What are *you* looking at?" Joe barks, and Sutton notices Dan Armstrong standing near Megan. Sutton doesn't know Dan even though he had been in some of her middle school classes. He's always been a quiet kid who looked like he'd rather have been anywhere but in class. They'd had that in common, but she can't remember ever having spoken to him. She wonders what he's doing at this party.

Joe reminds Dan that Dan hadn't been invited, and then he grabs for Sutton's hand and hauls her outside. The gesture doesn't feel romantic at all. It feels harsh and cold.

Joe drops her hand and sinks down into a chair close to the fire. Sutton looks around and finds an abandoned chair near a table, drags it over, and wedges it in close to Joe.

Joe stares into the fire, looking sullen. He doesn't make a move to touch Sutton even when she places one of her hands on his thigh. Instead, he tenses, and not in a good way.

She glances over at the lounge where they'd been intimate the night before and finds Holly Griffin kneeling on the cushion, doubled over with laughter at something Ryan Tolbert has just said. Sutton wants to tell her to get off the lounge. In fact, she wants all of these people to disappear so that she and Joe can have that lounge to themselves again.

She shuts her eyes and tries to recall the magic of the night before. The memory feels off while the word *option* reverberates in her mind.

After a few minutes, Ryan comes over and hands Joe a beer. He doesn't bring anything for her, and she glares at him. He doesn't notice. She doesn't like Ryan, and he obviously doesn't like her. She was good enough for him to have sex with after homecoming but isn't good enough for anything else.

She tells herself she's not going to listen to what he's saying to Joe, but she can't help it. He asks Joe what he's doing. She knows that Ryan means, *What are you doing with Sutton?*

Joe tells Ryan about Megan's college boyfriend, and Ryan casts doubt on that theory. "I don't know, man. Holly and Megan are pretty good friends, and she's never said anything about it. Where'd you hear that?"

Joe doesn't respond, but he doesn't have to. Ryan knows exactly who gave Joe that information. Ryan tells Joe that he's dumb, and Sutton rises suddenly. She needs a drink.

Nate Kasinski is carrying the second keg into the garage around the left side of the house in an effort to keep people from gathering in the kitchen. He sets it down, having already hoisted a cooler full of the malt alcohol into a corner. Sutton plunges her hand into the ice for a bottle and twists off the cap. The drink is still warm, but it's fizzy, and she drinks it quickly, trying to get the buzz back.

Nate straightens and looks at her. "Whoa," he says. "Slow down."

"Why?"

He blinks, then shrugs. "Or don't." He starts to walk away.

"Can I ask you something?" she calls after him.

He waits, but then three other boys from their class enter the garage in a loud tumble and refill their cups from the keg. They make some inane comment about the amount of alcohol that Doughy Chloe was able to score. Sutton had forgotten that it was Chloe who managed to get the beer. Maybe the girl isn't useless after all.

The group walks out of the garage, taking Nate with them and leaving Sutton alone. She finishes the bottle of the sweet beverage and opens another. When she gulps the second one, it goes straight to her head.

Dan Armstrong enters the garage. He glances in her direction and refills his cup without a word. He looks miserable, but that could just be his face. She's never seen him smile.

"Hey," she says.

He looks around to see those to whom she's talking. When he realizes that no one else is in the garage, he says, "Hi."

He's not a bad-looking guy. His wavy dark hair is cut short, and he's got a strong jaw and nice eyes. "Why *are* you here?" she asks, referring to Joe's earlier question to Dan.

Dan shrugs. "Why not? Seems like everyone else is."

She narrows her eyes, wondering if that's a dig at her. But he looks guileless, and she lets it go.

She glances back at the crew around the fire. Nate Kasinski has taken her seat, and Joe doesn't seem to notice that she's disappeared.

A group is heading toward them with empty cups.

"You want to hang out sometime?"

"Me?" Dan points at himself, and the gesture is exaggerated like he is a character in a bad situation comedy.

"Yeah, you."

The other group reaches the garage door, stepping between Dan and Sutton. Dan doesn't bother to respond. He walks through the side door and back into the house without looking in her direction again. She tilts her head back. Was she that awful? That nasty?

Well, Joe Wright certainly hadn't thought so the night before.

She drinks the rest of the bottle of flavored beer and grabs two more bottles in one hand along with a fresh cup of beer in the other. When she reaches the fire, Nate doesn't offer to move. She hands Joe the cup, which he takes, and then makes herself comfortable on his lap.

"Hey," he yells as the beer sloshes over the side of the cup. He shifts so that she's not crushing him, but he doesn't push her off. She twists the cap off her bottle, and when she swallows, the fizzy drink threatens to come back up. She swallows down quickly and burps.

Joe is still talking to Nate, but his arm snakes around her middle and settles her in closer. As they all continue to drink, she becomes a part of the conversation. Mostly, she's not sure what they're talking about, but she laughs when they laugh, and finally, she seems to be included in the group.

She starts drinking her fourth bottle, and someone else has brought a fresh round for Joe, Nate, and Ryan. Joe is finally relaxed. He seems to have forgotten about the people in his house and the alcohol in the kitchen. Most importantly, he's forgotten about Megan Richards.

Sutton's face is warm from the alcohol and the fire. The earlier clouds have dissipated, and the sky is clear and bright. The smoke from the fire curls up toward the heavens, and Joe's body is solid against hers.

"Joe," Nate says, and his voice has an edge. He points, and they all look in the direction of the house, where Megan is standing. She's swaying slightly and staring intently at Joe and Sutton. "Maybe you should go talk to her. She doesn't look so good."

Sutton feels suspended in time as she waits to see what Joe will do. She considers kissing him to keep him right where he is, but time is moving slowly, and she's having trouble moving at all.

Sutton feels Joe shift beneath her, and then she does lean back. She kisses him, thrusting her tongue in his mouth. She's not sure if he likes it, but a second later, he kisses her back. When he breaks the kiss, he catches Sutton's earlobe between his teeth and bites. It hurts, and she gasps. But she pretends that she likes it.

Ryan makes a gagging noise beside them. "Come on."

Joe lets her ear go and laughs. It is a cruel sound, and Sutton can't tell if he's laughing at Ryan or at her.

She looks over at Ryan who is still gagging. Her eyes are watering, and she wonders if she's bleeding. She's afraid to know.

She manages a smile at Ryan. "Jealous?"

"I had that once, remember? It wasn't up to my standards."

The smile fades from Sutton's lips, and Nate guffaws.

Dan Armstrong comes out of the house and says something to Megan. She doesn't seem to hear him at first, and then she looks up at him, falters and begins to fall. Dan catches her in his arms, and they smile at each other.

Sutton watches this interaction, and the familiar blade of jealousy twists in her gut. *It was never about Joe*, she realizes.

Joe has lost interest in Sutton and seems in a daze. "You think she's okay?" He's not talking to anyone in particular and his words are slurred. Sutton knows that the *she* he is referring to is Megan, not Sutton.

Megan and Dan are no longer standing near the doorway.

Nate stands. "I'll make a walk-through." He moves toward the house.

Sutton stays put. She has to pee, but she knows if she stands, Joe will wander off, probably in search of Megan. She needs to use the alcohol to her advantage. Time passes differently when you're drunk, and she's not sure how long they've been sitting there before she realizes that Joe is silently staring into the fire and Ryan has disappeared, too. One minute he was sitting beside them, now he's huddled with Holly in a dark corner of the deck.

Sutton's bladder feels like it might explode.

Nate returns. He's drinking a bottle of water and hands Joe a bottle, too.

Bleary-eyed, Joe looks up at Nate.

Nate shrugs. "She's with Dan Armstrong."

"Why would she be with that guy?"

"Probably because you're with that girl." Nate tips his bottle in Sutton's direction.

She wants to tell him that she doesn't appreciate him speaking about her as if she isn't right in front of him, but she can't make the words come out. She really has to go to the bathroom.

A few more minutes pass, and a female voice screeches from somewhere outside in the darkness. It's not quite a scream, but it's loud and panicked.

Nate stands, and this time Joe pushes at Sutton and stands, too, swaying slightly.

They move toward the voice, which has begun yelling, "You can't leave!"

Nate jogs forward, and Joe moves on unsteady legs. Sutton follows, doing her best to stay upright in the dark. Her vision is still slightly blinded from the bright glow of the fire, and she keeps her hands in front of her as she walks. Her legs feel like stumps as she tramps through the damp, slippery grass.

Crystal Karlik is in the front yard, still screeching at Dan Armstrong as he leads Megan toward his little red car at the top of the driveway. Suddenly, Sutton runs forward, stumbling as she goes.

Megan is her friend, she remembers, and the alcohol makes her feel sentimental and fiercely protective. Megan should not be leaving with Dan. "Get away from her," she yells. She nearly trips as she lunges toward Megan and manages to grab hold of her arm.

Megan stares at her, horrified. She shakes Sutton away. "Get off me."

Crystal is still yelling at Dan, but her words are a squealing jumble of sounds.

"Megan," Sutton slurs. "You cannot leave with him. I will take you home." It doesn't matter that she doesn't have a car. She will find a way.

She forgets about Joe, who doesn't want her anyway. Well, maybe she doesn't want him either.

But Megan's face is red and twisted. "For years, people have been asking me why I'm friends with you. I always defended you, Sutton. I said you were a good person. But you're not a good person. You're awful. I hope what you've done is worth it. Because I will never forgive you. I will never speak to you again. And I hope the rest of your life is as miserable as your dark and horrible mind."

Sutton is actually shocked even though she knows she shouldn't be.

But can't Megan see that she has everything, and Sutton has nothing? Just once, Sutton had wanted to feel like she was as good as her friend. Can't Megan understand that?

Megan slips out of her grasp, and Dan Armstrong leads Megan in the opposite direction toward his cherry-red car. Crystal follows after them, clutching at Dan's arm much the same way Sutton had clutched at Megan's.

He shakes off her grasp, too, helping Megan into the low bucket seat and dodging Crystal to walk around to the driver's seat. He slides in, and the car roars to life, its engine rumbling in the silence of Mitsin Ridge. The tires slide over the asphalt, and while it's not quite a burnout, the noise is loud enough that Joe swears under his breath and mumbles something about the neighbors calling the cops.

"Do you think we should go after them?" Joe asks.

"No, man. We've all been drinking. No one should leave now," Nate says.

Holly and Ryan come around the side of the house, arms wrapped around each other. "Who just left?" Holly asks.

"Megan left with Dan Armstrong," Nate responds.

Ryan cocks his head to the side. "Seriously?"

"I have to go after them." Joe stumbles toward the house, and Sutton lunges at him, but Nate gets to Joe first, nearly knocking Sutton out of the way. He guides Joe toward the back of the house and into the kitchen while Sutton follows lamely behind. She'd told her parents she'd be staying at Megan's that night, so they wouldn't be waiting up for her. Her plan had been to spend the night in Joe's bed, but as Nate instructs his friend to drink water, Sutton isn't sure what she should do.

Doughy Chloe, her cheeks flushed pink, flutters around pressing her hands together. "I really need to get home tonight," she says. She looks at Scott Murray at the same time Nate does. "You been drinking?" Nate asks.

Scott nods.

"Then you're staying."

Chloe moves her fingers to her mouth. "I told my parents I'd be home by midnight."

Sutton rolls her eyes and wanders down the hall toward the bathroom. It's mercifully empty, and she sits on the toilet for a long while. In the silence of the bathroom and the stillness of the back of the house, she hears the wail of a siren. Her first thought is that the cops are on their way, and she pulls her jeans over her hips and rushes from the bathroom, ignoring the flash of her reflection in the decorative mirror—the smudged lipstick and running eyeliner.

She finds Nate, the closest thing to an adult. He is wiping up a puddle of liquid that has spilled on the kitchen floor.

"The cops are coming," she says.

"What?" he asks.

"I heard the sirens."

Nate abandons a wad of paper towels and walks past Chloe, who is now crying. Sutton follows him outside. In the distance, there is a cacophony of wailing sirens. Nate's face tenses as he listens. "They're far away. I don't think they're coming here," he says. But he goes back into the house and instructs everyone left to call their parents, older siblings, or other adults for rides home.

There are groans and protests, but Nate doesn't budge.

A few minutes later, Joe emerges from the stairs, where he looks green but no longer as drunk. Sutton assumes he's thrown up the water and most of the alcohol. "What's going on?" he asks.

Nate looks at him. His face is grim. "The party is over."

It is that moment that Sutton realizes that something terrible has happened.

CHAPTER 34

JOE-NOW

Joe brews a fresh pot of coffee and wanders moodily around the kitchen. He misses Vivian, and he misses his girls. He is contemplating packing his stuff and heading home when his mother enters the kitchen. She looks both distracted and surprised to see him in the room. Or maybe she isn't able to get used to seeing him in the house.

Her phone is clutched tightly in her hand, and she says, "Have you seen your sister?"

"I think she's napping."

She nods and frowns.

"Anything wrong?"

"I just got a call from the director of the home care and hospice office. She said that Angela Schultz will no longer be assisting us. We'll retain Madison and the other aide—the one who hasn't visited yet. The director will be assigning us a new head nurse."

"Okay," Joe says slowly. "Is that a problem?"

He pours his mother a mug of coffee and stirs in cream and one sugar, the way he remembers her drinking it when he'd been a kid. She abandons her phone for the mug and takes a sip, cradling the cup between the palms of her hands. "It just seems odd, all these coincidences. You don't think Sutton would have told her, do you?"

"Does it matter?"

His mother lifts an elegant shoulder. Her silver hair brushes against the cap sleeve of her silk blouse. "I suppose not." She purses her lips. "If the girl was going to tell her, I imagine she would have done that years ago."

Joe doesn't bother mentioning that Sutton is well on her way to middle age. "Even if she'd recently told Angela about the pregnancy, I can't imagine the woman would refuse to treat Dad. She'd be angry with me, not with my parents."

Something about the way his mother evades his gaze and declines to comment causes the hair on the back of Joe's neck to stand up. "Right, Mom? There would be no reason to be upset with you and Dad."

"Of course not," she snaps.

Joe's heart sinks. All those years ago, he'd told his dad about Sutton's pregnancy. Emotions had still been raw from the accident. Everyone had walked around in a state of grief, shock, and disbelief. Joe continued to blame himself and mourn the loss of Megan while struggling with all of the subsequent events. There had been the responsibility for the party and his dad's involvement in shifting the focus away from Joe and onto the attendees. There had been the funeral and the somber graduation ceremony. There had been questions from the police, and news of the arrest of Dan Armstrong. There had been tears, but there had also been silent blame, regret, and shame.

Four weeks later, when Sutton had rather triumphantly announced to him the unplanned, unwanted pregnancy, he had freaked out. The thought of becoming a teenage parent with Sutton Schultz had very nearly pushed him over the edge.

He'd begged Sutton to make the situation go away, but she was adamant that she would keep the baby, with or without his involvement. She'd been sure that this was a sign—her destiny, a second chance to make things right.

All Joe had seen was the end of life as he'd known it. And after he'd failed to convince Sutton to abort the baby while they'd sat at a picnic table at the river park, he'd gone home, shut the door to his dad's office, and broken down. His dad had listened, the muscle in his jaw twitching to its own furious beat, and then he'd calmly told Joe to leave the room.

And Joe had left. He hadn't asked any questions. He had laid low for weeks. The next time he'd seen Sutton at the Independence Day fireworks celebration, she'd been wearing a pair of microshorts and a crop top. While it would have been too early for a pregnant belly to be prominent, Sutton had been glued to the side of a beefy kid that Joe didn't know. She certainly hadn't acted pregnant, and she hadn't looked in Joe's direction even though she'd definitely seen him.

He was out of the woods, and he knew better than to question how that had transpired.

But now he was a thirty-eight-year-old man with children of his own. "What did you do?" he asks his mother.

She doesn't answer the question. "Do you want some lunch?" She heads to the refrigerator and pulls out roast beef, provolone cheese, lettuce, and tomatoes. She also opens a bottle of wine, and while it isn't early, it's certainly not late enough for alcohol. She pours the pale-yellow liquid into a delicately stemmed glass and lifts the glass to her lips before she sets to work building the sandwiches. She hadn't waited for Joe's response, and a few minutes later, she sets a sandwich on a plate in front of him.

"She wasn't a bad person," Joe says, looking at the sandwich.

His mother replaces all of the ingredients in the refrigerator before she joins him at the island in the kitchen where he'd spent so much time as a boy. "Who?"

"Sutton Schultz."

Sandra waves a hand in front of her and takes another swallow of her wine. "Of course not."

"It's just that…she was a kid, too. We all were."

His mother takes a bite of the roast beef sandwich and chews thoughtfully. Joe does the same. After a minute, she says, "It was a long time ago."

"You know, everyone keeps saying that. But it doesn't feel like it, you know? It feels like just yesterday that this kitchen was filled with people during that party." He looks around as if the ghosts of those young adults are still in the room.

His mother doesn't answer right away, and they eat their sandwiches in silence. When they are finished, his mother clears the plates and pours herself another glass of wine. Joe watches her. He's never given his mother much thought. She'd been an extra in his life—the supporting cast. He hasn't spent much time thinking about her actions, thoughts, or feelings, except as they had pertained to his.

"Did you know that Dad gave the Richards money after Megan died?"

There is a slight pull in the tendon at the base of her neck. "I did."

"Did you know that Dad told the police and the district attorney to go after Chloe Nicholson and her family to keep the attention off our family?"

She looks at him levelly, coolly. "That's not entirely accurate, but yes."

"Did you know that Dad called the parents of every person who had been here for that party to check in and make sure they were all okay? Did you know he offered to pay for therapy for everyone who may have been upset or affected?"

She looks at him over the edge of her wine glass.

Despite the silver hair, her face is remarkably unlined. In addition to good genes, she's stayed out of the sun and taken extremely good care of her skin. She's still young in her early sixties, and Joe won't be surprised if she marries after his dad succumbs to his illness.

On the other hand, she may go on as her own powerful force. He is beginning to see that she may well have been the force behind his father. Just as Vivian is the force behind him.

When it comes to her family, Vivian is ferocious. She will do anything for her children. And for him. His mother, it seems, had done the same.

"Did you know Sutton's family back then?"

"You're determined to talk about this, aren't you?"

"It's important."

"Why?"

He doesn't have an answer to that question. He supposes some of it had been brought on by the simple act of coming home and facing a situation he'd avoided for the past twenty years. "I just need to know."

"Your dad offered her—Sutton—money," she says with a shrug. "She took it."

"Did he threaten her?"

"I honestly have no idea what he said to her."

He doesn't believe that for a second. "And what did you do?"

"What makes you think I did anything?"

"Because you answered my question with a question."

She opens her mouth to argue, then shuts it again. She looks away, and then looks back. In the quiet of the house, Joe hears his dad's uneven breath coming from the other room. Finally, his mother says, "All I did was make sure she followed through."

"What about her parents?"

"Sutton was over eighteen. It was her job to keep her parents informed. Not mine." His mother's mouth is a firm, thin line. She will double down on her decision until the day she dies, no matter how wrong she may have been.

"She was still just a kid." Joe repeats his earlier remark.

This lights a fire under Sandra. "She was old enough to know what she was doing," she says slowly, articulating every word. "And so were you. But you weren't old enough to deal with the consequences intelligently." She frowns deeply. "Can you imagine what your life would have been like if she'd had that baby? There would have been no college, at least not out east. There would have been no baseball, no fraternity, no travel. There likely would be no Vivian, Natalie, or Ava. You may have taken over management of the dealership, but the expansion would not have happened. You'd have stayed in Conway with an unwanted child and perhaps an unwanted wife."

She drains the rest of her glass, and Joe can tell she is contemplating another. "I know that what happened that summer is the reason you hate coming back here." There is a measure of regret in her voice, but there is also steel. "I know some of what your father and I did drove you away. Let me tell you—I'd do it again in a heartbeat to protect you.

"Sutton is not my child, nor is she my concern. I'm sorry the girl has issues, but I take no responsibility for that." Sandra Wright straightens, rinses her wine glass, and sets it carefully on the counter. Before she walks from the room, she says, "I love you, Joe. More than you realize. I'll make no apologies for that, either."

In the seconds that follow, he can hear her moving around in the living room. His dad's breath changes, and the voice of Joe's mother murmurs to her husband softly. Joe is both awed and mortified by his mother's recklessness and lack of remorse, and as always, he struggles between love and judgment. Even if his mother feels no responsibility for Sutton's current circumstances, Joe can't help questioning his own role in Sutton's life.

What if there *had* been a baby? It may have given Sutton a reason to stay grounded. Maybe she wouldn't have drifted off into whatever awful situation had awaited her. Then again, maybe she would have taken the child down with her. Who was to say?

He's not sure how long he's been staring off into space when Paige enters the room, her face creased on one side, her hair flattened. "Hey," she says, grabbing a bottle of sparkling water from the refrigerator. She taps out one of her cigarettes and places it between her fingers.

"You shouldn't smoke those," Joe says.

"Do you really care?"

"I do, actually."

She shrugs, but she puts the cigarette back down on the counter in front of her. "It's a bummer that Vivian left."

He nods and blows out a breath—a modified chuckle without much humor. He looks at his sister. "Mom's crazy."

"You're just realizing that?"

"I guess I am."

Paige tips the bottle toward him. "I've had three failed marriages, and I'm not even thirty-five. At some point, I started suspecting that I might be part of the problem." She shakes her head. "Not Mom. According to her, I can do no wrong, and all those guys are losers."

"Are they?" Joe asks.

She opens her mouth as if to make a smart-ass comment, but instead her face turns thoughtful. "No, actually they're not," she says instead. "They were all good guys in their own ways."

Joe had met all three of her exes but hadn't gotten to know any of them well enough to have an opinion. They'd seemed okay to him, if a little advanced in age for his young sister.

"According to Mom, they're the scum of the earth."

Just like Sutton, he thinks. "Is that good or bad?" he asks his sister.

"That she's like that?" Paige cocks her head. "I'm not sure if it's good or bad. It's just Mom."

He nods. Paige has a point—their mother is never going to change, and she's never going to admit that she might have been wrong. So if there was any movement—any correction of past mistakes or healing of old wounds—it was going to have to come from Joe.

He's not sure he's up to the task, but he at least has to try.

A few hours later, Paige and his mother are watching a documentary on some streaming service, and Joe is sitting on the sofa scrolling through the social media pages for the dealership. He'd spoken with Vivian who had assured him that everything was under control, both at home and at work. He knows that she will hold down the fort while he stays in Conway with his family. He has seen a noticeable decline in his dad's awareness over the last twenty-four hours. While the nurse, Madison, wouldn't give an estimate of how much time they might have left, Joe knows that Bill Wright's time has grown shorter. He's not sure if his mom needs him here, but Joe needs to be here. And Vivian is offering that opportunity. That gift.

His dad drifts in and out of consciousness while Sandra, Paige, and Joe sit sentinel on the sofa. It's a bizarre vigil, and Joe is both horrified and honored to be a part of the witnessing of these last days. But there's something oddly routine about the moments, too, and when Paige says that she's hungry, Joe is the one who offers to make a run to the grocery store to pick up a rotisserie chicken and some macaroni and cheese for dinner. Preprepared comfort food. Paige also requests rocky road ice cream and a bottle of chocolate syrup.

None of that food is anything Joe would have eaten at home, and had Vivian still been here, she would no doubt have offered to cook an elaborate and healthy meal that included a balance of food groups. To be honest, Joe is looking forward to a sodium-filled, carb-laden dinner that would make them feel full and bloated afterward. He doesn't mind forgetting about his diet for a few days.

He grabs his keys and winds through Mitsin Ridge and then down Falgan Road toward the grocery store. As he passes Megan's memorial tree, he glances over, for once not avoiding its existence. Someone has removed the deflated balloons, and the cross is now stark and bare against the trunk.

Looking at the tree is not as horrendous as he'd thought it might be. After twenty years, the trunk is thicker and the canopy fuller, but the tree is still just a tree.

Joe realizes he's once again been holding his breath, and he inhales and exhales deliberately the rest of the drive.

The grocery store is not crowded on a Sunday afternoon. He pulls into a spot close to the door and grabs a basket to walk through the foreign aisles. The place has the basics but is not as trendy or as upscale as the market near the city where he and Vivian normally do their shopping. Still, he's able to find what he'd come for.

After picking up all of the items, leaving Paige's ice cream for last, he walks out of the frozen food aisle and heads toward the front of the store.

Standing alone at a display filled with electronics accessories is a small, painfully thin figure with long, lank blond hair. The pink t-shirt that the woman is wearing covers bony arms, one of which is secured in a sling, and a narrow back, and the jeans ride low on her hips. He knows this person, he realizes, just as Sutton Schultz turns around. Her left eye and neck are a greenish purple, and she looks warn and exhausted. The shock of her appearance hits him just as it had in the hospital a few days earlier.

She averts her eyes and quickly turns back around, and he is about to pass by as if he didn't recognize her.

But the conversation he'd had earlier with his mother is still fresh in his mind. This woman had nearly had his baby, and his parents had erased that potential path that his life might have taken. He can admit that he's glad for it, but what had been the toll on this other person because of him and his family?

He stops abruptly and turns around.

Though she doesn't look up, he can tell by the slight stiffening of her body and a shift in energy that she is aware of him walking toward her.

She studies the phone chargers intently, looking as if she might will him to disappear through inattention.

"Sutton?" he asks.

She looks up. Her eyes are still blue, and there is something left of the girl that he used to know. This woman is tentative and scared, though. Far from the rebellious aggression that he remembers.

He smiles, and it's genuine and warm. "Hi."

CHAPTER 35

CHLOE-NOW

It is May 28. Twenty years since the day that changed Chloe's life. Her world is still turning, albeit in a slightly different direction than it may have been otherwise.

A week has passed since Chloe and Emma made their spontaneous trip to Conway and shared a disastrous meal with Jason and Becky. A week has passed since Chloe told Emma about Matt and the party, a story that she's managed to keep buried deep for all these years. A week has passed since she came face-to-face with Joe Wright. Her world has not imploded. In fact, she and Emma have gotten along remarkably well since Chloe agreed that Emma should spend the summer with her father.

It's taken a bit of time, but Chloe has resigned herself to a summer without her daughter. While she's not looking forward to it, she and Elaine have agreed that the time alone might be good for Chloe, too. Chloe knows that she'll throw herself into her work, but she might be able to do things that she's always intended to do but never made the time. How many years has she intended to plant a garden or take up yoga?

She glances at the time on her phone. Jason, who works from home, is expecting them at 9:00 a.m., after which Chloe will drive to her meeting in the neighboring school district to talk about the supplemental curriculum for her

Academic Achievement Academy.

Then she'll return alone to a silent house. She is terrified.

Emma comes down with her bags packed, her face drawn and glum.

"Ready?" Chloe asks, and Emma gives a small shrug of her shoulders.

Chloe had suspected that her daughter may have second thoughts. But instead of reveling in the development, she puts an arm around Emma. "Give it a try and give your dad and Becky a chance. But remember—you can come home whenever you'd like."

Emma gives her a small smile, and her eyes are grateful.

A surge of emotion bubbles from deep within Chloe's belly, and she moves briskly so that the tears don't come. "Come on," she says. "Let's get going."

They stop at a fast-food drive-through for breakfast and eat their egg and cheese biscuits while a woman on Emma's playlist sings about a boy marrying the wrong girl. The lyrics are deceptively simple. At thirty-eight, Chloe is finally beginning to realize that there is rarely true right or wrong in this life. There's only a reaction to the circumstances flung in your direction.

Traffic is heavy as people head back to work after the long Memorial Day weekend. And though Chloe had thought she'd allotted plenty of time for the commute, by the time they get to Conway, they are later than they'd planned.

They stand on the front stoop in front of Jason's two-story house, but when Emma knocks on the door, no one answers. Chloe can hear the twins crying and Harper yelling.

She looks at Emma. "Maybe we should just go in?"

Emma nods and goes first, turning the knob and stepping over the threshold. Chloe steps in tentatively behind her daughter. To the right, the living room is cluttered with toys, stuffed animals, and a laundry basket overflowing with clothes. From the blaring television, a blue dog talks with an unidentified accent to the empty room. In the room to the left, a dining room table is covered with papers, envelopes, and folders. A laptop glows at a desk in the corner, and an email pings its incoming arrival.

From the top of the stairs, Harper yells something unintelligible as one of the twins screams.

Chloe glances at Emma. "Maybe go up?" she asks, and Emma nods and climbs the stairs cautiously.

After Emma disappears in the direction of the noise, Harper, at least, stops yelling. A few seconds later, Emma and Harper appear at the top of the staircase, holding hands. Jason follows, his thinning hair sticking straight up as he holds a twin on each hip.

"Hey," he says. "I'm so sorry. Becky was called in to teach today, and as you can see, it's not going well here."

Chloe holds up a hand. "No need to apologize."

Emma and Harper descend the staircase and head to the living room where the talking blue dog continues to chatter. Jason follows carefully with his hands full of babies. "Would you mind?" he asks and hands Chloe one of the twins without waiting for her answer. "I need to get breakfast for them."

He heads through the living room toward the back of the house. Chloe and the baby—she's not sure if it's Gavin or Liam—look at each other. Then they follow, Chloe carefully stepping over plush animals and colorful gadgets.

In the kitchen, Chloe secures the squirmy little bundle of baby on her hip. Even though it's been twelve years since she's held a child of this young age, the muscle memory surprises her. He pats his slobbery hand on her shoulder and babbles happily.

The baby in Jason's arm makes a squawking sound that threatens to turn into a yowl. Jason moves deftly, heating up two plates—mushy puddles of green, orange, and yellow.

He nods to a highchair that is secured to the end of the table. "You can slide Liam there," he directs.

Chloe does as he says.

This is bizarre, she thinks, helping her ex-husband with his new children in his house. She can't remember one time when they'd been married that Jason had taken charge of any of Emma's care. Child-rearing had fallen solely to Chloe, and she remembers resenting it. But watching him now, the calm and competent way that he moves, she wonders if control of the child-rearing process had been more her decision than his.

He places the small, compartmentalized plates on the counter and slides Gavin into the matching seat next to his brother.

"Thanks," Jason says. "Sometimes you just need an extra pair of hands."

Harper giggles over the sound of the television in the other room, and as Jason alternates spoonfuls of food into the mouths of his sons, Chloe suddenly feels incredibly out of place. She finds herself wishing that Becky were here.

This is the signal to take her leave. Besides, she doesn't want to be late to her meeting.

Before she goes, she hesitates, then asks, "Did Becky say any more about the assembly at the high school?"

Jason glances up, looking confused. Chloe reminds him of the conversation from dinner the week before with Ryan Tolbert.

As the memory comes back to him, he frowns and nods slowly. "What did you want to know?"

"Like what time it may be happening."

He scrapes a smear of what may be pureed banana from Gavin's chin, and Liam fingerprints his tray with the orange puree.

"This afternoon sometime," he says noncommittally.

Her meeting with the superintendent of the neighboring school district is scheduled for 10:30 a.m. She estimates that it will last roughly an hour, though she's left some room for potential follow-up conversations with the guidance staff. In any case, the conversations should not extend past twelve thirty.

"I can find out," Jason offers.

She nods. "Yes, I would appreciate that. Thank you."

Unspoken words hang between them, and she's not sure if they are hers or his. But Jason speaks first. "For what it's worth, I think it would be good for you to attend the assembly."

Normally, Chloe would take this as an uninvited criticism. A commentary on a subject he could not possibly understand. Today, none of those walls are raised. "Why?" she asks, genuinely curious about his thoughts.

Again, the tentative glance up and then back down. She's really done a number on this guy.

"I wasn't there twenty years ago," he starts, qualifying his comments before he speaks. "But I'd always gotten the sense that the responsibility you've taken for the deaths of both Megan and Matt were...inflated." The last word is spoken carefully.

"Inflated," she repeats slowly.

"I'm not trying to diminish what happened or your feelings about it. It's just that a lot of other people had responsibility, too, in both of those situations. It wasn't just you, Chloe."

She can tell that he's bracing for her reaction. She can also tell that he isn't expecting what she says next. "You're right."

"I am?"

"Part of the reason I was thinking of attending is to get some perspective. Seeing Joe Wright and Ryan Tolbert last week and realizing that they had no idea who I was…" She shakes her head. "Once my ego got over that, I realized that meant they were not thinking about me at all, which also meant that any involvement I thought I might have had may have been, exactly as you said, inflated."

"Yes," Jason agrees a little too enthusiastically. When he clocks her frown, he mumbles, "Sorry."

"I guess I've just always thought if I reduced the responsibility, even in my own mind, I would be making excuses for what happened to Matt and, as a result, what also happened to my parents."

Jason shakes his head and spoons the last of the food into both babies' mouths. "Chloe," he breathes, slightly exasperated. "Matt was six years older than you. He knew what he was doing, and he knew the risk that he was taking. You were just a kid."

"But I can't blame *him*," she cries.

"So, you think you have to blame yourself," he finishes. "But you don't need to do that anymore. You can let go of that burden."

A second later Emma and Harper enter the room, and Harper says, "I'm hungry."

Jason looks at the sticky set of twins and then to his youngest daughter, whose hands are planted firmly on her hips.

"I can get her something," Emma offers, and the grateful look on Jason's face is almost comical. "That would be wonderful, sweetheart."

Chloe's fear that Emma might turn into a babysitter are not assuaged, but at this point, at least, Emma does not seem to mind.

Chloe kisses her daughter, promises to call every day, and then says goodbye to Jason.

She steps off the front stoop feeling lighter somehow, as if she's left something of herself behind in Jason's house.

When she climbs into her SUV, she switches her playlist to one she hasn't listened to in years. A tenor male voice croons a melancholy ballad about a teenage beauty queen who's always belonged to someone else.

Chloe thinks of Megan. Then the chorus plays.

She will be loved. Chloe smiles.

CHAPTER 36

SUTTON-NOW

It is May 28. Sutton is in a strange room, in an unfamiliar place, miles from home. She is completely and utterly alone.

She and her parents had left at 5:00 a.m. to make the six-hour drive across the state to the inpatient rehabilitation facility that will be her home for the next three months.

The last week has been exhausting. Sutton kept up with the methadone treatment each morning, where, at a small counter separated by plexiglass, she was handed a miniature plastic cup with two pills containing her prescribed dosage. After about twenty minutes, she would just barely feel the effects of the drug. Unlike the immediate surge of bliss and oblivion that came with a heroin high, the methadone brought an almost undetectable eventual relief that slowly crept through first her brain and then her body. Throughout the day, the effects would diminish, and by early evening, she would begin to pulse and itch with that indescribable craving.

Evenings had been hard, enduring the lonely hours sitting in the small dark living room of her parents' house. The hours that her mother worked were worse than the days her mother was home. At least when Angela Schultz had been there, Sutton felt as if she had a reason to subsist. She could perch herself on the edge of a kitchen chair while her mother prepared dinner, chopping vegetables or distracting herself with small tasks.

When her mother was gone, Sutton had felt alone and untethered.

But worse than the evenings alone were the evenings when she'd been at home with her father. The man had been at a loss as to what he should say to Sutton. She knows that she's been a disappointment to him and has always sensed that she let him down somehow just by existing. They'd rarely had words for each other. Now, the silence between them is deafening.

The seconds had ticked by each day—a painful countdown to May 28, as they had been every year. Sutton has always hated this month with its slow march toward the date, culminating in the painful insignificance of the day itself. The biggest insult of all was always the lack of acknowledgment on the part of the universe.

A knock sounds on the door, making Sutton, alone in her small room, jump. A woman with strawberry-blond hair pulled back in a low ponytail pokes her head in the door. She wears no makeup, and her top teeth are slightly crooked. "Just checking in," she says, and Sutton gives the intruder a brief smile.

Her name is Olivia, and she is at least ten years younger than Sutton. "How is your room?" the woman asks.

In response, Sutton inadvertently glances around the space, which is decorated in different shades of beige and blues—azure, cerulean, cobalt. An anonymous oceanscape painting hangs framed above the bed, and a desk and lamp are positioned in the corner near an overstuffed armchair. A door on the other side of the room leads to a well-lit bathroom that smells of lemon and bleach.

Sutton is housed in a private room, which had led to a great deal of confusion upon arrival that morning with her parents. "There must be some mistake," her mother had said. "We don't have the money to pay for private accommodations." But Andrew, the admissions director with the soft Irish lilt, had assured them that Sutton's arrangements were in order and the balance of her residency had been settled.

To Olivia, Sutton says, "The room is fine." She motions toward the window on the opposite side of the room. "I like the view."

The facility, which is aptly named Treetop Manor, has been built atop a hill and overlooks a town and river valley. Although they are on the other side of the state, Sutton thinks that the town below looks much like Conway would appear from a similar vantage point.

"Isn't it lovely?" Olivia agrees. She informs Sutton of the name of the river and town, which Sutton promptly forgets, and mentions that she lives in the valley a few streets south of the river with her husband and young daughter. "If the weather holds, we'll do a therapy session outside tomorrow, and maybe go for a hike."

Sutton raises an eyebrow. The facility had confiscated her phone upon admittance. She asks, "You trust a bunch of addicts outside?"

"You are patients. And this is not a prison."

Sutton doesn't respond. She is grateful to have been admitted, and she is trying to show the appropriate amount of appreciation, but she can't suppress that skeptical and jaded part of her that feels as if this is all a bit of a farce.

Olivia had been introduced as one of two primary therapists for their group of residential patients. She supervises a small staff of experimental specialists, holistic practitioners, and wellness consultants. Every three days for the next ninety days, Sutton and her fellow program participants will endure a rigorous and structured schedule of therapy and daily activities that include exercise, clean eating, and supplemental classes and career counseling.

Every three days, Sutton will meet with a medical doctor. After the program is complete, she will continue to attend weekly sessions with her appointed therapist who will consult with a caregiver at home until such time that all parties agree that the treatment is no longer needed.

Sutton isn't clear on what any of these people will actually do, or if any of this will work, but she is trying to keep an open mind.

"Dinner is in an hour," Olivia says. "I'll collect you, and we'll walk together to the dining room, where you'll meet the other patients in an informal setting."

Sutton raises her chin a notch and nods once. She does not want Olivia to know that she's terrified. Olivia seems to know anyway. "You are going to do just fine."

Over the past week, Sutton has inadvertently found herself practicing vulnerability. For most of her life, she has retreated inward when faced with a challenge. Somehow she had gotten the idea that it was a badge of honor if she was able to deal with challenges on her own. Part of that is her status as an only child. From a very early age, she'd wanted to seem perfect to her parents. Of course, that strategy failed long, long ago.

But there is another part of her that thought asking for help was a sign of weakness and failure. It has only been this past week that she's realized she's not the only person who struggles with the weight of time, emotion, and memory. And it's only been this past week that she's realized that sharing her feelings can make her feel less alone.

Without thinking about it, Sutton asks, "What if they don't like me?"

"You're lovely," Olivia responds enthusiastically. "Everyone will love you." She pauses. "But if they don't, that's okay, too. You're not obligated to like everyone, and they're not obligated to like you. Sometimes life is like that."

Sutton blinks at the honesty of that statement. It makes her feel better. "Okay," she says.

Olivia gives her another smile and turns to leave, but before she closes the door, Sutton says, "My best friend died on this day twenty years ago."

Olivia opens the door back up again. Sutton can see her weighing her response. Finally, she says, "What is her name?"

Mirroring Olivia's use of present tense, Sutton says, "Her name is Megan."

"When you're ready and comfortable, perhaps you can honor her memory and her spirit by telling her story to the group."

"If it weren't for me, she'd still be alive."

Olivia chews on her lip and then comes back into the room, closing the door softly behind her. She seems to be giving Sutton the space to share, but Sutton can't bring herself to say any more. At least not right now.

After a minute, Olivia speaks. "When I was fourteen, I was supposed to be watching my seven-year-old brother who wanted to play near the river. I got distracted by a phone call about something unimportant. He waded too far into the water and lost his footing. The current carried him away. They found his body three days later."

Sutton doesn't know what to say.

"I carry guilt with me every day," Olivia says. "But I also carry love and light and forgiveness." She touches her chest with the fingertips of both hands. "And I carry him with me."

Tears fill Sutton's eyes.

"We get to choose what we do with our grief," Olivia says quietly. "I choose to use mine to help others."

Sutton has been using her grief to harm herself. And she hasn't been the only one.

Olivia looks at her thoughtfully. "Thank you for sharing that with me."

"It seemed important."

"It *is* important." She gestures toward the desk and a leather-bound book that rests next to a black pen. "We encourage all guests to keep a journal. If you're so inclined, an entry on this subject might be a good place to start."

Sutton follows her gaze and hesitates. Documenting her feelings makes them so permanent.

Olivia says, "Only by facing our fears can we overcome them. Our fears know where to find us whether we acknowledge them or not."

Sutton exhales. "I'll try."

"That's all we can do." She gives Sutton another smile and then retreats, shutting the door behind her.

Sutton walks to the desk and sinks into the chair. She opens the journal to the thick, creamy first page and sits poised with pen above paper, considering the words that she should write. Then she realizes that the words themselves don't matter as much as the act of releasing them.

She writes: *One week ago, I made a plan to kill myself. I wanted to do it before today, May 28, so that I could no longer insult the anniversary of Megan's death with my continued existence. I had a plan to buy the drugs and die in the same spot where Megan died. A sacrifice to her and her family, and for everyone else who remembered what happened that night. A sacrifice so that we could all move on.*

Obviously, I didn't follow through or I wouldn't be writing these words. I have asked myself why I didn't go through with it. Why I'm now in this resi-

dential rehabilitation facility, as if I have something useful to offer to this life.

But the strangest thing happened as I was making my plans. I saw Joe Wright at the grocery store. Joe Wright, the boy who started it all. But this time, he did not ignore me. He did not pretend that I didn't exist. He did not act like I was beneath him. He apologized for everything—for Megan, for the baby, for how he'd treated me. He apologized because he thought it had all been his fault. The same feelings that have haunted me for all of these years have also haunted him.

It was such a relief to find out that I am not alone in those feelings.

Even after seeing Joe, I might still have gone through with the suicide, but every time I thought about it, he sent me a text message, like he'd known. He told me about his life; he told me about his family; he told me about his dad. He unburdened himself to me, and somehow, sharing his burden lightened my own.

I told him a little about my struggles, but I didn't tell him everything, and he didn't force it.

And when we got to the facility this morning, everything was paid for. The private room and board, the treatment, the aftercare. My parents were confused, but I knew who was responsible. I will never tell.

I can't thank him because I don't have my phone in here. But I guess I can repay him by trying my hardest to get through the next few months as best I can and coming out a better person. It won't bring Megan back. On the twentieth anniversary of her death, nothing will bring her back.

There is a part of me that still believes I don't deserve to live while she is gone. But I do hold her with me, in my heart. I remember her every day. Is that enough? Olivia said something that might be important—we choose what we do with our grief. I don't know what I should do with my own grief, but maybe by the end of this program I'll have some idea. In the meantime, I'm willing to try to figure it out. Not only for Megan, but for the wounded girl I was and for the incomplete woman I still am.

Whatever happens, Megan, you still have some of me. But not all of me. Not yet. And I think you'd be glad to know that. Because once upon a time, you loved me, and I loved you. I wasn't able to show it properly then. It's still not fair that you're gone and I'm still here. But maybe I can use my grief to honor you somehow. Maybe when I dream about you, it's less about you haunting me and more about me remembering you. Remembering how kind and beautiful you were, and trying to live the rest of my life in the same way.

Sutton stares at the words she's written and blinks. She has an overpowering urge to tear out the pages and crumple them. She feels small and helpless. She feels bleak and hopeless. She squeezes her eyes shut, threads her fingers into her hair, and tugs until it hurts. She wants to scream.

But before she can open her mouth, she has the distinct sensation of two hands on her shoulders. A chill creeps up her neck, and the sensation of the invisible hands covers her own. It coaxes her fingers away from her head and holds her lightly, so gentle that it's almost painful.

Sutton is terrified; she looks around anyway, half expecting to see Megan standing behind her. The room is empty, but the air is filled with her—her laughter, her kindness, her beauty.

"Megan?" she whispers.

Silence answers her, and Sutton waits, barely breathing.

It was just her imagination, she finally concludes.

She turns back to the journal, and as she does, a draft catches the page of the book, fluttering the leaf. The sheet of paper hesitates on a breath, suspended for less than a second between past and present. And then it floats down, settling on a new page, a clean sheet of paper. A fresh start.

Sutton stares at the book. She turns around again. Nothing. The room is quiet.

When she turns back to the journal—the blank page—she swears she hears just a hint of a whisper. *Your story is still unwritten.*

CHAPTER 37

JOE-NOW

William Edward Wright died peacefully on May 28 with his beloved wife and children by his side.

Joe stares at the solitary sentence on his laptop screen for a long time. Finally, he forces his fingers to press the keys.

A graduate of Conway High School, Bill was a proud member of the Conway community for his entire life. He was the founder and owner of Wright Automotive Group, a business that flourished under his leadership for thirty-five years until his well-deserved retirement. He enjoyed traveling with his wife, Sandra, and spending time with his family—his daughter Paige and son Joseph (Vivian), and his two grandchildren, Natalie and Ava.

He stops typing. The cursor blinks back at him after Ava's name, and his breath catches.

He reads the words he's written.

The first sentence is not accurate. His father had not gone peacefully. He'd held on to this life with every ounce of strength he could muster. As powerful of a force that his father had been in life, it should not have surprised Joe that Bill Wright would not go gentle into that good night.

But it isn't that small fabrication that bothers Joe. It is the last sentence.

His father had not spent enough time with Natalie and

Ava. Or Joe for that matter. And that had been all Joe's fault.

Vivian and the girls had visited a day earlier—Memorial Day. His daughters hadn't understood what had been happening, of course. Natalie had kept asking why Granddad was lying in a bed in the living room. And Ava, still shy at two, had mostly hidden behind Vivian's back as they'd sat on the sofa. Before she'd left, Vivian predicted that she'd be back the next day, but Joe had argued that his dad would hold on for another week.

In the end, Vivian had been correct. When Sandra had woken that morning, her husband's breath was shallow and his eyes unfocused. They'd all known that the time was very near. They'd called the nurse, Madison, who had rushed over but given them the privacy they'd needed. Then they'd taken turns saying their goodbyes, and their mother had held her husband's hand as he'd transitioned.

Madison had taken care of the rest.

All of the arrangements had been made long ago, so there wasn't much to do.

Joe had thought he was emotionally prepared, but it turns out that nothing really prepares you for the loss of a parent.

Now he is sitting at the kitchen island, trying to figure out how to bleed his feelings into a coherent death notice for the local newspaper.

His mother has been furiously cleaning since the funeral home arrived to take possession of her husband's body, and Paige fades in and out of rooms aimlessly, as if she's a ghost herself.

Joe is still staring at that blinking cursor when his sister appears beside him and lets out a shaky breath. Her eyes are red and swollen, but for now, they're dry. She clutches a damp wad of tissue in her fist. "I could really use a cigarette," she says. She doesn't look directly at him, and he avoids looking directly at her, lest he open the flood of her tears again.

"That's not going to help in the long run," he says. But he understands her craving. He doesn't have many vices himself, but if a bad habit could offer some comfort, he'd be open to starting a new one in this moment.

"How's this going?" she asks, her voice wobbly, nodding toward the laptop.

"I'm not sure I'm the one who should be writing this."

"Well, I certainly can't do it. I don't think Mom can either." From somewhere on the second floor, the vacuum hums.

Joe returns his gaze to the screen without really looking at it, and Paige says, "What time is Viv coming back?"

"Not until this evening. She'll come for dinner."

As word of their father's death has passed through the community, prompted by notification of the funeral director along with his sister's texts, phone calls, and social media posts, a limited number of food items had already been delivered to the house with gentle words of sorrow and sympathy.

These visits will increase throughout the day and crescendo when the initial death notice appears in the online edition of the local newspaper later that afternoon.

Paige glances over his shoulder, and a fresh deluge of tears begins as she reads Joe's words. He pushes the laptop to the side so that the screen points away from her. "I don't know why you're crying at that. There's nothing there."

"That's why I'm crying," she manages.

"I'm doing my best."

She shakes her head. "It's not that. How do you pack someone's whole life into a few paragraphs?"

With another watery sigh, she fades out of the room again, leaving Joe to stare at the screen alone.

The significance of the date itself is certainly not lost on him. Exactly twenty years to the day since that ill-fated party. The date that he'd dreaded every single year since Megan's death, and now he has double the reason to hate May 28.

He glances at his phone. He'd texted Sutton earlier with the news.

Since he'd encountered her in the grocery store just over a week ago, they'd embarked on a tentative friendship. He still isn't sure what had possessed him to talk to her when he'd seen her standing in that aisle, but the look on her sunken face when he'd said hello had been first one of disbelief and then one of incredible gratitude.

During that first awkward conversation, she'd asked after his father. That had moved him, especially knowing how his parents had treated her. In turn, he'd asked in general terms about her life. In those few minutes, she'd mentioned her addiction and attempts at treatment. She hadn't mentioned whatever it had been that had called Angela Schultz away from her work with Joe's father, but Joe could see the deep pain in Sutton's eyes.

It hadn't seemed right to leave the conversation on that note, so Joe had suggested he take her number to keep in touch. He'd had no intention of contacting her again, especially when Sutton's mother had rounded the corner and glared fiercely at him. If he'd had any question as to whether Angela knew about what had happened between the two of them in high school, the question was answered by the hatred in her eyes. He didn't blame her.

He'd walked away, but he hadn't been able to forget that initial look of gratitude on Sutton's face. As if she'd been waiting her entire life for someone to see her.

When he'd told Vivian about the encounter, she'd encouraged him to reach back out. She'd said it might give him closure, whatever that had meant. But his wife was a lot smarter than he was, because when he did text Sutton and the conversation continued, he actually felt better.

It isn't so much that he feels better about what had happened twenty years ago, but Sutton clearly needs help, and he is in a position to give it. He is wise enough to know that money can't fix everything. Sometimes money makes everything a lot worse. But in this case, all he had needed was the name of Sutton's inpatient treatment center.

One phone call on his part resulted in one less thing that Sutton and her family needed to worry about. It had been the very least he could do.

He looks back at the names of his children on the screen. Someday, one of them would likely be writing similar words for him. He wants them to be able to write about how he'd do anything for them—to protect them, to ensure that they grew up healthy, happy, and prosperous, despite all of the mistakes they might make on their own.

He starts typing.

William (Bill) Wright, 68, a lifelong resident of Conway, Pennsylvania, died peacefully with his devoted wife and children by his side on May 28. A graduate of Conway High School, Bill was a proud member of the Conway community throughout his lifetime, serving in various leadership positions in his beloved hometown.

The founder and owner of Wright Automotive Group for thirty-five years until his well-deserved retirement, Bill generously supported a number of causes—many anonymously—throughout the years. He was a supporter of the history, culture, and revitalization of the community, but the role that he dedicated himself to fully and completely was that of husband and father.

You would rarely see Bill around town without his adoring wife Sandra by his side. They were a package deal, a united front, and together they were a force to be reckoned with. Bill would have done (and sometimes did do) anything for his children, Paige Wright and Joseph (Vivian) Wright. There was rarely a weekend that Bill wasn't found supporting Paige at an equestrian competition somewhere along the east coast, cheering on both Paige and the family horse, Brodie. Similarly, he never missed one of Joe's baseball or football games or wrestling matches.

All children make mistakes, some of them bigger than others, but Bill was always there to offer a word of advice, a light out of the darkness, and sometimes a shoulder to cry on. Neither Paige nor Joe would be where they are without the steadfast support of their parents and the understanding and watchful eye of Bill Wright. While his grandchildren Natalie and Ava are too young to have known just how amazing their granddad really was, they'll grow up listening to stories about him—the man, the myth, the legend.

Rest in Peace, Dad. You'll be missed and remembered.

Joe is reading over the words so intently that he doesn't hear his mother come up behind him. Only when a soft, "Oh, Joe," escapes her lips does he startle and turn around.

She is staring at the screen. Her hands are pressed to her mouth, and her eyes shine.

His immediate reaction is embarrassment, but he suppresses it and instead says, "Is it okay?"

Her chin quivers Sandra she nods. "I didn't think you understood."

"I'm starting to," he says. He doesn't cry, but he can feel the emotions welling up in his throat as his mother wraps her arms around him. He hugs her back. While she is healthy, he can feel her fragility as he holds her. Their time together is not unlimited.

Paige floats back into the room and joins the family hug. Joe swears that he can hear his father's laugh from somewhere close by.

They've just broken apart, all three of them laughing and crying, when the doorbell sounds. Because both of the women have tears streaming down their faces, Joe blinks his own tears away and says, "I'll go."

When he opens the door, he finds an older woman he doesn't immediately recognize standing in front of him holding out a foil pan. She thrusts it forward. "It's a chicken and cheese noodle bake."

"Thank you." Joe waits for her to say something else, but she doesn't.

The pan now in his possession, she shoves her hands into the pockets of a shapeless blue dress. He inclines his head toward the open door behind him. "Would you like to come in?"

"Oh, no, I couldn't impose at a time like this." Still, she offers no other words of sympathy.

Joe is curious. Even though it's been years, he expects to recognize most of the friends of his parents. People didn't change *that* much over the years. "Did you know my dad well?" he asks.

"Not well, no," she says. She looks like she wants to say something else but then stares off into the distance, searching for the words.

Joe wants to help her out. "My mom is inside if you'd like to talk with her."

"Oh, no." The woman says this quickly. At Joe's confused face, she adds, "I'm sorry. I'm not good with this." She waves her hand around her.

He smiles and leans in. "I don't think any of us are."

She smiles back and then studies him. "You grew up to be a very handsome man."

His smile fades. "Have we met?"

"A long time ago. You probably don't remember me." She moves to put her hand out and then remembers the pan Joe's holding. "I'm Renee Richards," she says.

All of the saliva dries in his mouth, and he feels the blood drain from his face when he realizes that this is Megan's mother. He's not quite sure what to say, so he just says, "Thank you for coming, today of all days." The date is painfully present in his mind and between them.

Her gaze touches his and then skims away. "Strange coincidence."

The way that she says the words makes Joe think she doesn't believe in coincidences.

"Your dad made things a lot easier for us…afterward."

Joe just nods. He knows what she's referring to, but he doesn't let on.

"I thought I'd stop by before I head up to the high school for this assembly thing that Ryan Tolbert is doing." She shifts from one foot to the other. "I don't like to talk about that day, but if it helps someone after all these years…" Her voice trails off. "My husband was supposed to come with me, but he can't bring himself to stand on stage in front of all those kids." She blows out a breath. "Can't say I blame him."

The words falter between them, and she looks around the house and then to the road, as if she's imagining Megan's final retreat.

"I really liked your daughter," he says, wondering just how much this woman knows about the drama surrounding the last days of high school. It all seems so silly and insignificant now. It hadn't been then.

"Megan liked you, too. And you turned out just fine. I see your commercials with your beautiful wife. She looks a little like Megan—how I imagine Megan might look now."

Joe shifts from one foot to the other. Mrs. Richards isn't the first one to mention the resemblance between Megan and Vivian, and Joe isn't completely comfortable with the implication. He clears his throat. "I didn't treat Megan well…in the end."

She puts up a hand. "Don't you dare do that." Her voice is gentle but fierce. "You were kids. All of you." She shakes her head. "Stupid, innocent, ridiculous, sweet kids who didn't know any better. It's all such a shame. So many lives affected."

They look at each other for a beat longer than Joe would like, and Renee Richards says, "Please pass along my condolences to your mother and sister." Her smile is weak when she adds, "And wish me luck."

As she walks away, Joe says, "Mrs. Richards?"

She turns around.

"What time does the assembly start?"

"Half past one." She gives a little wave and heads to her car. She drives away slowly, and Joe shuts the door behind him and walks to the kitchen with the pan. "Cheesy chicken bake," he announces, setting the pan on the counter.

Both Paige and his mother have pulled themselves together and opened a bottle of wine. Joe doesn't think that is a great idea, but he only shakes his head when they offer him a glass.

"Who was that?" his mother asks.

"Renee Richards," he says. He doesn't mention Megan's name. Instead, he says, "Dad helped her out a long time ago."

"He was a good man who helped a lot of people." Sandra toasts the air.

Joe glances at his phone and notes the time. It's one o'clock. "I think I'm going to take a drive, unless you need me here."

His mother waves him away. "The minister is coming at three to talk through the arrangements for the service, but I don't think we need you here for that."

He eyes the glass in her hand and glances at Paige who waves him away. She scrunches up her face with a look that says, *It's fine.*

Joe decides that he'll return by three.

He makes the drive through town and pulls into the visitor parking lot at the high school. His heart is thumping, and his hands are sweating on the steering wheel. He cuts the engine and sits in silence. *This is a mistake.*

He's about to start the engine again and back out when a small red SUV whips into the space beside him. He glances over and makes eye contact with a woman who seems very familiar. She looks away quickly and stares straight ahead.

It takes him a minute, but he realizes this is the woman that he'd seen a week ago during dinner at the Crawford Inn. He'd recognized her only after he'd had the chance to connect her face with the memories. Chloe Nicholson.

This is also the woman his dad had asked Joe to apologize to. "Wow, Dad," he mumbles out loud, thinking of Renee Richards at the front door and now Chloe Nicholson in the car beside him. "You're not even trying to be subtle," he says to the spirit of his father.

He waits for the woman to glance over again. He knows that she's seen him. But she doesn't. She looks as if she might leave.

He climbs from the car and taps his knuckle against the

passenger window of Chloe's vehicle.

In the brief pause that follows, he thinks she might ignore him. Then she powers down the glass, barely looking at him. "Yes?"

"Chloe?"

Her eyebrows shoot up. Her lips are pressed tightly together, and the tendons in her neck are taut.

"It's Joe Wright. I'm not sure if you remember me from high school."

"I remember," she finally says. "I remember everything." This is said quietly, almost to herself.

"Are you going in for the assembly?"

She opens her mouth, then shuts it again. She looks around as if she's surprised to find herself in the parking lot of the high school. He feels the same way and says as much.

This bit of vulnerability seems to soften her, and she opens the door of the car and steps out. They start walking toward the front entrance to the school in silence.

Joe says, "My dad died this morning." He's not sure why he blurts it out like that.

"I'm sorry to hear that."

"He wanted me to apologize to you."

"To me?"

"For what happened to your brother. He felt partially responsible."

She says nothing.

They reach the front doors and find them locked. There's a camera and intercom button on the wall to the left. Joe is closest to the intercom and presses the button. A woman's disembodied voice says, "Can I help you?"

"Joe Wright and Chloe Nicholson here for the assembly at the request of Principal Tolbert."

There is a pause. "Just a minute, please."

In the silence that follows, Chloe says, "I've spent a lot

of time thinking about your family over the years."

From her clipped tone, Joe can tell that those thoughts were not good.

"My brother has been gone twenty years, and my parents nearly that long."

Joe dips his head. He's just lost his dad today, but in a way, he severed ties that long ago as well. He knows it's not the same thing at all, and he doesn't vocalize his thoughts to Chloe. Instead, he says, "I'm so sorry."

"You didn't recognize me last week. At the Crawford Inn."

"It took me a while," he admits.

She shakes her head. "I've wasted so much time."

Joe isn't sure what that means, but he suspects it has something to do with him. "To be fair," he says, "the last time I'd seen you, we were kids, and you were not yet a knockout."

She glares at him. "Stop."

But it's true. Her highlighted hair is cut in an elegant blunt style, her features are meticulously enhanced with neutral makeup, and she's wearing a cream-colored tailored suit that is cut perfectly to her small, curvy frame. She is not the same body type as his tall, willowy wife, but she's definitely attractive. He would have never connected her to the girl he'd known in high school. He shrugs.

"It's just…what happened back then changed my life."

"It changed all of our lives."

She rolls her eyes. "We are not the same."

"No, we're not the same as we were back then." He deliberately misunderstands her. "We're twenty years older and maybe twenty minutes wiser."

Chloe laughs, and Joe feels pleased at this small victory. He tentatively places a hand lightly on her shoulder. She does not move away from him.

Finally, there is a buzzing sound and the latch of the door clicks. Joe pulls it open. He and Chloe Nicholson walk through the door of Conway High School one more time.

CHAPTER 38

CRYSTAL-NOW

It is May 28, and Crystal has barely heard from Dan over the past week. Some of her text messages to him were returned with one-word responses, which was only slightly better than the messages that had received no response at all. He had ignored her invitations to dinners and a Memorial Day cookout with Frank's family. She had even teased confidential legal information about Amber's divorce case, or lack thereof.

He'd been infuriatingly reticent.

"You have to let this go," Frank had said as she'd fretted about Dan's state of mind. "He's not a kid. He can take care of himself. And if he can't, that's not your problem."

Crystal knows that her husband is right. But now it's the twentieth anniversary of that goddamned party, and she is officially anxious.

After making Frank's breakfast, she dresses and exits the front door, leaving Frank to watch some conspiracy theory documentary. She's not even sure that he's aware that she's left despite the fact that he acknowledged her farewell.

As she walks down the porch steps, she realizes that she is extremely lonely, and by the time she gets into her car, she is nearly in tears.

She starts the engine and sits there for just a minute. The late spring air is cool, but she knows that the temperature will be in the seventies and the sky will be sunny later in the day. Her sadness tips toward anger. She should be enjoying the start of the summer season. She should be looking forward to blue skies and warm afternoons. She should be…so much more than she is right now.

And to hell with Dan, too, for making her feel like she'd done something unforgivable. She was right to confront him about his drinking. And Frank was right to insist that he stay somewhere else if he kept on behaving badly.

She runs her hands up and down the cool plastic of the steering wheel.

Hadn't they been right?

She glances at the clock on her dashboard. It's 8:39 a.m.

Before she can think better of it, she snatches her phone from where she'd placed it in the center console and navigates to her favorites list, scrolling until she finds the number she needs. It rings twice before the woman picks up.

"Marie Munson speaking."

"Hi, Marie, this is Crystal Neumann."

There is a pause. "Hi, Crystal. Won't I be seeing you in just a few minutes?" The voice is a tad too cheerful.

"That's actually why I'm calling. I wasn't feeling well when I woke up. I thought I'd be fine to make it in, but as the morning went on, I started to feel worse. I'm hoping that it won't be too much trouble if I take a sick day."

There is another pause, and Crystal can tell that Marie doesn't believe her. She feels slightly indignant. She's been there nearly three months, and she's barely taken any time off at all—only for Frank's doctor appointments and once for her own dentist appointment. She's only left early twice and has only been late a handful of times. This is, in fact, the first sick day that she's taken.

"Look, Crystal, I understand that everyone gets sick. I

really do. But it's extremely late notice to find someone to fill in for you."

Crystal is quiet even though she can tell Marie is waiting for her to say something.

"Crystal?" Marie finally says.

"I'm here."

Marie sighs. "If you're sick, you're sick, I guess. We'll manage. But, Crystal, when you come back tomorrow, you and I need to talk about the expectations for this position. There have been some other things…potential conflicts that Mr. Temple has brought to my attention as well."

Crystal's jaw is clenched. "Understood," she replies then disconnects the call, angry all over again. But she won't let Marie get to her. She has something to do now.

As she drives, she tries Dan's cell again. It rings five times and then goes to voicemail. He should be awake and an hour into his shift at the rail yard. She recognizes that he might not be able to answer her call, so she pulls into the employee parking lot at the rail yard and wanders around until a grizzled man in a blue jumpsuit emblazoned with a company logo and the name *Rick* notices her and says, "Can I help you?"

"I'm looking for Dan Armstrong."

He frowns. "Don't know that I've seen him today. You his wife or something?"

The question catches Crystal off guard because it's so ludicrous. "Or something," she answers, and the guy arches a brow with an understanding that Crystal had not intended.

She starts to protest, but he dismisses her words with a wry grin. "I'll go check on him for you." He walks away, leaving her to hope that she didn't just start a rumor that might get back to Amber. That's all Dan needs.

When the man comes back a few minutes later, he

shrugs at her. "Dan's off today," he says.

Crystal chews on her lower lip, worried all over again. Dan has never been one to miss work, no matter what is going on in his personal life. "Off, as in he took a vacation day? Or off, as in he didn't show up?"

Rick says, "I'm just telling you what they told me."

"Because requesting a day off is different than not showing up."

"Lady, he's not here. That's all I know."

"Can you go check?"

When he gives her an annoyed look, she says, "Or I will, if you tell me who I need to talk to." She points in the direction of the office and starts walking.

Muttering something under his breath, the man turns around. "Just hold on a minute," he says over his shoulder.

While she waits, Crystal continues to chew the inside of her bottom lip until it's good and raw.

When Rick comes back, his expression is stony. "Chuck said Dan requested early last week to take today as a vacation day."

"He didn't say what for?"

"That's all the information I have for you, lady. If Dan didn't tell you any of this himself, it's certainly not my job to keep you updated."

Crystal considers him thoughtfully, gauging his willingness to answer questions about Dan's attendance and attitude this past week. But the man's brow is furrowed, and the grin on his face has long since vanished. She decides not to push her luck. "Thanks for your help." She actually does appreciate the information he's given her, but her words come across as sarcastic.

He makes a grunting noise and walks away, clearly sorry that he'd approached her in the first place.

Crystal climbs back into her car and holds an internal

debate with herself. She could give up and go into the office. Marie would likely be irritated by her appearance but ultimately glad that she didn't have to answer the phones and greet clients herself. Crystal then considers driving to Dan's house where Amber was most likely at home. Crystal's not sure how Amber would feel about seeing her. She doubts Dan's wife will appreciate any excessive concern coming from Crystal. Then again, maybe Dan is back home by now. Amber had canceled her last scheduled appointment with Temple.

Maybe during the past week, Dan and Amber had resolved their differences and Dan's request for time off was actually a positive development.

Crystal makes the short drive to the south side of town where Dan's house is tucked away on a quiet side street, shaded by mature oak and maple trees. She drives slowly past and notes Amber's minivan. Dan's truck is nowhere to be seen. She keeps driving, unsure of her next move, until she finds herself heading out of town and up the back side of the mountain. By the time she realizes where she's headed, it's too late to turn back, and so she keeps on going.

She follows slow-moving school buses, logging trucks, and tri-axles with loads of rock and gravel up and over the winding mountain roads. Nearly forty minutes have passed by the time she makes the turn into the community of Highland Rocks. It's been years since she's been in this neighborhood. When she and Dan were kids, her mother would often drive into the mountain community to collect Dan from his father, but Crystal had never once left the safety of the car.

The roads look very much the same, though there are newer houses nestled amongst the trees. The community is a diverse collection of ostentatious-looking homes masquerading as rustic log cabins and more modest cabins, many of which had been built by the hands of their owners' ancestors. Crystal remembers it being a beautiful, if remote, place in all seasons, but it's certainly lovely now in the late spring growth.

But the place is also connected with her memories of the disappearance of her aunt, which fills Crystal with unease.

Deep muscle memory leads her to the house of Dan's father, one of the humble homes on the street. If it wasn't for the large concrete garage located to the right of the property, she might not have noticed the house at all. But there, parked in the driveway, is Dan's truck. Multiple other vehicles in various states of roadworthiness are parked around the garage.

Crystal has no way of knowing if Greg Armstrong is also home. The thought of encountering the man fills her with dread.

But when she parks and starts walking slowly up the driveway, it is the weathered, age-toughened figure of Greg that pushes the storm door open before she even has a chance to knock.

She can tell he doesn't recognize her. Why would he? The last time she'd seen the man had been during Dan's sentencing hearing, and Crystal isn't sure Greg had ever known she'd existed.

He has less hair, and what's left is gray, but it's still cut in the same short menacing crewcut.

"Help you?" he asks. He's wary but not unfriendly.

"I'm looking for Dan."

As she gets closer to the door, Greg squints at her. "I'll be damned. You're Brenda's daughter." He snaps his fingers. "Crystal."

She affirms his deduction, and he shakes his head. "You look just like her. Like both of them," he adds in a voice that is less gruff.

Crystal does not have fond memories of Greg, so she says, "I just want to talk to Dan."

He holds the door open for her, but she stays on the small covered porch. He gives her a curious glance but lets the door bang shut behind him.

A minute later, Dan is framed in the storm door, and he steps outside. He is dressed well in a pair of light brown trousers and a button-down green shirt, the cuffs of which are pushed up to his elbows. His hair is still slightly damp above his ears, as if he's just showered.

At least her fears that he has been wallowing in a deep depression have been subdued. Dan looks healthy and well rested; not at all like a man who has been drowning his sorrows in a bottle. On the other hand, this means that he's been very deliberately ignoring her messages.

"What are you doing here?" He looks at her business-casual black slacks and pink blouse. "Don't you work today?"

"I came up here to make sure you were okay, since you aren't responding to my messages."

He shakes his head slightly and looks off into the distance. "Crystal, I'm fine. I told you that in my last three replies to you."

"You didn't pick up when I called you this morning."

"I was getting dressed." There is a forced patience in his voice that infuriates her.

"I'm not some annoyance, Dan. I'm your cousin who has always had your back and who loves you very much."

He holds his hands out in front of him, palms down. "You're right, and I'm sorry. I just needed some time."

"And you've chosen to spend that time here? With your good-for-nothing father? I told you to come back to the house. I told you that I'd talked to Frank—"

"Crystal," he interrupts. "This is exactly where I need to

be." At her mystified glance around the property, he continues, "There was a lot that I didn't understand about my mother and my father. Their relationship. Her disappearance. I'll never have all the answers, but I have more now than I did before. I needed this time."

"But what about Amber? What about the kids?"

"We've been talking. I wouldn't say there's a resolution, but at least there's communication."

Crystal blinks. She should feel happy about this news, but instead she feels let down. And left out.

Dan must sense this, too, because he reaches out and puts a hand on her arm. "This was good for me, Crystal. If I had stayed with you, there's a lot I still wouldn't understand. It doesn't change anything. My childhood was still awful. But it does make me appreciate even more how important you and Aunt B were to me."

This mollifies her slightly, and she knows she's acting like a petulant child. "What about today?" she asks. "The date."

Dan exhales through his nose. After a moment, he says, "You know the assembly that Ryan Tolbert told us about in Bud's? The one Henry found out about?"

She nods.

"I'm going to speak."

"In front of the school?"

She can see the lump in his throat as he swallows. "It's part of the reason I haven't wanted to talk. I'm terrified."

"Are you sure it's a good idea?"

"It's something I have to do."

"What are you going to say?"

From his pocket he pulls out some folded pieces of notebook paper scribbled with smudged black ink. Crystal can see that words have been crossed out and added in the margins and that the pages have been unfolded and refolded multiple times. "I'm not sure what's going to come out when I get up there."

"Do the Richards know that you're going to be there?"

"I sure hope so. Ryan supposedly arranged everything."

Crystal gazes off into the distance. "I think that's great, Dan, that you're moving forward. It's about time." Again, she gets that feeling of unease, as if she's been dismissed.

"I wouldn't have been able to do it without you."

She gives him a half smile.

"Come with me?" he asks.

"To the assembly? Do you want me to be there?"

"Honestly? I'd prefer that no one at all be there." He laughs. "But it would be nice to know there's a friendly face in that crowd."

She nods. "I'd love to."

He holds the door open for her. "It doesn't start for a while. Want to come in and help me practice a few times?"

Crystal hesitates as she looks at the inside of Dan's childhood home.

"No monsters," Dan says softly. "I've killed them all." He laughs, but Crystal doesn't. He adds, "Maybe it's time for you to kill yours, too."

For some reason, that makes her want to laugh and cry at the same time. "Oh, Dan," she says with a sigh. "You and me—we are not the same."

He rubs her shoulder as she walks through the door. "Thank God for that. I wouldn't wish that destiny on anybody, especially the person I love most in this world." And he laughs, which makes her laugh too.

"We're going to be just fine," he says.

Crystal believes that.

CHAPTER 39

DAN-NOW

I t is May 28, the anniversary of the day that changed Dan's life forever, and he is on his way to talk to a few hundred high-school kids about his mistakes. He might throw up. At the very least, he may pass out.

The scenery whizzes by as Crystal navigates the twisting and ill-maintained back roads leading from Highland Rocks to Conway High School. He regrets the decision not to drive separately. At least he might have had some illusion of control in this alien situation.

What had he been thinking?

He doesn't even like to talk one-on-one, let alone stand in front of an audience. An audience of high school kids, no less. And this particular subject…

He shuts his eyes as Crystal takes a sharp right turn and the tires of her car just barely hug the road.

He will be speaking in front of Megan Richards' mother and his own son. The normal fear of judgment and insecurity brought on by the thought of public speaking is magnified significantly by considering those two listeners.

It's not just the nerves that are getting to him. What threatens to bring him to his knees is the shame.

Crystal glances over at him. "Breathe."

He does, and she adds, "Slowly."

She inhales and exhales to demonstrate, and his breathing begins to match hers. When the oxygen flows through his limbs, he starts to feel more grounded.

Crystal doesn't talk much on the drive. She's always been good at reading the body language and emotions of the people around her. It's what makes her a good caretaker. She's been assuming the role of protector, fixer, nurturer, nurse, angel—whatever you want to call it—for years.

When they enter the high school parking lot, she steers her car between a black pickup truck and a silver luxury-model SUV. Dan doesn't pay attention to the make or model of the car, but he does note the Wright Automotive Group bracket around the license plate.

Another wave of anxiety hits him, and he stops for a minute before he and Crystal exit the car and walk toward the front doors.

He breathes in and out rapidly through his nose, and she puts a hand on his shoulder and instructs him to breathe through his mouth. Then she says, "You don't have to do this, you know."

She's right. He doesn't. He could get back into the car and return to Greg's house. But something feels ominous about that choice. If he leaves this parking lot right now, he may never leave the house in Highland Rocks.

"But if you do this, Dan, there is no reason that you can't do anything in your life."

He looks at her, and she repeats, "Anything."

Dan exhales and keeps walking, Crystal a half step behind him. They approach the main front entrance of the school and press the call button to announce themselves. Ryan Tolbert appears less than a minute later and ushers them into the flow of a river of students who are all making their way through a set of doors just down the hallway.

The blood is rushing through Dan's ears, and he just barely hears Ryan's words. "I'm so glad you decided to come. Your presence will make such an impact on the kids. You have the power to change lives today." The other man's words escape on a rush of breath, as though if he doesn't get them out quickly enough, Dan might turn around and walk out.

And, in fact, the words serve as a reminder to Dan that he is here to make an impact on just one student. He's here to show Henry that he can move forward.

The smell of the building and the voices of the students are much the same as they had been twenty years ago, the last time he'd been in this building. The sense of familiarity and foreboding envelops him, filling him with unwanted emotions. The past and present coalesce around him in the form of the young people walking past. Their voices are taunting, jeering, mocking. Every bark of laughter is directed at him. Every squeal is a sound of disgust at his presence. They feel like ghosts, gauzy and blurred.

Crystal is at his side telling him to breathe. When he does, the sensation dissipates and the specter of the past retreats so that it is just outside his field of vision. The students are just students, and they are not looking at him at all.

But he can feel the spirits around him.

Ryan has not stopped talking. Dan hasn't heard a word that he's said until he directs Crystal to the auditorium doors where the stream of students is also flowing. She squeezes his hand and mouths that she loves him, and then she is gone.

He follows Ryan down a hallway and to the right, in the opposite direction of a few straggling students, who don't look at him, and a few teachers, who stare curiously. Dan doesn't see Henry, and he doesn't recognize any of the other faces.

They head down a darker, narrower passageway, and

Ryan opens a heavy door leading to a short flight of stairs. When they emerge at the top of the staircase, they are at the back of the auditorium's stage. A heavy dark blue curtain is all that separates them from the swell of voices on the other side.

Dan feels as if he might be dreaming.

Ryan introduces him to a few people, and Dan manages to make all of the appropriate responses. But he has no idea who he's just met or even the words that have emerged from his mouth. He moves in slow motion.

They walk toward a woman with short silver hair. She is tall and ramrod straight, wearing a long blue dress. Her face is deeply lined, and her eyes are impossibly sad. She stares at Dan warily.

This is Megan's mother. Ryan provides hesitant and tense introductions.

The woman continues to stare at Dan, and he bows his head and lowers his eyes. He's not sure what to say.

She speaks first. "I'm glad you're here."

That surprises him, and he utters a mystified, "Why?"

She seems to consider this. "Twenty years is a long time to miss someone. It's also a long time to have lost yourself."

Dan assumes that she's talking about herself, but the realization hits that he's been lost, too.

"I've spent a lot of time alone in that moment— imagining Megan's last breath. There have been times that I've thought that if I could concentrate hard enough, I could change it. I might be able to go back in time and alter that reality." She looks at him. "I would imagine you've spent a lot of time in that moment, too."

Dan's eyes burn. He nods.

"Well." She looks at the curtain, as if she can see what's beyond. "This is a new moment, and it's a step forward. It's better not to take that step alone."

She does not absolve him of his actions, nor does she attempt to assuage his guilt or regret. It is simply a gentle acknowledgment of their shared and tragic connection. It's a kindness and a generosity that she does not owe him but that perhaps he owes himself. He is not the same person that he was twenty years ago, though that scared kid still lives inside him. Maybe Dan owes that kid the same kindness that this woman has just gifted to him.

Ryan steps in with the logistics of the event. Dan will offer his remarks, and then Mrs. Richards will speak.

Dan reaches in his pocket for the notes and pulls them out. His palms are damp, and his fingers tremble.

Ryan places his hand briefly on Dan's shoulder. "I will introduce you, and then you can come out, just around the side there." He points to stage right, where there is a gap in the curtain.

Ryan disappears around the curtain's edge a moment later, and the roar of the crowd quiets. His words are crisp and clear.

Dan hears Megan's name. He hears a brief overview of the accident. Dan concentrates on breathing.

Then he hears his own name and the silence that follows. His feet are frozen to the floor. Seconds tick by before a hand touches his arm. It is the hand of Renee Richards. "You can do this," she says, and when Dan looks at the woman, her face transforms into the shining, smiling face of her daughter.

Dan blinks the likeness away, nods once, takes two deep breaths, and then walks through the gap in the curtain.

There is a smattering of applause, but mostly blank faces stare back at him. He clutches the notes in his fist, and Ryan gestures toward the microphone, a look of relief on his face.

Dan takes his place and clears his throat.

Crystal had suggested that he try to find Henry in the audience, since he is here to speak to his son. But as Dan scans the faces, he swears that he can see Megan's face in the second row. He shifts his gaze, and there she is a few rows back. His eyes dart to the right and to the left, and Megan looks back at him. She is smiling encouragingly. *You can do this*, she seems to silently communicate to him.

A low murmur reaches his ears, and a movement to his right distracts him. Ryan is standing off to one side, and he is poised to return to the stage. Next to him, Megan stands, and she puts a hand on Ryan's arm, like she's holding him back. She nods at Dan.

Dan looks back at the sea of faces, and every single one of them is Megan—all of them filled with light, love, and forgiveness.

He looks down at his notes, and then he stuffs them back into his pocket.

This time when he looks up, he spots Henry, who is watching him anxiously. In the back of the room, he sees Joe Wright, Chloe Nicholson, Nate Kasinski, and Crystal.

He leans forward. Into the microphone, he starts to speak.

"My name is Dan Armstrong, and twenty years ago, I was in an accident that killed one of the kindest, gentlest, and most intelligent people I've ever had the pleasure to know."

There is silence.

Dan breathes into the microphone, and his breath is amplified through the auditorium.

"Last week, for the first time in two decades, I visited the scene of that accident. Someone had left a framed copy of the yearbook memorial page that included Megan's senior quote—*You were born with the ability to change someone's life. Don't ever waste that.*"

He glances up, finds Henry's encouraging face. Then he looks back at Chloe Nicholson and Joe Wright, who are holding hands tightly. Beside them stands his dear cousin Crystal. He addresses the trio. "We've all changed a lot of lives. And we may not be the same, but when it's all said and done, we're not so different, either."

THE END

ACKNOWLEDGEMENTS

I'd like to acknowledge all of the steadfast supporters of this hobby of mine, that sometimes feels more like an obsession. You know who you are. Special thanks to Jim, Mom, Sue, and Nate.

As always to my children—Rachel, Noah, and Adam. I love you more than all the words and beyond all human meaning.

Sydney, Lydia, and Gracie—thank you for inspiring me with your hearts and creativity. The future is so bright for you. May you do great things with the gift of the life you've been given.

To my dear friends who loyally read my books. You also know who you are, but I'll name a few of you here: Natalie B., Ann, Kate, Mark, Anita, Robyn, Robert, Jo, Kristy, Kathy, Sandy, Cheryl, Linda, Lisa, Natalie M. You never fail to lift me up when imposter syndrome brings me down.

Great appreciation to my cover designer Kerry Ellis, who created the final compelling cover that so eloquently represents the spirit of the novel. I highly recommend her to anyone looking for graphic design work: coveredbykerry.com.

I've borrowed from a few real-life events (drastically altered) to recreate this work of fiction. For those of you who may think you recognize an event or an occurrence: Maybe you do, and maybe you don't. But a nod to those situations that manifested inspiration, even when I may not have been aware of it myself.

And finally, to Connellsville, on which the town of Conway is based. I lived in Connellsville for many transformational years. It wasn't until I left that I realized the tremendous imprint this beautiful, imperfect place has left on my soul. From the Youghiogheny River and the Great Allegheny Passage to the salt-of-the-earth people who would rather life stay as it is than progress too quickly. You were (are) my home. No matter where I end up, you will always be a part of me.